Published in Birkerød Denmark

With deepest thanks to Lise, Asta and Kristian.

Also by T J Slee

CRIME/ESPIONAGE

Cloister
Volume II of the Charlie Jones series

Fissure
Volume III of the Charlie Jones series

FANTASY

The Vanirim
Book 1 of the Midgard Cycle

Visit me at Facebook.com/teejayslee/

Purchas
Multnomah C
Tiny Title Wave

D1167202

About 'B.U.G.'
Volume one in the Charlie Jones series

"Slee's contemporary spy-tale has a lightness of touch mixed with a little Aussie needle - as if he nibbled cucumber sandwiches with Chesteron and Wodehouse while the covers went on, before heading to the pub for pool and a pint with Shane Maloney and Lennie Lower.

There's enough in-house knowledge for me to fear greatly for this country's security while in the hands of our bumbling would-be protectors.

Slee has come up with a new genre: Espio-nudge."

Dave Warner

Award winning author of 'City of Light', and the Andrew 'The Lizard' Zurk series including 'Murder in the Off Season'

About TJ Slee

"Slee captures the processes, techniques, frustrations and idiosyncrasies that characterise the world inhabited by the secret intelligence services. The author has brought a rolling counter terrorism yarn to life with verve, healthy cynicism and lashings of good humour. Hang on for a very entertaining ride."

Neil Fergus

International Security Expert, CEO 'Intelligent Risks Pty Ltd'

Book I

"Bless me Father for I have sinned, it is, uhmm…"

"Two days."

"Really? OK, two days since my last confession. Thanks Father."

"You're welcome Jones. Jones…"

"These are my sins. I called a guy a paedophile."

"What? Is he?"

"Why, think you might know him Father?"

"That's not funny Jones."

"Sorry Father. No, I don't know if he is or not. Probably not, I just did it to piss him off. What sort of sin is that? Is it one of the venials?"

"It sounds like slander."

"Is slander a sin?"

"It's illegal."

"So, I should confess to the police?"

"Pass. What else do you have?"

"Well, I told a lie to the Attorney General and now I have less than 48 hours to find an ex-Kurdish-traffic-cop who probably knows where this missing US Delta Forces soldier is, unless these Kurdish PKK terrorists have already got him. Or the US Defense Clandestine Service. Or the Turks."

"That sounds…stressful. Jones, what do you want?"

"Forgiveness, basically. Both retrospective and prospective."

"I absolve you of your sins, in the name of the Father Son and Holy Ghost Amen. For your penance say three Hail Marys. Now let me go back to breakfast."

"Have a good one Father."

"And Jones? You don't have to ring me every time you sin, just save them up and bring them in to the church a few at a time."

"OK. This was your idea Father."

"Good day Jones."

"G'day Father."

Four weeks earlier

A room, about the size of a billiards hall and just about as well lit. Desks where the pool tables should be, laptops sitting on them where the balls should be racked. Not a lot of paper lying around, because it has to be put away at the end of every day. Next to every desk a safe, where the paper goes. Two baskets next to the safes, one for waste, one for shredding. I throw my coffee cup in the shredding basket every time, don't know why.

"So explain to me," I say to Jenno, "How *this* guy, whatsisname…"

"Merdem Barrak," Jenno grunts. "Easy name to remember, Jones."

"Right, Barrak… how he gets his name in an Office of National Assessments Report and I never heard of him?" I ask, because I'm sitting there reading the weekly ONA Situation Report that goes to the Attorney-General and there's a piece in there, if the Attorney actually reads this stuff, this guy Barrak's soon gonna be world famous.

"*Associated with PKK*," Jenno says, points at the page. "Says so right here. I know you used to be in surveillance Jones, but you got to be able to read to be a case officer." He reads out the title of the report, "*Coming home: recent returnees from the conflicts in Syria and Iraq.*"

"That's what I mean," I say, "I'm the PKK case officer and I never heard of the guy. Where do they get this stuff?"

4

"There's *phone-calls* to Kobani," Jenno intones. "To people in the Partiya Yekîtiya Demokrat. So I'm guessing it's some signals intel you never saw, or you ignored." Smirks.

"Cousins, I bet," I say, not letting go. "Guys like that have 20 cousins, half of 'em gotta be in some sort of militia over there. Who isn't? Rings his cousin, *Hey Ahmed, my mother said to ring her once in a while you wanker, she can't sleep worrying about you...*that sort of thing, now he's in an ONA report?"

"Not just phone calls," he reads out loud again. "*Barrak is reported by a reliable source to have been a member of Jabhat al-Akrad, the PKK aligned militia which currently controls Aleppo.*"

"So," I say, trying to stay unconvinced. "He was a Kurdish militia guy who got out and now he's here. I got five of them living here already. Big deal."

But I make a brain scrawl - ask George (my best PKK source, bad personal hygiene, good information) about this Barrak guy before someone on high asks me.

You have to forgive my frustration, because I spend half my damn life now running down people who know people who maybe might have heard about someone who went to the Middle East to fight, and that list is longer than a roll of single ply toilet paper, and it's just about as thin. Call a travel agent about flights to Syria? Travelled to southern Turkey to visit relatives? Post a tweet that your second cousin is visiting from Aleppo? Ooh, bad luck. You're *associated*, man. And if you live in Sydney, chances are Charlie Jones (that's me, should have introduced myself earlier) is gonna be coming to interview you.

Like now, I'm standing in the doorway of a flat in Campbelltown some dog, no, make that *all* the dogs in Campbelltown use like their own Facebook page. Name on the door says Tony Collins (*Tones*, written in thick red pen) but that must be the old tenant because the phone is registered to Serwan Askari, late of Aleppo, Syria, now three years a driver for Silvertail Cabs and according to New South Wales Police, a light smoker-but-not-dealer in hash (one possession charge, no conviction) who is, according to my mate George, a nice young guy who likes discos and wires money home to his grandmother so she can migrate one day.

Tip number one for people who don't want to be interviewed by C Jones – don't wire money anywhere, don't buy a big money order, don't send money home any way except up someone else's date.

Grandmother must be saving up to migrate to the moon, the amount of money Serwan is sending home. Why I'm here.

I knock on the door. Ring on the bell. Bang on the window pane. OK, finally he comes, in his pyjamas. Poor bastard must be driving night shifts and I come banging on the door middle of the afternoon. Yes, I am a swine.

"Who are you?" he says.

"Johns is my name," I say and show him my ID and he looks at the ID and he looks at me and at the ID again and says, "What you want?"

"Glass of water, and a chat," I say and he says, "Oh, *shit*, man. Why?"

And I say, "Because it's your turn Mr. Serwan, that's all," and I start to explain about the *Community Interview Programme* (the way I say it, you can hear the capital letters) like I really am interviewing every single member of the Middle East community in Sydney for their own protection, and I say, "So we can talk right here where all the neighbours can see us or you can invite me in and give me that glass of water," and I let it hang right there.

And he says, "Or, I can say no. I know my rights." And gentle as you like, he shuts the door in my face.

Which ironically, just makes him more interesting.

So I scrawl on the brain pan, *Note to Jones: Take a Silvertail Cab to the Trivial Pursuit Night at the Three Weeds hotel tonight and ask Silvertail Cabs for the nice Mr. Serwan to drive you.*

The job's not all bad though. George my best Syrian source is a nice guy, always lets me take him to this good cheap place for lunch. Has a deal with the owner, puts a 100 x 40 cardboard sign in the window of the kitchen, calls it an advertisement and claims it on tax, eats at the restaurant for half price. I like that kind of thinking.

The cover story is, anyone sees me, I'm his rehab officer - George on long term disability leave since '06 after an accident at a building site.

We're talking blue-painted walls, posters of orange groves mounted on warped particle board, plastic table cloths with that zig zaggy black and white border you see on the urns in the museums. Smell of fried eggplant and kebab. I don't know if I love Middle Eastern food because of the job, or I love the job because of Middle Eastern food.

"Khashkhash," says George and then, "Khashkhash?" to me and I say "Yeah, what-the-hell, beef, extra chilli," and the waiter doesn't even ask, just brings us two Cokes and two iced water like always.

"We got a refugee protest Sunday week, you heard that?" says George and I nod like I did, which I didn't.

I say, "Tell me the latest."

"Gonna dress some women and kids up in life jackets. Gonna go down the harbor, they all gonna jump in. Right by the Opera House," George says. "Go right down the middle of George Street mate down to the Opera House. You tell the cops gonna be a *thousand* people there, get us the permit right?"

"Get your own permits," I say. "Takes 21 working days you know that and no way they're gonna let you do a protest with women and kids drowning at Circular Quay on a Sunday mate. Think of the tourists."

"Gonna do it anyway," says George. "Can't hold 'em back mate. *You* try to hold 'em back. Navy turns back a boat of 100 brothers

7

and sisters and their kids, back to Indonesia, they nearly died mate. That causes a lot of angst, alright?"

Angst. George tries a new word a month. This is August and *angst*.

Food comes and George stabs a pine nut with his fork so hard he could split the china and the peppers and lamb slide off to the side, like they know who's next but he gets them anyway and it takes him five minutes to chew and swallow, the stuff is chewy like leather. Reason why God made lambs so cute is so you don't want to eat 'em, but tell that to George.

"Alright," I say, sounding tired. "So George Street to the Quay Sunday week, where you starting?"

"Hyde Park mate, Martin Place, then George Street. No cars, just on foot. Oh yeah, maybe one truck, like, maybe put a dinghy on it with some people in it. Maybe cover it in freakin blood, eh? Got a guy works at the abattoir, he can get buckets of it. Your angsty touros will like that. Put it full of holes so blood leaks out. Maybe cover the kids in blood too. You not eating?"

So I ring the police Counter Terrorist Co-ordination Command (who comes up with these names?) from my limo on the way back and this new guy is there, Kanno or Ganno or whatever and I tell him about the demo and he says "You know what's bloody on at the Opera House Sunday week don't you mate?" And I say "Yeah" like I do, which I don't, and he says "Bloody *Placido Domingo* mate and we're doing protection on about 10 politicians gonna be there - I reckon the Immigration Minister might even be on the list, have to check. Damn," he says, like it's my fault.

"Yeah, well," I say, "Your job sucks. Ring you again when I get back to the office," and I hang up and put the radio on JJJ and one arm out the window doing aeroplanes in the wind and the sun while I do my CS on the way home (that's Counter-Surveillance, which is spook talk for Coffee-run), and Newtown is buzzing with slackers eating lentil soup on the sidewalk. And the lights are red, I pull up and the girl with the shaved head is waiting tables at the corner again and yeah, one day I'm gonna go in there and say hello to that girl.

Think of something cool to say.

Damn, I forgot to ask George about Barrak.

"Harold Holt!," I say, when the guy at the Pub Quiz asks who was the only Australian Prime Minister to have a US Naval Base named after him.

"Bullshit," says Jenno, "They never. You don't name a naval base after a guy who was supposed to have been kidnapped by a Chinese submarine."

"They bloody did," I say, "And not only that, it's a submarine comms base."

"Bullshit," says his sister Money but the quiz guy says, "*Correct, ten points!*"

"Well now I change my opinion of Americans," Money says and she licks the rim of her marguerita glass. "I thought they didn't get irony."

"George Bush Snr., George Bush Jnr., Jeb Bush... "

"Jeb who?"

"...and Donald Trump."

"Fair enough."

The referee calls a break and Jenno gets up to get a round of drinks in. He and I are drinking Coopers Ale, and his sister Money is on the margueritas which she doesn't often have to buy herself, because there's usually a sponsor out there somewhere. *Love is the bread of life, but Money is the honey.* Has that tattooed on her butt.

So, we're at a pub in Rozelle, little room up the back where they used to put the bands and comedians, then it was slot machines until they built a bigger room for the slot machines so now it can host audience participation nights with Trivia Tuesdays and Speaker's Corner and Author Author.

Me, Money and Jenno come every Tuesday for the trivia night. Money is Jenno's little sister but they get along just fine. And whatever he doesn't know, she usually does because between them he *owns* Grand Finals and Beers and Wines, and she *owns* Famous Murders and Scabrous Diseases and I can chip in now and then with Dead People and Cultures (which is why we like the trivia night at this pub, is the categories.)

It's warm in the bar and Money is just in jeans and a white singlet you can see her little tits through, and with her cropped black hair it makes her look pretty butch, which together with the bright red lipstick really makes you wonder which team she plays for. I can tell you though, she's straight as the Stuart Highway.

How she knows her diseases, she did a bachelor of medicine a few years before she discovered she is an artist, and she still reads the journals. Freaks out a lot of boyfriends, what she has on the bookshelf beside the bed. If she has doubts about a guy, leaves the journal open to a picture of a hernia operation, or pustules, watches his face as he clocks the pictures for the first time. Guy can write himself in or out of her good books just on the way he reacts.

"You ever been to America?" I ask Money.

"Yeah," she says. "Toured the east coast with a show in '09? No, '08? I don't know. Anyway, yeah. Why?"

"Meet any actual Americans?" I ask and she smiles.

"Well," she says, looks around. Leans over. "Met this cop at a club," she winks, "One of those riot cops, rides a horse. We end up against the wall in the back room of this club, there's no room to even sit. He was gorgeous, I'm getting nailed really nice, but I can't get the horse smell out of my head, and I start thinking about the old nursery rhyme, you know, can't get it out of my head, *Ride a cock horse to Banberry Cross, see a fine lady upon a white horse* . . .then I realize I'm saying it out loud. I laughed, and that was it. He got the shits." She swirls the ice with her finger. "I think he took it personally."

"That guy, he was the one came here on holiday and you left Jenno to look after him?" I ask.

"Yeah," she says, holding her nose, "That one."

Jenno comes back with the drinks and we get to pick the category this time, but I already cleared 'Dead People' and Jenno picks 'Football Grand Finals', so now I can tune right out and think about tonight's cab ride.

How I drove myself all the way out to Pennant Hills before I called his cab, gave myself a nice long ride in and plenty of time to talk to Mr Serwan Askari, friend of the PKK.

Serwan doesn't recognise me when I get into his cab, or maybe doesn't even look, he just thumbs the meter and starts driving. Says, "You asked for me personal? Thanks, it's been a slow night." Then he looks, says, "I know you?"

Got my jeans and an old Hilltop Hoods T-Shirt on, so I forgive him for not being quicker on the uptake.

"Yeah, Johns," I say. Nothing. So I try again, "Asked you for a glass of water and a chat the other day? You declined. I figured I must have interrupted your beauty sleep so I didn't push it." He looks at me again, gives a little frown, and then cool as you like glides the cab into the curb and puts it in neutral.

"Guess you'll be walking to Rozelle then," he says. "Out of my cab, please."

Please is nice. *Please* I can work with. I say, "Now now, it's just a talk. Clear something up for me. Ten minutes, then we can keep driving, you drop me off where I'm going, we're all finished."

"I'm all finished now, any of my mates see *you* in this cab," he says. "I asked around, plenty of my people know you, Johns. See you in here, they start asking questions about me. Doesn't matter why. I don't need the hassle, so, out please."

Still saying please. That's good. I get right into it then, "You know Serwan, you send more than ten grand overseas through a bank, it has to notify the finance department?"

"So? I pay my taxes," he says.

"Yeah, but they have this computer thing now, you send that much money to places in the Middle East, automatically rings a bell in our office, and you or your mates get a visit from me."

"I need a lawyer?" he asks. Nice guy, asking me that. I shrug, "I'm not investigating you," I say. "Yet. What was the money for? If it's clean, I don't care."

He waits, decides on an answer. "Family in Ifrin," he says. "You know, a little bit for food, coffee, keep the rent paid. A little bit to bribe the Syrian soldiers at the check points, so people can get out and visit relatives, go to work. Got an uncle shot in the eye two months ago, he's got medical bills. Some of it they save, get themselves out of that shithole one day. Some they give for our people in the camps. That OK with you?"

"Sorry if I'm a bit nosy, you're talking grocery money, but we checked the transfers from that account and you sent 57 grand in the last six months. That's a lot of chick peas."

"Hey," he says. "It's not all *my* money, alright?" He pulls his sleeves up now, showing a watch, a bracelet and a faint phone number on his arm he probably wrote after a bit of limbo in a night club the night before.

In my experience, when they roll up their sleeves, they're getting ready for business. Which is good. Or a fight. Which is not.

"So you're part of some group, raising this money," I ask.

"You make it sound like some secret organization - a *group*. Call it a group, yeah, we're a group," he says, "But we don't all know each other. Each week we all put in, three times so far I get to send the money to who I want, rest of the time, it's like someone else. You invite new people to join, after a while, it's their turn. You know. Like a pyramid thing, stay in long enough, everyone wins."

I don't know if this young Arab is taking the piss with the pyramid thing, so I don't bite. "How many in this scheme then?" I ask.

"Three, at the top" he says. "About forty maybe, total."

"You don't know them all?" I ask, "Sounds risky."

"All from back home," he says, "I know the families, don't always know the guys."

"Names?" I say, taking out a piece of paper and a pen.

"Bugger off," he says.

"OK, but who does all the fundraising, must be one of you," I say. "I need to know, so I can check the name is clean and then it isn't my business anymore. It sounds like a full on legitimate thing to me, nice boys all sending money home to your families, I appreciate that, but you understand I have to close this somehow, with a name. Or, I'll just put it against *your* name shall I?"

"You going to freeze our money?" he asks. "I heard from a Pakistani driver youse froze some other Paki guy's money. Guy was saving years to get a deposit on a house, I heard. Sends it home to his bride's family. Now youse froze it, and he's living in shame with his sister and her kids. What, he's going to buy a nuke for $10,000 bucks? Smuggle it into Sydney in his baggy freakin pants?" he says, winding himself up now. "You people," shakes his head, stares out the windscreen. "Got no freakin idea. Better you get out, now."

I open the door of the cab and step over the shit in the gutter, lean in the window as I close the door. "OK, it's up to you, but you want me to come back at you, don't give me a name. You want me to go away, give me a name."

I wait, so does he. It gets boring, so I stand up, away from the window.

He leans over to wind up the window, says to me, "Yeah, and good luck finding another cab…I'm going to call it in that some drugged up freak in a Hilltop Hoods T-Shirt vomited in my car and ran off without paying the fare. Something like that gets around on a quiet night."

He drives off.

I ring Money, get her to pick me up. Bring me a different shirt so I can get home later.

She wants me to pay her petrol. Guess how she got *her* nickname.

"Who you calling now?" Money asks on the way back to Pennant Hills to fetch my car after the quiz night ends in controversy.

Like, who needs to know how to spell *Jesaulenko* anyway. Name of some random Australian football player? We spelt it with a 'z'. Some guy in the audience says there is no 'Z'. Money rings the Australian Football League itself, but they can't even spell it. Wikipedia has it spelt three different ways. Fiasco.

"Jesus Jones why can't you get a *real* job – leave your car all the way out in the bush like this?" she mutters.

I ignore her, call the number Mr. Serwan had written on his arm. Why not?

> *Tip number two for Bad Guys. Don't write important phone numbers on your forearm and forget to wash them off.*

"Yeah?" comes an answer. This guy sounds old, clears his throat. "Who this?"

"Serwan," I say, my best imitation of a Syrian guy ten years younger than me, who I only met twice. But I figure it doesn't wash, because the old guy on the other end is all quiet. I look at the display on the phone, he hung up or what?

"You got some bloody balls you *something something something else*," the old guy rolls into Kurdish, really warming himself up. You know how didgeridoo players can breathe in through the nose the same time they are blowing out through the mouth? He must be a professional nostril breather - no breaks at all in the words until finally, he spits. Like I can almost see him looking down at the phone and actually spitting on it, and *then* he hangs up.

I look at the number again. It's the kind you get with a pre-paid mobile. They think I can't look that up or find out where it lives. Geniuses.

Later, same night, I'm sitting under a Hills Hoist on a rooftop in Artarmon, dirty laundry around the outside, but the top's open so it's like some bloody Bedouin tent with the roof blown off. I'm peering through a pair of binos at a shop window, at some guys playing cards. Why? Doing Robbo a favour because one of his guys is sick is why. (I'll introduce you to him and his pack of maniacs later too but trust me, we don't want to rush it).

My mood is not improved by having to constantly wait for the Hills Hoist to swing around to the right angle so that I can keep the target in sight *under* someone's old panties instead of *around* their piss-stained bedsheet.

My mum worries that my job is dangerous. Worst thing can happen to me up here is I catch scabies.

No, your honour I did not see the accused actually put the bomb in his bag because at that exact moment my view was blocked by a G-string.

It's an institution. Sure, they call them Cottages not wards, and the nurses are in casual clothes, but they're not fooling anyone. Gwen gives me the signal when I walk in, lets me know Mum's *in a mood*. She's a good room-mate, ol' Gwenny, cheers Mum up when she has the blues, which is most of the time nowadays, state the world is in.

Mum's sitting by her window watching some birds. They're Noisy Miners. Another thing that gets her down. It used to be rainbow lorikeets and white cockatoos out that window, now it's all Noisy Miners.

"Oh it's you," she says, without turning, "Look at those cheeky buggers."

"Yeah."

"Arseholes."

"Mum…" pointing my thumb over my shoulder at Gwen.

"Sorry Gwen."

" 'S alright Dawn," Gwen says, automatic.

"Well, they are."

"I brought you the morning paper, Mum."

She looks at it, looks away again.

Put it on her lap anyway. "Got to stay current Mum."

"Let me guess," she says, "We won the cricket, we lost the tennis. Or the other way around. The Middle East is a mess. The farmers need rain or it's the end of the world. And the prime minister is still an arsehole."

"Mum!"

"Dawn!"

"Sorry Gwenny. The prime minister is a…a Noisy Miner."

"'S alright Dawn, he is a bit of a Noisy Miner," says Gwen.

I make sure she's well stocked with candy and cigarettes and Gwen walks me to the door of the cottage.

"How's work love? You still keeping us safe from them jihadis?"

"You're safe in here Gwen."

"Have some of my apple crumble to take with you? Can't fight A Death Cult on an empty stomach luv."

"Trying to give it up Gwenny."

"Good-o pet. Look, try and get your mum out a bit more often will you? She's starting to give me the shits."

"Oh you look awful," Shirl says when I come wandering in, my late night/early morning knock off drink still got its claws in my brain, I'm chomping on a burger and it isn't even 10 in the morning yet. "You went out after that job up on the roof?" she asks and I nod, throw my keys, phone, parking garage door beeper thing and wallet on the desk and go into the toilet, to finish my burger and get a half hour peace maybe. Shirl follows me in. (She's *that* kind of admin assistant; looks like Anne Hathaway, temperament like a honey badger.)

"Shirl," I say, "Gimme a break. It's the toilet. Get outa here, or go get me a Coke."

"Jones," she says, "You should be at the airport, not here - you're *on duty*. You never listen to your messages."

"On *what?*," I say, going into the stall, dropping my strides. "What duty? Stand back, Shirl," I say, "You are warned. I'm not feeling super solid today." She steps back quickish and closes the door to the stall.

"I mean you're doing airport duty rest of this week, and the weekend, Wes has done his back," Shirl says and I can feel her grin burn through the plywood.

Wes and his bloody buggered back. Guy has been living airport liaison for twenty years; how can you do your back staring at passports, Passenger Entry cards, CCTV monitors?

"You win?" Shirl asks.

"What?"

"The trivia night?"

"Spell Jesaulenko," I ask, thinking, half or full flush? What the hell, give it the works.

"J-e-s-a-u-lenko," Shirl says over the gurgling water. "My dad was an Australian Football nut."

"Ooh, you're good. But you're never around when I need you Shirl." Going back to my desk, I pick up the keys, the phone, the

17

garage door beeper thing, my wallet. Hand Shirl the piece of paper with the phone number of The Spitter. "Do me a subscriber check will you?" I ask her. "Tell me where this phone usually lives."

On the way out I go past Jenno's desk, swap *my* door beeper thing for *his* door beeper thing 'cause the batteries in mine are dead. Let him try and get out of the garage tonight.

"Jesaulenko with an 's', eh," I say. "What are you doing next Tuesday night? I think we're gonna have to take Money off the team. She said it must be with a Z because Mount Kosciuszko is with a Z and that's Polish and so was he. Which is dead logical except he was Austrian."

So Kingsford Smith Airport, behind the departure lounges, what it's most like is a hospital where people wear suits. Mostly blue, with wide lapels so they can pin multi-coloured badges on. Mean and green, I'm a cleaner. Hellow yellow, I'm an Airport Authority fellow. Lots of people pushing trolleys like hotel room service, never understood why. Colour of *my* badge, security liaison? I can't remember because tell the truth I lost the bastard two years ago and the shit you have to go through to get it replaced, forget it. Takes forever and they take $25 from your pay for replacing lost badges.

Oh yeah, purple, I think, fishing it out of my pocket. Jensen (not Jones), it says under the picture that also and most definitely looks nothing like me; but in two years using Jenno's badge no-one has even questioned it. See Jenno, he's the kind of conscientious guy, when he loses an airport security pass, he fills in all the paperwork, pays $25 and gets a new one. And our state of the art security system just issues him one without cancelling the old one. Border security, tight as a fishnet stocking.

I walk into the security room, where some neat as a pin Border Force guy I never saw before is sitting, but it's like six months since I last worked the airport, so that's no surprise. He nods. "I hear Wes is crook," he says.

"Yeah, slacker," I say.

Guy stands and holds out his hand, "Sean Phillips," he says.

"Ah, uhm, Jenno," I say, remembering my badge. Let's face it, with this guy and his starched white shirt with blue epaulettes and trimmed sideburns attitude, I don't want to have to explain the badge thing. "I just made coffee," he says, pointing at a pot.

He sits down again in front of a bank of monitors, flipping through some digitized stills on one of them. On the others the feed is live; bored tourists standing in queues waiting to get their passports punched, or waiting for bags, looking at watches, with that jeeeesus-man-can-it-really-take-so-freaking-looooong, look on their faces.

Sean 'Epaulettes' Phillips leans over, pushes a printout of some flight numbers at me. "Amman, via Singapore, only one should interest you so far this morning," he says.

So I boot up the old PC and get ready to one-finger type a bunch of passenger names into our system to check them. Why I still do this in the age of computerised passenger lists? Manually check every name? Because airlines suck at the details, no one ever does their online check in right, and surprise surprise the passport scan they do at immigration isn't linked to the database we use. *Sekandari, A, 07.01.32.* Nup. This is the thin blue line, I reflect. Some hungover underpaid spook single-finger-typing misspelt names into a Pentium 486 PC from back when Bill Gates still had acne. *Selfati, M, 18.09.67.* Nup.

I look over my shoulder at Mr. Clean, flipping through his stills.

"What you looking for?" I ask. The answer doesn't come straight away and I know he's thinking, *ooooh, should I say* ? He goes out on a limb, "Ice coming in from Bangkok, since the cops put a lot of the locals out of business last year?" he says. "AFP flagged this guy, is suddenly doing one trip a month, but we keep coming up empty on him." He flips the screen a few shots back and points at it, some guy in a Hawaii shirt standing up against a rail. "Him," he says.

"So what are you looking for?" I ask again.

19

"Anyone he talks to?" the guy says. "You know, these are today's shots, he came in this morning. Someone on the same flight? That kind of thing. Sometimes you see things in the stills, that you don't see on video."

He's buzzing back and forth through the shots now, all clipped from security camera footage. Mr. Hawaii reaching into his pocket, Mr. Hawaii chewing gum, Mr. Hawaii staring into space, Mr. Hawaii taking a pee, Mr. Hawaii standing in front of a businessman talking into a phone...

"Oh, you bastard," I say. Lift his hand quickly from the mouse so he doesn't move it, and look at the screen close. "You cheeky son of a bitch *bastard.*"

"I'm sorry?" Sean Phillips says. "What? You see something?" He leans forward.

On the screen, Mr. Hawaii and the businessman. "Can you print that?" I ask, "And copy the video for me to take home?"

"What is it?" he asks, so I tell him.

"Not Ice, Sean old son," I say, pointing to the portly black haired businessman on the screen behind Mr Hawaii, "Something much more interesting. Code name *Opium.*"

"It's not him," Speed says.

Speed is my Director, and we gave him his nickname for the same reason we call the six-foot-six Greek tech officer Flea. We're talking a guy mid-50s, his shirt parts at the bottom of his belly because the button's too tight. Grey hair, half-moon specs. Father Christmas face with a scowl. Salt of the earth, slower than a one legged dog on tranquilizers. "I'm telling you," I say, pointing at the prints on his desk. "It's Opium. He flew in this morning."

"You check the passenger list?" he asks.

"Of course I checked the bloody passenger list. Says his name is Levysohn, Adam, of Walla Walla Washington," I say.

"A US civilian," Speed says. "You want to put surveillance on a US civilian."

"He's not a US civilian," I sigh. "He's a bloody American covert ops officer!"

"Opium is a *declared* senior American Defence Clandestine Services operations officer," Speed says. "He was a liaison here for three years and has visited regularly ever since. I took him to a footy final five years ago. When he's coming here for a visit, he lets our liaison in Washington know. He calls ahead so we can meet and greet and he doesn't have to pay his own taxi from the airport. He gives us his itinerary, and a list of who he wants to talk to. He flies in his own name, brings flowers for the Attorney General's wife and baseball shirts for his kids."

I open my mouth to begin, but he puts up his hand, continues, "He does not just bowl in unannounced, under a dick cover name and a false passport, to get up to mischief. That would be dumb."

"Or cheeky," I say. "As hell. Which he is."

Speed looks at me over his grandpa glasses, "If it is him. Which it isn't." Turns to his screen and clicks the big 'DENIED' button on the form I sent him. "No dogs," he says. "You are not putting surveillance onto a US intelligence officer. If it is him, which it isn't, he probably just screwed up the paperwork."

('Dogs' is the polite name for the Mobile Surveillance Detachment, or MSD, which sounds so professional, and wrong, whereas 'Dogs' is just so right.)

"I'm gonna check with the SIS," I say. "See where *they* think Opium is." I figure if a US covert operative is in town, our own sister service would probably know about it.

Speed pushes the prints over to me, sighs, "You do that Jones."

Go back to my own desk on the floor below. Sit down, reach for the phone. "Got a job for you Robbo," I tell the Boss Dog.

"Paperwork will catch up later." See, I know that when Speed says DENIED, what he really means is APPROVED, he just doesn't know it yet.

"Who?" he asks. "We got a lot on. You know bloody Pavarotti is in town? Every VIP in the country lining up to meet him."

"Placido Domingo, ignoramus," I point out to him. "Don't know your sopranos?"

"Whoever. What you got?"

"Friend of yours," I say. "Opium."

"*That* cheeky bastard," Robbo says. "Thanks."

It's the next night. I'm sitting in a booth at the Colombian Hotel on the Oxford St strip with Karn. Money set me up with Karn about a month ago, and we're working through it. Got off to a blazing start at a house party fuelled by retro vodka jelly shots, but now we are at the 'do-we or don't-we' stage.

Karn is giving me a pep talk. Money warned me it was coming. I go up the bar and get a couple of vodkas in, bartender short changes me and I try to point out to him that that may have been a life or death move, seeing as it was Karn's $50 and she's a redhead. We argue a bit back and forth and then he looks over at her, "You tell her to come up to the bar, we can talk about whether it was a $20 or $50."

She's straight back with change for her $50, and his phone number.

She's a gorgeous woman, right? Long dark red curly hair, alabaster skin with freckles, and a big smile which when you see it makes you feel like you won a prize, coz you don't see it that often. She's taller than me by a good couple of inches and is wearing her clubbing kit which means taut belly and thigh, shiny black boots with f-off heels. She does stage and set design for theatre groups, just started up her own little company with a mate.

And maybe that's the whole quandry right there – what's she doing here with me? She'd look more natural hanging with Jenno and his six-pack, they could have little red-blonde designer babies, rent themselves out to Abercrombie for in-store appearances.

"So what I was saying," she yells in my ear. Smells good too, did I talk about that? "I don't want to waste *all this energy* getting you to open up, tell me what you really think, really feel, and then I finally find out maybe I don't like who you are and I've wasted all that time."

Green eyes. No surprises there. You knew she would have lovely big green eyes. And breasts like five star hotel pillows . . .

"Jones?"

"Sorry, was that a question?"

"My point completely!" she sighs, does the big green eyes rolling thing. "Honesty. Tell me what you think about us. Up front. Here and now. Try it."

"Or, we could just take a shortcut," I try to lighten the mood a bit, "Start with couples therapy, forget all the dating, struggles about commitment and disappointing sex, get straight into the breakup, and divide up our furniture?"

OK, that got a smile, no teeth but still a smile.

"You have five minutes and my undivided attention," she says. "Show me something real Charlie Jones."

She's got this long black lacey coat on, which right *then* slides off to reveal one creamy shoulder. Coincidence? Who cares, I'm lost.

I think about it. Now on the one hand we *are* talking an Überbabe. On the other, there is some pretty big time cringe value in this whole scary-arse *show me something real Charlie Jones* conversation. I mean, I'd be right into it if I thought I really was worthy of this big red beauty, but something is telling me she's too much woman for my mere mortal self to aspire to.

Nah. My time would be better spent following up on that waitress in Newtown with the tongue stud doing something useless at Uni. Or Money's mate Jane's sister, whatsername. I think maybe I saw something there the other night.

Thinking, *forget it, this is all a bit intense.* Leaning back, looking over Karn's shoulder as she eases the lace coat back up. Now, didn't I see those swarthy looking guys over there earlier in the evening? Two guys, both in leather jackets, one brown and one black? But before, the brown jacket was facing me, and this time it's the black jacket and which pub was it…nah, the restaurant, they were at the Malaysian restaurant. What the hell, it's Oxford street right, they're on a date. Relax Jones. Twice is only a coincidence, three times is the charm.

I lean across just before the silence gets awkward, "Camping."

"What?"

"You and me in Kosciuszko national park, bushwalking, hanging out by a campfire, two or three days. Really get to know someone when you go camping together," I say. Yeah, right. See *her* on Kosciusko in her high heel F-off boots. Not A Chance. "We'll see where it goes after that. Doesn't get more 'real' than camping."

"OK," she says. "Cool!" And what she does, leans over the table and wraps her arms around my neck and gives me one that puts the SSSSS in kiss.

"Ok!?"

"Yeah," pulls her beat up diary out of her big tote bag, "Used to go camping all the time, when we were kids. We're getting a cabin though. Not some mouldy tent. So, when?"

No, this *is* the third time. I also saw those guys when we were in the bottle shop.

Karn puts the pencil between her teeth and wrinkles her brow as she flicks the pages over in her diary. Too. Gorgeous. I give in to it. Wouldn't you?

Maybe it's karma. In my last life I was like, a goat herd, and my love buddy had horns and built-in woolly grips. So now I deserve an upgrade. The world turns.

"Him? Yeah, I know him," George says. We're at the Paddington Returned Soldiers Club. Another reason I like running George, he doesn't mind I want a beer, want to sit in a club. Long as it's nowhere near his mosque, of course. George is visibly on Coke, slice of lemon, never drinks it all the way to the bottom before he orders another. Never know who will walk in.

"Tell me about him," I say. Asking him about this Barrak guy at last, the guy from the ONA report, who according to 'reliable sources' – therefore not one of mine - was a low ranking member of PKK before he ran out on them and came to the promised land down under.

"Quiet guy, moved here couple of years ago? More, probably. Comes in every second or third Friday for prayers," George says. "No fanatic, you know, works at a car repair shop. Applied for permanent residency, I heard his wife is moving here soon."

"I hate the quiet ones. What did he used to do back home?"

"Hmm, why you want to know?" George is a bastard, never gives nothing for nothing. Got to know how much something is worth. How hard I'm gonna work for it. He slurps his Coke and gets a half lemon wedged at the back of his mouth, screws up his wrinkled Levantine face, hawks it out.

"We think he killed his gay lover and is on the run," I say.

George never smiles, because it would show his teeth, which he doesn't have. "You aren't going to tell me. Such trust."

"I'm just asking, George," I say. He just sits, there, blinking at me. "Alright, I'll tell you straight out. He's supposed to be PKK."

"PKK?" looks down into his Coke like he's not really interested, so I know he is. "*Which part* of PKK?"

"Jabhat al-Akrad," I tell him. "What they called, used to be Free Syrian Army?"

He laughs, a wheezy, toothless horrible laugh.

"That's amusing?" I ask.

"Not for him," George says, looks up again. "If youse are thinking that."

"George?"

"It's a good story," George says, "PKK. Yeah you could say that."

"So?" I ask.

"Yeah," he does the rubbing money thing with his finger and thumb and eyebrows that gives me the complete shits.

"Ok, the usual," I say.

"Good. Reason I laughed, see," George leans over, now that the money question is out of the way, "He's down here *hiding out* from Jabhat al-Akrad. If they knew he was here, he'd be dead meat, and if youse have already worked it out it's just a matter of time before the nutters in Jabhat al-Akrad find out he's here."

"Right," I say. "Wait. So he's *not* Jabhat al-Akrad." That's good, at least the ONA got that wrong.

"No he's YPG. And not even military. He was a cop."

"People's Protection Unit? I thought YPG and Jabhat al-Akrad were all buddies together under the PKK flag now?"

"Ah, see…" rubs his fingers again. "This is interesting huh? This is some good shit."

"I already agreed to compensate you."

He looks fake hurt, "I'm not asking more money. You think I just do this for money. You insult me. Insult my honour. I do this for my country mate. You can keep your bloody money."

He sulks a bit more but he wants to tell it, so eventually he does. "YPG and Jabhat al-Akrad are buddies like you say, as long as they stay out of each other's business, you know. So YPG they run things how they like in Dagh, Jazira, and Kobane. Jabhat al-Akrad, they having their party now in Aleppo, Tal-abyad and

26

Raqqa. They aren't really on the same side, what keeps them together is they both fighting against Daesh, Islamic State. You know, the enemy of my enemy, that sort of thing...

"How does Barrak come into this?" I say, a little impatient as George gives me his usual who's who in the PKK lesson, because he thinks I'm so slow.

"OK, you got it so far? So there's this jail in Hasakeh, was an old factory, but locked up like bloody Fort Knox," George continues, "Hasakeh is YPG country, so they run the jail. And this poor bastard Barrak, he's just militia, a traffic cop, they got him doing traffic at this big intersection in Hasakeh. He doesn't mind, at least no Daesh shooting at him, and he's making money on the fines. Then one day they say to him, hey they need you up at the jail mate, go on up there pronto. So he gets there and they say to him we're short of guards, just stand here, watch these cells, or something, so he does. He has no freak-en idea."

"What does this have to do with Jabhat al-Akrad?" I ask, gritting my teeth.

"He only killed four of them in the jail there," George says, drains his Coke, waves to the barman for a new one. "Including one of their big shot commanders. Hey, you, no lemon this time," he calls down the bar.

A space out near Kingsford Smith airport, used to be an airline maintenance shed, machine shed, that kind of thing. Now it's got a sprung board stage and some old soccer stadium seats for the punters, acoustics like an airline maintenance shed, but at least it's cheap.

Money is performing. A lot of people wouldn't call it that. The name of Money's piece of the evening is Girl On A Wire, but if I were a Martian and just came down to earth, walked into the theatre and had to describe what I saw I might call it Girl Covered In Mud Having Sex With a Tightrope. I wouldn't call it art. But hey, what the hell Martians know about art, right?

Thing is, she really can take the mud and rope and the slamming into the floor and walls and turn it into a bit of physical poetry that leaves you in awe at how beautifully the human body can move when you put someone behind the wheel who really knows how to drive. Unless you are a pervert, in which case you're just wishing there was a hose in the room somewhere. No worries, there are plenty of other performances and exhibits to look at, don't involve mud.

The after-show is in some busted arse warehouse in Balmain, and Money wants me to come, and Karn said she would meet me there, but I go home first have a shower, and then a beer, see half a soccer match on the box, and it takes the willpower equivalent of an earthquake to get my arse out of the sofa about 1 a.m. and back into my car and across town. But I do.

Guy on the door, what passes for a door, anyway, isn't interested in letting me in. I often get that. He wants cash or a ticket.

"It's my sister's party," I lie, "I don't pay to go to my own sister's party."

"Who's yer sister?" guy asks.

"Money, Money Jensen." For god's sake. Five gigglers behind me get sick of waiting and try to squeeze past, up some stairs, and he grabs them too, got six of us now held up in this rat infested pipe they're using as an entrance, and then he sees someone over my shoulder and calls out, "Oi Money! This one is family?"

I turn, see Money at the top of the stairs, almost wish she'd say "Nup" so I can go home, but she doesn't, says *"Jones, get your tardy arse up here!"* The guy shrugs and I go on up. She takes my arm, and I walk in on a room full of people standing around yet another 'happening'.

Your Martian would call it, *"A Room Full of People Watching A Large Man Wrap Himself in a Bloody Sheet."* So I start to watch; what the hell, maybe he'll set himself on fire or something. But Money drags me into the next room, which is more my style. Drunk, bent and happy people hanging on a bar, loud music, lots of fog and a few dozen lunatics out on the dance floor. Money gets me a Grey Goose, with my cash, and parks us both in a corner, "I'm your sister now?"

"Well," I say, "You'll never sleep with me, and Jenno's like my brother, so yeah."

Clinks her glass on mine, "You're probably right. I'm not your type," she says.

"My type, what is *my* type?" I ask, but she's looking around the room.

"Your girlfriend was here earlier, asking for you? But she's not here now…"

"Karn?" I ask, "Not 'girlfriend' yet. And I don't think I'm *her* type." Thinking back to a couple of nights ago, in the kitchen of Karn's flat in Redfern.

Thinking, *why is it, the breasts of red headed women are like clouds you can fall into and just keep falling?* Then I remember how she said, after the breasts had been worked up to cumulo nimbuses in my head "Jones, you have too many walls. I'm sick of climbing over the walls of dumb silent types like you." And me thinking, *I don't want you to climb over my walls, I want you to climb over my. . .*

"Hello?" Money says, waving a hand in front of my face.

"Yeah?"

"You said you're not her type?" Money asks and I nod. "That's good Jones. Tell you why, stay here," she says and goes for another round, parks one in my fist, which she paid for herself - a bad bad sign. She raises her glass, downs her drink in one, so I have to as well, or be outdone by a little girl. She leans in close, "That's good because she was waiting for you but you were unforgivably late and when you didn't turn up, she got pissed off and left, about a half hour ago, with Anthony. He sold a painting today. He's celebrating. Back in a minute," she says, and heads over to some other mates. I know that's my quality time with Money for the night.

Anthony eh? Write the name on the table in vodka, An-tho-ny. Nice name, for a dead man.

29

I do a couple of circuits of the warehouse, just in case there's any of Money's mates I might talk to, but no. Have to leave the car and get a cab home. Ask Jenno tomorrow who this An-tho-ny wanker is.

And speaking of cabs…who do I see?

"Hello Serwan," I say, creeping up behind the poor bastard. Got a little girlie bailed up against a wall and is running a hand with gold rings on the knuckles up and down her bare stomach while they talk. So he doesn't send *all* the money to his poor old granny. He turns and he is Not Happy.

"Johns, you can't do this," he says.

I shrug, "Whatever that means. Private party, seems we were both invited. Who'd guess we hang in the same circles?" I say. Lean in to the girl so she can hear me, but Serwan can't. Whisper to her, "*Did he ask you if you have a little brother yet? Pity, a guy with his looks being into little boys, isn't it?*" Slap her on the back, wink, and walk away.

Oh yeah. Forgot. Turn, go back to him, still watching me, as dark as. "By the way, I talked to a friend of yours the other night. Old guy. When he gets angry, he loses his English, starts swearing in Kurdish or something? I mentioned your name and he's very *very* pissed off at you, mate. I'd be careful around him if I were you." Smile at them both, the girl looking a little weirded out now, and wave as I walk away.

Unorthodox, Jones, I say to myself going down the stairs. But worth a try.

Good name for my memoirs. *C Jones. It Was Worth A Try*.

Speed's office is a little glass cube with room for desk, safe, wastepaper baskets, a whiteboard on the wall which he never uses and a bookcase with books by Russian defectors from the 80s with little tabs sticking out for the tiny bits about Australia. I remember that, he says, when I catch him reading one. But not quite how Smirnov/Oleg/Dmitri tells it.

"Barrak is not *with* Jabhat al-Akrad, he's down here hiding out from them. They want to kill him," telling Speed and Jenno.

"Says who?" asks Speed.

"Says AX1377," I say, the number for George, "And he's usually right, you have to admit."

"I do," says Speed and leans his chair to the back wall, yells into the next office, "Tell Witless to get in here." Witless is what I call Whitfield and it has stuck; guy can't even find the right office for a meeting. He comes in, the only one who wears a tie in summer. Only one never has rain on his raincoat in winter. Is a registered member of a gun club. Shoots kangaroos with a Steyr. Sleeps in combat pyjamas. Are we getting the picture?

"Sorry," he says, coming in, "I was . . ."

"Whitfield," Speed says, "Is going to be joining you and Jenno on team Syria."

We both look at each other like, WTF. But Speed smiles, knowing what we're thinking and visibly not giving a shit.

"Sir," Witless also calls Speed sir, if you needed any more proof, "I'm not sure..."

Speed holding up his hand, "Whitfield, sit. Jones, tell."

So I tell them what George told me. It's like this, the way Barrak told it to George.

The jailhouse in Hasakeh. If you can imagine a three story concrete industrial site, they put an iron door on the front, block all the windows with sheet metal on the top two floors, put in more metal doors, and call all the rooms on those floors cells.

Bottom two floors are bunks and offices for the cops working there, a couple of holding rooms, armoury.

Barrak is called in there because they're short on cops at the YPG jail and his brother in law runs the place. Never been to the place before. Gets told, go up to the third floor interrogation room. Goes up and there is a YPG guard on a door, and this guard says, "What? They're sending traffic cops now? Ah, who cares. I was supposed to be home three hours ago," and takes off. So Barrak is like, alright, I'll just stand here then, stands next to the door.

Looks through the peephole into the cell, can't believe his eyes. There's a guy in a US Army uniform covered in blood where his arm is nearly torn off, curled up on a bunk, sleeping or unconscious. Now Barrak just about flips out. Because a couple of months ago, a US Army V-22 Osprey aircraft crashed in Kurdish controlled Syria and three Delta Force soldiers were captured. The PKK's YPG made a big deal about handing back two of the Delta Force prisoners and the bodies of the pilots, and scored a big arms shipment in return. But the third one was supposedly never found. So who's this guy and what's he doing here?

Barrak gets real focused, all of a sudden. He's been in this game a long time, because even on road duty, where traffic arguments are settled with automatic weapons, you learn a few things. He slips a round into the chamber of his rifle, and puts the safety on. And that's it for the next few hours.

Until the heavies arrive. Some bad boys from Jabhat al-Akrad. About five of them piling down the corridor, with his brother-in-law the commander of the YPG jail tagging along behind them and he's not looking happy. They stop at the door, four of them, and nod at Barrak to open it. Barrak looks at the head jail cop, he nods too, and these Jabhat al-Akrad lads go in. The head cop closes the door behind them.

"You stay here," he whispers. "And so does the American."

"What do you mean?" says Barrak.

"I mean, no matter what happens, you don't leave this door," the boss says, "And the American does not leave that cell, alright? No matter what. I called you here because I trust you Merdem. Jabhat al-Akrad found this guy so they think they still have visiting rights, but I need to ring YPG headquarters about it." He shuffles off.

Alright, thinks Barrak. No-matter-what. That's pretty clear.

There's about an hour of some pretty ugly noises coming out of the cell, but nothing Barrak hasn't heard before and don't misunderstand, he isn't feeling any sympathy for the American. Americans no better than the Saudis really, give them guns but no bullets, give them artillery shells but no artillery. Can't make up their minds which side they're on. He's listening to the prisoner getting knocked around, thinking, they should give the bastards suicide pills, something like that. That's about as much sympathy as he can dredge up.

OK, then there is a knock on the cell door. The Jabhat al-Akradis want to come out, so Barrak lets them. Except they don't come out alone. They got the American soldier hanging between two of them, out cold or dead, Barrak can't tell, and they're walking off down the corridor.

"Hey," Barrak yells, "Stop! You can't …"

The Jabhat al-Akrad commander is a small, mean looking guy with long sideburns and a moustache – kind of a rockabilly beard. He turns, but the others keep walking, "It's OK," he says nice and calm, "It's been arranged." And he turns to go. Barrak is thinking like, what the hell do I do, but the jail commander was pretty clear on this point, so Barrak draws down on the al-Akradis with his rifle, and flicks off the safety "Stop!" he yells, "Bring the American back, or I fire!"

Now, that gets them finally to all stop and look at him. The commander looks at Barrak, and he's joking now, "My friend, is that a traffic police uniform? Just write us a ticket." The others laugh. All nice and smiling but Barrak sees he's pulled out his pistol from his waist band and seems ready to use it. Not a friendly gesture, even in the Middle East. Barrak sees the gun coming up and plugs the Jabhat al-Akrad commander through the head and chest with a spread of three from the rifle.

For about two milliseconds, it is very quiet in the corridor.

Then it gets very noisy.

"This," Speed is saying, "Is going to send the Americans ballistic, they find out this guy might know something about one of their MIAs."

"Yeah," says Jenno, "Well, unless they're sleeping, they already know about him. That ONA assessment about Barrak was copied to the Americans."

"But this adds a whole extra level of *granularity*," Speed smiles. He's almost rubbing his hands. I start to feel worried. If I've uncovered an actual piece of real intel, this is going to mean a shitload more work for me. Suddenly I'm glad Witless is here, looking so enthusiastic.

Way Barrak told George, the remaining al-Akradis all drop to the floor and start returning fire. Barrak falls backwards into the open cell he was guarding, thinking oh shit what did I just do? Downstairs, about forty cops have all spilt their mint tea and are grabbing flak jackets and guns and standing around looking at each other like, what the hell is going on up there? They all know about the prisoner upstairs and they're thinking it's the Americans have come. The jail boss rounds them up, puts most of them at the doors and windows on the ground floor to watch for American special forces dropping out of the sky, and then takes a few others and starts going up the stairs. But slow.

About half way up, they find the American. To get him out of the way, the al-Akradis have pushed him down the stair well, and he's fallen down the first flight of stairs and is lying on the landing. He's still breathing, but if he broke anything, he probably wouldn't have felt it anyway.

Well, that's good enough for the jail boss. He grabs the American prisoner and hauls arse down stairs again, knowing what his priorities are. Calls the local YPG military commander for help, then calls his boss.

Up in the cells, Barrak is not having a good time. One of the al-Akradi militia has worked up the corridor within two cells of his. The other two are yelling at their buddy to give it up, they still have to get out of this bloody building full of YPG, but the first guy is going mental at them, saying no way any bastard son of a shit eating YPG *traffic cop* is going to kill their commander and live.

Barrak looks down the corridor, the guy is two doors down and diagonally across, with a beautiful angle on Barrak, and the next few shots from his US made carbine go clean through the metal sliding door Barrak is hiding behind and start zinging around the concrete room.

That's enough. Barrak pulls a grenade from his belt and blows all three al-Akradis, what's left of their leader, and half the third floor, to hell.

Which should tell you it's a bad idea to run a red light in Hasakeh, the traffic cops carrying grenades.

The shooting stops, and after about five minutes, enough time for everyone to be properly dead, about twenty YPG militia come running up the steps and his brother-in-law finds Barrak sitting in a pool of his own piss in the cell, mumbling to himself. Deaf, slightly deranged, but not a mark on him. Given his last words to Barrak, it's pretty clear what happened though. He's got to admit, the guy knows how to follow orders.

Two other cells have been blown open, and there's four wounded prisoners in them. There's four dead Jabhat al-Akrad militiamen as well though, which is worse. The jail boss just has time to run downstairs, drag the half dead American up again, throw him in a cell, and put his hand around one of the dead al-Akradi's guns, before any more al-Akradi turn up to find out what happened. Why is he covering for Barrak? The guy is his wife's brother. He doesn't want his wife saying he left one of her family with his arse hanging out - because sure as hell YPG command is going to be looking for someone to blame for this and Barrak has 'my bad' written all over him.

There is a lot of shouting and pointing. Finally the jail boss tells everyone to shut up, if anyone asks, the American prisoner got a gun and a grenade off one of the al-Akradi fools and started shooting. Barrak does not remember much what happens after that.

His brother-in-law puts him in an ambulance and his parting words are, "Get the hell as far away from here as you can, you stupid bastard." So Barrak gets himself to Turkey, works out he's got an Aunt in Australia who'll sponsor his visa, and buys himself a one way ticket.

"So he's been here two years. Doesn't matter what flavour of PKK the guy is, important thing is he's probably still connected, and he might know where the American was taken. Is that Delta Force soldier alive or dead, sort of thing," Speed says. "Your US Forces tend to like precision around that kind of detail."

Jenno turns to Speed, "This explains why Opium is here. We're talking a missing guy from Delta Force, so they've sent the Defence Clandestine Service in to sniff around..."

Speed looks at Jenno, looks at me and Witless, "*If* he is here at all, why would he come in undeclared? Makes no sense. He can just bowl in, flash his credentials and get Security Intelligence Liaison to hand over everything we got."

"Maybe, but come on...you think it is a coincidence ONA sends out an assessment with Barrak's name in it, which goes to the whole security committee of cabinet and everyone in the Five

Eyes so it's about as a secret as a Kardashian boob job, and suddenly a week later the Americans are running an operation here?"

"If they are, which I don't believe," Speed crosses his arms.

Everyone looks at everyone else, like, ok so what do we do now?

"It's actually easy to check," Jenno says, "You got the guy's number in Washington. Call him up. Tell him you got an urgent request."

We all stare at Jenno.

"He calls you back, you can trace the call. Not likely he's going to reroute a simple call to an old mate, right?"

"Jenno," I say, "The way your mind works, I hope you never have children."

He's right though. Speed calls Opium, gets an answering machine. Couple hours later, Opium calls back, asks him what's up. Speed gives him some made up name, asks him can he check does US DCS have any information about the guy. About fifteen minutes after the call, we've got Opium triangulated. He's calling from a zone somewhere near Brighton Le Sands. Sydney. Australia.

"Doesn't mean he's here for Barrak," Speed says.

"Sure," Jenno says, "He's probably an Opera Fan, in town to hear Pavarotti like everyone else."

Alright we can't avoid it anymore. Let me tell you about Robbo. Robbo doesn't like *all* Americans. Robbo hasn't liked all Americans, especially those of the Defence Clandestine Service, since 2005. In 2005 Robbo was a young surveillance officer, straight out of the basic course. And the US Defence Clandestine Service, back then it was called the US Defence Intelligence Agency. One day this anonymous caller leaves a message on a hotline saying some guys in Sydney are storing weapons for an attack on some US Navy ships visiting Australia. The caller names one of the guys. It's one of those calls that get people excited, because the guy is already known as an extremist. But not too excited, because since 2001 we get hundreds of these calls. Resources are tight so the newbie, Robbo, gets the job of following this guy around for a few days, all on his own, see what's what.

Except, he's following this young Lebanese guy around Western Sydney for a while, and starts to get this sinking feeling because buggered if the guy isn't being followed by someone else. Robbo keeps seeing this brown hire car and the two white guys in it, everywhere he goes - and he's just been taught not to believe in coincidences. But shit, he needs to be sure before he goes and makes an idiot of himself by telling the rest of the guys he reckons he's detected surveillance on the target. It's probably the cops. Maybe he should just call base, ask them to check if any cops are also on this guy? That would be typical, both of them following him around. Two white bread white guys in a brown hire car wandering around in the Sydney middle east community screams 'we're cops'. At least Robbo is half Coptic Egyptian, looks like he could live around here.

Goes round for a whole day thinking, *OK, what should I do – stay on the target, or follow the brown hire car home.* After a while, that seems like the best option. Yeah, see where it lives, get some details on those guys, that's the idea. It's probably just cops, no harm done, he can just warn them they've been made. Score some brownie points. The target is just visiting second hand car yards, looks like he's just buying a car anyway, so at the end of the day Robbo gets behind the mysterious brown hire car and when it seems it is peeling off to head home for the day, he stays with it.

Getting dark now, street lights come on. They go Parramatta road, then turn into a dead end side street. Shit, he should have realised that, so he pulls to the kerb, and they make a u-turn and come back at him. Shit shit shit, so he's looking straight ahead, not even at them, lifts a street directory up like *oh yeah, don't worry about me, I'm just sitting here in the dark, looking up a street, not following you.* They get level with his car and – then – they – stop. Guy in the passenger seat winds his window down. Cool as you like, motions Robbo to wind his window down, like he's going to ask directions.

Robbo puts his map book down, winds down his window, ready to be the helpful citizen, says, "Yeah?"

Guy looks at him cold as a Double Bay barmaid, says, "You are goddamn useless at this, you know that?" Deep South USA accent. Robbo doesn't say anything so he goes, "Don't you guys talk to each other? Jee-zus. You stay out of our problems, we stay out of yours, OK? You're just getting in the way, young man."

Robbo says, "Sorry mate, what *are* you on about?" But inside he gets that blown feeling, the kick in the guts which says *I screwed up.*

So they drive off. Robbo thinks, what now? But *they* broke the rules, talking to him, so what the hell, Robbo heads off after them, virtually tailgating. They don't seem to care he's there, he's sitting right behind them like they're mates on a convoy to the beach, and nice as you please the Americans cruise into central Sydney and drive into the underground car park at 19 Martin Place Sydney. It's a big building, and Robbo has had enough, so he calls it a day and goes back to base.

Gets home, ready to fess up and tell how he got made by some Americans, but he's hardly parked the car when the shit hits. Turns out 19 Martin Place is the US Consulate. In the fifteen minutes it took him to get from Martin Place back to work, the DCS officers have called Security Intelligence Joint Operations, who called Canberra, who called the Regional Director for Sydney, who is waiting there and opens the door for him as he pulls on the handbrake. Then spends ten minutes explaining to Robbo what a complete embarrassment he is, gets blown in his own backyard by a couple of Yank tourists.

Robbo got taken off that job, but things only ramped up more. The question of who was doing what got sorted out, and five months later the New South Wales Police moved in and arrested about half a dozen guys and rounded up a shed full of guns, ammunition and photos of the Garden Island Naval base. Turns out they learned on the US Pacific Fleet Facebook that Ticonderoga Class Missile Cruiser USS Port Royal was going to be visiting Sydney in March 2006. And on the US State Dept. Facebook page that US Secretary of State Condoleeza Rice would be attending the Ministerial Trilateral Strategic Dialogue between Australia and Japan in March 2006. They put 1 and 1 together and figured the best place to cause maximum mayhem would be to attack the USS Port Royal while it was berthed mid-city at Garden Island base with Rice on board. Bag themselves some US sailors maybe. Sink that guided missile cruiser with a .22 rifle.

The sarky southern gentleman in the passenger seat of the brown hire car? That was the *first* time Robbo met Opium.

Now it's ten odd years later, the Defence Intelligence Agency is now the Defence Clandestine Service, and Robbo is in charge of the dogs; sitting on his arse making rosters and deciding which insurance deal is likely to give them the least grief next time one of the lads or lasses stacks an Operational Motor Vehicle. Or decides what to do about the latest brainwaves coming from Canberra – like, this one from the external comms department, an email asking shouldn't they all be driving electric cars, it's better for the environment, help the Minister meet his Sustainability Target. 'Good idea', he emails back, 'pls approve the purchase of 63 Teslas, Model S'. Pencil heads.

Clicks send, then walks into the ops room. They got nothing from hotels around Brighton Le Sands. But after a quick call around Sydney hotels in walking distance of the US Consulate, they found Opium staying at the CC Hotel on Hyde Park. Three star boutique, small lobby, fire escape to the ground letting out into a back alley behind Wentworth St, free parking for guests, elevator directly from the car park to the guest rooms, no need to go through the lobby. Perfect fit for a DCS operations officer looking for a base.

Herbal is in the ops room, blowing his eternally running nose. Radio mumbling away in the background, and Herbal has a map of the city on his screen, mouse pointer resting on Double Bay.

"Where is he at?" Robbo asks.

"Who?" sniffs Herbal. It's disgusting. Why the others always want to leave him at home. Idiot won't see a doctor.

"Opium," Robbo says patiently.

"Cell phone shop on New South Head Road. Just left."

"Nugget still on him? Gimme the thing."

"Yeah, you want him to ask what the guy bought?"

"No, Herbal, I want him to get me a phone charger. Gimme the thing," Robbo says, taking the mike. "What's his tag?"

"Rabbit...uh (sniffs) ....rabbit 3."

"Rabbit 3 this is base, you got a sitrep?"

"Yeah. Did you know you can get 10 GB data for 20 bucks a month, flat rate nothing more to pay if you change to Lebana prepaid cellular?"

"Fascinating Nugget..."

"That's actually a good deal," Herbal says, tugging his sleeve to get the mike.

"Shut up both of you," Robbo growls. "*Target* sitrep Nugget."

"Oh, right. Well the package was here for about 30 minutes and left with six Blackberries and a bunch of sim cards."

"Six?!"

"I just checked with the guy. I'm waiting for his boss. Might be able to slide a look over his shoulder at the invoice, get the numbers for you, unofficial like."

"Brilliant stuff Nugget. Store got CCTV? See if you can..."

"Already asked for it. Think I'm wet?"

"Alright. Stop yapping and get back to work, base out."

"Rabbit 3, out."

"That *was* a good deal for 10GB data," Herbal says.

Robbo ignores him, lays down on his couch, "Why the hell is a senior DCS ops officer buying off-the-shelf comms gear from a bloody shop?"

"Maybe for his kids? Cheaper here than in the States?"

"Opposite Herbal. No, if he was running a sanctioned DCS op, he'd be getting his gear from the US Defence attaché here, or CIA."

Herbal sucks back some mucus, "*Gnnn*, yeah, unless hey, unless they want this one to be deniable."

"What?"

"Yeah, we find them with a whole lot of spook kit, on some sort of undeclared op, then it is official and there could be all sorts of shit. But if they are using off the shelf gear, they can always say it was unsanctioned..."

Just then the radio crackles again, "Base, Rabbit – 3, you still there Robbo?"

Herbal leans over to the mike, "Yeah, we're here, go ahead Rabbit-3"

"Got some good news/bad news," he says. "Good news, I got the phone numbers. Bad news, he bought the BBM enterprise package. Rabbit-3 out."

"What?" asks Robbo, "Why is that bad news?"

Herbal throws down the mike, knocking over a half plastic cup of coffee, which he ignores, just moves out the way and watches it slow leak itself off the table.

"Hey! Why is a 'BBM enterprise package' bad news?" Robbo repeats.

"You got to start turning up to your own team meetings," Herbal tells him. "We had that cyber guy from Canberra here last week, telling us what's the latest encryption kit people can buy on the open market, and he said," he takes a big sniff, and pushes some coffee onto the floor with a pen. "He said Blackberry has just updated its enterprise grade messenger app, that's for business level contracts, to FIPS 140, 2 cryptographic library-enabled messaging," he recites, by memory.

"That sounds like the shit," Robbo says.

"It *is* the shit," Herbal replies. "They're offering it to like private security companies, defence contractors sort of thing. It means great, we got the phone numbers, we get warrants, we can listen in if they're stupid enough to use voice. But if they use Blackberry Messenger with FIPS 140 encryption, it will take days, maybe weeks for the DSD supercomputers to break it down. It's a freaking nightmare, uses a separate encrypt code for each message back and forth so you crack one code, it only gives you *one* message. You need to crack like a dozen codes just to read a single conversation. No way you can do it in real time."

"Still, we *can* do it if we throw enough time and bandwidth at it?" Herbal nods. "And it is off the shelf gear, so my question is the same. He's here on DCS business? Why isn't he using Agency kit?"

"He's going off reservation," Herbal declares, coffee dripping onto his shoes now, "I told you. I got a sense about this stuff. It's spooky, my instincts."

The angle I'm moving on, before I get told to do it anyway, is the Barrak angle. Take Jenno and decide to cold call him 9 o'clock on a Wednesday night. I warn George we're going in, so he can prepare to drop by his work the day after, get a quote on fixing his car, get the guy's reaction.

We take our Immigration ID, no sense freaking him out yet. Home in his new promised land is a weatherboard in Ethel St., Allawah, opposite the high school. The people inside are Bosnians though, just rent the granny flat to Barrak. Yeah sure, we can go back there, they don't mind. We knock on the flywire door, can hear the telly on inside. Guy looks like he fell asleep on his sofa after a hard day bashing panels into shape. Mid 30s, solid, black fuzz on his jaws, tight wiry black hair...looks like that Aussie actor plays the Muslim in all the TV shows.

We show him our IDs. "Yeah, is there some problem?" he asks. Not aggressive, a bit concerned.

"Sorry to call so late," Jenno says, "We just finished another interview and we were nearby, can we come in?"

Opens his door wide and indicates with his head it's OK. We all sit in the kitchen. Plain, simple neat. You get the idea the guy lives a simple life, works hard. "We get reports all the time about people, anonymous reports, have to check them out, hope you understand," I tell him. "You were granted a family carer visa yes? To look after..." I check the papers I brought with me, "Eli el Safadi?"

"My Aunt," he says.

"Your Aunt, yeah," I nod, "How is she?"

"Alright," he says. "She's old, why?

Jenno leans forward, "Just, on your visa application, you might not remember, you had to answer a question whether you were ever a member of the Defence, Police or Intelligence Services of your country, and you said "no.""

Did his eyes narrow a little bit? Maybe. He nods, "Sure, because I wasn't."

"OK, well you have to be precise around that, sometimes it can be confusing, especially with Syria, we appreciate that. So let me ask, you were never in the Syrian Army, police, intelligence services, or even like a Syrian militia, you know Syrian Free Army, that sort of thing."

He's definitely wary now, "Someone is lying to you," he says. "Whatever they said, I was never a member of any of those things. I worked in a garage in Hasakeh, where I grew up. I fixed cars there. I fix cars here. No army, no police, no militia."

I raise my eyebrows, "No? You're an ethnic Kurd right? What about PKK, YPG, any of those?"

He's sticking with it, "Sure, I'm Kurdish. But I stayed away from all that trouble. And I was happy to come here for my aunt, get away from it for good."

"So your official answer," Jenno repeats, "Is still you were not a member of any of those kind of organisations?"

"No. Never."

He is staring back a bit defiant now. I'd almost believe him, if I didn't believe George more. George isn't smart enough to make up a story like he told about this guy.

I look at Jenno and nod, and he reaches out his hand to the guy to shake, "OK, then, thanks for your time." We stand up to go.

The guy looks confused, walks with us to the door. "So…what happens now?" he asks, "My residence permit…"

"Oh, nothing more," I tell him, "We get told stuff like this all the time. Unless we get some other information makes us ask the same questions. Then it might be more serious," I tell him. "But we'll just put your answer on file and that might be all for now." I smile my best helpful public servant smile. "Have a nice night, sorry again to bother you."

"He's good," Jenno says, as we get in our limo, "Very cool."

"Yeah, we need to find a way in," I agree. "George aint it. Some other way. If that guy knows about the Delta Force soldier, it's better for him we hear it first."

Funny thing, as we are doing our counter surveillance run on the way home (McDonald's drive through, get the burgers, oops forgot the shakes, go through twice) Jenno is convinced he sees this black SUV pull into McDonalds, pull out again when we get our burgers, and pull in again when we go for the shakes. He's watching to see does it follow us away the second time, but he doesn't see it again. So we forget it, start moaning to each other about how they changed their BBQ sauce to this crappy mayonnaisy stuff now. What is this, France? We're supposed to like mayonnaise on burgers? He drops me at our place and then heads off for some icecream. We'll check Barrak's phone records, see did he call anyone we know after we visited, but it's another busted night of not getting very far at all.

Story of my life.

"Barber shop in Crow's Nest," Shirl says the next morning.

She knows my brain doesn't start working until 10 a.m., likes throwing things at me like that as I walk through the door 0830.

She's really rocking the Anne Hathaway look today, got black boots with heels, those faux leather pants, white blouse with a black jacket over it. Older than me and Jenno, but still young enough to get away with it. She could get a job with an ad agency, running million dollar accounts, but I guess she just loves working with me and Jenno too much.

Right…

"What, Jenno gone for a haircut?" I ask. Why should I care where Jenno goes for a haircut?

"That mobile phone you asked me about, where it lives," she says. "The number you filched off Serwan Askari's wrist? I tracked it down."

"Move around much?" I say, going over to her desk. Looking at her screen, shows a map with a few blotches on it, where the mobile has been faithfully reporting to the network its location.

"Nup, couple of trips into town the last couple of weeks, otherwise, at the barber shop." I look at the blotches. Pretty big blotches.

"How do you know it's a barber shop? Those spots on the map, they cover what? Few hundred meter radius?"

"Two hundred. I looked up the streets. Got a hit on an operation we were running on a barber shop on Willoughby Road. *You* were there, couple of weeks ago, night job before your Pub Quiz? On the roof, remember?"

"The Lebbos? I remember camping out all night in someone's dirty laundry, watching a whole lot of nothing, yeah."

"Not Lebanese; they were Kurdish Peshmerga, Jones, read the damn briefs," Shirl points at the screen. "Zerevani Forces. Officially they're Kurdish Red Crescent. *Unofficially* they're on a national tour recruiting for the Peshmerga. You sit staring at a window for 12 hours and you don't even know who you're looking at. OK, I know I'm no analyst but the middle of that mobile phone blob is a barber shop which you had on 24 hour surveillance when John Kerry came to town. Or maybe that is just a coincidence?"

"John Kerry was in town that night? That's why I was lying on a roof under a hills hoist full of stained jocks?"

"I just sent you the file. Read it, Jones."

Read it; right. One question, "Hey who is John Kerry?"

A shopfront on Willoughby Road, between a burger joint and a used-book shop that sells nothing but second hand porn, the pages stuck together. Fading letters on the window say *Barber Shop Unisex: Men's <u>and</u> Women's Cuts*.

It's a bad haircut. Higher on the neck than I usually have it and that means the maniac cutting it, who doesn't wet his razor, burns about an acre of neck skin as he scrapes away the fuzz.

I must have missed the sign saying: *Customers <u>Not</u> Welcome*. Cause I walk in, there's five Kurdish guys playing cards, some flies hanging off a long spiral of flypaper, and no one having their hair cut. Maybe this *is* the place I was looking for after all. So I point at an empty barber stool and they all look at each other like 'what the?' Too slow to kick me out though. Some kind of code goes from eyes to eyes and one of them loses, and has to do the haircut. Others stop playing cards, just sit there smoking, watching. Like, hey lookit, Xemu is going to cut hair, this should be interesting.

47

Make it easy for the guy, I ask for a number three buzzcut. He looks at the others, they translate for him, he gets stuck in with the electric razor.

Now my usually spooky instincts are telling me this is the place, but which of them is the guy I'm looking for – the one I was talking to who spat into the phone when he thought I was Serwan Askari? They're whispering away in low voices and I'm trying to pick out a voice I heard on the phone once. Any one of them could be the one I'm looking for, but three of 'em look a little young. The fourth though, he's this wrinkly old geezer, and when he says shut up, they shut up. He points at my neck, like, *there's a bit there you didn't burn Xemu*, and the guy goes at it with the shaver again. Yeah, this could be the elderly Kurdish profanitor I've come here for.

Xemu puts down the shaver, steps back, looking kind of surprised it's over, and I'm not dead or bald. Says, "Ah, twenty bucks?" So I give him a hundred and apologise and they're all reaching for wallets to help Xemu make change and looking at me like, what kind of pork eating dirtbag pays for a buzz-cut with a hundred? Xemu poking around in the cash register, which anyone can see is empty. I mosey on over to the old guy's table while they argue who should give me change, and I say to Wrinkles, "I have a message for you from Serwan Askari."

Now, suddenly, the only sound is flies trying to unstick themselves from flypaper. Bullseye. Ol' Wrinkles lifts his eyebrows, "What message?"

"Serwan says to tell you to screw yourself."

Wrinkles gets a little squinty around the eyes, but no other reaction. And that's all I notice, because around about then, must have been when Xemu the Bad Barber hits me on the back of the head with the cash drawer.

I wake up. It's bright but fuzzy and it hurts. Someone is throwing water in my face. Voice says, "…wake up. Hey you, here, look here, Serwan told you to say anything else?"

"No," I say, rubbing my head, trying to focus, his face is just a pale blob, "Or, yeah, actually he said something about your mother, and a goat."

Lights out again.

I wake up. Now its bright and red and it really hurts. But pain is *good*. 'Pain is life', some philosopher once said, and vice versa, so I must be alive. Probably a Norwegian philosopher. Philosophy like that doesn't come from a country with good surf. Try to open my eyes, realize they *are* open, and with a whack like a Sherrin football in the face the whole annoying world comes suddenly into focus and there's Speed and a bunch of flowers and Jenno (with chocolates), Money, a nurse, plus four minions from *Despicable Me* doing a mamba on my brain pan. Whitfield is there too. That's nice, considering I called him a jerk, more than once.

"Ow," says Money, looking at my bandaged head.

"Shut up Money," I say. "That's my line. Ow."

I'm in a hospital room at St Vincent's hospital, big enough for four beds and a bedside table and two black plastic visitor's stools. Bed with a 'privacy' curtain on three sides. Little window with white nylon curtains looks out over a patch of gravel at the base of the big chimney where they burn the human off-cuts and bandages.

"The good news for the taxpayers, Jones, is that you got multiple contusions on your face, a cracked skull, broken ribs, and first degree burns on your neck, but you won't miss much work," says Speed.

Nurse comes over and starts dabbing some stinging purple stuff on my cheekbones and forehead where there seem to be a

49

million bruises and cuts and all I remember is Xemu and the cash draw so they must have partied on my face some other time I forgot. Small blessing, memory loss.

"Bad news," Speed continues, "Is that you walked into the middle of a joint op being run by us, the Federal and New South Wales Police, picked a fight, got thrown in a garbage bin and if we didn't have the shop under 24 hour surveillance you'd be mince in the back of a garbage truck by now. And now it looks like that barber shop is suddenly closed for summer."

Nurse straightens up, looks at Speed like, *should you be saying this with me in here?* Adjusts a tube I hadn't even noticed was in my nose. But Speed is pissed off, a journalist from the Herald could be standing there, he couldn't care. Jenno puts a hand on the nurse's arm, points to my cut-up chin, "You missed a big cut, right there. Don't be shy with the stingy stuff."

Speed is waiting. "I'm waiting," he says.

"I complained about my haircut," I gurgle. "Guy was an artist. They're a temperamental people."

Speed looks patient, or sleepy. Both are dangerous looks, so take your pick. "Shirl told me you were out following up on a community interview," he says. "So, you want to tell me what you were doing, why you didn't do a formal check on the address before you went barging in there, and why they took such violent exception to you?"

"I'm leaving," says the nurse and Money goes with her, kisses my knee on the way through, and takes my chocolates with a wink.

"Good question sir," I whisper. "Well, I got this," I hand him the piece of paper which I fished out of my jeans when I woke up. I'm thinking Wrinkles must have put it in my pocket. "It confirms a connection between this guy I interviewed, Serwan, who is raising funds for the Kurds, and the five Peshmerga recruiters." It says:

Tell Serwan he has 48 hours.

Speed reads it a couple of times, like he wants to ask the question, but knows that really, he doesn't actually want to ask.

He hands it to Whitfield. "The words 'intensely interested'," says Speed, "Do not do justice to the way I feel about reading your report." Whitfield drops it on the floor, and steps on it.

Jenno watches everyone leave. "Karn is waiting outside," he says. "Told her I'd let her know if you were up to seeing visitors or not. You know, you look like something that got blown up and then eaten in a Mad Max movie."

"She do it with An-tho-ny?" I ask.

"Who? Nah, apparently not. Money reckons you're still in," goes to the door, "Shall I tell Karn to come in? She's pretty pissed off at you about something though."

You have to love redheads. Girl leaves the party with some narcomaniac low life artiste because I'm a bit late, now I'm lying bashed to a pulp in the acute care ward, but *she's* pissed off.

"What the hell. Tell her come on in."

I take the nurse call button in my hand though, might need that in a minute, mood she's in.

"Bless me Father for I have sinned. You know how you said you wanted me to share my moral dilemmas? Even the work ones?"

"Hello Jones, yes, if it helps you."

He tries to sound bored, but come on, the guy loves it when I talk work.

"OK, so here is where we are at: I was out doing this boring old interview and it turns out the guy I was interviewing is linked to this group of bad ass Kurdish barbers somehow. I went to talk to them but they beat the crap out of me and disappeared."

"Jones! Are you hurt?"

"Sorry Father, missed that, had to move one of my feeding tubes because it was rubbing on the bandage on my face."

"They didn't break your funny bone then."

51

"No. Anyway, this is my dilemma. I really should be spending my time finding these Kurdish barber shop guys, because it was my fault they've gone underground. But what I really want to do is see if we can track down this US Delta Forces guy who is missing."

"I see, I see…" He's really giving it some thought. "Now, which do you think is the greater good?"

"Well, if I rounded up the Kurdish militia recruiters, that would be pretty good, but if we found out what happened to the Delta Forces guy before anyone else, that would be *great*."

He sighs. "Not good for you, Jones, good for the community. Good for the safety and well-being of your fellow man. Remember we are working on getting you to think beyond your own immediate needs and desires."

OK. Tough call. I mean, taking Serwan and the PKK Barbershop Quintet off the streets could definitely help World Karma. But we still don't know that they are doing anything really bad. Ask me, the more people who go to Iraq and get themselves killed, it just helps the gene pool.

Scoring major bonus points by getting Barrack to cough up the intel on the Delta Forces soldier though, before Opium gets to him...

"Well, Father, my fellow man would probably care more about me finding five harmless PKK barbers than a missing American soldier, so by your logic I should go after them."

"Harmless? Didn't they put you in hospital Jones?"

"Well. Yes. But I was rather rude to them, and that's a whole 'nother confession Father. Soon as I get off the drip."

Picture a blonde haired, steely eyed man in jeans and blue Oxford shirt, white t shirt underneath, six six, square jaw with a three o'clock shadow. Keeps his wallet in his briefcase so it doesn't wreck the fit of the jeans across his arse. That's Jenno.

And I'm not even making that up. That guy plays Wolverine ever loses his job, Jenno could walk right into it. He's standing in front of a whiteboard, doing what I should be doing, if I weren't in the car wreck ward of St Vincent's. It's late. The fluoros are stuttering and a Yo Yo biscuit is going soft on the table. Jenno whips up the felt pen from the table and twirls it around in his hand. "Righto Jones, what do I have to cover for you?" Looking at the notes Shirley gave him and talking to the air.

First he makes a list of what Jones and him, and now Witless, are working on:

- Kurdish barbershop quintet (recruiting for Peshmerga, or something more evil?)
- Serwan (connected to above?)
- Opium (unsanctioned op?)
- Barrak (target of Opium, key to US MIA?)

Kurdish barbershop quintet, and some names. Next to that he writes: *AWOL.* They have to be a high priority. Put an 'A' next to that one because as much as he loves Jones, that operation got royally screwed by Jones waltzing in there and scaring them into hiding. The barbershop is now closed for business. So they have to be found, pronto in case they got scared into doing something stupid. But the police are all over that.

Then there's this young guy Jones went out to see, the time Money had to fetch him. Serwan the taxi driver. According to Shirl, he's got a link to the Peshmerga guys, but he's raising money, not trying to recruit for the Peshmerga so the connection isn't clear. What else they got in common except they all seem to be pissed off at Jones? OK, nothing dramatic there. Draws a line between them anyway. Raising funds, that's a B job, keep that guy for when Jones gets out.

Third: *Opium et al.* And what the hell do we know except there might be five American DCS covert ops agents running around Sydney doing who knows what? Jenno is convinced it is too much of a coincidence with Barrak popping up at the same time, but they could be up to anything. Jones was more motivated about that one than Jenno is, probably because Jones used to be in surveillance and is mates with Robbo who got royally humiliated by *Opium* that time. Nah, let Opium do what he wants, after all he's on our side, right? Right. There are no sides.

Hmmm. Barrak. Jensen knows George a bit, and is betting George's info is solid. So it's pretty certain Barrack is PKK (YPG faction) on the run from a rival Kurdish faction. He was one of the last ones to see the Delta Force soldier alive? Jones is right, if they can get Barrack talking, it'll be Australia Day medals for everyone.

So he needs to get some face time with Merdem Barrak. Alone. Because Barrack must have looked at Jones that time and thought, 'Nothing to fear'. Jones means well, sure, but isn't exactly intimidating. Let's see how Mr. Barrak the Kurdish traffic cop likes having six feet of blonde haired blue eyed 20th generation Viking breathing down his neck.

Picks up his car keys. And the useless piece of shit garage door opener which always seems to be dying on him. Then the phone rings.

Robbo is dark. He doesn't mind losing a target, part of the game, he can admire the art in it sometimes. Doesn't mind getting sprung by Joe public, confronted, yelled at, abused - coz if you aint dyin' you aint tryin', as the Anzacs used to say. Annoying getting the cops called on his people by old ladies who have nothing better to do than look out their blinds and wonder why someone is sitting in a car outside their house, but what really gets him, is when he's doing a job on someone, and they work out they're being followed, and they go ahead do their business right under his nose, like they don't give a shit.

And when it's a Yank intelligence service, and *Opium* in particular, it really gets on Robbo's nerves.

So he's in a room off a basement parking lot, looks like computer nerd heaven. Fluoro lights, workbenches full of wires and circuit boards, smell of sulphur, burnt.

"See here's the bit," Herbal is saying to him, rewinding the
CCTV video from the telephone shop. Picture frozen of an older
guy in a white short sleeve shirt picking up some brochures.
"Right, he grabs this brochure, looks at the phone again, ok yeah,
that's the one he wants, and then…" Herbal sniffs and points,
"Right…there."

And hello- there it is, the guy turns to walk down the aisle, in the
middle of picking up comms gear to support a covert op, and he
looks up, straight…into…the…security…camera. Kind of half
pauses, but what does he do? Does he go, oh shit a CCTV
camera, that's buggered it, the whole thing is blown? Nup, he's
already clocked that the camera is there. He looks up at it, and he
winks.

Herbal sniffs, pauses the video, "Bloody amateur, you ask me,"
he says, "Knows the camera is there, but goes ahead with his
business anyway? Can't find a shop without CCTV? Vastly
overrated, yer US Defence Clandestine Service."

Robbo sneers, "Herbal, he's no amateur – he just didn't give a
damn about the camera. Maybe he thinks we aren't bothered
about him, maybe he knows we are, but shouldn't be. He just
didn't care."

Herbal chews on this for a minute. Unwraps the paper on some
horrible green wad of organic gum and jams it in his mouth to
help process the problem. "So why," he pounces, triumphant,
"I'm thinking, if he knows we know, and he doesn't care, why
not just come to us anyway. Tell us his business, maybe ask for
some help."

"Six phones. Way we'd do it, that's one phone each, one spare for contingencies, so I'd say he's got at least a five person team here," Robbo points out. "Whatever it is, it's big, and he doesn't need our help."

Roof of the hospital is a kind of gravel garden thing, few half dead plants in concrete boxes that only get water when it rains, and a lot of cigarette butts, the staff mostly using the place to have a fag instead of going all the way down to the ground floor. I crawled my busted arse up here to get away from the lunatics in the ward they moved me into, but I'm starting to feel much better, can turn my head to both sides now without passing out. I want to get out of here, not least because of the company on my ward. Ted's a guy wears rugby shirts with crocodiles on the left breast, should be in a St Ives private hospital but had his accident while on a pub crawl in the Cross, ended up in St Vinnies hospital. Tells sex jokes and talks about 'rugger' and is baiting Rob the druggie in the bed across the room who broke both ankles jumping out a window and can't walk, calling him a poofter, asking him does he pay for his drugs by sucking dick. I decide to get out of the ward, so Rob is free and clear to hobble over to Ted's bed on his double plastered feet and stab Ted with the plastic fork I saw him hiding under his pillow after lunch.

Money is visiting, and she brought my chocolates back. Or some to replace them anyway. Got her head back against some clay pot with a dried out cactus, eyes closed, soaking in the sun, hair is getting a little longer now and it's going honey blonde again, the Jensen's natural colour. Got one little bead of sweat between her breasts down there where the wonderbra joins up.

"You like watching people Jones?"

Move around a bit on the bench, so it hurts less, "Nah, more of an animal watcher, me. Pigeons, cats, that sort of thing…"

Turns and looks right at me, like she does, cheeky as, "You were watching *me*."

I blush. "Yeah, well. True. Your boobs anyway. But I think of you like a sister, right, so I think of your boobs like I would a sister's boobs, so it was more of an objective appraisal type of look, you know. See how they're doing."

"BS. Aren't you getting enough from Karn?"

Karn. She spends a half hour in the hospital telling me that never in her *life* did anyone *ever* turn up *four hours* late to meet *her*, what sort of egomaniac thinks *anyone* will wait *four hours* for them? The nurse comes in, so luckily that stops her, then in front of the nurse, Karn gives me a kiss so pornographic it would be banned in Tasmania. Like a dog pissing on a fencepost, I suppose. Marks her territory in front of the nurse, and she leaves.

"Plenty," I say, "Of something. Hard to define it though."

"Not sex then."

"Nah. Does sex have a parallel?"

"What?"

"Like is there a state between two people which is definitely not celibacy but which is not actually proper sex? That's where we're at."

"Jones," she sighs. "Get the girl drunk. Tell her you're crazy about her. She's just waiting to hear it."

"Right. How about I get *you* drunk and *you* tell her 'Hey, Jonesy is crazy about you', so I can deny it later if I need to?"

"We do it that way, I'm more likely to have sex with her before you do."

I blink a couple of times and she shakes her head, "It will really creep me out if you turn that comment into some sweaty fantasy, Jones."

Heartless. Hands it to you on a plate and then throws it against the wall.

So I'm on the hospital roof talking rubbish with his sister, meanwhile down below Jenno is taken out of play.

An old Commodore, piece of shit built like an M1 tank with a bull bar, must have been doing fifty when it hits Jenno's door at a perfect 90 degrees. Takes his piece of shit government car and flattens it against the wall of a carpark and the other driver, whoever it was, because of course no one saw anything, jumps out the car and runs. Into the car park. The car is out of registration and last time it was resold was 1989, so forget finding out who was driving it. It's got thirty years of prints on it and not a single piece of paper in it.

That's funny, eh? Like when did you ever see an old rusty Commodore that wasn't full of condom and chip wrappers, crumpled tallyho packs, smelly blue singlets and sun-dried parking tickets? When did you ever see a *clean* rusty Commodore? This one I could have taken mum to church in. If she hadn't been excommunicated in '03. For calling the Archbishop a bum bandit. To his face.

So I get a phone call to tell me Jenno's in the same hospital as me, but not in the *'could walk away and get back to work if he wasn't a lazy bastard'* ward like me, more in the *'will probably have to drink his beer through a tube rest of his life'* ward. He was unconscious when they found him, got a busted wrist, but they can't wake him up so they're thinking major head trauma.

Takes us ages to find him. When they finally let us in to see him, a nurse gives us the latest. "His skull isn't fractured and we've given him a scan, there's no internal haemorrhaging, but he won't wake, so we're monitoring brain activity. It looks suppressed, but we don't have a cause yet." She hands me a pillowcase, "It's his clothes. He was pretty banged up when he came in, so we had to you know, cut the clothes off, save a little time checking him. Anyway…" she says looking at her watch and wandering off.

No shit he was banged up. Bruised all over, left hand in plaster, and a machine going beep with about twenty wires glued to his head.

I look in the bag.

"Bastard."

Money looks up from her phone. She's sat herself on his bed making lists of stuff she needs to do for Jenno now, stuff she needs to do when Jenno gets out, and stuff she needs to do to the bastard in the Commodore when she finds out who he was. "What?" she asks.

"They cut it clean up the back. My shirt. Swine was wearing one of *my* shirts."

Now in the Denzel Washington version, the faithful friend of recently torpedoed intelligence agent goes back to the office to file a report (who, and I mean it, who out there thinks anyone really does the admin?) and looks over at his mate's empty desk and sees a hastily scrawled note in his friend's writing by the phone... "3 p.m., meet Scarface at Woolly Bay Hotel, come alone." This leads Denzel on a revenge fuelled rampage through the underbelly of the city culminating in a fight to the death finish between Scarface and Denzel in an abandoned warehouse festooned with handily placed steel pipes and rocket propelled grenades.

Easing my still tender frame into his chair, I however find the following hastily scrawled note by Jenno's phone, "Medium marinara pizza, extra olives."

Shirley comes over and sits on the desk, crossing her legs daintily. When we talk about Shirley, I want you to think Audrey Hepburn with attitude. And a bosom. And hips. OK, nothing like Audrey Hepburn, but she's got movie star genes. She wears her age and her clothes well, and I do find myself wondering...you know. She's divorced with a kid and a kelpie in St Ives though, so she outgrew losers like me back when Springsteen released *The Rising*.

"He's OK?" she asks. "Jensen?"

"Won't know until they try to wake him up. He's in a coma at the moment," I tell her. "Then again it's Jenno - if he is brain damaged, how will we know?"

She gives me the look, lets me know that was Inappropriate. Hands me a piece of paper full of numbers. "You'll want this. I ran it for the police but I knew you'd want a copy."

"Of what."

"Jensen's inbound calls this morning, up to when he left and had the accident. They're treating it as a hit run, car not registered and insured sort of thing, but because of who he is, also that it might have been deliberate. I got full details for the telephone numbers too, all except one," she points down the page, "This one, he got just before he left. Took the call, then stood up and said he had an urgent meeting. I'd normally need a warrant to get details on that one. I'm blind on it."

Yeah, the incoming calls list. That would have been exactly the first thing I thought of, straight after staring blankly into space and scratching my arse. Thank God there are professionals like Shirl working here. I lean over, "Who has a number that *you* can't look up?"

"There's only two types of number I need warrants for," She puts her pencil in her mouth, "First is politicians and second is diplomats."

"Diplomats? Jenno doing any joint ops with any other intelligence services, that you know about?"

"None, that I know about," Shirley says carefully.

Take Shirley by the elbow and walk her to the stairs, "But, if for example someone wanted detail on that phone number without, you know, having to bother a busy man like the Attorney General for a warrant, that person would … um…take someone shopping perhaps?"

"Jones…stop whispering."

"Or a very expensive restaurant?" I whisper.

"Jones."

"Of her choosing, of course…"

She peels my hand off her elbow and goes up a couple of steps, "This is Jensen. I've already asked the telecoms liaison to do what they can through the back door …and by the way, I'm flattered, but not at all tempted."

Turns at the top of the steps, "Of course, if you worked out a little more…" Winks and disappears.

Don't believe her. I'm not carrying a single surplus kilo. Tone, that's all I lack. Tone.

To misquote a famous sociopath, in the world of secret intelligence there are known knowns, known unknowns, and unknown unknowns. So let's review where we are at this point in the game.

Known knowns. There is a pyramid of Syrian Kurds raising money to send home to support their ailing grandparents (yeah, right) and a taxi driver called Serwan sitting at the top of it. There is a bunch of rather violent newly-arrived Kurdish barbers who are (were) using a barber shop in Crow's Nest as a recruitment center for the Peshmerga armed forces. Serwan has been in contact with them, but I scared them into hiding by allowing them to beat me senseless (yeah, right). There is a Kurdish traffic cop (Barrak) hiding out in Australia who may or may not know the whereabouts of a missing US soldier, and *coincidentally* (yeah, right) a American DCS (c)overt ops team arrived in town and got very busy shortly after this.

And Jenno was called for an urgent meeting by 'someone', possibly diplomat, possibly politician, immediately before 'someone' put him in hospital with a very nicely executed hit and run.

Known unknowns. Are any of these things connected? Is Serwan working with the Kurdish barbers? Are the Kurdish barbers really here recruiting, or is that just a cover for something else? Does Serwan know where the Kurdish barbers are now? Why are

Opium and his Defence Clandestine Service team really here and why haven't they declared themselves? Is any of this connected with Barrak? And does Barrak actually have any info on the missing Delta Force soldier?

And most important of all, what the hell am I going to do about Karn?

Unknown unknowns: Er, unknown.

There's not much of a queue Wednesdays so I can pop in and out during my lunch hour.

I open the door and can tell by the aftershave this isn't one of the regulars.

"You new then?" I ask.

"I'm just filling in for the day," comes the voice, "Please, begin?"

"OK before we start I should remind you that everything we say in here is covered by privilege and you can't repeat it outside this…"

"One usually starts with 'Bless me Father'. You must be Charlie Jones."

"Yes Father, how do you do?"

"Father Thomas told me about you."

"Righto, so anyway, it's three days since my last confession, here are my sins…"

"Go on."

"Lust and uhm, what's the one where you want to kill someone."

"Wrath? Malice of Forethought?"

"If wrath means there is a Commodore driving bastard out there who doesn't know I am after him but when I catch him he will gladly dig his own grave with the bleeding stumps of his fingers and then cut his own throat with a rusty knife rather than face my wrath, then yes, wrath is the one."

"Let's get back to the lust first."

"Sure. You guys are all the same."

"Not sure what you mean. Now, what or who is it you lust after and do you honestly regret it enough to repent of your sin?"

"Father Thomas usually just takes my word for it."

"I am not he."

"Right thou are. Well, the object of my lust is a girl called Karn who I have been seeing a lot lately but we haven't got past a bit of a fondle and it's killing me."

"Karn is a girl?" He sounds a bit surprised. Must be new out of the seminary, this one.

"Yeah, I know, it's a dumb name but apparently her parents forgot to put the 'E' on the birth certificate, so what can you do? OK, can we move onto the wrath?"

"You must, uhm, show contrition for your lust. Are you truly sorry for feeling this way about your friend?"

"Hell yes Father. I wish the sight of her didn't burn a hole in my halo, but I guarantee if you saw her, you'd have something to talk about at *your* next confession. We're talking goddess here."

"Hmm. And how do you intend to avoid being placed in the situation of lusting after her next time you see her? That is also important to consider."

"Well, call me a dreamer, but next time I hope to be confessing to fornication."

"I can see you think this is funny."

"No. Father Thomas said I should be honest in here. Can we move to the wrath please? I seriously think I am going to kill someone for what they did to Jenno."

"I think, perhaps you had better come back when Father Thomas is here next week."

Update on the known unknowns: Shirl's back door contacts came through. We now know it was a *Turkish consulate* number that called Jenno right before his accident. Turks? Why would the Turks want to put Jenno in hospital? I mean, yes, he does lock all the windows and then fart when you're sharing a car with him, but would you try to kill him for that?

Ten hours after discharge and I'm meeting George and George says "Hey mate, nice bruises" and I say "Yeah," and that's about it until I've got the prawns and the bread rolls in and I already got the Cokes under my arm so it's down to the docks in the sunshine where I can swing my feet over the edge and throw bread at the seagulls and listen to George suck the prawn heads dry.

"You not eating those prawn heads?" he asks, and leans across and takes mine.

"So how was the protest?"

"You didn't see the news?" Assumes I do nothing but watch the 2 a.m. news on SBS.

"Nah mate, I was busy *not* shagging a redhead," I tell him.

"Well, all messed up wasn't it. Call this a democracy? It's a bloody police state mate. Bloody Pavarotti's rights come before the rights of decent tax paying Australians mate…"

I let him rave on for about fifteen minutes and he eventually winds down and slurps a prawn head, swigs his Coke and mumbles from somewhere inside a bread roll…

"Could have bloody told me, by the way, youse were going to knock down the door of that Barrak bloke."

"What?"

"I'm in the traffic office yesterday paying a speeding fine, and he's there."

"And?"

"And I had to pay it meself, no thanks to you. Won't even help a bloke with a speeding fine?"

"No, George, what about Barrak?"

"Oh, him. I says to him, how's it goin mate haven't seen you at prayers and he says to me, nah mate I been a bit nervous lately, tryin' to lay low, and I says what for nervous, and he says ah mate, the bloody Aussie security mukhabarat mate, they come last night and got me outa bed and start asking me about that American soldier."

He throws a prawn head in the water, "You shoulda told me youse was going to see him again so I coulda prepared, I stood there like a dork, didn't know what to say." Got flour on his moustache. Looks at the bruises on my face, "Supposed to be a *team*. Hey, did his missus beat up on you or what?"

"Wasn't us," I say. Because it wasn't (was it?) "Besides, better if you look surprised, why should you know anything?"

"Anyway, he says they were youse guys. Two of 'em. They showed him some badges, government writing and all."

"We don't have badges," I tell him. I show him my ID again.

"Like I care," George says, "He says they had badges. You told me, George, just report what they say. Don't embellish. It's what he said."

We go over it again.

I had to lure my Mum out to the car with the promise I'd visit my Dad's grave with her. What I had in mind was to distract her with a little trip to Coogee, maybe some fish and chips on the beach, exchange a few profanities about the Prime Minister and then home, but she wouldn't be in that.

"How long since you visited your father?" she said.

"He's compost mum."

"Don't be gross, you know what I mean."

So now I am standing next to his plot in the cemetery at Waverly, which I can imagine just might, a hundred years ago, have had a view of the sea, but that was before six blocks of flats went in between it and the coast.

My dad lies on a corner, next to an Italian bloke.

"Always did like the aisle seat, your dad." Mum leans down to pick a soursob out of the gravel.

"Was that luck or did you ask for it?"

"Oh, had to pay a bit extra for a plot on a corner, but I couldn't imagine the idea of your dad wedged in between two strangers," she says. "Just seemed...wrong."

Her small soft hand steals into mine. The skin feels like velvet, warm and a bit buttery.

"Women always outlast their men. You have to think about that," she says absently.

"Not likely a problem, mum," I point out to her.

She looks at me sadly, "Don't say that. A mother lives in hope."

"If wishes were fishes..."

She smiles, "Yes, he used to say that, didn't he. He had lots of little sayings."

"Yes."

"Drove me bloody bonkers."

"Mum..."

"Drove you away from home too."

"Hmm."

"Well, he did. I know it."

"It wasn't his little sayings, Mum."

"I know Charlie. Let's not talk about it."

"It was the bloody limericks."

"Ha ha."

She walks over to the Italian bloke's grave, where someone has recently placed a big bunch of fresh chrysanthemums. Picks up the vase and places it carefully on her husband's headstone, then puts her arm in mine and turns me back toward the car.

When I get back to work Speed tells me in very plain language what my priorities are. The Kurdish Barbershop Quintet have closed up shop and disappeared. The ones I was watching through the panties and who gave me a kicking after they gave me a haircut. I should have realised the barber shop was the same shop I was watching that night, but I didn't. Shirley warned me but I didn't register there were ongoing operations attached. I should have asked Jenno about it at some time or other, it being his operation and he and me spending most of every day together. But I didn't. Everyone's human, right.

Anyway, no one can find them now, so I am very popular with Speed and Team Syria at the NSW Police. Not.

The only live lead we have on these guys is my new friend Serwan the taxi driver and not surprisingly, Serwan has gone to ground too. I call his work, he hasn't clocked on for three days and if you hear from him, the taxi guy says, tell the bugger he's fired. Call his mum she just hangs up when she hears me speaking English. Go to his flat, I can hear the spiders knitting through the window.

One thing I learned about people who go into hiding though. They'll give up the bond on their flat, move interstate, change their name eventually but the last thing they'll give up is their mobile phone – the untraceable one they bought from a mate which they keep changing the prepaid SIM cards for.

*Tip number 10 for villains: No matter what
SIM card you put into a phone, when you turn it
on it faithfully reports back to the network, "Hi,
phone 555 here, checking in. I'm using a new
SIM card now, write it down." You want to stay
anonymous, throw the SIM card AND the
phone away.*

Shirl finds him after about two hours of not even trying very hard. "Subscriber check says Wollongong," she says. "He didn't go far. His phone shows him in this suburb, mostly at night, but he seems to be all over."

And here's another bloody amazing thing about people trying to hide. They need money, so they gotta work, so what do they do? Well what would you do, if you were a cabbie in Sydney, you gotta find a job in Wollongong? So I ring around and on about the third Wollongong cab company I get a bingo, they just hired a young middle eastern guy a few days ago.

Speed still doesn't know I've got Robbo running around after Opium, so Serwan I have to find myself. Nice drive actually, once I get onto the freeway and floor it. First time in my life I ever went down to Wollongong too, which I should probably feel bad about, but then again why. Poor old busted arse Wollongong. It's got bigger things to worry about than whether I visit it.

Of course I'm wrong and as I drop down the road from the escarpment to the sea I'm already thinking, hey nice, if you gotta hide, hide where there is surf and dolphins. I don't want to scare the cab company any more so I pull into the first cab rank I see and ask does anyone there know a new guy called Serwan, I got some money for him. Here's the third amabloodymazing thing about people on the run – they will change their last name, but they keep their first.

On the third rank I get a hit. Yeah, Serwan is working today. The call goes out on the radio, 'Hey tell that new guy Serwan there is a bloke here with some money for him," and if Serwan pulled up five minutes later in his cab, this part of the story would be completely different and much simpler.

I'm parked at the cab rank having a snooze in the sun and the door behind me opens and someone gets in (shoulda locked that). "Don't turn around," he says so of course I start to turn around and something pointy sticks into my upper back right between the C3 and C4 vertebrae. "I said don't turn around dumbo," he points out.

"Serwan?" I ask, but even as I say it I know it isn't him. The bits I can see in the mirror are fat and dark, a bit sweaty, a bit bald.

"Nah, just a friend," says baldy. "You got some money for him eh, or what?"

"No," I say, "Just a message from his mum."

"What."

"Well, she said, tell my son Serwan to stop fondling the little boys."

Give the guy credit, he doesn't mess around. Reverses the knife so the big knobby end is facing forward and plants it hard behind my ear.

Lights out.

I'm getting good at this. Soon be able to do it on command.

Waking up is hard to do. That should have been the name of that song. Breaking up is easy. Breaking up doesn't usually leave you feeling someone has driven over your skull with a steamroller and dried it in a wood fired pizza oven.

I am still in the car. Still in the front seat. My cards and the contents of my glove box and my pockets are in the back seat, though my cash is gone. Lucky I didn't bring any ID with me. I can't be bothered trying to reach it all though, just looking back there makes everything go white so I want to throw up. Couple of lungfulls of fresh Wollongong sea air. That does make me throw up. Get that done, wind up the window again, look in the rearview mirror and see it's now afternoon. Parked at the rank, behind me, just one cab. I watch, it starts up, pulls around me and drives slowly up the road.

Serwan.

Just getting the keys into the lock gives me the shakes but I get the limo started and follow along after him. Not that he's trying to lose me. We get to a beach car park with a closed up icecream shop and a few kids kicking a football and park out of sight behind some scraggly pines. Think to myself, *let Mohammed come to this mountain because the mountain is going to throw up again, if it has to move itself out of this car.*

He realises I'm not getting out of my car, so he walks around and gets into the passenger seat.

"Car smells like sick," he says.

"Yeah, I hit your friend's knife with my head."

"Sorry, that's Mustafa," he shrugs. "He said tell you it's nuthin personal. Knocking you out. He just doesn't like foul mouthed racist kafirs."

"Fuck him and the camel he rode in on."

"Nice. How'd you find me so quick?" Of course that's what he's worried about.

"It's what we do friend. But I have to tell you, it wasn't hard," let him think about that. "Blind Freddy could have found you."

He thinks. "I'm buggered aren't I?"

"I dunno. Are you?"

Sighs. "Yeah mate. Got five angry Peshmerga on my arse haven't I? I think you met them." Mimes me getting hit on the head with a cash drawer.

"Want to tell me why?"

"Because of *you*, right!?"

"No, I'm not the one who they're angry at. So why would they be angry at you Serwan?"

"I dunno. Or maybe I do. OK, if I tell you, what can you do for me?" Now, this conversation I've had plenty of times, so I lay it out.

"OK, here's the deal. They're recruiting for a foreign conflict? That's illegal, you need to witness against them if we decide to go the legal route. You can do that anonymously, secret court hearing. No one knows it was you. Say they're involved in something worse, like planning to blow shit up, and you know what it is, same deal. If you have to witness against them, I can get you full witness protection. New name, new job, new State. If it's just minor, or we don't think we can make it stick and we just deport them, I can give you a reward, like ten or twenty grand and no one will ever know. But there's a but…

He sighs, "There had to be…"

"But…if you're into something criminal with them, and this is just because you aren't love buddies anymore, I don't give a rat's arse. Go tell it to your imam, or the cops. I'm only interested in terrorism."

He thinks about what he's got, and what it'll get him. "OK, so I think I got something you can use to kick them out of the country, maybe even lock them up but you have to keep my part totally secret, or they *will* kill me. You seen these guys. That's no joke. Also, that money scheme I was telling you about? If you shut that down, I'm out 50 thou I been waiting five years to collect. So that's my price. 50 big ones."

I'll spare you details of the haggling. Not the haggling with Serwan. That was the easiest. I mean the haggling with Speed and our financial controller, and our Regional Director, and an Assistant Director General in Canberra, and his financial controller. I kill time with three more meets in Wollongong docks and parks and car parks with Serwan, getting him to hang in there, and there is a lot of yada yada yada. Finally at a beach in Bulli, Serwan signs on for $30,000.

So how you feeling right now Mr. or Ms Taxpayer, when you see how we're spending your hard earned money on Serwan there, so he can move to Surfers, get a new life and blow it all on casinos and hookers? You sleeping better?

Well, hey, could have cost you $50,000 if I wasn't such a good negotiator. Think of it that way.

Robbo is in a royal funk. His dogs are all over Opium like bluebottle jellyfish on a Japanese tourist, and what Opium does, he goes Circular Quay to George, on foot, up George to the Queen Vic building. Cool, Robbo's got him boxed in nice with three on the leg and two limo teams ready for a fast lift if he hops in a cab. Bugger gets to the Queen Victoria shopping center building and does he go inside? No, he starts walking down the car park ramp. OK that looks a bit dodgy but a man can make a genuine mistake, we've all walked down the entrance ramp as a shortcut back to our car, right? Now Robbo's team have a problem though, because how do they follow him down a traffic ramp where they shouldn't walk, which also looks dodgy?

Of course, it might also be a sign he knows he is being followed.

Now, Robbo cut his milk teeth on the Chinese, who wrote the book on anti-surveillance, so he doesn't panic, just sends a limo down the ramp right behind Opium, a team of 3 in it, and soon as they peg Opium walking over to the stairs inside the carpark they are out of the car with two behind him on the stairs and a third going ahead in the elevator. OK, one of his mobile units is no longer mobile, but he's back in control.

And the bugger goes up two levels then stops on the steps to tie his shoes. Robbo hears over the radio as his two people approach Opium, no choice but to keep going, and the cheeky shit says in his slow southern drawl, "Sorry gentlemen, let me get out of your way. Y'all look like you're in a hurry." Waits until they pass, then goes back *down* the stairs. OK so now he's made it clear he's screwing with them but Robbo is spread thin, too thin. Has a team useless at street level and his second team split on two floors of the Queen Vic with one man still turning his car around down in the car park.

"Spud, package on the way back out to you." Robbo radios the driver in the carpark. "He's pissing around with us, just stay close."

"Still stacking Boss," Spud jams his car into a vacant spot, looks in his rearview mirror, got a good line on the stairs, sees the package, "Yeah I got it, coming out the stairwell, what you want me to do?"

"Leave the car, stay with the package, you're on your own for a while, so get right up it," Robbo tells him. Calls the team in the Vic back to the street.

"'K"

Spud's a porky lad, likes his chips. He waddles on behind Opium who's in a helpfully distinctive blue jacket, twirling his keys as Opium heads for the passage linking the Queen Vic to the subway. "Gonna lose you Boss, going underground to Town Hall station," Spud tells his team. Smart arse Yank probably knows the radio link will be crap this deep underground, but it's a dead end play because by the time they get to the other end of the tunnel Spud knows Robbo will have the second team in place at the other end to pick Opium up again. What's he thinking?

There's a few commuters in the tunnel, everyone just walking head down and in a hurry. Opium is about ten metres ahead, the only one who seems he's not in a rush. In fact, he's going so slow it's pissing people off, got to squeeze around him. Scratches the little bald spot on his curly black nut and pulls up the collar on his coat. Spud's alarm is ringing but he isn't sure why, maybe because Opium is making him walk unnaturally slow. Spud starts scanning the people coming their way, looking for anyone who looks a little funny. Maybe it's a hand-off, the guy slowing down so he can palm something to someone walking past. Hand off one of those phones maybe? No that isn't it. His intuition is jangling now, *Something is wrong something is wrong!*

Opium doesn't have a bald spot.

"Shit shit shit shit shit," spins on his heels, points his fat arse back down the tunnel until he emerges into the empty carpark again, gets a signal on his set, "Spud, Robbo. They switched in the stairs, it wasn't Opium that came out, *the package is still in the Vic somewhere!* Package might have lost its wrapper," he adds. Yeah, changed coats as they passed, banking the dark swarthy build, black curly hair would be close enough in the dark car park as they peeled the surveillance apart.

Robbo swearing now on the open channel. There are 22 possible exits from the Queen Vic building and Opium has just given himself a five minute start. That gives a two hundred square metre five story search grid and he has only three people in the right place. In another five minutes it will be a four hundred square metre grid.

Opium is lost.

"So where's me money?" Serwan's opening line.

I slide $50 across the table. "That's it. Buy some breath mints will you."

"Bugger off."

"No. You don't get anything until *we* get something. I told you that."

"I gotta live alright? Can't even drive a cab now…" Serwan says aggrieved, like it's my fault.

"We're paying your hotel bill and three meals. That's tea money. Get the organic mint, should last you a month."

"Freaking hilarious."

"No, serious. We been in this shithole hotel two days and I still got nothing about no-one."

"I told you how it all works," Serwan says.

I look at him, then look across at the whiteboard where he's been scratching out the details of his pyramid scheme. True enough, it was all there, and enough names to make the whole thing come tumbling down. Two or three years of fundraising for the PKK, and two or three other causes in Syria including a couple of legit

74

ones. Names of all the people involved. Quite clever really. You come in at the bottom of the pyramid, just throwing a few grand in yourself, work yourself up, start raising money at the mosque, get to keep 15% of what you raise. Work your way up again, 20%, 30% until you're sitting at the top of the pyramid and you keep 50% of what everyone raises, then you shut the whole thing down and start again. Money always goes to someone's aunty, never direct to anyone political. And that's where a prosecutor is going to have the nightmare, prove it went to buy guns, bombs or votes.

"You didn't tell me yet," I say, reaching for the coffee, "Why five Peshmerga barbers kicked my head in just for using your name."

"You offended them."

"No, they didn't know me. They kicked my head in because *you* offended them."

Silence. Looks at me, looks out the window. Looks at me again. Sighs.

"They were screwing it all up, alright?"

"How?"

"OK, right, we got this good thing happening, yeah? Everyone making money, everyone a hero at home because we're shipping all this cash back. I tell you mate, I go back there last year, I fly in to the Queen Latifa airport in Jordan, guy picks me up in a Mercedes, they take me to this restaurant, my whole family is there, speeches and shit. My aunty crying, picture of me in my cab on the table my mother sent her. I never been there before in my life, there's all these strangers clapping me on the back. All these guys I never met, take my arm, tell me I'm a freakin' hero, right. Put me on the plane again on the way out, they organise an upgrade for me, business class back to Istanbul. Freaking cool or what."

"So you're a hero."

"Freaking right. Then these Peshmerga guys turn up. I'm not paying any attention at first. Someone says they're Barzani, someone else says they're Gulani, turns out they're Zerevani.

They're trying to get guys to go to Iraq to fight Daesh, sure, pay your own airfare and pay your own funeral. But then the word comes from over there, they need money. Someone there has done a deal, and we're supposed to take what we're raking in, and just give it *all* to them. I ring home to check and they say, "Yeah, just do what they tell you, keep your mouth shut, you don't want to mess with those guys."

"So?"

"So this happens when it's finally *my* turn to collect, man. Five years I worked for this, you think they're going to let me take my cut? No! They say to me, I got to give it *all* to them, and I'm like bugger off half that is mine, and they get ugly, call me a bloody thief, bloody traitor, make my family ashamed, you guess the rest."

"How much are we talking?"

"Half of 100 thou right? So mine was 50, which is why I asked you for 50."

I whistle. That is not small money. "But you didn't give it to them yet, so are you trying to scam 100 thousand plus our 30? Or what?" I ask, confused. "Planning to disappear on us?"

"No," he says, slow so even someone thick like I gets it, "I got to give them everything or I'm dead. If you gave me 50, that would be my share. Except you're only giving me 30, so I give them 100, I'm still down 20 mate. But they don't know yet exactly how much we got, they think it's like 50-60 thou. I'm top of the pyramid mate, I'm the only one knows we are talking 100. It's been a good year, right, everyone digging deep coz of all the shit happening over there. So I'm thinking, I'll try to get them to take 80, tell them that's everything. Keep back 20. They're happy, I'm happy. Smart eh?"

I look at him, "Don't try to get clever. You want to quit while you are ahead mate."

"Right," he sighs, looks around. "Livin' the high life."

"They ask you for anything else?" I ask him. "Apart from the money?"

"Like what?"

"Guns, explosives, help getting vehicles, that sort of thing."

He thinks about it. "Nah. Or yeah. Yeah, actually."

"Yeah?"

"Yeah, they asked me, did I know a Syrian guy called Barrak? Could I find where he lives?"

I have one of those, *did he just say that* moments. But yeah, he did.

"Barrak? And you know anyone with that name?"

"Nah. But I can find out easy. You think I should huh?"

Speed doesn't look at it the same way I do when I tell him my plan is for Serwan to hand the money over to the Peshmerga.

"We're going to approve our agent to give 100,000 dollars to a bunch of terrorists?"

"Right."

"Dream on. Why would I sign off on that?"

"It's a lure. Serwan can put the word out that he's changed his mind, is willing to give them the money. For 100 thousand they'll get in touch pretty bloody quick. We get 'em in the bag, and you can take the money back."

"Hmmm, or, they take the cash and use it to buy themselves some fertiliser, diesel and a detonator and they blow up Merdem Barrak's car, it's my signature on the chit that paid for it? No way Jones."

"We know what they're after now. PKK knows Barrak is here too, so they sent these goons down here for some payback. They're not Peshmerga, I bet they're al-Akradi."

"I don't like it."

"What? You like it better that a PKK hit squad kills Barrak in his repair shop, maybe takes out the whole shop and everyone in it? When could bring the whole bunch of them in?"

"Oh, *we* could?" Speed does his putting the papers in a pile routine. So I know I got him now, he's just pissing around. Lifts some files off the desk, bounces them a couple of times, gets the edges all lined up, puts them back. "How exactly could *we*?"

"Serwan is going to go back in, tell 'em here's your money, you need any other help, I'm your man. Going to get himself inside."

"And why would he do that?"

"You're going to give him the full fifty he asked for. If he goes back in, and after we got one or more locked up."

"Ah."

I know I got Speed on the hook. Question now is, when Serwan goes back with his bag full of money and then offers to be the local gofer for the barbershop quintet, will they welcome him back as the prodigal son?

Or take the money, put a brick through his skull, cut him up and dump the bits in the Pacific off the back of a tuna boat and kill Barrak anyway?

Robbo looks at me like *I'm* the one who made a fool of his lads. Like I gave him this shit detail and he can't blame Opium, so he's focusing all the love on me.

"He went through us like a priest through a nunnery," he says. "Like yesterday was the first time we ever hit the street."

"Hey," I point out, "You recovered him."

"Pure bloody luck, and three hours later," Robbo says back. "We have no idea what he did for that three hours."

"Bought fruit," I'm trying to help. "He's a juicer. American guys get embarrassed about that girly shit, he didn't want you looking over his shoulder."

What happened - Spud's in Bondi getting a take away souvlaki after the debrief of the screw-up at the Queen Vic building, heading back to his car, and who does he see keying his way into a block of flats two streets back from the beach, but Opium, the real one this time, carrying two bags of shopping, you can see the pineapple head sticking out the top of one, the broccoli out of the other.

Sometimes you get lucky.

So now we have not only the hotel where Opium is staying, not only the hotels of his two teamsters, but an apartment he's also using. I look at my watch. It's Saturday night about 5 pm. Thinking, o.k. he's either going to end up at the hotel or he's at the flat. Do we want him to know that we know about the flat? Or do we want him to keep thinking what a clever dick he is and how dumb we are. Yes to that last one, Jones.

"So what I want," I tell Robbo, "Is you leave the flat alone and just watch the hotel, he didn't check out of the hotel, yet, right?" Robbo shakes his head no. "Good, so, next time you see him at the hotel, call me."

"And you will?"

"I asked Canberra is Security Liaison doing anything local with US DCS and they said nothing they know of. So whatever he is doing is *not* kosher and ten to one says he's going after Barrak. I'm sick of messing around with Opium and his goons when we've got all this other stuff going on with Serwan and the PKK. So, I'm just going to take him some room service at the hotel. Vegemite chocolate, eucalyptus marmalade, Tim Tams, shit like that. Courtesy package from the Organization. Have a little chat. And while I am, you will work out how to get into his flat at Bondi and wire it for sound and vision."

"You got your own personal bed reserved at the hospital, yeah?" Robbo asks. "Can I use it? Because chances are pretty good that Opium's ops team is holed up at that flat and they might not react well to us drilling holes in their walls."

"My bed is your bed," I tell him. "That nurse in emergency was a babe," I wink. "Ask Jenno."

"I will, *if* he ever wakes up. There's easier ways to meet women," Robbo observes, "Than getting a kicking."

He's right, but I'm sitting there, smiling at Robbo, happy with my little plan. What can go wrong?

They're going to try to wake Jenno up today. They wanted to put an electrode into his thalamus and shock him awake, but his parents said no to that. So instead they are going to dose him with amantadine, a Parkinson's drug, and see if that can 'excite his cortex'. I told them I can think of other ways to 'excite his cortex' but they said his insurance wouldn't cover those.

You know how, when an Armenian woman is giving birth, the whole family is in the waiting room, listening to every grunt? (No? OK, then trust me on that one). So even though he doesn't know it, he's got Money and Jane here (you know, Money's friend, known Jenno since he was in diapers), and his parents who just assume it must have been *my* fault, or why else am I here. And two girls who apparently both think they are a long-term chance with Jenno, if he doesn't croak, giving each other the evil eye. Plus me and Robbo and Speed and Witless (he gets some points back for that) and Shirl.

Only immediate family is allowed in. What happens, they make up a solution, feed it to him gradually straight into the stomach, make sure he doesn't go into seizure, watch his ticker doesn't give up, keep an eye on the brainwaves, see if they start spiking. All this takes hours. What they want is for him to cough or sick up and open his eyes, look around and say, "Where am I?"

Jane and I are outside. Money comes out with the medical bulletins every time she needs coffee. This tube is *out*, that one is *in*. Now the beep machine is off. He started shaking, now he's stopped shaking again. Door opens and she comes out again, smiling.

"He's might be OK," she says.

80

"He's awake?" Jane jumps up. She's the pepper to Money's salt. Dark and lithe and wiry, could crack walnuts with her toes. She grabs Money's face in her hands, "What did he say?"

"He's not awake yet," she smiles, "But they said he's dreaming. There are some electrical signals weren't there before. That's a good sign, they reckon, but there's still something keeping him in la la land."

"How do they know," I ask, "He's dreaming?"

"They can see it from the pattern on the machine, not that they need to. Bed sheets over his groin just rose six inches," Money says, "My mum is sitting there making out it isn't happening, poor luv."

A nurse comes out, hears Money talking, keeps walking past, but remarks, "She's right. You could spin plates on it." Disappears into a staff room with a smirk.

Jane whirls to high five me but I have to be honest, something about celebrating my mate getting a boner is just too metro. I cough and head off to the loo.

Later, he's lying there with a big lopsided grin on the bits of face I can see between the electrodes. Slack jawed, and he's still completely dopey, sliding in and out of sleep.

"Well, the lights are on," I say, leaning over him, looking into his blank eyes. "But I think a possum is nesting in there."

The doc looks up from his clip board, "He can probably hear you."

"Will he remember?"

"Can't say."

I lean over by his ear and whisper, "Hey Jenno, your mum and I got it on last night. She was a bit upset so I took her for a drink. You know how it is, when their guard is down…"

Nothing, he just keeps smiling.

"Nah," I tell the doc as he leaves, "He's still off with the pixies."

He blows a bubble. I wipe it off his chin with a cloth. He blows another one. Disgusting. I drop the cloth and lean over to pick it up and then I hear him say it.

"Grrrl-p" Bubble pops on the 'p'. He's looking up at the ceiling, not focused on anything, but he says it again, "Grrrl-blap." Pop.

I lean in again, "What is it mate?"

But that's it. He closes his eyes and he's off with the pixies again. I look at my watch, two hours til Money comes in, takes over.

Two more hours with the bubble boy. On the bright side, the little fella's better company than usual.

So, to detect or deter surveillance there are two kinds of activity – *counter* surveillance and *anti* surveillance.

Counter surveillance, if done well, should be almost impossible for the dogs to detect. Because counter surveillance is purely intended to help you identify if you are being followed. It isn't intended to help you lose the surveillance, because that would tell the people who are following you that you are trying to lose them, and that would be suspicious.

Counter surveillance means that the target goes about their normal daily routine, doing normal daily things, in normal daily ways designed to help the target spot people around him doing un-normal things, like lurking, skulking, watching and waiting. A trained ops officer sets their every day routine up to provide multiple opportunities to detect surveillance without doing anything out of the ordinary, and if they see it, they adjust their plans accordingly, but if they don't they can confidently go through with whatever nefarious deed they have planned.

Now, what the movies usually show as counter-surveillance, is actually *anti*-surveillance. Anti-surveillance is where Jason Bourne gets on and then off the train before it leaves the station, takes a bus one way and a taxi back again, or does a u-turn on the middle of the Harbour Bridge, or stops and goes into a pipe tobacco shop even though he doesn't smoke a pipe, so he can run out the back door. Anti-surveillance is a last ditch measure designed to throw off anyone following you and it is a complete admission of guilt. Anti-surveillance is a neon light saying, "Ok, I am about to commit a nefarious deed and I know you are following me and I don't want you to see it."

So what Opium did to us in the Queen Vic building, that was a big shining disco ball of guilt.

Then there's two types of surveillance – your *covert* and your *overt*. *Covert* surveillance is the one you usually see in the spy movies, where the dogs with the lapel mikes are buzzing all around the target like a bunch of invisible bees, being unobtrusive, like city noise or restaurant wallpaper, and the target has no idea it's there.

The opposite of covert is of course *overt* or *prophylactic* surveillance. Overt surveillance is surveillance which is conducted with the intent of letting the target know you are following them. If anti-surveillance is an admission of guilt, then overt surveillance is an accusation. It says, "We know who you are, and we are all over you, so you better just pack up and go home." Even though, usually, you just have a suspicion, not a concrete certainty, and letting the target know you are onto them is just a way to test your instincts and try and goad them into something stupid. Or prevent it from happening.

Now, Opium doing anti-surveillance, seems to indicate he had worked out we were following him. He might even have been thinking, wow, they are being rather overt. The fact he doesn't seem to have packed up and gone home indicates what he is doing is a) important or b) he doesn't give a shit. Winking at the camera that time, seems to indicate we are more in the ballpark of b).

Going ahead with his op right now, knowing we are all over him, is a lot like wilfully having sex without a condom, when you know you have AIDS.

Shirley thought a gift basket would be nice. He won't shoot someone bringing him a gift basket she said. Not one with a fluffy koala and chocolate macadamias in it.

So I'm standing outside Opium's hotel room with a gift basket. Freaking *pink* koala. She did that on purpose.

I knock. I know he's in, coz Robbo's team just saw him go up five minutes ago. Probably on the crapper. Knock again. There's a shuffle behind the door and the chain goes over. "Who is it?"

"Mr. Levysohn, my name is Charlie Johns, from the Australian Government. I wonder if you would open the door please, we need to talk." Hold my ID up to the peephole. Smile like a wally.

A head of curly black hair and freckles, or could be liver spots, anyway Opium pokes his head around the door. "Yes, what is it? I was about to take a shower."

"Can I come inside for a minute?" Hold up the pink koala-in-a-basket, and my Govt. ID side by side.

Looks at one, then the other, raises his eyebrows, but gives me a big armed wave on in. "Please do," he says, all gentlemanly.

He's not alone. Robbo and his crew didn't pick up on that. Dammit.

Big guy, looks like a Mafia goomba, with a wart on his nose, sitting in a corner of the suite watching MTV. Stands, but Opium motions him to sit down again so he does. "This is my associate, Mr. Bakani. Now, what is this about please?" Bakani, Kurdish name. OK, thanks for the pointer. He could have been here on any sort of business but he's hanging out with a big Kurdish guy.

Put the basket down, walk to the window. From here I can look straight out across Hyde Park. Straight down at Robbo's dogs, sitting on a bench under the tree watching the front exit. One of 'em eating a yiros, looking up at us. He might as well wave. OK, let's call them *made*. Turn around.

"I work for the Department of Immigration Mr. Levysohn. I just want to clear up a misunderstanding." He sits, I sit. Everyone's sitting, which is nice because it makes the hitting harder to do.

84

"Misunderstanding?"

"Yes," I take a folder out from under the basket (actually it's got my expense reports in it – first thing I grabbed when I was on my way out the door). "You see we have you coming into Australia under the name and passport of Mr. Adam Levysohn, is that correct?"

"Yes."

"Yes. But our facial recognition system at Kingsford Smith Airport came up with a different name." (OK, we don't actually have a facial recognition system, I saw that on an episode of *Homeland*, but hey, does he know that?)

"Oh, really ?" Looks at his mate, and smiles. Arrogant shit.

"Yes. I have it here. Let me see. Yes," Ruffle through a few Burger Bar receipts, and one from 8 Ball Heaven, that was a good night. Last time I played 8 ball was with Jenno. Girl at the table next to us in a mini dropped a ball, did a straight-leg bendover right in front of us and showed us both her G spot. "Ah, it says here you are actually a credentialed officer of the US Department of Defence Clandestine Service?"

"Really?" Acts surprised. OK, play it that way. "I think you have the wrong person, what name do you have there?" he asks. Not sure what I have on him.

"Uhm, let me see," I flick a page, "Yes, here it is – *Heeza Jerk*."

His eyes narrow, "Sorry, what did you say?"

"Maybe it's my pronunciation, I'm not so good with ethnic names," now he's getting a bit of colour up. "Should it be Heesa? Heesa Jerk?"

"Are you trying to be funny?" Stands up, and so does his boofy boy. "What is this about? You have something to say friend, say it or go."

So I stand too. Now everyone is standing which unfortunately makes the hitting easier. In fact, wart nose takes a step forward which puts him within hitting range. "Well, actually I'm here as a personal favour to the blokes who are following you around

85

town at the moment. You've probably seen them here and there."

"I've seen them," he says through his teeth, *"Everywhere.* They are goddamn useless."

"Ah well, depends on whether they wanted you to see them, or not, doesn't it? What do you think?" He says nothing so I continue, "Because actually they are pretty good at not being seen, unless we want to send a message. And apparently, some people are so thick, they need the message spelt out in big letters." I shrug, apologetically, "Which is why I'm here."

"I have no idea what you are rambling about," he says. "What message?"

"Well, the message is simple - we know who you are. We know who your support crew is. We know why you are here," counting off the fingers on my hand, "And we don't like declared DCS officers coming in under a false name and conducting covert ops without clearing it with us. Your little operation is as blown as a Brit in Hollywood mate, and we tried to let you know the polite way, but you didn't get the hint. So because we are nice people, we are giving you 24 hours to leave Australia, or on my next visit I'll be here to deport you."

The whole thing about the 'visible surveillance' is a favour to Robbo, to make his dogs look better. Cover up the fact they just did a hopeless job.

"I have no idea what you are talking about," he says, with a hard man look. Wart nose shuffles forward a little more.

"Don't waste your time," I say to him, "I'm just the messenger. Enjoy the nuts," I nod at the basket before turning for the door, "Joe Banana there might like the koala. Matches his eyes." Give him a wink. Both stand there looking from me to the pink koala and back, speechless. "24 hours. On a plane, or you'll be in a police cell. Your fake passport doesn't give you any sort of immunity."

Put my hand on the door, expecting to feel a fist in my hair just before my nose smacks flat into the green enamel, but instead I'm out into the hallway and it swings quietly shut behind me.

Gotta hand it to Shirl. Who'd have thought the best tactic against getting thrown off a 19th floor balcony by the big bad US Defence Clandestine Service was a pink fluffy koala? In fact, I am so satisfied with myself, I go down to my car, have a chat with Robbo, then give Karn a call and meet her down at the Oyster Bar in the Opera House forecourt and try to get her drunk like Money suggested.

And it works quite well.

I mean, I do go home alone, again. But I think we nudged the dial a bit more into the danger zone.

The Turkish snatch team has no idea exactly who they are about to snatch. Well, not completely true, they have been following the Australian security service officers ever since they made the unannounced call on Barrak; logging routines, associates, place of work, home address, known associates. So of course they picked up on the red head. Very interesting. Last night they followed Jones down to the harbour, watched a nice romantic dinner for two over Oysters and then followed both of the targets home. The snatch has been planned thoroughly. They know when she goes to work, what time she usually goes home. She drives a little red Fiat with a blown gasket. Fast and furious.

They're going to take her on her way to home, get her to a safehouse and keep her there a few days. Long enough to thoroughly distract the security service. That's all they know, and that's all they need to know.

Despite the rushed planning, it should be an easy pick up, and they rehearsed it in a vacant warehouse. Timed it. Ran it three times today, at different times, on location. Checked the timing, ran it again. The first few minutes are where it could go wrong, get past that, she's in the bag.

Burcu waits by the park, in an old Transit van. She's the driver, because the target is a woman, and might get spooked if the driver turns out to be some big boofy guy, but little Burcu, she won't spook anyone. Throw in she's a cute little Turkish girl, does her 'oh I'm very sorry' routine. Target doesn't stand a chance. If they nail this one, Burcu will be batting 'two for two' in Australia. They'll call her the crash queen. 'Crash Queen', she likes the sound of that, even if she did have to come up with it herself.

She's got her phone in her lap, waiting for the signal, radio in the stolen car is on a pop radio station, Sia's new one. Trying to learn the words, keep herself calm that way. Like, this isn't Suruc, down on the border near Syrian Kobane, this is a holiday after Suruc, but she always gets nervous when she gets to the pointy part. She got her first break in Suruc running messages, and when they saw she could do that without screwing up, they started giving her some real jobs, a little more training, and now after two years, this cushy little job in Australia.

Keeps an empty orange juice bottle in the door in case she needs to pee last minute; learned that her first time out. Your Orange juice bottle has got a nice wide bore on it. Try pissing in a Coke bottle, see what that gets you. Wet, is what.

Voice in her ear.

Target passing Boundary Hotel

"Two in motion," she responds.

Target on Cleveland

"OK"

Checks her mirror, pulls the van out into the dark street. It's a one way street around the park, one road in, one road out, and they already swept the park for drunks and joggers. Only eyes around are tabby cats.

We are green.

We are green? she murmurs out loud. What a jerk. Calls over her shoulder to the two guys in the back of the van, "Buckle up boys."

She laps the park, slowly, 18km/h should be about right and yeah, it is, she reaches the corner just ahead of the target, doesn't even have to wait, pulls easy as you like in front of her. Indicates right, then left, like she doesn't know. The little Fiat tries to go around her, *easy girl, patience!* She pulls left into the one way road around the park, the little Fiat tucked right in behind, impatient to swing past again. Gets to the part of the road where they took out the street lights, nice and dark and…now! Swings right, jams her foot down and mashes the gears, and in her mirror she sees the Fiat leap forward to go round her, but she's cut if off and the Fiat rear ends her so hard - *WHAM* – she head-butts the damn steering wheel as it slams into her rear end – not part of the plan - she bounces against the headrest of her seat and whips forward into the wheel again with a sick thud.

Seeing stars. *Bitch!* Did she even *use* her own brakes? Burcu slips the seat belt; it feels like she's cracked a rib too.

Climbs out all wobbly and doesn't have to act at all, it hurts like hell just to turn her head. This wasn't part of the plan. She stands there bent over with her hands on her hips trying to feel if anything is broken, saying to herself, *come on, get it together,* when suddenly there is this firestorm of swearing coming her way and she just manages to straighten up before it hits her.

"….freaking mother of a bloody *loser* puts on their brakes in the middle of the god damn bloody *road*…wrecked the whole *bloody* front of my already *buggered up* car so I am totally…hey, you ok?"

Burcu just looks at her. She's standing there about a foot taller than Burcu, who is bleeding a bit from the nose now, she can feel it dripping but she can't get her hand to come up and wipe it. Burcu can't help just looking at the other girl. She's about eye level with a big Elizabethan bustier laced up with different coloured boot laces but it's the hair she can't get past. It's like a big red thundercloud from where Burcu is standing, with the streetlights behind it. The girl puts her hand on Burcu's arm, "I think you'd better sit down girl," she says and leads Burcu over to the curb between the busted Fiat and the buckled van. Burcu knows she shouldn't be sitting, but man, her head hurts. Ok, just a little sit, that's probably a good idea.

The girl is pulling a telephone out from between her breasts. Well, probably not enough pockets in an Elizabethan bustier, so that's why, Burcu thinks. Put it between your boobs. Why not? Or is it Edwardian. The bustier. Ponders that. Her head is banging now. *Bang bang bang. Bang bang bang.* No, not her head, the doors. Someone is trying to kick open the doors of the van, from inside, but they're all jammed up.

Burcu frowns. Oh yeah, better let them out. She remembers that part of the plan at least. The girl is looking at the doors too now, like, what's the commotion in there? Someone is yelling.

"It's OK," Burcu says quietly, trying to stand up, "OK, OK, OK. They're with me." Gets one hand on the curb and one leg under her but they don't seem to want to work together, and then she puts her weight on the arm to lever herself up and something screams inside her like it's tearing and she falls on her back on the grass. "Oh, son of a bitch," she says. Now it *is* her head pounding, and the doors, and feet, there are feet running out from some of the houses she can see.

Oh oh. That's *not* in the plan. She blacks out. And then wakes to a siren. That's *definitely* not in the plan. She laughs. So, the plan is history. Well, the plan isn't all that's history. . .oh, that's nice, someone laying her head back down now. Gentle hands.

Nice perfume.

Meanwhile at the hospital Money is wearing a white singlet, no bra and jeans. And Ylang Ylang oil. Thank God she is picking some crud out from under her big toe nail, or I would have to go out and jump the nearest girl scout, the effect she is having on me. The toenail picking makes it bearable, that and the fact her Ylang Ylang is balanced by the putrid sweet smell of Jenno's fibre-glassed wrist about two feet away in the hospital bed.

Robbo doesn't even seem to notice her. "I can't believe you got out of there without a thumping," he says, nose buried in a paper. "Heeza Jerk?"

"It was the pink koala," I say. "Got a good word in for the dogs too."

Now he looks up, "Oh, yeah?"

"Yeah, told Opium you were overt on him, in case he was wondering."

"Overt?"

"Right, as in, we wanted him to know we knew."

"Knew what?"

"Knew it all."

"So…we were overt on him because we wanted to scare him off?"

"Right."

"But we weren't. We just buggered up. And we didn't scare him off; he didn't give a rats."

I sigh, "I know that, Robbo. But *he* doesn't have to."

"OK, thanks," knits his brow, looks down at his paper again, "I think."

"Are you finished?" Money says, sliding her feet into some sandals. "Because one of you needs to buy me a coffee."

We walk out the front into the park where the little café in the rotunda. Money's got her arm in mine and she rests her head against my shoulder as I wait for traffic.

"You a bit sad?" I ask once I've got the espressos in.

"Bit. Yeah," she sighs, "He's supposed to be awake by now."

"He is awake," I point out.

"Yeah, but you know what I mean. Awake, but not humming to himself."

It's true. Jenno is better, in that he's not blowing bubbles anymore, and he's sitting up. But he just stares at the wall, and hums an old Pearl Jam song over and over. 'Alive', which is pretty ironic.

"We used to listen to that song every day on the way into work for about a month, we were living in Rose Bay, remember?"

"I remember Rose Bay, yeah."

"That jealous ex of yours spiked the tire on Jenno's motorbike? Didn't know it was your brother's, thought it was some other guy up there with you." Try to get her off thinking about something else.

"Yeah, I remember. He paid for the tire though. He was a nice guy." Only Money can think a guy who spikes someone else's motorcycle tire with an awl, is nice.

"Jenno'll be OK. Nurse said he could snap out of it any day."

"Or never, Jones." Looks at me, "You're always the bloody optimist. He may *never* get better."

Stirs some sugar into her coffee and then spoons in a little more. I remember from science classes in high school you can dissolve sugar or salt into hot water only up to a point and then it gets to where it is more sugar than water and you can't dissolve any more – it's called super saturation. Money is looking pretty super saturated.

"Two half bricks," she says.

"What?"

"We used to say to each other, if we ever had an accident, and one of us became a vegetable, the other one had to get two half bricks and whack - both sides of the head. Good night."

"Shit, Money."

Looks up at me, "Don't worry, the bricks were his dumb idea. I'll just smother him with a pillow."

We hit the corridor where Jenno's ward is, and I can hear him yelling. Money breaks into a run, and I trot after her.

"Get the *hell* off my *freaking* leg and get me the *hell* out of this *freaking* bed so I can kill that *freaking* bitch!"

This is what I see. Robbo is lying across the lower half of Jenno. Jenno is trying to push him off. A nurse is holding his fluid bag in one hand, the stand has fallen on the ground and she's trying to push Jenno's head back to the pillow with the other but she's losing that fight. It's a two bed ward but up to now the other bed has been empty. Now there is a dark skinned woman in the other bed, her gurney has just been wheeled in, it looks like, and the orderly who wheeled her in is crouched behind the bed using her as a human shield. The woman is still completely out of it, neck in a brace, must have just come in from an operation.

Jenno picks a book off his bedside table and hurls it across the room where it smacks into the wall behind the woman. "Freaking missed!" he yells and tries for the vase but the nurse lets go of his head and whips the vase out of range.

I get shoved in the back and a doc and two nurses come running in. They all throw themselves on Jenno, and he disappears in a welter of white coats, dresses and legs clad in support hose. One of the nurses must have had something in a syringe because gradually the mess on the bed gets still and they peel themselves off, she's holding an empty needle, and Jenno is out again.

Everyone looks at everyone.

Robbo breaks the silence, "He was humming. She came in. He actually turned his head and looked at her. Then he went nuts."

"Freaking nuts is right!" the orderly says, getting up from behind the gurney.

"Maybe we should move her?" one nurse asks.

"Where are we going to put her," another nurse says, "She's worse than him. Put *him* in the corridor."

"At least he's making progress," the doc says, smoothing his coat.

"That's progress?" Money asks.

Right then Karn walks in, doesn't even notice the kerfuffle, dumps her coat, her bag, her phone, some flowers, and for some reason, a plastic bag full of stuff looks like she emptied out of her glove box. "What a *bastard* of a night," she says, to no one in particular. Then she looks across at the little middle eastern woman still lying quietly on her cot, still out from the anaesthetic or something, her neck in a brace. Karn walks over to her and frowns.

"Hey, that's the bitch who just buggered up my car. Small world," she says, and then looks at us, all looking at her. "What?"

"I rang your house, you weren't there, I rang your work, you weren't there and *when* are you going to tell those jerks on reception at your office to put through my calls?" Karn is steaming. "I always get the *can I take a message* routine."

"How's your car?"

"Wrecked. I called to see if I could borrow yours, I'm going to that birthday thing tonight, but you weren't there so I figured, bugger you, I've just had the worst night of my life and you don't even care, I'm taking your ute."

"*My* ute?"

"Yeah, you never use it, always got your guvvy car haven't you?"

"How were you going to take it?"

"With this key, genius." Holds up the keyring I gave her about two nights ago, in a gesture of complete surrender. It has my house key on it, but I forgot it had my spare car key on it too.

"So when it's fixed, let me know." She continues.

"When what is fixed?"

"Your car, duh. I got to your place and two boys in blue overalls were standing in your garage, so I said hi, but I could see they were working on your car and now it was late so I went back up and got a cab here instead. What a bloody day."

"Wait. *First*, tell me about your accident. *Then*, tell me about the guys in the overalls." I point at the unconscious girl who Jenno tried to swat with the book, "And who the hell is *she*?"

"Hi mum, it's me. I just need a chat."

"Well that's nice, Charlie. Just let me turn the iron off." Can hear her shuffling around her loungeroom, radio in the background. "OK, I'm back. So what's up Charlie? Is your friend better?"

I told mum about Jenno a couple of days ago. "There's been a development. Someone tried to kidnap Karn, but it went wrong and they crashed into her car and she ended up in hospital."

"Oh dear. Karn did?"

"No, she's alright. The kidnapper ended up in hospital. Then Jenno tried to kill her."

"Kill Karn?"

"No Mum. You're fixated. The kidnapper. Jenno tried to kill her, with a book. He recognized her."

"From where?"

"We're thinking if she makes a habit out of crashing cars, maybe she was the driver who put Jenno in hospital. He recognized her, and went mental."

"Where is the poor girl now?"

"Poor girl? She tried to kill Jenno and kidnap my girlfriend Mum! There's only so far the other cheek will turn…"

"Not her. Karn. She must be very upset."

Actually of all the people buzzing around the ward, Karn appears the least upset. She's on the phone to an importer, ordering some cloth. Sees me looking and gives me a little wave.

"No Mum, she's pissed off but fine. Which seems to be her default setting. I'm the one calling you, remember? This is all adding up to one big bad day."

"Right, well. You take her home Charlie and make her a good cup of tea. And keep your eye on her, the shock of these things sometimes sets in days or even weeks later, I'm told."

"Right. Thanks mum."

This is how easy it is to find a monofilament microphone in the body of a 2006 Ford Falcon utility. First, pluck a nice thick pubic hair from your groin. Now go down to the nearest sports ground – soccer is OK, but Australian Rules Footy or Rugby League are better. Walk into the middle of the ground and drop the pubic hair. Now go to the nearest pub, and drink until you are legless. Then go back to the footy ground, and find the hair.

Flea takes three hours, which he says is a world record. The filament is in the lining of the vinyl above the driver's door. The little button battery is cut into the rubber, attached to the guts of a tiny 4G chip programmed to call home and dump its memory every 2 hours.

"Nice," he says after taking out the battery. "This is primo kit. You can't get this online." He points to it, "You want me to take it with me, or put it back?" he whispers when the door is closed again.

"Put it back. I've got this."

I pull the CD I just bought out of the shopping bag. *Dolly Parton, Greatest Hits.*

"What the hell is that?" Flea says as I put the keys in the ignition.

"Psychological warfare." I tell him.

"So let me get this straight, someone tried to take your girlfriend hostage. Crashed into her in a stolen van. We got the driver, but the guys in the back legged it."

"She's not exactly my girlfriend."

"And someone has bugged her car."

"*My* car. My ute." I slide the photo Flea took across the table.

Speed is not taking this well, being as little of it makes any sense.

"Your car. And Jenno is sharing a ward with the woman who tried to take your girlfriend hostage."

"Not any more, they moved him so we could keep her isolated, but yeah. It's the acute care ward, so she can't be moved too far yet. We need to get her out as quick as we can though, she's the best link we got and I'm worried she'll do a runner on us. The two guys in the back of her van disappeared when the cops showed, but the girl was out cold."

"And Jenno tried to kill her."

"With a copy of Da Vinci Code. And a vase. So, they gave him some elephant juice. He's still sleeping it off. Didn't speed his recovery any."

"She's got no ID, is claiming she can't remember who she is but she was driving a stolen van. You think it might be the *same woman* who crashed into Jenno, the one who tried to kidnap your girlfriend?"

"Right. Why else would he go mental? I'm getting a DNA match done on her and some hair we found in the Commodore."

Speed has his half-moon glasses on and looks at me over the top of them. Ignores the question.

"So your theory is?"

"American DCS. They got at least five people in their team, is our theory, including Opium."

"You know I don't buy your theory about Opium."

"OK, you accept that the PKK has sent a hit team here to take Barrak out, but you don't believe the US DCS would come here for the same guy?"

"No, I don't believe the man in those airport photos was Opium," he insists.

I push some photos across the table that Robbo's lads and lasses took over the last week. "Tell me this isn't him."

Speed flicks through them, "OK. It's him. You can tell me later how you got these when I expressly said no surveillance. But why would Opium want to do something like this to Jenno, or your girlfriend?"

"Well, Jenno I can't explain, but it is possible I might have provoked him," I confess. "Personally. If he is thin skinned."

Speed wipes his hand across his face, waves at me with a tired hand, "And how?"

"Well I might have called him a jerk and told him he had 24 hours to leave the country, sort of thing."

Speed, to his credit, stays in his chair and sighs. "What else don't I know?"

"Well, someone false-flagged Barrak, did an interview, showed him some faked up Australian IDs. I'm thinking that's DCS too, which is why I took the liberty of telling them to pack up and get out of town."

Speed picks up Opium's photo. Sucks a tooth. That's a good sign. When Speed's annoyed, he sucks a tooth. "So these cheeky buggers are running a major counter-terrorist op right under our own noses and because we are annoying them, they have put one of my officers in hospital, and tried to kidnap the other's girlfriend for leverage?"

"Yeah. Cheeky buggers, eh? She's not my girlfriend."

98

I get the girl, who while she was still groggy after the accident told Karn her name was Burcu, moved to the infirmary at Long Bay prison.

Thinking about that name. Burcu. That's Turkish. I guess if you're Opium, and you want to intimidate a Kurd, one way to do it is to use Turkish operations officers. Plus they probably speak a bit of Kurdish too.

I tell Karn I think someone was trying to kidnap her, and for her safety she needs to move into a safe house for a while and take a holiday from work, and she takes it relatively well.

I'll be on solid food again in no time.

Then Barrak is taken.

"It wasn't us, George."

"I know it wasn't youse. Youse would of buggered it up."

George has called me on the phone, all fired up. "Thanks very much, just tell me what you heard."

"Wasn't what I heard, it's what I saw. I was the first one there. His mates at work didn't know who else to call so they called George. They all call Georgie," gives a big toothless Levantine wheeze.

"And…"

"And I go round there. Back door is smacked in, like with a sledgehammer, hanging off one hinge. Secretary says they was talking in the front office, and three guys in black ski masks bust in, slap her down and take him."

"That's it? She didn't say what they looked like, how they left, anything else?"

"Hey, she was busy getting slapped. Woman is in shock."

"What did the cops say?"

"Cops? What freaking world do you live in? You don't call the cops on something like this. Guy lives alone, keeps to himself, just got here a couple years ago from Syria? Everyone is shitting themselves it's crime, drugs. A gang thing. Who gonna call the cops?"

He's keeping something back. "She must have told you something. Come on George."

"Well, there was one thing."

"Yes."

"She said, they didn't say much when they came through the door, just told her to shut up and lie down on the ground, right?"

"Let me guess. They were Americans."

"Americans?" he spits, "What? No. They spoke Kurdish."

Opium finds me before I find him. Come out of our office and he's standing there on the sidewalk, as calm as you please. 'Cept he's not smiling.

"Nice office you have," he says. I start walking up toward Pacific Highway and he falls in step, "I need to talk."

"Oh, talk? Had enough of assault and kidnapping?"

"What are you talking about?" He looks genuinely frustrated and confused. I'm not buying it. I motion to a café and step inside. If Robbo is half as good as he thinks he is, there must be at least one of his teams in the area since Speed made Opium a VIP, so I feel pretty safe.

"Your people will come in a moment," Opium sighs, watching my eyes. "The rather portly gentleman and the girl with curly hair."

Sure enough, Spud and his mate bowl in on cue, take a seat up the back and start leafing through magazines. Portly? Well there's the pot calling the kettle. Opium is a gentleman of weight.

"They just want to make sure you get to the airport on time," I tell him.

"Look, I need your cooperation and I can't go through normal channels," he says.

I just look at him sideways as we get the coffees in. Balls like a Brahmin bull, I got to give him that. "Our cooperation? I've got one mate in hospital and another holed up in a flat across town so that *you* can't find her, and you want my help?"

He does the frown again, "Whatever you're talking about, that wasn't us. We don't treat friends that way."

"Really."

"Of course not."

"French Embassy, Libya?"

He puckers the small mouth in his big round face, "Libya? Not following you."

I draw a circle in coffee on the table. "1986, you decide to bomb Gaddafi's compound in Libya with jets based in Britain. This is Gaddafi's compound," I say, putting a dot on one side of the circle. "You ask the French, hey do you guys mind if we fly over France to get to Libya and President Mitterrand says 'Non! Ce n'est pas possible.' Which is French for 'screw that', and a royal pain in the arse because now you have to go the long way around Spain and refuel in flight."

"I vaguely remember..." he says, smiling.

"OK, so you get it all organised anyway and blow the shit out of Gaddafi's tents over here," I point at my wet dot in the circle, then make another dot way over on the other side of the circle, "But unfortunately one of your laser guided J-DAM smart bombs misses the target by about ten miles and what does it hit, way over here?"

101

"Well if I recall, that was coincidentally the French embassy, wasn't it? You have a very good memory for detail," he says.

"You telling me the French are not your friends?" I ask.

He shrugs, "Are the French really friends with anyone?" he asks.

"Touché," I say, "But I'm not buying your 'I know nothing' routine."

"Look, I will be very honest," he says, "We don't know each other so why should you trust me? But I come to you, because I can sense you are the one in charge on the ground working this case and I don't have time to go through your chain of command."

"I'm waiting."

"Ok. We came here to talk to a man. That is all. Your ONA sent a report out, it was circulated to Defense Intelligence, and it landed on my desk. His name is Merdem Barrak."

So. *Badaboom*. I'm not often wrong, but I was right this time. "We know. We also know you already went and talked to him, made out you were from the Australian Government."

He leans back, "That's true. One of our Kurdish speakers did the talking. We didn't want to scare him into hiding."

"So this guy is pretty important?"

"To me, yes, he's *very* important."

"Important enough for assault, and kidnapping? We have your driver you know. She's being well cared for."

"Driver? What driver? Assault, kidnapping? We haven't been doing anything like that. Your surveillance didn't bother me at all. I came here to interview Barrak, I just needed a day or two with him, some questions, nothing rough. I had no time to go the official route. At our first interview, we arranged a day to meet. The second meeting was to be tomorrow."

"But he's been kidnapped."

"He...yes."

"And that wasn't you."

"No, believe me. If we had him would I be here?"

His coffee is a flat black with a shot of caramel which he throws down in a gulp. Mine is a small frothy cappuccino which I instantly regret because there is no way to look hard and drink cappuccino. Should have ordered an espresso. Double. I push it away to let it get cold.

"I'd like to believe you, but what I see is you coming in on a fake passport, running anti-surveillance on us, setting up a safe house in Bondi – yeah, we know about that too, give us some credit – all this without as much as a courtesy call. We don't like people pissing in our pool, Mr. *Levysohn*."

"I couldn't go through normal channels, I'm trying to tell you. Officially I am not here, even as far as my own service is concerned."

Now that is interesting. "So why are you here?"

"You know about our missing Delta Force soldier? I think Barrak was the last one to see him alive."

"Or dead," I remark, and regret that later.

He pauses, "Yeah, or dead. And I have to know. Was he dead, or was he alive, when he left the jail? Where did they take him? Who might know what happened to him after that?"

"Sound like legitimate questions to me, why not fly in with your DCS credentials, have a pot of tea with Security Intelligence Liaison, and ask them to help?"

He swirls the dregs of his cup, "Because Delta Force has given up on him. They say by now, with no word for two years, no ransom, no intel…they say he's dead." Now it's my turn to frown so he looks up from the cup, "He's my *brother*. I'll never give up until I know what happened to him."

103

Karn and Money and Jane are having tea on the balcony of Karn's temporary flat in Manly when I walk in. Except no one in Sydney outside of me and Karn are supposed to know where it is. But let's face it, I'm not going to fight them on this one.

"How's Jenno?"

Money smiles, "He said hello today."

"Yeah?"

"Yeah. I walked in and he looked straight at me and said hello."

Start unpacking the groceries I bought for Karn, "Like he knew who you were?"

"I don't think so. But like, he felt like he *should* know who I am. Hard to explain. I think that knock out shot they gave him put him back on the ropes."

Karn comes over and puts her arms around my neck, "Wow. You bought green tea."

"Matches your eyes," I say. "And raisin bread."

"Why raisin bread?" she asks.

"Uh, matches your freckles?" She whacks me with the loaf.

Money and Jane look at each other and stand, "Sounds like foreplay to me," Jane says.

"Nah," Money shrugs on her jacket, "Jones hasn't made a move yet."

I watch them walk to the door, Laurel and Hardy freakin har.

Jane's turn, "Oh, Karn told you that too?"

"Yeah, she's dying for it, but she's starting to wonder if Jones will ever make a move."

"Hmmm, she'd be the only one Jones *hasn't* made a move on then. Must be true love." Piss themselves all the way down the stairs.

I turn to Karn, expecting her to be fuming, but she's got this sort of completely wrong glow about her. Like here she is in a shitty flat in Manly, her car wrecked, business might going down the tube, all because of me and she's looking at me like I'm a warm scone buttered with strawberries and cream. She runs her fingers lightly over the short hairs at the back of my neck, where the Peshmerga barber burned them black.

"Are you ovulating or something?" I ask.

I catch him as he is walking into church through the back door, "Father, a quick word?"

"Ah, Jones, how are you?"

"Won't keep you, just…needed to see you face to face, about something."

He sighs, "So, meet me after the service."

"Well, I'd love to but I have to go and convince a man to throw his life away for the good of the country."

"Jones, I'm about to do a wedding."

"Can see that Father, not completely stupid you know, had to park two blocks away because of all the stupid cars. It's just, I'd like you to break another oath."

That stops him. See I'm Father Thomas's personal project. We met about two years ago when I needed him to do a little favour for me by giving me some information about one of his parishioners. That wasn't exactly in his playbook so it took a lot of talking, and quite a few bottles of port, before he trusted me enough to break one of his vows – sanctity of the confessional and all that. But there was a condition. More than one actually. I had to start coming to confession. I had to do the penance he gave me, and, even though the op was over, I had to keep coming to see him.

Now, the confessions I can cope with. In fact as you might have guessed, I quite enjoy them. It was a bit weird at first, all that 'Bless me Father' stuff but when you get into the swing of it, it has a kind of liberating soul cleansing aspect to it which (don't tell him I said this) makes me feel like no matter how bad the day was I can always confess it and then have a beer in good conscience afterwards. And to be honest, I thought he would crack before I did, because let's face it, how much fun can it be listening to *me* unburden myself a couple of times a week?

But no, he's hung in there and now I get the impression he's made my redemption some sort of life goal. Which is why I know this next one will be a big ask.

"I'm thinking, if I ever decided to get married, not now, but you know, some time…would you do the honours?"

"Is it that girl you have been talking about?"

"That's the one."

Full credit to him, he just blinks a bit and then says, "Jones, you are…that's out of the question."

"I know I know, I'm not baptised Catholic, but you could still do it couldn't you? *She's* Catholic, if that helps…"

"Never…"

"But I would, I mean, I am Father. See she's Irish descent, quite a religious girl, though you wouldn't know it the way she dresses, and I know this would mean a lot to her."

"No."

"We wouldn't need the whole white wedding and photos at Balmoral Beach gig," I say, waving a hand at the church full of people waiting on the other side of the doors. "Just the three of us and a couple of witnesses and then off to the pub for some champers sort of thing."

"My God, you are serious," he whispers, like the congregation might hear us through five inches of oak door.

"Yes Father, I actually think I am," I whisper back at him.

"I can't marry you," he says, opening the door to go into the church, "Never in a million years, not unless you convert to the

Catholic church – which you have told me time and again you never will - and embrace our beliefs and *all* those beliefs entail."

"I'll rock up with her every Sunday, is that enough?"

"I'd be defrocked. No way. I'm sorry, Jones." He gives me a meaningful look and disappears inside.

I smile. I'm a great believer in nudging. He's about to crack.

What Opium was talking about is all very well and good, but my ute and the Turkish hijacker are what I'm left with, if Opium is to be believed. Which he is not, for a minute. But if it wasn't the Americans, my bugged ute and the girl are my best chances of finding out who torpedoed Jenno, and who snatched Barrak. Not that they have to be the same crew. Probably aren't – that is what is so fargin annoying about this job. No nice neat ends.

> *Review of the new known unknowns: Who is Burcu the Turkish girl (and her two mates from the back of the van who legged it before the cops came) if they aren't working for the Americans and why did they try to kidnap Karn? Who the hell kidnapped Barrak if it wasn't Opium – suspects include the Turks/PKK/drug gangs or an angry customer with a bad panel job? Can Opium be trusted? Who bugged my car? And are they enjoying the Dolly Parton?*

Denzel would have had it all wrapped up by now and the camera would be zooming from a burning car, into his stark and terrible gaze for the final fade out.

My stark and terrible gaze is falling on Serwan. Because despite everything else, the job must go on, and I am still missing five bad-arse barbers who haven't surfaced yet.

"I called him, alright?"

"The old wrinkly guy?"

"Harith, yeah."

"Harith. And you told him you had his money and you wanted to make things right?"

"Sort of. Not directly."

"Sort of?"

"I rang this guy I know, might know where he is. I told this guy, tell him I need to talk to him."

"And?"

"So I'm waiting for the call back."

I listen to the six lane highway going past the door, look at the flypaper hanging from the ceiling fan. "You like this place so much, you just sit here all day and wait for the phone to ring?"

"This place is a shithole man. I want to talk to you about that. I aint even got money for bus fare to go to the shops. I…"

"…*You* need to get something happening," I point out to him, "Instead of sitting on your arse. Sooner you do, sooner you'll be lying on a beach showing off your tan and gold chains."

"I *could* make another call," he says. "I been saving it."

I run my fingers through my stubbly hair, "Saving it. Why?"

"There's this guy, I don't hardly know him, OK. I just know he's a guy who knows *everyone*. He's got a piece of everything that's going on. If I ring him, OK, suddenly I owe him a favour. And one day he'll call it in."

"Who's the guy?"

"No way I'm telling you. Anyway you said, if it's criminal, you don't care."

"He's some kind of crime boss?"

"Something like that." His knee is bouncing up and down. "Like Lebanese biker gang assassin, sort of thing."

"Good. So call him."

"Now?!"

"Yes, now," throw him the phone. "Call him now and get it happening."

He's sweating. Pulls a piece of paper out from the side of the chair, got numbers all over it, dials one of them, "Probably no way I'll get through."

"Try."

"It's ringing, all right?" Holds the phone out so I can hear. "You can't trace this call."

"You asking?"

"No, I mean it man. He'll know, he's got people paid everywhere, phone companies, cops, everything. If you trace it, he'll know I'm working with youse. I'm dead meat and you're finished and everything."

He gets through. After he gets over the shock and says hello, the rest of the conversation is in Arabic. I can see he spends the first minute explaining who he is, then he sounds like he is promising his virgin sister to the man. The rest of the conversation is over in about two minutes.

He puts the phone down, "OK, I done it. Fuck."

"What did he say?"

"He said I should wait for a call. He also said I should be glad I'm still alive, what he's heard about those Peshmerga guys."

"I keep telling you how lucky you are."

Looks down at his shaking hands, "Keep reminding me."

There's worse fates than this. That's what I am trying to explain to Burcu, later in the day. Her busted head lying on nice clean white sheets in Long Bay medical center, costs the taxpayer $1,500 a day to keep her here, not including the flowers I got her.

She doesn't quite see it that way.

"This is kidnapping," she says, all snappy.

109

"Well, you should know. So, ring your embassy, tell them you want to talk to someone," I suggest helpfully.

"What embassy?" She's quite cute, got the whole light skin, dark brown eyes, dark brown hair with a little mole on her top lip thing working for her, and now the dark brown eyebrows are all wrinkled up. Right, what embassy.

"You tell *me* what embassy. Hey, have you always been cross-eyed?"

"What are you talking about, cross-eyed?"

I focus on my nose, "Like this. I was just wondering, is it just since the accident?"

"I'm not cross-eyed you asshole."

I squint at her eyes again, then shrug. "OK, and I guess you *aren't* working for the Americans."

Now she really does look at me like I'm crazy, says in her broadest Turkish accent, which I have to admit is a pretty good one, "Do I *sound* like an American you freak?!" Yells at the top of her lungs, "*Help! Someone get me a lawyer!* Ow, son of a ...!" Holds her head in her hands and squeezes her eyes shut. Tries to loosen her neck brace. She's got a cracked skull, so all this yelling can't be fun.

The corrections officer outside in the corridor, Stewart it says on his name tag, pops his head through the door, "Everything alright?"

"No worries Stewie, Burcu here was just venting," I tell him. Looking down at her, I realize she's actually crying. I feel like a swine now, "Ah, get the nurse will you, Stew?" He ducks back out again.

"I've got family," she says, "They'll be going crazy with worry."

I think about how close she and her crew were to abducting Karn. Sympathy? Got none.

"Suck it up honey," I sit on the bed next to her, "This is your situation. You are being held under warrant in an Australian government correction facility for suspicion of being engaged in politically motivated violence. Under the 2002 amendment to the Australian Security Intelligence Organization Act, I can hold you here for questioning for, uh, seven days, while we talk. If you clam up, I can get the Attorney General to extend that indefinitely. Or, hey, just tell me, which embassy do you want me to call?"

Stops sobbing. Maybe it was just an act. Talking through her teeth now, "I'm an Australian citizen."

"Yeah, you keep saying, but you got no ID and you won't give us an address, family contact details, nothing. But I'm willing to believe you, that's why I mentioned sedition. Se-dish-un. That's when an Australian plans to carry out an attack on their own government mate."

"I'm not talking to you any more until I see a lawyer. *Mate*." Her tears have suddenly dried up.

Stewie opens the door for the nurse, a hard little Scottish bloke called Andy who looks like he might have been a guest in prison here himself once. "Someone called?"

I point my thumb at her, "Yeah, her head hurts. Can you give her a jab or something?"

"I'll see," he goes to the bottom of the bed, looks at her chart, "Not yet, it's only an hour since her last one. Give her a codeine tablet is about all I can do."

I start walking for the door.

"I don't want a headache tablet!" she sits right up and yells at him, "Can't you see I'm being held prisoner here? I need a telephone, I need a lawyer!"

He puts a hand on her shoulder, eases her back down onto the pillow, "Lassie, there's nothing *but* prisoners in here, just relax."

I hear him still talking softly to her as I step out into the corridor, "Umm, have you always been cross-eyed?" He's good value Andy. Only cost me a six pack to get him to say that.

"She's a what?!"

"Says here a local admin officer, but I'd say, from the look of this, she's a Turkish MIT cooptee."

"Shit. Which one is the MIT again?"

"Shit is right, Jones," Speed says. "MIT is the Turkish National Intelligence Organisation. And we got one of their people in Long Bay infirmary. I don't think we have ever been this deep in the shit."

Usually it would cheer me up, Speed using the 'we' word, but this is way beyond cheer-up-able. This has me wondering how fast I can clean out my bank account and who I know in Broome who would put me up for a few years.

Speed throws the Turkish Consular briefing note across the table. I already read it, but I read it again. *Consular Officer Missing…*

"Damn. I was sure she was working with Opium. OK, so the Turks don't know we got her, yet. We have Karn's witness statement that she was the one rammed her, we got the van, and the kidnap kit in it, we got all we need."

"All we need? We have *Burcu Last Name Unknown* on a warrant the A-G was looking at yesterday, and today this comes across his desk. 'Missing consular officer, last name *Sima* First name *Burcu*'," He points upstairs to the Regional Director's office, "Bob's on a plane to Auckland right now, or I'd be getting the come hither already, bet my arse. We're screwed Jones."

Now my righteous anger kicks in, uselessly but I have to vent it or it will turn my lunchtime toasted cheese sandwich into acid, "How come it's *us* in the shit, when a Turkish Consulate employee tried to kidnap *my* girlfriend and for all we know, they t-boned Jenno too!?"

"Oh, she's your girlfriend suddenly now?"

"What?!"

"Forget it. You can't prove any of that. You haven't got a single reason the Turks would want to do us harm. This woman had a car accident, ran into your girlfriend's car. Coincidence."

"With a big dog cage, duct tape, a black cotton bag, and plastic ties in the back of the van?"

"So, she has a big dog. Needs to restrain it."

"She duct tapes her dog?" I've got two chances in hell of not getting fired, is what I'm really thinking, and so is Speed.

"Maybe you can arrest her on animal welfare charges. She isn't talking and you don't have that DNA result back from the Commodore yet. I reckon we have about two or three hours before you and me and anyone who's name is on her arrest warrant get marched into Foreign Affairs with a rope around our necks. Between now and then, you have to get her to admit she was trying to kidnap your girlfriend and if you can link her to Jenno's crash that will be a bonus."

"I can do it," I say, without much conviction.

"I know you can." I can see Speed has as much faith in me as I do myself, because he is starting to look through his drawers, like he's already working out what to take with him when he goes. He pulls out a bottle of headache tablets, sleeping tablets, something like that.

Gives me a sudden flash of inspiration, "Wait, I really think I can!"

He looks up, defeated, "Sure you can Jones. I'm counting on you." Pulls a photocopy paper box out from under his desk and starts dumping office supplies into it.

"You want me to *what?*" Money is looking at me over a glass of champagne at the Opera House where I found her waiting to go in for some charity show.

I'm hopping from one foot to the other because I already wasted an hour going to the pharmacy and then tracking her down and my limo is parked on the forecourt at the bottom of the steps leading up to the Opera House and a cop on a horse said he would give me three minutes to get in, get out or get nicked for parking there, Security Service ID or not.

"Come with me, I'll bloody explain in the car…" I say, looking pointedly at her friend Darren who last time I met him, was face down in a toilet bowl in a pub in the Cross.

"Wants you to dress up as a nurse, darling," Darren says, grinning at me over his marguerita. "If she won't Jonesy, *I* will."

Somehow I manhandle her out of the theatre, down the stairs, and into the passenger seat of the limo without her swinging at me. It helped I told her I think I know who crashed Jenno, or at least, I know how to find out.

The horse cop has let his mount drop a steaming shit-cake right by my driver's door, and you got to be impressed by horsemanship like that. I step over it, climb in, then wind down the window. Look up at him, sitting there all stony faced, but I know he's cacking himself inside. I smile at him, "I guess you wanted a clean poo tube for when love him up later tonight, eh?" I don't hang around to see what he does next, but I'm pretty sure he's reaching for his gun.

"What do you mean, you know who crashed him?" Money says.

"I think that Turkish girl knows." I'm tearing up Macquarie heading for Broadway and the prison beyond. I've already rung ahead. They should be getting her ready.

"The girl he went mental at?"

"Yeah, she tried to kidnap Karn, right? Crashed right into her, but buggered it up. Too much of a coincidence, he goes mental at her soon as he sees her too. We got her locked up in a hospital for safe keeping but unless I get something out of her, she's probably getting out tonight."

Money looks spooked now, "I don't know Jones, this sounds a bit iffy. Where do I come in?"

114

"I need someone to act like a nurse. You're the only actor I know. I need someone who can just play it by ear, see what happens, go wherever it goes. And you got a medical degree, or nearly. You can do that."

"I don't know."

"Hey, it's for Jenno, right?"

"..."

Point at some clothes in the back seat, "I got an outfit from work, it should fit you. You should change now. Gotta arrive looking like a nurse."

She pulls the crumpled green uniform from between the seats, wrinkles her nose, "Yeah, it would fit, if I was a fat arse cow." Stares out the window, but I can see I got her now.

"Attagirl, get it on will you?"

She sighs and climbs over into the back seat, pushing my mirror up before she does, so I can't watch her change, "You had a fake nurse uniform just lying around at work? You have one fucked up job Jones, I keep telling you that."

"Oh, you wouldn't believe the crap we got downstairs," I say. "I would have got you matching green frilly panties but I think Herbal has borrowed them."

Now I'm tearing down the freeway, closing on Long Bay. Money is still in the back seat trying to get the old lady nurse pantyhose to stay up by tucking the waistband into her bra. I reach over to my phone and hammer out Karn's number.

"Hi mate, how are you? Nah, still at work. Yeah, you know, maybe a bit late, but definitely come past before you go to sleep, if you want. Yeah? Wait on, I need a pen." Rummage around in the glovebox, find half a pencil and a parking ticket.
"Right...yep...ok, milk, bread, vodka. Just the essentials, eh?"

Look over the seat at Money, trying to pin on a name badge, can't decide if it should be the left boob or the right, settles on the right. "Money? Nah, I haven't seen her…isn't she at the Opera House tonight, some charity show? You could try her mobile. Yeah…yeah. Or, I'll probably see her tomorrow, I can ask her then. OK, see you later. 'Course. Bye." Throw the phone in my glovebox and the shopping list on the dash. Somewhere down on the floor, Money's phone rings, then goes quiet.

"That was Karn," I tell her. "She wants to know, do you want to come to dinner tomorrow at her (quote) 'miserable pokey shithole of a government flat'?"

Money legs over into the front seat again and slips on her shoes, "Fucked up job, and one *seriously* fucked up love life, Jones."

There's an overly protective Protective Services guy waiting at the door as we walk into the hospital wing at the prison. If he's this stressed by me being 20 minutes late I feel sorry for him. Imagine how he's going to be trying to explain to the Royal Commission later, how he helped drug a Turkish consular official.

"You're late," The Protective Services guy says, can't help himself. Checking my paperwork, which Speed actually signed (without looking) so for once it is kosher.

Beside him is a guy I recognise as the prison doctor. Money climbs out at the same time as me, bold as, and walks over to stand beside me, looks the doc straight in the eye. Doc just looks at her for a second, "You brought your own nurse? I thought I would be going in with you…"

"Protocol," I tell him. "She has top secret clearance, you don't. Have to have a nurse with us whenever we question a sick suspect in case anything happens, it doesn't come back on us. How is she?"

He sniffs, "She's mildly sedated. She's fine to speak with, or I wouldn't allow this, but keep it short." Hands me a clipboard to sign and looks at Money. "Half an hour, max."

Money glares her death glare at him. Damn she's good. Takes the clipboard from him and reads it in the light from inside the corridor.

I go through, the Protective Services guy follows me. "Restraints?" I ask.

He jerks a thumb over his shoulder to the room beyond, "I got her plasticuffed to the bed. Plus her neck is still in a brace. That good enough for you?" Looks at me like I'm a little fraidy cat.

"Mate, maybe you haven't read your brief," I say, all holier than thou, "But that little lady is a trained Turkish spy. In case you didn't realise it, they are at war in Southern Turkey and they take that shit seriously. I'm willing to bet that if she wasn't totally messed up from a car crash, and drugged witless, she'd have had *you* tied that freaking bed by now and she'd be halfway to Ankara."

The Doctor at least has the decency to go a bit pale, but the Protective Services guy tries to look unimpressed, shrugs and walks off together with the Doc. Yeah, right. I bet he tells all his mates about it.

I wait until the door to the corridor closes and Money and I are alone. I've already checked there is no CCTV either here or on the ward. "Right. I need you to give her this." From my pocket I pull a small vial of clear liquid, hand it to Money. With a syringe. "What do you reckon she weighs, 45-50?"

She holds it up to the light, "Forty six. What is it?"

"Quinalbarbitone solution. It'll relax her, get her talking. Five mils per 10 kilos. Give her 20 ml, any more will put her to sleep if she's already sedated."

"Where did you get it?"

"Doctor I've helped out in the past, right? He promised me it's safe enough, you just dose her like I said."

"Shit, Jones, I don't think I can."

Squeeze her arm, "You had that junkie boyfriend for two years, don't tell me you can't give an injection."

"No, I mean…you're sure she's the one hurt my brother?"

"Yes. No. I won't lie to you. I'm not. But I mean to find out." Money's got big brown eyes, and they waver, just for a second.

"OK. Intravenous or sub-cut?"

"What?"

"In a vein or in her arse?"

"Uh, arse. I think."

She hitches up the pantyhose and we go in. I follow her in, swing the door closed behind me.

Burcu is lying on one of those half jacked up hospital beds, turns her head and looks over at me, then Money. She's got a belt around her waist, arms under the belt, and her wrists cuffed to the frame of the gurney with plastic ties. She looks kind of groggy, pointing at me with a finger, "I know who that one is. Who the hell are *you?*" she spits at Money.

Money digs around in some drawers and finds what she's looking for, pulls some rubber gloves from a box. Pops the foil bag and pulls the syringe out. It's got a needle on it, so tiny I can hardly see it, but that just makes it more terrifying, you ask me. She leans over and holds the needle and vial where Burcu can get a good look at them.

"I'm here to look after you darling," she says, all Florence Nightingale. "This will keep you comfortable for the trip." Lifts the girl's gown up to the top of her thighs. Puts the needle into the vial and fills the syringe, squeezes a bit out. Burcu's eyes trying to follow everything she is doing. She looks like she thinks she should be protesting, but Money tilts her on her side and it's over before she knows it and Money is holding a gauze to the little welt on her butt cheek.

118

I scootch up next to Burcu and she looks at me suspiciously. "What the hell do you want?" she says. Give her a few minutes, till her eyelids start to flutter, the doc said. "What freaking trip?"

"We're taking you to the consulate," I say. "Your people have kicked up a royal stink and we have to take you back. I owe you an apology."

She might be getting groggy, but she isn't completely out of it, perks up a bit, "Consulate?"

"Turkish Consulate Ms Sima. Burcu Sima? Nice name. I'd never have guessed you were Turkish," I fib.

She lays her head back, "You thought I was American!"

Laugh, "Yeah, pretty random right?"

"Very random," she says, lifts her hands up far as she can, "Take these off!"

"Sure, uh, you got some scissors nurse?" Money blinks, starts fecking around in boxes until she comes up with some big clippers you'd use for cutting off plaster casts. Reaches over to the girl's hands and shears through the plasticuffs, and the girl pulls her hands out from under the belt, folds them over her chest. Money heard what I said about Burcu Sima though, and I can't help notice she keeps the big scissors handy.

"Better?" I ask. "We just have to wait for the driver."

"Hmmm. God I'm tired." Breathes out and then in, nice and slow.

I break in, before she fades away, "But you have to admit, it looked a bit funny, the whole thing with that redhead. She was a middle east peace activist, so we figured *you* had to be American DCS. One professional to another, a bit of a screw-up eh, that crash?" Money looks at me, the idea of me calling Karn a peace activist is making her cough.

"Bit of a screw-up?" Burcu snorts, she's quiet for a very long minute and I wonder if I've lost her. Then she breathes in and laughs, "Complete screw-up is more like it. A peace activist eh?"

"You didn't know? I guess it's the same for you MIT guys as it is for us, they never tell us anything."

"They don't tell us *anything*," she says, "And me least of all, because I'm just a helper."

"Out of interest, what *did* they tell you? Is this girl someone we should be watching, or what?"

She sighs contented, the soothing rumble of the ambulance over the bitumen as it winds through traffic, she's still with us but I don't know how long, "Watching...watching...no, they told us something about how her significant other is getting in the way of some Operation we are running, so she was supposed to be a distraction. Disrupt, and distract."

"Disrupt and distract?"

"You know, freak you out, keep everyone busy until our op is over." She giggles. "Usually works."

Take the chance, "And that other guy? That was a distraction too?"

Half murmurs, on the edge of dropping off, "Other guy?"

"Yeah, the one you crashed into in Darlinghurst."

It's a long shot. She just frowns, looking vague, or confused, or both. Then she smiles, "Oh, him. The cute one. Nah, that was the disruption part." I put a hand out to Money, who has reversed her grip on the scissors and is ready to jump off her seat. "Bam, *nailed* him." Burcu lifts a finger in the air. "Dis-rupted his cute ass."

I laugh, "Yeah, that you did. Hey, what were you driving, an old Chrysler Charger? It was a miracle you even got it to run."

"Don't know. Local car, big one. I didn't source it. He's OK though, just shook up a bit...I checked him...before I jabbed him...with the knock-out juice."

"Sorry? What?"

"Got to him...before he could even get his seatbelt off...really...you call that babaganoush? That aint babaganoush...." Now she's gone, talking rubbish. I lift an eyelid and all I see is white. Money looks worried.

"She's OK, just sleeping," I say. "It's actually pretty mild. Must be because of the other stuff they gave her, knocked her out so quick."

Money is still looking black death at her, "I wish it was battery acid in that syringe." I gently take away the scissors.

Pull the recorder from my belt, "Did she say *I checked him before I jabbed him?*"

Two minutes later, I'm standing on a curb yelling into my phone. "I want a background check on every nurse, doctor and bloody floor-mopper that works the acute care ward at St Vinnies where Jenno is," I tell Shirley. "I think I might know why he is still a babbling mess."

The first time I met the Attorney General was the day I finished my BIC, my Basic Induction Course, five years ago. He handed me a naff certificate and shook my hand. Later, I brought him a beer and a savaloy and we talked rugby. I liked him, because the word that sprang to my mind about him was 'profane'. He clearly doesn't remember me, and I wish it could stay that way. Not much chance.

"Well, this is a freaking mess, isn't it?" He's holding the transcript of my conversation from Long Bay infirmary. We dropped Burcu around the corner from her Consulate in Woollahra, gave her a big overcoat and a pair of sunglasses and pushed her in the right direction. She toddled off, humming to herself. Not at all out of place in Woollahra; looked like a drug-addled actress.

"Been better, Sir," says my Regional Director, Teflon Bob. He's a career toadie, no responsibility so big he can't avoid it. Dresses like a men's clotheswear salesperson and uses cufflinks and hair oil. On the way in to see the A-G he said to me and Speed, "I want you blokes to know, no matter how hot it gets in there, we are in this together. I'll back you up 100%."

So you know he's looking for a way out already.

The A-G is sitting in Bob's leather chair. His spin doctor is sitting beside him, guy called Alasdair, and yeah, that is *exactly* how he spells it. Him I've seen in the paper, when he had his own column. And outside in another meeting room, drinking coffee and waiting for us all to join him, is the local head of the Foreign Affairs Dept who has been dealing with some pretty vexed Turks the last few days.

I shouldn't even be here. This sort of meet usually takes place in Canberra, but the A-G happens to live in Balmain and is back home for a conjugal visit with his wife I guess. So here I am.

"Where's the Turkish girl now?" A-G asks.

Bob looks at Speed, who clears his throat, "Dual citizen sir, Syrian-Turkish. Grew up Syria, then Turkey, where MIT recruited her. She's been returned safe and sound to her Consulate."

"Reassure me. She's *not* actually Turkish MIT."

"No, according to our sources she's just a co-optee. Contractor. They probably recruited her when she did a stint for the Turkish border authority in southern Turkey."

"Diplomatic status?"

"None. Here on a 457 visa as a temp attached to the consulate."

"And you think she did what?" he's looking at me.

"Her and a couple of other MIT agents are running some sort of operation here. Jenno and me seem to have stumbled into it, not quite sure how, and they decided to scare us off, or in her own words, 'distract and disrupt'. They organised a crash that put Jenno in hospital, and they were planning to kidnap a close friend of mine, but that went wrong, which is why we held her."

"Jensen," Bob explains, "Is the other officer, the one in hospital."

"You got this all on tape." He's saying it, not asking it. "So the Turks can't come back at us and say it's all bullshit."

"Yes. All her own words."

He nods, "That's the only reason I haven't shut down this whole region and called in the Inspector General, you know that?" To Teflon Bob, who squirms nervously. He leans back in the chair, which creaks, because it wasn't made to be leaned back in. "I got to take the helicopter view of this, right?" the A-G says.

"Certainly, Sir," Teflon replies, "View from the top. The Big Picture."

"No, Bob, the how-will-I-make-anyone-believe-this-fucked-up-looking-thing-flies, view," The A-G says. *That's* why I like him.

He shifts on his seat, "So, let me get this straight. I got American Defence Clandestine Service, chasing this ex PKK guy called Barrak, which they never had the courtesy to tell us about. And Barrak, he's gone off the radar, so now DCS want *our* help to find him. Or, you think they already have him and they're pulling our chain?" He's looking at me.

"Maybe. I don't know," I say.

He nods, noted. "And, it seems I got the bloody Turks, also running around Sydney up to something and putting my officers in hospital, trying to kidnap your, um, fiancé, because you are interfering in some Op of theirs, which by the way *they* haven't told us about."

Alasdair hands him a piece of paper.

"Back to matters at hand," looks at the paper, then at Teflon, "We also have a team of Peshmerga bomb chuckers who have gone to ground in Sydney, and they are also looking for this Barrak guy? I image the Turks might be a bit interested in *them*, could that be related?"

"Ah," Bob says, looking at Speed, who looks at me, "Don't know that they are...'bomb chuckers' as such. Recruiters, recruiting foreign fighters. I haven't seen an update on that in the last couple of hours, uh, gentlemen?"

I sound stone cold certain, which scares me later when I think back to it, "We've confirmed they are still in Sydney. We're confident they are here for Barrak. And we'll have a location on them very soon through a human source."

A-G closes his eyes, gets in touch with his political Force. Opens his eyes and says, "All of these things are connected."

Speed doesn't see the headlights in time, steps right in front of them, "Well, maybe not, Sir, we see no link yet between the Kurds at the barbershop, the Americans, Barrak and whatever the hell the Turkish MIT…"

The A-G frowns, and Alasdair coughs, "The A-G believes, ah, that these events cannot be coincidental, and that the disparate elements of these investigations will be best managed as one combined operation, ah, which based on the information presented at this briefing amounts to the gravest, ah, single threat to national security since, ah…"

"The Lucas Heights bomb chuckers," the A-G adds, helpfully.

"Right, ah, the Al-Qaeda style plot to attack the Lucas Heights nuclear facility," Alasdair continues, "Requiring us to engage in extreme, ah, measures, such as…"

"Locking up Turkish citizens for their own protection and telling their bastard Turkish employers about it later," the A-G says.

"Yes, taking into protective custody a potential informant, ah, who we had reason to believe may have information regarding…"

"The Peshmerga bomb chuckers we are really worried about and whom our friends the Americans are actively cooperating with us to help locate, in a joint operation on Australian soil between our two services," the A-G finishes. "Which joint operation I authorized before they arrived here, in a briefing note which will be dated appropriately and on my desk in an hour."

"Right, the Americans who, ah, in return for their help finding these suspected terrorists have asked for access to uhm, this Merdem Barrak fellow, which access we are happily facilitating," Alasdair concludes, smiling. "Forthwith."

"As soon as you find the cunt," the A-G adds. "So, gentlemen, are we fully aligned on this before we go and talk to that Foreign Affairs department wally outside? Warn him I'm going to publicly confirm we detained and then released Ms Burcu Sima, Turkish consular employee, for her own protection. See how her secret agent career goes once she's had her name and photo on the front page of the Herald. You might want to put down plastic, he's going to shit kittens."

Me, Speed and Teflon take no time at all to adjust to the new reality that my series of three different disasters is now a tightly coordinated international counter terrorist operation. We nod vigorously.

The A-G looks at Alasdair. "The PM just took a big hit in the polls on that climate thing, he'd love nothing better than a good security alert right now, make him look all statesmanly."

"Uh, Operational Name?" Alasdair says, stands and smooths his suit. "It's a big combined inter-service op, should already have been given an Operational Name for media use."

"We have a random name generator we use," Teflon tells him. "So no one can guess what the operation is about..."

A-G smiles, "Right, like 'Desert Storm'? Iraqis never guessed that one...I know, let's call it 'Operation B.U.G.' Short for Buggered. Up. Good." He shrugs on his jacket, "Which you'll all be if you don't tie all this into a nice gift wrapped package for me before the week is out." Says to Alasdair before they reach the door, "Get me a half hour with the PM. Get my cheeky friend Opium on the phone, so I can tell him about his offer of assistance and ask him what the hell he is up to. Get SCC to bang out an interagency briefing with a low classification so everyone in the country with a clearance hears about Operation BUG. And book me a one-on-one with the Turkish MIT head of station in Canberra. Tell him to wear his Kevlar freaking underpants."

"Your mob's in the paper," Karn says over coffee.

Folds it and hands me page three. Headline says, *Arrest creates diplomatic rift*. Describes how the Turkish Government is outraged at the detention of one of their staff, followed by assurances from the Turkish ambassador that he regards the incident as minor and is certain any concerns will be ironed out. Followed by a quote from the A-G saying that while normally he would not comment on issues of national security, he anticipates the full cooperation of Turkish government authorities. Thus leaving the reader in no doubt the Turks have been up to something but no one can prove it yet. Nothing about Operation BUG yet.

"Actually, it's down to you," I say, handing it back to her. "You hadn't been so quick calling the ambulance and the cops on that girl Burcu, the bad guys would've spirited her away and today would be just another Tuesday."

"It's Wednesday," she says. "So if it's in the papers, it must mean I can go home now?"

"Why I came over," I smile, "Escort you off the premises and back to your own digs. No more living off the taxpayer you."

She looks out the kitchen window at the rusting bathroom pipes of the flats next door, "And I was just getting used to the good life."

In the car, winding round the harbour toward the bridge, she drops her sunglasses to the bridge of her freckled nose, "So, Money and I have been talking and we agree you have to give up this job."

Cough, laugh, "Yeah? Do we? Why do we reckon that?"

"Well you have to admit it's a weird life, and we reckon you aren't made for it, like say, Jenno is."

Reminds me, I have to go and talk to the hospital about Jenno. Get the list from Shirley. I knew I forgot something.

"No?"

"No. For a start, you're not menacing enough. He's tall and handsome, and kind of ruthless. You're short and…not. *He's* what people expect when they open the door to a spook."

"I can be ruthless," I mumble. "Just ask anyone I've ruthed."

"Your heart's not in it. Jenno, he can do it because he really feels he's saving the world. Why do you do it?"

Grip the wheel tighter, I've never been good under cross examination of my motives, "Uh, the fringe benefits? Guvvy car and free parking in North Sydney?"

"See what I mean. You can't even say why you do it. Want me to tell you? Actually, it was Money who worked it out."

"She's an artist, not a shrink."

"She's intuitive. For you, it's like a club. It's the mateship. You, Jenno and that Robbo guy, just like Harry Potter and his mate Ron and that Hermione girl. You feel like you fit in there."

"Uh huh. Which one am I then? Don't answer that. I'm the ranga, aren't I?"

Karn puts the glasses back up and leans back in her chair, "Money said you'd be facetious, but I told her I'd say it anyway."

Money's right, of course. It is a club. The only one that ever let me be a member.

Shirley hands me the summary of background checks on the hospital staff, "Bingo. Got a nurse on Jenno's ward with the name Ayse Donmez. She's not in our files but Immigration database shows her place of birth as Kirrikale, Turkey."

"Yeah? I was hoping we'd get a little more solid than that."

"What do you want? She's got *I heart MIT* tattooed on her bottom?" Shirley is the kind of classy lady says 'bottom'. "Jones, there are six nurses working Jenno's ward and *she's* one of them. What are the chances?"

I'm thinking about the tattoo. "Thanks Shirl. Hey do you have a tattoo?"

She blushes.

"You do! You bad girl! Show me yours I'll show you mine," I say, untucking my shirt.

She spins around and heads for the door, "Never in my lifetime Jones."

"Well, then I'll sneak a peek at your funeral," I yell at her as she disappears, "You know I'd do it."

At the hospital I take the head of the acute care ward down to the cafeteria. It's a quiet day, steer him to a corner table.

"So, this is about Mr. Jensen?" He's about fifty. Sinewy and intense. I'd bet he still does half marathons.

"Yeah, thanks Doctor Sizlek. What I was wondering, if you wanted to keep him babbling like an idiot, is there a drug that could do that?"

"You mean, a drug that could induce the state we are seeing now?"

"Right."

Thinks. "I can think of several. Most any of the psychotropics. But they all have a short half life, and you'd have to give most of them as tablets - like every few hours – or at least in solution. Why?"

"OK, but if you wanted to be more subtle, could they be mixed in with the other stuff he's getting, or would they have to be given separate?"

"I have to ask why *anyone* would do that?" he says and I shrug. "OK, you could, well you could mix something liquid like *buflomedil* into his steroid drip, but I have no idea what effect that would have on the steroid, the *buflomedil*, or your colleague…"

"And how quickly, if you stopped giving him the stuff, would he stop babbling and come around?"

"Well, could be hours, could be a day, depends on the person and the drug. Impossible to say when I don't know what drug we're talking about. The intervention we gave him does seem to have stimulated his cortex but there is something…"

Pull a picture of Shirley's Turkish nurse out of my pocket, "This one of your nurses?"

"I've seen her." Looking at the picture properly for the first time, I suddenly realise I've seen her too. Sprawled over Jenno with a needle in her hand shooting him full of elephant juice to stop him murdering the little Turkish crash bandit.

"She been at the hospital long?"

"She's a contract nurse, I'm not even sure of her name, to be honest. She just started…"

"It's Ayse," I tell him. "I'm sorry to inconvenience you, but we have to do background checks on anyone caring for one of our officers in a situation like this, and she didn't pass the check."

"Really? Why not?"

"Sorry, can't say. Can you move Ayse to another part of the hospital?"

"Not without a lot of questions. I'd need a legitimate reason, but of course if you think…"

"I want to speak with her first. Maybe we can solve the problem today."

"Now?"

"Yep, I'll wait here. If you could get her, take her to your office?"

"I'm not even sure if she is…"

"She is," I assure him, because we checked. "Don't tell her what it's about, just ask her to come up to help with some admin BS. Tell her it's like, a salary issue. Something with her roster, kind of thing."

Looks a little wary at me, but we head off anyway, and he leaves me at this office, buttoning up his jacket, straightening his hair.

I fix myself a cup of tea, and steal a biscuit from his personal stash. Thing I've learned from bitter late night experience is that most places the coffee tastes like shit, but it's hard to bugger up a tea bag and hot water, even in a hospital. Bit later, she walks in and the doc introduces her, and I can see why he hasn't even bothered to learn her name yet. You'd forget her the minute you turned your back on her. Short, stocky, plain, friendly face, late forties. She stands at the door of the office, not certain what to expect. I stand and smile, and she walks in with a slight frown.

Dr Sizlek makes his excuses and leaves, closes the door behind him. I indicate the chair opposite me, and I take the one nearest the door, "Hi, Ayse? My name's Johns, please sit." Show her the ID.

"Security Service? Is this a practical joke or something?" she smiles, "Dr Sizlek said it was a HR thing," Her accent is very mild, you would hardly know she wasn't born here. Perfect. Shirley was right about this one.

"I know. Just didn't want you doing a runner on me."

"Doing a runner?"

"Running out. Disappearing."

"Why would I?"

"Don't know. Uhm, maybe because you're a Turkish intelligence agent who has been administering psychotropic drugs to a government officer?"

She blinks. "Let me see your ID again?" she says, so I hold it up for her. "What do you actually want, Mr. Johns? Is it that boy who came in? They told me he is one of yours…"

"Born in Kirrikale, eh?"

"What?"

"Know people at the Turkish consulate?" take the photo of Burcu out of my pocket, all bruised and puffy from her car accident. "Her, for example. Ring a bell?"

Her eyes widen a little, "Not personally. But I read in the paper she was arrested. What did you do to her?"

"Oh, she did that to herself."

"What?"

"Ayse, I know you are Turkish MIT. While you and I are sitting here, having a nice little chat, a police forensic team is downstairs taking samples of the drugs being administered to my colleague. And when we analyse them, I'm betting we'll find he's being given something he shouldn't." Let her think I have an entire army of lab coated techs swarming through the hospital.

She just looks at me, a little annoyed almost.

"Don't look so shirty. It was Burcu who told us, the little girl who drove the crash car. Told us he was injected just after the accident to knock him out, in case busting his head apart didn't do the job. Were you there too?"

"I haven't done anything!" she says, on the verge of tears. I'm supposed to feel like a mugger beating up a sweet little lady. What, do they all get the same training at Turkish spook school? If in trouble, cry? Maybe that shit works on your average guy. I'm not that guy.

"Then there's no problem. And I guess we'll find nothing at your flat - in Auburn isn't it? Unless you've been just a bit careless. Left a couple of bottles of the stuff sitting in your fridge next to the milk."

Can see her eyes, just for a second, flick up and right, like…which shelf was the milk on again? She rallies now, crosses her arms. "I want to talk to my husband. He'll sort you out."

So I laugh. "Your 'husband' MIT too? This isn't a TV crime show Ayse. You don't have the right to a phone call. No right to remain silent. But the parliament of Australia has been kind enough to give *me* the right to walk you out of here and lock you up for a week without access to anything more than a toilet, just so we can get to know you better."

She repeats, like a trained parrot, "I'm not talking to you until I've spoken to my husband. And even then."

Lean back in the chair, "Actually, I don't want you to talk to me. Or I would have had the police in here too."

"Then what is this about?"

"Actually I want you to bugger off out of here. Get out of this hospital. Go back to your MIT boss, whoever it is – and tell him to stop pissing in our pool. We don't have time to waste on you right now, and you, and the entire Turkish mission here, is in a world of shit already."

"I have no idea what that all means, but…" she says, standing. "I'm leaving. I'm going to call my husband." She reaches into her purse for a phone.

I stand too, grab her arm, "Fine, make the call. Tell whoever is running this operation, all they managed to do was piss us off. Tell them…"

Wham. I have no idea where it came from but her arm swings up out of her bag holding a short fat syringe, and she slams it into my neck. Doesn't hurt really, just the surprise of it. The last thing I see as the floor comes up to say hello, is her opening the door of the office and stepping out.

Lights out.

I wake up in a bed next to Jenno, about an hour later. At least this time I was already in the hospital. Saved the taxpayer an ambulance ride.

The nurse with the brown eyes who looks like Mila Kunis (yeah, I know I should know them by name by now), is looking down at me. Lips moving so there must be words, and gradually they come into focus, "…that's it, looking at me, can you hear

132

me…yes, that's it, now we're checking you for head injury because you gave yourself quite a knock on the table there, so I'm going to…are you there…ok …looking at me…going to ask you a few questions, just say yes if you're with me Charlie."

Thinking, OK, so I'm a regular now, we're on a first name basis. "Yes, I'm with you."

"Good then, so, do you know where you are?"

I hate a pop quiz. "Uhm, deep shit, again?"

"Har dee har, and what year is it?"

"Year of the Goat."

"O…kay. So, who is the Prime Minister."

"A bastard, according to my mum."

"Spot on, last question…who am I?"

I point at her forehead, where a piece of paper is stuck on with surgical tape, "Well, the sign says *The Terminator* but you're way better looking."

She frowns at me, then slaps her hand to her forehead and looks at the piece of paper, "Shit, sorry. Bit quiet until you came in, we were playing 'famous names'."

"What is your real name then," I ask.

"Michelle."

"Michelle, that was one weird-arse conversation to wake up to. Maybe we should try again some time when I'm vertical."

She blushes, "I'll…I'll go tell the doctor you're fine." She winks, "But I'll be back."

I groan, and she goes, but not before I detect a bit of a linger. Hmmm.

Robbo is there too, "You're getting good at this. Went down this time without even a visible bruise." Points at my neck, "Except for that. Looks like a wasp got ya."

Feel my neck, lump on it like a paintball whanged it. "Where is she?"

"Gone mate. This is a bloody big hospital. I didn't even try to find her. You told me to wait in the car. I waited in the car. Got a call from the office, who got a call from that Doc. Came up here and found you slacking off, sleeping on the floor of his office, big audience of bystanders around you. Got you moved here. Then you woke up."

Up on my elbow, "Get the dogs to Auburn?"

"Did that, you think I'm a complete loser?" He's got a banana and is peeling it. Stole it off Jenno's side table, "Nothing there yet but we got techs all over it looking for your drugs. She'd be stupid to go back there."

I look at him, annoyed.

He looks annoyed back, "Yeah, *alright*. We'll stay on it."

My mother on the phone. "Charlie, they told me you are in hospital *again*?"

"Yeah Mum, the nurses here got me a coffee mug with my name on it."

"You are a silly freaking sausage aren't you dear?"

"Yes mum."

"You've made some strange life choices Charlie. I just wish..."

"I'm not giving it up mum."

"I mean the job, dear."

"That either."

Sitting in my car later that night, parked under the bridge by Milson Point. Clock's ticking, or I would have stayed home, nursing a beer and a grudge. Got a turtle neck sweater on to hide the bump on my neck. Cow.

134

Serwan is quietly shitting himself. "I have a meeting."

"About time. When, where?"

"Tomorrow morning at 9. The old man rang me himself. I'm supposed to call back."

"The wrinkly old Barbers' boss?"

"Harith. It means, *He Who Cultivates.*"

I have that in a file somewhere. All I remember is that he sat on his chair while the others did the kicking, which makes him the boss.

"Something you should know," I say, "Before you meet him."

"Oh no. What?"

"It's going to be on the news pretty soon, all channels. AG is putting the country on 'Extreme Alert: terrorist incident imminent.' Your mates the Peshmerger barbers are going to be famous wanted terrorists. All their pictures from the airport cameras."

"Oh, no." All he can say.

"Yep. A-G didn't want to take a chance, he's giving a news conference tonight and he'll be up there with the PM, in front of about twenty Australian flags, warning people to watch out for them because they are planning something bad. He'll make it sound like it's up there with Martin Place or Bali, but worse."

"Oh, no."

"Oh yes - stop saying that. He'll be telling them to turn themselves in, speed things up a bit, avoid getting themselves shot. Think they will?"

"They are just recruiting people to help in Iraq!" he protests. "With humanitarian work."

"Peshmerga is the Kurdish army. They running orphanages now?"

Sits back and crosses his arms, "Does the Australian Army help with floods and fires?"

135

"Yes, but you don't need training in how to fire a Kalashnikov to fight floods and fires. Besides, if that is why they are here, why do they suddenly need your money? Why did they ask you about this Barrak guy?"

"I figured they just wanted to recruit him or something. You put them on TV, you're really going to send them underground."

"That's why you're here."

"They won't show up," he says, sounding almost relieved. "They see themselves on the TV, they won't show up."

"Sure they will. They need that money, they'll turn up. Unless you tip them off."

"No. I wouldn't..."

"Right, then." Hand him a phone, "Call."

"We might get *one* of the Peshmerga barbers at the handover of the cash, or if we're patient, we can get all five, up to you," I tell Speed over the phone. Robbo is in Speed's office too, I can hear him opening a chocolate bar. Got to be him. Ook Ook.

"Right now, I'll settle for one. We don't know they're doing any more than just putting the hard word on the locals to get 'em to cough up more cash. Waste of time if you ask me," Speed says. "A-G will be happy we get just one of them."

"What about Opium?"

"What about him?"

"Well, aren't the Americans supposed to be helping us? We can call them, it's an extra team at the least."

"Yeah, they're pretty good, dammit," Robbo adds, in the background.

"Forget that," Speed grunts, "I got resources out the wazoo. We're just supposed to *say* they're helping us, we're not actually supposed to put 'em in harms' way. Least, no one told me to. Cops are giving us a tac team."

"I want more. More cops. Buckets of cops. I've already had one serious kicking from these lads," I remind him. "And that was before we went public and made them desperate."

Speed relents, "Alright, call your Greek cop friend and set it up."

"I like your bravery by the way…" I say, offhand.

I can hear Speed was about to hang up, brings the phone back, "What bravery?"

"Just bagging one of them. Leaving at least four on the hoof to do whatever it is they were going to do? Kill Barrak live on the internet, probably, if it's them who have him."

"Yeah, pretty brave," Robbo chimes in. "If they start blowing shit up or go crazy in a shopping center carving people up with machetes. You got balls of ice boss."

"You bastards. How solid is your man Serwan?" Speed asks.

I count off on my fingers, "He's on the run already. He's taken our money already. No close family. He's connected. About as good a chance as we're ever going to get…but I'm going to have to promise him a big payout."

"How much of an Islamist is he? How radical?"

"You know what they say about Kurds – compared to a non-believer, the Kurds are Muslims. He's about as radical as you. His goals in life do not include a high explosive trip to paradise."

"What then?"

"More like, a condo on the gold coast and a lifetime pension," I say.

"OK," Speed decides, "See if he bites. We can talk real estate later."

Stop by the hospital on my way home. Walking into Jenno's room is like walking into a dressing room at the Moulin Rouge. Money and Jane are both performing tonight, and Money is wearing a skintight black lycra bodysuit, with a leather jacket and bikie boots. Jane is pulling off a pair of jeans as I walk in, pulling on a simple white satin dress and black slip-on shoes. I can see she has on a gold thong and gold wonderbra before the satin slides down over her shoulders. Karn is sitting with her long bare legs up on Jenno's bed, skirt falling around her thighs, bottom buttons on her linen shirt open to show the navel ring on her stomach shining in the fluoro light and her phone lying on her bosom with buds in her ears as she reads a magazine. The only thing that ruins this vision is Robbo, three chins resting on his chest, sleeping off his lunch. Oblivious to the festival of flesh around him.

"Hey all."

"Hey. Jones," he wakes and slurbles, "He's better."

Jenno looks just the same to me, lying unconscious with tubes out his nose and in his arms, but Money runs over and gives me a hug, "He woke up! Asked for orange juice!" Looks over at him, "Then he fell asleep again."

"He did pee," Jane says, holding up a bag I really didn't need to see.

"And he said," Robbo adds, "*What the hell are you all looking at?* Then he dozed off again."

Hard to say what the feeling inside me is. On the one hand, a kind of scared longing, with Karn smiling at me over her magazine. On the other hand, pitiful relief, that maybe I was right about Jenno being drugged and that getting rid of that Turkish nurse really worked. And if I had a third hand, on the third hand, kind of loneliness, because only Jenno could understand how tired and shit scared I am right now, but he's sleeping it off, so all I can do is go home, go to bed and get up in the morning and do what has to be done.

So I do.

Opium calls me at 2 a.m.

"Who the hell?" I mumble. Recognise the voice, even though I am still half giddy.

"It's me, at your service," he says. "Turkish MIT is parked in a car directly opposite your flat, watching you. They are apparently still annoyed at you."

"What?" I roll out of bed, crawl to the window. Peek out. Can't see shit. "How do you know?"

"Because some of my people are in another car, a hundred meters down, watching *them*," he says. "We'll keep an eye on them for y'all. But you might want to stay inside and lock your door. Good night."

It's a sign how tired I am, that despite the threat of more monstering by a carful of Turks angry I busted and drugged their girl Burcu, I feel reassured by the idea Opium is watching over me, check the chains on my door and just roll straight back into bed, and sleep. At 4 a.m. he calls again, telling me they have moved on, and I'm wide awake now so I just start getting ready for the day.

Watch the A-G hold his press conference on the breakfast news, looking all statesmanly. Talking about how everyone should stay calm and alert at the same time as he is scaring the crap out of them. Tells us the police and security services are working together with the full assistance of foreign services to stop the evildoers from evildoing and everyone should give them every support.

Wait, that's me, Jenno, Witless, Shirl, Serwan the Brave, Opium and a handful of no-freaking-idea cops he's talking about. Go the A-team.

I realise Money and Karn are right. my job is pretty weird. And they're wrong. I'm nowhere near ready to give it up.

"I'm glad you're back."

"Thankyou Jones."

"I need to talk."

"So I hear. Can it wait, I'm eating an egg muffin."

"Having a bit of a crisis here Father, need your advice."

"Say three Hail Marys"

"This is definitely more than a three hail Mary crisis, Father."

"Oh dear." Said with feeling.

"So, Bless me Father for I have sinned, it is, uhmm…"

"Two days."

"Really? OK, two days since my last confession. Thanks Father."

"You're welcome Jones. Jones…"

"These are my sins. I called a guy a paedophile."

"What? Is he?"

"Why, think you might know him Father?"

"That's not funny Jones."

"Sorry Father. No, I don't know if he is or not. Probably not, I just did it to piss him off. What sort of sin is that? Is it one of the venials?"

"It sounds like slander."

"Is slander a sin?"

"It is illegal."

"So is tax evasion, but the church does that."

"Hmm. What else?"

"Well, I told a lie to the Attorney General and now I have less than 48 hours to find an ex-Kurdish-traffic-cop who probably knows where this missing US Delta Forces soldier is, unless these Kurdish PKK terrorists have already got him. Or one of the others who is looking for him like US Defense Clandestine Service. Or the Turks."

"That sounds…stressful. Jones, what do you want?"

"Forgiveness, basically. Both retrospective and prospective."

"I absolve you of your sins, in the name of the father son and holy ghost good night. For your penance say three Hail Marys. Now let me go back to breakfast."

"Have a good one Father."

"And Jones? You don't have to ring me every time you sin, just save them up and bring them in to the church a few at a time."

"OK. This was your idea Father."

"Good bye Jones. Wait, Jones, have you thought any more about my suggestion?"

"No, Father."

"Just consider it Jones."

"Thanks anyway, but no."

"It was a calling that brought you to the Church at this point in your life, Jones. You shouldn't deny it. That calling may be more than just a call to prayer."

"The only call I hear right now is the call of nature, Father. So, it's three Hail Marys and join an order?"

"You're being flippant," says the man, chewing on his muffin while dispensing spiritual guidance.

"I'll stick with the Hail Marys, thanks Father."

Grab an egg muffin myself and meet up with Serwan, still shitting besser blocks.

"OK, so this is what we do," telling Serwan, "You give them the money. All of it. Grovel. Apologise for the misunderstanding."

"OK," his knee is shaking. He holds it tight. Sitting in the back of a white electrician's van about two kilometres from the meet.

Put a hand on his shoulder, "This is going to be OK. Remember, you do this right, you'll be set for life."

"Or, I'll be dead," he says.

"Never happen," I lie, "Now, you don't want to be too eager. You just give them the money, grovel for a while, and then you tell them, they need anything else, anything at all, you are their man. Tell them you owe them. *Anything* they want."

"What if they want me to go with them?"

"Say yes please I'd love to. Find out where they are and then make any excuse you can to get out of there again. We'll have a hundred cops there in five minutes. Be like Butch Cassidy and Sundance."

"Bullshit 'I'd love to'."

"Hey, you got a GPS chip in your collar. We'll know exactly where you are. You get an offer like that, you take it."

"What if he's not alone?"

"The more the merrier. You're in less danger than Princess Mary of Denmark at the Melbourne Cup."

I don't tell him we've also rigged his phone to be a passive transmitter, got surveillance all over him, and we'll be following Mr Wrinkles all the way home.

"And if they don't let me leave?"

"We'll know where you are," I tell him again. "If you don't come out, we'll come in and get you. You hear any loud bangs, just lie down quick and don't move, like I taught you." Look him in the eye, "You ready?"

"No."

"Screw it. Get out there," push him toward the van door, "It's a long walk, get a move on."

He's meeting the old man in a café on Darling Street in Balmain. Suggested Lakemba but the old guy said nah, they were nowhere near Lakemba, that would be too obvious. Serwan has to walk from where I let him out by Victoria Road up to Darling Street, take the 433 bus down to where the café is opposite the London Hotel.

Now I just wait, Robbo's team already at the café, behind the bar, on the street, in the breakfast joint next door.

Peel an apple, thinking, did Opium call me last night and tell me there were Turks outside my house, or did I dream that?

At work earlier, I passed Whitfield in a corridor while we're all kitting up, some ungodly hour of the morning. Leaning up against a wall, acting like he's trying to stay out of the way, but actually being as obtrusive as he physically can.

"Hey Jones."

"Hey Whitfield. Nice night for it. What are you doing here?"

"Me, oh, not much. Got a call in to the Saudis, if they ever ring back, see what they have on Barrak."

"Why not ring from home?"

Looks at me shocked, "That wouldn't be secure!"

"Pretty sure there's an app for that mate. Anyway, see ya."

"Big day today then?"

Tap my nose, "You know how it is Whitfield. Need-to-Know and all that."

"I wasn't…I mean, just…good luck, you know."

See him standing there, jealousy with a capital J on his forehead. Put a hand on his shoulder, "Whitfield, you don't want to know about this one. Most likely, anyone who has anything to do with this, is going to be lucky to get a job as a bouncer in Bondi when it's over. Personally, I've already packed my desk up…"

143

"Oh sure," he sighs.

"Here, I'll prove it." I reach into my pocket and pull out a dog-eared cappuccino points card. You know, the ones where every time you buy a coffee they stamp it and then after about 50 coffees they give you a free one? "You can have this. I'm only one coffee away from a free one at Tony's."

He looks at it suspiciously. Reads the name written carefully in ballpoint pen on the back. "Hey, this is mine! I lost it like three weeks ago…"

I clap him on the back as I walk away, "Exactly. Would I have confessed to that if I thought I was still going to be working here tomorrow?"

Sitting in my van with a cup of cold tea, a sleeping Nugget, and a girly magazine one of the dogs has left behind. Can hear the clink and buzz of the coffee shop from the directional mike that one of Robbo's waiters has sitting on the bar. Should probably have told Serwan he would be under multilayer surveillance, but then again, not. Just freak him even more.

This is the bit which I think must be like being pregnant – lots of waiting, feeling kind of sick, a bit excited, and a lot terrified. Thinking of all the things can go wrong.

I'm down to reading the rub and tug ads when finally I hear a cough on the radio, "Red Three, the first package has arrived." Nugget stirs to life, leans over the radio kit.

Then Robbo's voice, sitting nice and comfy back in Paddington, "Thanks Red Three, please describe."

"Uh green paper, blue ribbon, dark colour, looks like it comes from the Mid-East, about six foot long. Yeah it's ours." Serwan, a bit early. Must have hurried.

I don't know where Robbo's team have got the mike but I can hear Serwan order an espresso clear as a bell. Must be using the good kit today.

Seems like forever before the next cough, "OK, I got another package from the Middle East."

"Thanks Red Three, describe."

"This one's young. Brown paper, black ribbon with white stripes on the sides. Looks like it was made in about 1990. It's going to go on the same table as the first package. Sending you an image."

"OK Red Three, maintain."

On a monitor in the van, a laptop shows the picture of the contact who has just sat down at Serwan's table. Bugger. Not Harith. They're using a cutout. I grab the mike, "That is not one of the known packages," I say. "I repeat, we have an unknown package." What is going on? Serwan said the old guy was coming, but this is not even one of the other Barbers I took a beating from. This is some total newbie. Then I hear nothing, or I can hear the whole cafe actually, as the mike swings around to line up on Serwan and his new friend. Finally I hear it coming through. A lot of good it does me, the whole thing in Kurdish. But listening to the ebb and flow, it isn't too hard to get the gist, so in my head I put it together like this:

Contact: Harith sent me. You got the money?

Serwan: God be with the Venerable Wrinkled One. And with you. My respects to your mother, may God bless her munificent loins.

Contact: Yeah yeah, you got the money? I don't got all day. Wait, tell this guy to get me a coffee.

S: Indeed I have the money for He Who Cultivates Success. (English: Uh excuse me, can I have two more espressos? Thanks mate.) And yea I have cried tears like the flooded Tigris at my foolishness in not providing it to him with the utmost haste. I was greedy and selfish and hope he can find it in his large and bountiful heart to forgive me. But, where is Harith? I was told he would be here.

C: Would you come here yourself, every cop in the country looking for you? You think he's stupid? Just give me the bag.

S: Of course, of course.

C: Lucky we don't chop you into bits and feed you to the freaking sharks. Wait until I tell your Uncle Altan what a loser his nephew turned out to be. If *we* don't kill you, he will for sure, I ever tell him about this.

S: I deserve to die slowly and horribly, it is true. Here you are. 100,000 big ones.

C: Not here you idiot! Put it in the bag under the table.

S: No worries, my bad.

C: This is not the end of it. Don't leave town again.

S: I would not dream of it. Harith is the Owner of My Pitiful Arse. I only hope I can be of service to him again at some time. I hope you know that if Harith told me to chop off my own left nut, I would.

C: Whatever, just pick up the bloody phone if we ever call you again. Which, between you and me, I hope we never do, you coward. Damn the coffee in this country tastes like shit.

S: Indeed it does. Can I buy you a pastry? They taste like goat excrement compared to our own but perhaps you can choke one down?

C: I didn't come here to get fat. Look at these people. Decadent porkers. (Spits)

S: Yes. It shames me to live among them. They are unclean wastrels. (Spits)

C: Well get your arse back to Syria then. They could use a boy like you next time they need someone to drive a suicide car. Ha ha.

S: Ha ha. Good one. Ha ha. If only that were possible. Uncle Altan says I can do more good here raising the funds needed to arm our brave brothers and sisters.

C: You'd probably just steal the suicide car and sell it, more like it. Get out of my sight.

S: As you wish. God be with Harith. Please tell him I give my respects to his daughters, whose beauty is legendary throughout the wide world.

C: Go already. (Serwan leaves) Randy git.

W: (English) You, waiter. A baklava please.

"Stay on the target," I tell Robbo. "I don't know who it is, but he must have been sent by the Peshmerga." OK well, this should still be smooth as silk – we follow him from the café to his secret hideout where we catch him and the rest of the barbershop quintet knee deep in fertiliser and fuel oil and every one of us gets an Order of Australia.

Sure.

What happens is the young guy walks down to the ferry, gets the ferry to Circular Quay. We are on him. He buys a roll at a café. Sitting there, he takes the money out of the bag Serwan gave him, puts it into a Woolworths shopping bag. Throws the bag with our GPS chip in it, into a bin. OK, no problem. We are still on him. He goes up to the train platform, and waits for the T2 Inner West and South train. Looks like he's getting on, but changes his mind and sits down again. Oldest trick in the book. Our guys get on the train, another team takes their place. Bloody amateur. He gets on the next train. Sits down, looking around. After about ten minutes, gets up, changes carriages. We are on him. He gets off at Canley Vale and walks into the *Australian Persians and Descendants Mutual Association*. OK, we aren't going in there, but within about five minutes we have the whole place covered from north to south and even got a quadcopter drone in the air overhead. We are still on him.

Got enough vision of him to be able to make a really good ID, find out who he is. Then the tech in the van reviewing the video suddenly says, "Hey, he lost the bag."

"What?" I feel kind of pale.

"When he went into that Australian Persians and Descendants Mutual Association building he wasn't carrying any Woolworths bag. But back when he got on the train, he was."

Surveillance is not a science. If it ever works, it is a bloody miracle.

The news that every cop in the country is now on the lookout for five Middle Eastern terrorist suspects, probably planning something unspecifically heinous, gets repeated on every radio and TV channel, all night, and all next day. The media tries to make a link to the Turkish Consular Officer incident, and the A-G doesn't deny it.

We can't roll up the young guy who met with Serwan, even though we identified him now, because if we do, we blow the whole operation open. Turns out we know him, he's a low level PKK sympathiser. So we're watching him, but all he does is go to an internet café and play Counterstrike all day. He's done his job, collected and handed off 100 thousand bucks. Not a bad day's work.

At 4 p.m. one of the barbershop Kurds rings Serwan. Tells him thanks for the money, Harith is willing to spare his pathetic life if he can get them five passports, gives him rough descriptions of how the guys in the passports should look. Tells him they will call him again, tell him where to drop the passports.

Ka-ching.

It's not exactly what I want, but it's contact. Plus the guy called from a pay phone in Hurstville and Serwan reckons they have mentioned Hurstville a few times, which is starting to narrow things down a bit. I reckon pretty soon even Robbo will be able to find them.

Next steps. I tell Serwan to tap his mates in the Lakemba Buyer's Club for the passports. Reality is it will actually be easier for Serwan to round up five suitable passports from his network, than it would be for me to get the Dept. of Foreign Affairs to fake me up five freshly used ones. For me it would take a forest of paperwork and arse licking and they'd still manage to give me at least one with a smiling blonde German girl's photo it.

"I have some more interesting information for you, in the spirit of our new relationship," the message on my voicemail says. "Please call me at my hotel."

I yell at Shirley, sitting at her desk across the room, "How does the US DCS get my bloody direct line number?"

"How does your mother always know when you are back at your desk?" she shrugs.

Fair enough. I call Opium, "What information?"

"Hello Johns, I'm fine thanks, how are you?"

"Spiffing. Actually, that's not true. I'm not sleeping too well. Keep getting crank calls in the middle of the night."

"How annoying. But then, some of us didn't sleep at all last night. I'm happy to hear you did." Chuckly feller this morning. I can hear he knows something I need to know and he also knows how badly I need to know it.

"Ok what's up?"

"So much for the pleasantries then. I was wondering, how close are you to procuring us a few minutes together with my friend the traffic policeman?"

"You have questions? I thought you were going to *tell* me something."

"Well, the information is not without, shall we say, obligations."

Of course. "Oh, as soon as I find him you'll be at the front of the queue."

"So, no progress? How disappointing. Ah well, then I have wasted your time, I'm so sorry."

"That's it? You get nothing, so I get nothing?"

"I'm afraid that is it, yes."

"Big bloody deal."

"Oh, it is Johns, in light of what our mutual friend the Attorney General told me on the phone yesterday, it is indeed a big bloody deal."

He's like a cat playing with a brain dead rat, I got to give him credit, "OK, how big a deal? I have to know how motivated I should be to find one Kurdish traffic cop. He's not the main game. We got real live terrorists to catch, you know. Find them, we'll probably find him."

I can hear him stop smiling, "You should be very motivated my friend. I can tell you why the Turks have been so emotional about keeping you and your partner out of their way. I think you are still at risk."

"So tell me," mendacious bastard.

"Hmm, but that would involve me sharing information from a very very sensitive source. My service would never normally consider that. The risk to the source, you understand. But a man in my situation, well, he might go beyond the normal limits in a time of extreme *personal* need. Y'all know where to reach me, Johns." Click.

He's lying. He doesn't know shit. Turks have forgotten all about me and Jenno.

He's not lying. He wants to save his brother.

If he even has a brother, which I seriously doubt.

Anyway I have no idea where Barrak is, no way to find him. And I still don't have any of the Kurdish barbers in the bag and I still have no idea what the US DCS or Turkish MIT are really up to.

This job sucks. Or more likely, I suck at this job.

"My job sucks," I yell at Jane's sister Melanie across the pool table. Karn doesn't like playing pool, and is working tonight anyway to catch up on the time I cost her hiding from the Turks. Melanie's got Jane's Scandinavian cheekbones and blonde hair,

150

but is skinny as a broomstick except for a wonderful DD bust which must be where all the food goes. It isn't like a clandestine date or anything, Melanie knows Karn, probably better than me. Actually I'm hoping she'll be able to give me a few Karn pointers.

"Your job sucks? *Tell* me about it," Melanie says, which is one of those quirks of the English language which appears to be an invitation to unburden yourself but is actually an opening to ask her about how much her own job sucks.

So I do, and I have to admit, being a social worker in a closed psychiatric ward, which Melanie is, does sound like it blows bigger chunks than being beaten up by Arabs and drugged witless by Turks. At least my bruises are only physical.

I stop feeling sorry for myself. For as long as it takes for Melanie to wipe me off the table five games to three, which means I pay for the table *and* the drinks.

Sitting at a shawarma place later, I look up from my coffee, "Midnight. Yay, it's my birthday."

She smiles, "Nice try Jones - you're cute, and you know I might be tempted, but hell, Karn scares me. Besides that, if *she* didn't kill me, Jane or your ninja friend Money would. So for your birthday I can give you a hug, that's about it." Ninja, ha. Tell that one to Money, she'd like that.

There are so many possible responses to all this information that I can't process them, so I just mutter, "Thanks, I think, or as Hugh Grant says, bugger. No I mean, really, it *is* my birthday. I just realised."

"You can't *just realise* it's your birthday. Only a complete loser forgets their own birthday. Didn't anyone ask you what you want? Don't you have a mother who knits you stuff and sends it to you a week early?"

"Yeah, and, no. Karn asked me when my birthday is, about a month ago, but she's probably forgotten. My mum says birthdays are a capitalist plot created to generate wealth for the global industrial establishment. We never celebrated birthdays. I guess that's why I forget."

She smiles. "Alright, here you go - happy birthday loser," and she leans across and gives me a kiss which proves 8 ball isn't her only talent. "Damn that was nice," she says, closing her eyes for a second, "You sure know how to kiss a girl."

"Comes with the territory," I shrug. What *are* you doing Jones you idiot?

Luckily she gets up and picks up her coat and handbag. "I better walk myself home before I do something we regret. Thanks for a nice night Jones."

So let's examine the romantic known knowns; there's Karn who more or less has ownage but so far won't have actual real sex with me, and then there's Jane who would kill me if she knew I were out with her sister Melanie, who hardly knows me but it seems might actually have sex with me, except she's scared of all the other girls, principally Money, with whom I have no physical relationship whatsoever.

I say this out loud to myself a few times and a few different ways on the walk home, but it doesn't get any better no matter how many ways I re-say it.

Outside my place I see flowers on my car under the wipers. The note says, "Came past at midnight with flowers and champagne (wearing almost *nothing*) to help you celebrate your birthday. Read your text messages. Karn."

There are five text messages, the first one says, "Fuck me, it's your birthday!" What? How should I read that?! As in, 'everyone deserves one on their birthday', or 'bloody hell I forgot it's your birthday'.

The last one says, "F U, where R U."

I bend my wipers back into shape, and slope into the apartment, alone.

Breakfast with George is never a joy, given how noisy he eats, but who knows, today may be different. It's my birthday, right?

"You aren't going to believe this," he says, so I know I won't, because George is reliably literal. "Why I called you, urgent?"

"Go on," push the coffee pot over to him.

"Got this friend, Ahmin, lazy slob, never worked a real day in his life, got this nightshift cleaning job at Bankstown airport, where he just *sleeps* all bloody night."

"And?"

"So he's got all these little corners he takes off to, for nap. Keeps moving around, the shift supervisor never knows where he'll be sleeping next, right? He does like the total minimum, and they can't catch him sleeping so they can't fire him."

"And?" He'll get there.

"So one of these places is an old workshop, belongs to an outfit went bankrupt this year, *Ride On Air* or something."

"*Ride On…*"

"*Air*. Yeah, crap name, light planes had flights to Tamworth or something. Who wants to fly to Tamworth?"

"Tamworthians?"

"Not enough of 'em. Anyway so he sneaks in there to have a kip and bowls on through the back door, he's got all the keys, right, coz of his job, and buggered if there's not someone living in there. Couple of blokes, they got beds and a little camp stove and shit."

"And this is unbelievable because?" Shove a plate of croissants at him.

"They tell him to bugger off go clean someplace else, and show him some sort of airport security badge which he says was fake.

And you won't believe who he thinks he sees on one of the beds, fast asleep."

"I'm sure I won't."

Gives the gap toothed smile, "Of course, it was kind of dark, he didn't get a real good look."

"George."

"And he doesn't know the guy all that well, just saw him a few times around. And the guy was lying down, right?"

"God's sake George. The usual fee, OK?"

"Just raggin ya. It's not about the money, you know that, but I got expenses. Anyway he says to me hey Georgie, in that hangar, I saw that guy you was asking about, your friend the panel beater. Sleeping like a bloody baby he was."

Barrak.

Happy Birthday Jones :)

"Oh, well, it's solved then," Speed throws an intel printout across the desk at me.

"What's solved?" Look up from the surveillance tasking screen I was working on. Robbo telling me he doesn't have anyone able to get out to the hangar at Bankstown, check it out.

"Operation B.U.G. Your Barbershop Kurds are apparently accredited representatives of the Syrian Arab Red Crescent here on a legitimate cultural exchange. That's what it says on their visas, and SIS has a source in Damascus who has confirmed it. Says so in this report ONA just sent through."

Look at it and frown, "ONA and SIS believe what these guys wrote on their visa applications?"

"Apparently. Don't fret. The A-G is disinclined to believe Red Crescent flunkies would assault one of his intelligence officers and put them in a trash bin and threaten to kill a guy unless he gives them 100 thou."

"I like the A-G, you know that."

"So B.U.G. is still operational. Tell me we are closer to finding them and that bloody money."

"Yeah totally all over it. Have them any minute now. What about my airport thing?" Trying to change the subject.

Speed sighs, "You got all our people out checking out Mosques and coffee shops in Hurstville and precinct and you want to pull them off to go look at an aircraft hangar at Bankstown because some friend of EX1188 thinks he saw this guy Barrak sleeping on a cot?"

"OK. *I'll go.*" Which I have no intention of doing. "Alone. Into a whole nest of terrorists probably. But am I afraid? Hell no..."

"Sleeping - on a cot," Speed emphasizes, "In the corner of a dark hanger. Does that sound likely to you?"

"Said I'll go." I shuffle doorwards. He better call my bluff.

Look outside, it's raining again. It'll take two hours to get to Bankstown. A whole afternoon lost and I only got about three days left before the Teflon Bob tells the A-G he's thinking Case Officer Jones would make a lovely scapegoat.

"I'll go too," comes a voice from the door. Look across and there is Jenno. OK, a bit wobbly on his pins, got a bandaged wrist, but his lopsided grin still works. "Where we going?" he asks.

"Bankstown," I tell him, grinning, "Bout time you got off your arse."

Operation B.U.G. Intelligence Context for Heads of Departments

Operation B.U.G: Wires Red Crossed?

Information from a sensitive source indicates that five individuals currently the subject of an alert issued by the Australian Security Service and Federal Police, and suspected of being Kurdish Peshmerga recruiters or operatives, may in fact be Syrian Arab Red Crescent (Red Cross) representatives, as their visa applications state.

The reasons for accepting their bona fides include:

- **A sensitive source in Damascus**, *with access to Syrian Arab Red Crescent staff lists, has confirmed the named individuals are listed as employees of the Syrian Arab Red Crescent in Damascus.*

- **The Syrian Arab Red Crescent** *is not known to allow its credentials to be used to provide cover for PKK operations, nor amenable to employing known Peshmerga representatives or supporters. The SARC has previously denied any links to Kurdish militias or material support for paramilitary or insurgency operations in northern Syria.*

- **We are unaware of any other example** *of Peshmerga supporters or operatives using SARC credentials for cover.*

While none of this information can be used to completely rule out the possibility that the named Kurdish individuals are Peshmerga supporters or operatives, it increases the likelihood that this is in fact, not the case.

(We refer to the usual disclaimer that the situation on the ground in Syria is highly fluid and subject to constant change, so the intelligence provided in this bulletin while accurate at the time of writing, may or may not be credible and reliable at the time of reading.)

In the limo heading down the M4, telling myself Jenno looks like he actually put on weight while he was on the drip. Bit chubby around the jowls, I think to myself, jealously. Seriously how does a guy spend days in emergency in a coma and then come out looking like he's been at a health spa? Apart from the banged up wrist. He's thumbing through the music on my phone, muttering to himself about my hopeless taste. "Do you listen to *anyone* except female singer songwriters who wear thick black rimmed glasses?"

"I got some Iggy Azalea on there…she's hot."

"That sentence was wrong in so many ways," he says, "What did I miss while I was out?"

I shrug, "Nuthin. That bloke Barrak the murderous Kurdish traffic cop got kidnapped, we think he might be in Bankstown, where we're going."

"So, that's nuthin?"

"Nup. Pretty quiet actually."

"Last I remember you were in hospital after getting a kicking from those Kurdish hair dressers."

"Barbers."

"Barbers. Shirley tells me you had another trip to the hospital too, Turkish MIT tried to kill you."

"Oh, that. She's exaggerating. It was just a little love stab. I wasn't even properly unconscious."

"Hm hm. And Money tells me they also kidnapped Karn."

"Pah. Tried to. They messed it up, she went ballistic on them. She's fine."

"And we caught one of them?"

"Yeah. Oh, they bugged my car too. I Dolly Partoned them. Now they're really pissed off."

"OK, so, not much going on then. And why would they do that, Jones? Try to kidnap Karn?"

157

"Opium thinks it's all to do with Barrak. OK, so he's an ex-Kurdish YPG cop, but why would the Turk's care, when actually all he did was kill a bunch of other Kurds? Opium knows but he won't tell me."

He winds down the passenger window which is a good thing, given the smell off his plaster cast wrist. "But Robbo tells me Opium is your best mate now, calls you up every day, even middle of the night, check you are OK."

"Damn, you didn't waste any time getting plugged back in did you?"

"And you had a meeting with the Attorney General?"

"Oh, forgot all about that. Yeah, he was in town, we did coffee. He's a Tigers fan too you know."

"Well, that's two of you." Finally he finds an old Cold Play album on my phone I didn't know I had, and thumbs play, "And, who the hell used all my shaving cream, by the way?"

Thing is, I never learned how not to blush. Blush like a bloody nun at a buck's party anyone catches me, "What shaving cream?"

"You're pink as a baboon's arse Jones. I go to the flat to freshen up after getting out of hospital, go to use my shaving cream and it's just an empty can. Couldn't have a shave. It *was* a new one."

"Oh that. Yeah, I think Karn shaved her legs. She's *your* sister's friend, I told her to use *your* shaving cream."

"She used a whole can?"

Shrug, "Really *long* legs. She used your razor too. That's probably buggered as well. Lucky you didn't try it, would have ripped your face off."

"Jones?"

"What?"

"Why is Karn shaving her legs at our place?"

"Um. They were hairy?"

"She's a redhead. They have no visible body hair."

158

No way am I going to tell him what we did with the shaving cream. "Oh yeah, there was *one* thing happened while you were goofing off in hospital. You should know."

"Uh huh. What?"

"Your bank suspended your credit card. Rang up to let you know. I took the call."

"They *what?*"

"They said unless you paid a minimum 200 bucks in three days it was suspended. That was a week ago."

"So you paid it, right?"

"Hey, I been a bit busy fighting the war on terror, mate. I'm supposed to say, sorry Attorney General I can't do coffee today, I have to go to the bank to bail out Jenno's credit card?"

"Shit Jones. My card shouldn't have been $200 over." Looks as thoughtful as he can get. Big manly brow all wrinkled up.

"Well, it was."

"How do you know?"

"Girl in the shop told me it was already maxed, so I had to use all my charm to get her to put my stuff through on a paper slip."

"You used *my* card while I was lying in hospital?"

"Shit yeah. Had to buy myself some clothes to replace the ones you bled all over in your car crash didn't I?"

Karn has a dark side, by the way.

I know you are all sitting here thinking, she's just about miss perfect, redhead with the long legs and lace bodice and all that, a successful small business entrepreneur no less. OK she won't actually have real sex with poor ol' Jonesy, but apart from that, she's just about the bees knees. Right?

Nope. Girl likes karaoke.

Last night after midnight, I prise the flowers off the car and call her up and she's mad at me, I didn't get her text messages. Mad enough she's not going to come around my place, but not so mad she doesn't want to meet up despite it's two a.m. So, I climb into the car, meet her at this little bar she knows in the Cross, I never heard of. I walk in, and my lightning sharp sixth sense immediately tells me something is wrong. Place is full of Japanese and Korean businessmen.

They all look at me kind of bleary as I walk in, only westerner in the place. But that's nothing compared to the reaction when Karn walks in. Jaws drop. Necks put out of joint. Beer is spilled. The guy who was murdering Tom Jones stops. One lonely guy on the stage keeps singing, "Think I gonna dance now!" They all piss themselves laughing.

Used to it, she ignores them. Gives me a big long kiss. That shuts 'em up. "That's all you're getting tonight, Jones," she says and winks. Bastard.

Hour later it's 2.30 a.m. and I'm actually thinking this isn't too bad, Karn sitting on my lap, laughing at the Korean drunks singing karaoke. And she hasn't even asked where I was earlier, so I haven't bothered to tell her about my not-date with Melanie. Probably she already knows. Small town. Girls talk. Damn, she's probably waiting for me to mention it. Should I mention it? Day's first dilemma.

Table next to us is some students from Singapore, and they're actually good fun, keep trying to get us up there and finally Karn says, alright, I'm ready.

Ready? It's a set up. She goes up to the machine and puts her four bucks in, already knows what song she wants, punches it in. It's an old Missy Higgins and she sings it like she really means it. Which isn't to say she sings it good. But I know who it's meant for when she gets to the chorus:

But I will learn to breathe, this ugliness I see
and we can both be there and we can both share the dark
And in our honesty, together we will rise

160

out of our night-mind and into the light
at the end of the fight

See, when Missy wrote that song, she didn't expect it to be karaokied in a bar in Kings Cross, by a leggy redhead, to a morally challenged spook. Some songs, like some voices, aren't made for karaoke. And what I don't want, is for Karn to come back to the table now and tell me why she chose that song, so I jump up, can't believe I'm really doing it, and I grab three of the Singaporeans and we keep Karn up on the stage and between the five of us, we do a belting rendition of 'I Will Survive.' Which is a born karaoke song, if ever there was. The house cheers and I hit the bar for two glasses of champagne while Karn takes a pee.

"I will survive, eh?" she says when I get back to the table. "Clee-shay."

"Betcha. Don't worry about me, I'm a survivor. Cheers. Happy Birthday to me."

She smiles, kind of sad, but a smile. Tips her glass, "Birthday Jones."

Which the Singaporeans hear, "It you birday? *Happy Birday*!!" And pretty soon the whole bar is up on stage singing me a Pacific Rim version of Happy Birday and trying to kiss Karn who keeps explaining it isn't *her* birday. But I have to admit, as I stagger home arm in arm with the tempestuous non-musical Karn, it is probably the best damn birday I ever had.

Back in the car with Jenno the next afternoon, heading out to Bankstown airport, he wants to know what the plan is. Which is fair enough since we are probably about to walk into a nest of terrorists.

"I'm a real estate agent. Showing you the premises."

"We got no keys."

"So, if they're there they'll let us in. If they aren't there, we don't need to go in. They wouldn't leave him there alone."

161

"And who exactly, is *'they'*?"

It's a fair question, to which I have a fairly vague answer, "al-Akradi, probably. Or it could be another Kurdish faction, like if he's got a reward on him. Or, because Opium says it absolutely wasn't him kidnapped Barrak, it probably was. So it could be the Americans. Or the Turks."

"And the reason we don't have like 50 heavily armed Special Protection Group ninjas headed out there with us?"

"They're all in Bankstown. This one is regarded as a 'zero-probability sighting'. Except it came from George."

"Typical. You got a real estate agent business card?"

I point at the glovebox, "I don't know, find something in there."

Opens the glovebox and the nurse's uniform falls out, the one Money used when we lifted Burcu. He holds it up and looks at it. Looks at me. Shrugs, doesn't even ask. Picks through all the paper in the glovebox, finds a stack of cards with rubber bands around them. Thumbs through until he comes to one he likes, "Charlie Johns, Investment Consultant. That'll work." Looks at me, "You got a jacket in the car? You don't have the look."

"What look?"

"Investment consultant look. Smart, successful, sharp."

Silence.

"OK smart guy, you be the investment consultant. In your plaster cast. Who am I then?"

"Manager of an online sex shop looking for a new warehouse to store the dildos."

"Thanks a lot."

The hangar is, no surprise, away in a forgotten corner of the airport - so I stack the car in the main carpark and we walk/hobble. Jenno's got his leather attaché with him, designer jeans, Hugo Boss jacket. He's still a bit unsteady on his pins.

Norfolk Island Air is the next door neighbour. Big letters over the hangar doors still say *Ride On Air – Tamworth and Surrounds*. Big 'For Lease' sign on the side too, Blackworth Realty. Jenno points it out; that and the black Toyota RAV4 parked by the door at the side of the hangar. Reflective side and back windows. Discreet but surplus to requirements satellite aerial on the roof next to the radio aerial. Bingo.

"That's no suicide bomber's car. That's a spook car, right?" Jenno asks as I walk around it. "I swear I've seen it before, can't remember where?"

"Drive-through burger joint, about a week ago," I remind him. I don't have many talents but all those years in surveillance you develop a memory for that stuff. "Get the plate number."

He takes a photo of it. "Not terrorists then. It's either DCS or MIT. We're in and out, right?"

"Sure thing. Got to get in first Jenno."

"Nothing clever. Play it cool."

Look at Jenno over the top of my sunglasses, "Jenno. Shut up."

"OK OK. I'm a bit nervous, alright? We should have cops here with us. According to you it's probably some tooled up foreign agents in there with a hostage."

Try and see through a window on the way to the side door, but it's newly papered over with brown paper. "Or no-one."

Jenno walks up and bangs on the door. Sounds like a gun going off. Then there's voices inside. Nothing happens. Jenno looks at me and shrugs. Bangs again.

After a couple of minutes the door opens a crack, shows a big ethnic looking guy, "Yeah waddisit?" Sounds Turkish, or Syrian. Or Iraqi, Lebanese, Jordanian or... OK I have no idea. Not Chinese.

"Sorry to disturb you mate, I'm here to show a client the property," Jenno says, handing the guy the card, and then leaning on the door, taking the guy by surprise. It flies open and Jenno steps in, cheeky as you like, making a big thing out of his busted wrist. "Can you hold the door? Thanks mate. Come on in." Motions to me and I step quick up behind him.

Gambino at the door is not happy, but Jenno is away, "So as you can see, it's in excellent condition, completely, um, storm-proof." Turns to the guy, "How's the water pressure?"

"Uh, fine, look, this is nodda good time, I'm gonna ask you to leave," the guy is saying, but Jenno just rolls right over him.

"Five minutes mate." He points to the office at the back of the hangar, "Office facilities too, with broadband internet and fibre to the node," he ad libs. "You need that for an online business, right? Come this way."

I'm two steps ahead of him as the guy grabs at Jenno's sleeve, "I said this aint a good time. *Mate.*" Accent is kind of middle-eastern European. Polish Lebanese? Giving me nothing here.

But he's too late, coz I'm at the office door and as I put my hand on it, it swings open, "Can I help you?" Another guy is in there, this time in a suit, no tie. Looks like Pierce Brosnan used to look, except with a smashed flat nose.

I turn to Jenno, who is still being held by the sleeve, "My agent was showing me the property. It is for lease, isn't it?"

He manages me out, and pulls the door behind him, but he's still standing in the door jamb and through the door I can see two people. One, a woman in her twenties, is making a cup of tea. Luckily, it isn't Burcu. And a man is sitting at a table with playing cards.

And that man is Merdem Barrak.

He looks as though he's going to say something, then the tea lady steps behind him and rests her hot cup against his neck. He closes his trap and looks down at his cards.

"No, it's *not* for lease," the suit says. He's in his early thirties, dark curly hair, bit of a pot but not bad shape. Looks like ex-military gone to seed. "We've rented it for the whole of this month." He's not middle eastern though. I'm thinking 'contractor'.

"Oh," I say, all contrite. "I'm sorry, the real estate agents said...never mind."

"Do you mind if we look around a bit anyway," Jenno asks. "Save us coming back?"

Pot gut is already walking me to the hangar door now, collecting Jenno on the way, "Actually, it's bad timing. Our month is up soon, try again in a week."

I look pissed off, Jenno makes apologetic mouth noises to me as we leave. Gives the guy his card and asks him to call if he's vacating early. Both guys stand in the doorway watching us walk away. We stop a good distance away, Jenno pulls some stuff out of his attaché and starts flapping it round like he's showing me something, some other bargain basement shithole he's found for me.

"Are they coming over?" Jenno whispers.

"Nah, just watching us."

"That was Barrak right?"

"Sure was. Didn't look too happy did he?"

"No, poor little feller. Think he recognised us?"

"He'd be stupid to show it if he did."

Chew on that a minute, "They look American to you?" I ask Jenno.

"Them?"

"I'm trying to think, who the hell would whip Barrak out from his work in broad daylight, his workmates gonna call the cops, start a whole kidnapping investigation. Who else except them? But Opium swears it isn't."

Back at the car now, Jenno standing with a hand on the door says, "Aint their style. They want to disappear you, you just

165

disappear, out walking the dog or something, never seen again. They don't bust a door down and take you from work, all these guys with wrenches and rivet guns around you. Especially if you're like Opium, trying to do the whole op on the quiet."

"Except, he's kind of spooked according to George, not going to the mosque, not going anywhere probably. How you gonna snatch him, he never leaves home?"

"He still had to *go* to work, right? Get him on the way there. No they wanted to be seen snatching him. Send some kind of message."

"Yeah I guess. So who were those guys?"

"Sounded Middle Eastern to me." Jenno says. "Except the chubby white guy with the James Bond hair. He sounded Aussie."

"George said they spoke Kurdish," I point out. "The ones who took him."

"That fits," he shrugs. "Or it's supposed to throw us off." We both pile in the car. Do a routine counter-surveillance route on the way home (two cappos, muffin for me, fruit and yoghurt for Jenno), but either lazy, busy or confused, the guys in the hangar don't try to follow us.

We run the plates on the Toyota. It's registered to Doubletree Printing and Offset, Parramatta. Like those guys really looked like they were in the stationery business. But interestingly, Doubletree Printing and Offset is a subsidiary of TKS Holdings, which strangely enough is registered in . . . Ankara, Turkey.

This is another WTF moment. So both the Turks and the Americans *are* after Barrak? Not to mention the Kurdish PKK barbershop quartet too. And it's the Turks who bagged him? No wonder all sorts of pain started happening when Jenno and me got in the middle of all that...

Now I'm thinking, why would Turkish MIT risk trying to kidnap a Mr Nobody ex-Kurdish cop. Risk it so bad they were willing to come in here all gunned up and start roughing up Australian citizens, taking out the local intelligence spooks when we started nosing around. They must have wanted him bad.

"Barrak is out at Bankstown," I tell Speed when we get back to base.

He's happy we might have found Barrak. He's not so happy the guy is being held captive.

"They're kidnapping more people? Apart from your girlfriend?" he shakes his head.

"Jonesy's got a girl-friend..." Jenno says, singing it.

"Karaoke buddy," I mutter. "So what do you want to do? Give it to the cops?"

Speed picks up the phone, "Hell yes. Kidnapping's criminal. I don't care who's babysitting him. We're out of it. I'll talk to Teflon about it, he'll have a pow wow with Canberra and the DDG, I mean, this involves a foreign service farking around on our soil kind of thing, but I'm sure we'll be happy to hand this little package of shit to the police or foreign affairs or Security Intelligence and *we* can get back to finding your PKK."

"Really? Two big league foreign intelligence agencies are falling over each other to get a hold of this guy and you're just going to hand it off?"

"You bet. Faster than a babysitter's boyfriend when the parents get home," he smiles. "I agree, he is no ordinary Kurdish traffic cop. But neither do I see him as a credible threat to the Australian way of life. So, we have two foreign intelligence services here willing to break all the rules just to get a hold of him? Let the cops sort them out. Whenever I hear about this guy Barrak, I hear the horrible sound of career doors slamming for everyone who has anything to do with him."

"So the cops or SIS take over, foreign affairs makes sure the Turks just get a slap on the wrist, Opium gets away with pissing all over us, and we still have to pay all the hospital bills?" I take the phone from him, put it back down, "Wait. I got a better idea."

Speed looks dubious, "I doubt that…"

"I'll whisper it so you can deny later I ever suggested it, and then I won't ever mention Barrak to you again."

Robbo is spewing. Serwan got instructions for the handover of the passports, and Robbo was hoping it would be a Hurstville shopping center, a nice multi-ethnic environment for his guys and girls to blend into.

But it isn't.

"A Mosque? They're doing the meet inside the bloody Bosnian Mosque in Penshurst?"

"Newly renovated," I point out. "Very popular I hear. Should be a congregation of hundreds."

"I thought they were *Arabs*. What they doing at a Bosnian mosque in Hurstville?" He spits.

"Meeting with some old war buddies from Sarajevo? How the hell should I know Robbo?"

Blobs onto the sofa in his garage office, "I've had two teams in Hurstville all yesterday and half of today and there's no sign of them. You're telling me they are right there."

His office is not going to win any Better Homes awards. There's the fire engine red leatherette sofa, complementing the bar fridge covered in Beer Coasters of the World. It's not going to win any PC awards either, with Miss Fitness USA jockeying for wall space with The Rock and a nice big poster of Janet Jackson's wardrobe malfunction duet with Justin Bieber satisfying both the Janet and the Justin fans. Behind it is Robbo's Command Module – a cubicle, desk, huge map of Sydney, pins all over it, two way encrypted radio and espresso machine and a dusty $5,000 ergonomic Swedish chair which Robbo made the Organization

168

buy for his back, buggered up by the fact he did all his work lying in the sofa with a mike in his hand, and still does.

"So, stop whining, tell me you aren't gonna lose the geezers this time."

"Alright, alright."

"Damn kid, still not old enough to drive, has to take the train, you don't even see him hand off that money."

"These guys kicked your arse in that hairdressing salon, far as I recall. Glass houses Jones."

I rub my ribs and smile, "Nah, it took four battle hardened Arab terrorists to take me out mate, only took one pimply adolescent to show your guys up." And by the way, that kid now does nothing but hang out in fast food joints and play Counterstrike, so whoever he is, we aren't going to hit the jackpot following him around.

Robbo shifts his arse and points at Hurstville on the map, "It's not a total nightmare. They go east the only way out is around the airport, south they have to go over Tom Ugly's bridge, West the Salt Pan Creek bridge. We got natural choke points there if we lose them. But if they go north, like via Bankstown, Liverpool…"

"That's assuming you can even get close to the mosque to see the hand off," I remind him.

"Nah, that's easy. Cops have an Observation Post on Forest Road can see anyone going in and out. Had it since the Bosnian war. But we won't have eyes on your agent while he's in there."

"They still have to get in, and out."

"True, yeah…but what if they use another clean-skin. Some guy we never saw before?"

"This time is different. Flea is swapping out the e-tag in the passports and putting in GPS chips. Wherever those passports go, we'll know. We're gonna get these guys this time Robbo, I feel it in my water."

Wipes his hands on his greasy jeans, "All right then! Bout time."

"You put your plan together, I'll get the warrants started, say, three thirty to meet with the cops?"

"Nah, two. Best thing will be if your boy can stay with them this time."

"He'll try, he's buying his surf shop with this one."

"Or just a pine box six feet down, if he screws up," Robbo points out.

And that just leaves time for the phone call.

"Hi, is that Levysohn?"

"Ah, Johns. Lovely to hear your voice."

"Yeah, right. You in town or at the beach?"

"You mean you don't know?" Can hear him smiling.

"Relax Superspy, we haven't been on you for three days. Got more important things to do. You want to meet or not? Bondi, half an hour?" Let his ego leak out his pants for a few minutes.

30 minutes later I park in a back street of Bondi and walk slow and clean to his little safe house. Opens the door in a suit and tie, ready for business.

"Got a date?" I ask him. He doesn't blink. Points at the sofa, but I walk to his balcony. We've got wires all over his place, and I want this conversation to be off the record. The flat is barebones, except for a table with a microphone, laptop, and medical kit, ready for guests.

"I hope so," he says, joining me, "Do I?"

"Up to you. What are you like at crashing parties?"

"Crashing?" Frowns.

"You know, busting in unannounced. Could be a useful talent, you want to spend some quality time with Mr. Barrak."

"Oh, crashing. Yessir, I think we are accomplished crashers, when crashing is called for." Leans back on the balcony, keen, but relaxed, full on Cat on a Hot Tin Roof relaxed.

The salt wind off the beach blows a chip packet up and over the roof next door. I get the feeling it's not a lucky wind, but then, I'm not a chip packet. Screw luck.

"OK, this is the deal. I tell you where Barrak is. Tell you what you're up against. You can go and get him."

"That seems," he hesitates, "too simple."

"Here's the catch, no doing a disappearing act on us. You get him, you bring him back here, and talk to him all you like. One of my colleagues will be here too, with a nice warrant that lets you keep Barrak here for a week if you want to. But he stays in Australia, and at the end, goes back to beating the shit out of car panels like nothing happened."

Flicks his toe at a soursob sticking up between the concrete slabs of the balcony, "And if it proves difficult to respect these conditions?"

"Then, I guess you'll do whatever you want to and I'm a bloody idiot for trusting you," I say and glare him, like I'm daring him to make a fool out of me. I give him the full 100 watts of my big blue orbs. Only thing I really got going for me is those orbs, Jenno told me that once in a drunken moment of honesty. People can't look away, if I light 'em right up.

But he sounds amenable, "Your real name is Jones, am I right? Well, Jones, it isn't often I betray a trust. Yours is a trust I'll earn. That I promise."

What the hell does that mean? Why does everyone in the US South talk so fancy? Ah, what do I care, Barrak is a sideshow now. The main game is in Hurstville.

"OK, here's the catch. You want Barrak, you got to go through my new Turkish friends from the MIT to get him."

"You mean set up a meeting?"

171

"No, I mean physically *go through them*. They're holding Barrak in a hangar at Bankstown airport and I'm betting they're not that interested in letting you have him without a fight. I'm also betting they're planning on getting him out of town, seeing as they're holding him at an airport and all. So you better not waste any time."

He thinks about it, "I think I have assets available who could..."

I hold up my hand, "Don't need to know. I gave you Barrack. Now you tell *me* what *you* know."

"In good time, Jones, in good time. When we have Mr Barrak, you'll get what you want."

Fine. I'm about to bundle up the barbershop quintet anyway so maybe I won't need him. I love it when a plan comes together.

What I'm really looking forward to? Turkish MIT is running around town kidnapping people, crashing cars, injecting psychotropic drugs and other random shit? Well, let that chubby Turkish fool in the hangar be at the pointy end of an American DCS interdiction. See if he has time on his busy schedule for that.

It went like this, far as I can guess from what Barrak told us after. Barrak is sitting playing solitaire again, it's about 3 a.m., he's bored shitless but worried, why he can't sleep. He has no idea who these people are, just knows they're Turkish, and that can't be good. They don't talk, hardly even to each other. One speaks Kurdish, they ask him he wants to pee, he wants to eat, and that's it. They won't tell him what they want. Now he's convinced they're waiting for someone, and maybe after that he's going to die. There's three of them now, and only one ever sleeps. He hasn't seen a gun since they bust into his house and threw a bag on his head, but he hasn't seen a chance to run, so who knows.

One thing he doesn't understand. They bust into his work, hit the receptionist on the head, bag Barrak and tie him up, drag him to a big dark shed who knows where. But when they cook, they use Halal meat. Don't actually say anything of course, just show him the Halal label once, so he knows it's OK to eat. What the hell is that about? He's supposed to be grateful, how they thought of his diet while he was imprisoned?

The older guy, always in a suit, he's reading a paper. On the phone all the time; speaks Arabic, Farsi, Urdu, Kurdish, all pretty good. The woman, she's sitting at the table with Barrak, playing some game on her phone. No one's really keeping an eye out, they're relaxed again now, though they were a bit jumpy after those real estate people came in yesterday. The big guy watched them go, nothing else happened, they calmed down a bit.

OK, then they come into the office where there is always him, and one other. At the moment, it's the woman. The other two give her some signal, like 'OK let's go.' She motions to the chair and he moves off the bunk, sits on the chair. She ties his wrists behind him, one of the guys ties his feet. They rope the chair to the bed, which is bolted to the floor. They put the bloody brown hessian potato bag over his head again, then they all leave.

He's like that maybe 30 minutes. The place sounds completely empty, like they have taken off. Then the office starts to fill with smoke.

The hell? They're going to burn the place down with him in it? He starts yelling, desperate to get the ropes off, just manages to tip the chair halfway over so he is hanging off to the side, really painful, arms stretched in all the wrong ways. Trying to get his feet under him.,

Two big bangs, like doors being hammered open, one of them loud, like it's right near him.

In Kurdish he hears someone say, "He's here! In here!" Someone pushes him upright. He's so stupid he starts saying "Thankyou, thankyou. Get this bag off my head, untie me."

That aint going to happen. Whoever it is cuts him free of the chair, but they haul him to his feet and push him through the hangar and outside, coughing his lungs out. Smoke, kerosene smell.

Next he knows he's in another car.

This all happening while we're getting ready to go to prayers at the mosque.

"You have to get close enough to put this on their car as they're leaving," I hand Serwan the sticky little radio tracker, size of a camera battery. "Drop it inside the door, back seat, something. Worst case, stick it on the roof. Won't matter if they find it later, because there won't be a later."

"Then what? You going to arrest them?"

"Good idea. Wish we'd thought of it."

"What if they take me with them? How the cops know I'm one of youse? Who says some idiot won't shoot me?"

"I'm not that lucky."

"Freaking comedian. *You* go."

Sigh. "The dream scenario is they take you with them. They want the passports and they want to do whatever they're doing and get out of town, every cop in the country looking for them - they need your help. But the fact that guy in the coffee shop you gave the money was a ringer, that tells us you aren't the only one helping them. So make yourself indispensable, whatever they ask you just say yes."

"Just so we're clear, just in case, you tell the cops *I'm* the good guy," he says.

"Let's not get carried away here."

"Why can't you just put a microchip or something inside the passports, why I have to piss around with this thing?" He looks at the radio button like it's the size of a Frisbee.

Smile, "Microchip?"

"Yeah, tiny transmitter thing."

"You saw that in a movie?"

"Yeah, Bourne Identity. Good idea, or what? Can you do that?"

"No, we can't do that. Put a GPS chip in a passport? Do I *look* like Matt Damon?"

"Actually…"

"Get lost. One other thing I should tell you. These guys aren't Peshmerga. We think they are al-Akradi."

He goes pale, "Al-Akradi!? Those guys are psycho!"

"So keep them happy."

"I'm going to die," he mumbles.

"Or retire to the Gold Coast," I remind him. I pat him on the back. I don't know about you, but right now I'm thinking my cowardly, greedy, mixed-motive taxi-driving human source is a rolled-gold freaking hero.

Give Serwan a phone he can use, if he gets in trouble. Just has to flip it open and it'll dial home automatic. He's got the GPS sewn into his shirt lapel, the phone has also got a tracker in it, so we know where the phone is, hopefully that's where Serwan is too. So all I can do now is put him on the train to Hurstville with the passports, radio tracker, a shopping bag full of GPS chipped passports, and the phone.

Go back to Robbo's command module and listen to it happen.

Like watching a slow motion train wreck.

Sohrab is sitting in the module with Robbo and Speed. He's one of the younger Kurdish linguists, the one I trust most not to completely fabricate the translation. Most of them, the older linguists, they hate their targets so deep, it burns through their translations, and all of them like to spin it as badly for the target as they can. Sohrab is a young second generation immigrant, wants to do Engineering at Uni of NSW, got an engineer's attitude to his job – they say it, he translates it, no enhancing.

175

NSW Police liaison, Jimmy Panagyris, is there too, stacked on the sofa with a folder of papers in his lap, feet up but I can see he's tense too. This is as big as it gets, right, taking down five guys who are probably PKK. Big As It Gets. Got all five of Robbo's teams in Hurstville and area, got NSW Police tactical response unit in a chopper, ten unmarked cars cruising the south-east. Got Water Police on every wet bit from Botany Bay to the Georges River. Teflon Bob has a feed going into his office upstairs in North Sydney, sitting sipping Scotch with the NSW Police Commissioner. They want to make the call together to the A-G, if we bag any of them.

I got time to do a coffee run, and then a sandwich run, by the time the GPS screen shows Serwan near the mosque. On foot from Hurstville station, he'll be arriving just after the start of prayers, meeting the targets straight after.

"OK, I can hear him singing to himself. How many targets again?" Sohrab asks, settling the headphones over his ears.

"Five," Panagyris, says.

"No idea," I correct him, "We don't know who's going to be there. Could be just the old guy again, could be all of them. Could be a clean-skin."

"How's Kingsford Smith?" I ask Panagyris.

"Got flights out to um," Looks at his folder, "Singapore, Frankfurt, Vancouver, Fiji, London, Hong Kong, KL, next two hours or so. No bookings in the names we got, and they don't have the new passport names yet, right?"

"Can always buy tickets at the airport," Robbo points out.

"That's why we have guys at the ticketing desks, and at check-in for Qantas, Singapore, BA." Jenno is out there too, in the Border Force office, watching the monitors.

"What about light aircraft?" Speed asks. In all our pre-op planning, no-one raised that.

"Light aircraft? They gonna fly to Broken Hill?" Panagyris asks, sarcastic.

"How about PNG, smart arse?" I shoot back. "Hop a boat to Indonesia."

Panagyris not so cocky now, "They do that?"

"Biggest Muslim country in the world, got their own independent Sharia state about an hour from Jakarta, so yeah, maybe?"

"Your agent is at the mosque," Robbo announces, pointing at the blip on the GPS screen.

"Any sign of the barbers?"

"Not yet."

"OK, shit, I'll get someone over to the light aircraft terminal," Panagyris rolls off the couch to get at his phone.

But they must be there. One of them must be, or a helper. Prayers have already started, they must already be inside? We hear Serwan washing himself, getting ready to go in.

"Quiet please," Sohrab says softly, taps on his computer to start recording the feed. "He's talking to someone, uhm, *hey you can put your shoes here.* Talking English. Guy says *Here,* Serwan says *No worries.* Still in the foyer, I can hear noises from outside."

Sohrab describes Serwan going in, says hello to a couple of people, goes in to prayers. Imam is an Albanian, talking about Rugova like he was a saint, but nothing radical.

Eventually Sohrab says, "OK we're finished now. Your man is standing where everyone is talking, bit hard to hear. OK, here we go, I think:

hello Serwan

hello Mam Harith...mam, it means Uncle...he's sucking up

...shall we walk to my car? I want to stay with the crowd.

yes, of course, Uncle. how are you?

well, they don't have us yet, laughing

no and they won't Uncle, they are fools

we'll see Serwan, we'll see, do you have the papers?

yes, Uncle, here, one is a little older than you asked for but it is the best I could do…um… … Sorry, can't really hear. Maybe *How much did it cost you.*

about 5 grand. OK, car door opening. *hello, I am Serwan.* Could be introducing himself to someone else in the car. Yes there is someone else there, I hear another voice. Serwan talking again. *I paid it myself Uncle, a contribution to the cause. This car, it is like the one I had at University, a Toyota, yes? I believe so. Except mine was red, not blue. It is a good car, the Toyota.*

these are very good papers Serwan, we have to get out of here, where are you going now?

the train station Uncle.

You will come with us, we might need you again.

Uh, anything Uncle. Of course.

Just get in. get us out of here. Stick with the other cars leaving. OK that's it, sounds like a door shutting, no, two doors now, and like the car is driving off.

Serwan saying, *where are we going Uncle.* He's in the car.

I'm doing a little groundhog dance. It's the real thing this time – the old Wrinkly guy! It seems Serwan's 100,000 big ones has bought him a little trust.

"Oh, you beauty," Robbo says out loud. Sohrab looks sharpish at him, "Not you Sohrab, Serwan the Kurdish Uber agent there. He's in." Robbo squinting at his screen, leaning to his mike now, "OK I got a track. Moving, uhm, west southwest on Legrange? Probably a blue Toyota. Who's got it?"

Radio sits quiet a minute, "Bug-3-1 base, I have a light blue Toyota going west Forest Road, turning into Stoney Creek. I'm one out two back, need to overtake to verify. Bug 3-3 you're cover."

"Bug 3-3 roger."

"Bug 3-1 moving up. Tag reads LFX-2233. Confirm sky blue Toyota Corolla, three door."

178

Sohrab still whispering quietly, still translating ...*these really are very good Serwan. You are very resourceful. I have a job for you.*

Uncle, my time is yours.

"Bug 3-4 parallel on Boundary Road."

"Bug 3-1 roger 3-4 . 3-1 blowing past, I have a white haired Mediterranean male, looks like Target 2, with, confirming now, our man in the back seat. Driver is middle eastern, about 35, could be uh...target 4. OK visual lost, will take the next right, uhm, Bonds Road, you got it 3-3?"

"3-3 roger, one out one back."

"3-4 on cover now, four back."

"Ok 3-1, doing a blockie."

Robbo does his thing, moving three other teams southwest to parallel and in front of team 3, leaving one team at the mosque for now, in case they double back because they forgot something. Switches channels, "Tac-2 you have this on GPS and audio?"

Police chopper unit leader is a throaty bloke, voice like a Maori, "Tac-2, got the feed, suggest we get airborne."

"OK Tac-2, wind it up."

Robbo looks at me, "Your boy is either going to be a hero, or he's gonna be dead."

Right then, my mobile rings. It's my own home phone. Jenno?

I whisper, "Hi mate, aren't you supposed to be at the airport?"

"No Jones, it's me, Money, there's a guy here and he isn't happy," comes her voice, and she doesn't sound happy either.

"Here, where is here?"

"Your place, I'm at your place, and so is this guy and he's...he wants to talk to you anyway." Hear the phone being passed hand to hand.

"Hello Jones," voice doesn't register for a moment.

"Who the hell is this?"

"Sorry, it's 'Adam Levysohn', here with your lovely companion. I wish I could enjoy the moment more, but my mood is not good." Hear his hand cover the receiver, "Would you excuse me miss, I need to talk to your friend in confidence."

Confusion. Opium is in *my* flat? With Money? On my phone?

"Sorry for the interruption, yes…I was saying you have…"

"What the *hell* are you doing at my flat?!"

"To be honest, Jones, it is not my choice. It's quite disgusting, how you live. But I hope you have some answers. Can you come here rather urgently?"

"Now? No, I'm, things are pretty chaotic right now. Why?"

"Chaos. Y'all have no concept of the *meaning* of that word. Where I have just been, that was chaos. Now I suggest you join me, and quickly. Your lady friend is making us a pot of tea. You would not want it to get cold."

Was that a threat? Not Money too. How screwed up can a week get?!

Lean over to Speed, whisper in his ear, "Opium is at my flat, with Jenno's sister, something bad has happened. I have to go there."

Looks at me like I'm mad, "Now?! In the middle of this?!"

"Get Witless down here. You know he wants to be here, he's probably hanging around outside the door. I'm going to ring Jenno and get him to meet me at our place." He's still looking at me like I'm mad, as I hit the door.

And he's right, I am mad.

But not mad crazy.

Out of the cab running, door to my flat is open, I walk in. Opium sitting on my couch in black overalls, black t-shirt, dirt on the knees. Drinking tea with Jenno.

"Where's Money?"

"She left in a huff," Jenno shrugs. "She was only here to pick up some mail. She let him in. Man, I hate herbal tea. It never delivers."

"What is this about?" to Opium.

"I asked Mr Jensen to wait until you got here, to save explaining everything twice. I was hoping you would already know what happened…but, I can see from your faces, perhaps not."

"Assume not."

So Opium explains, how his tactical team and him head out to Bankstown early, lay the groundwork for their little light urban assault operation. Check it out, see who is moving around, start to make a plan for getting in, getting Barrak, getting out. He splits his team in two, one outside the airport boundary, checking ingress/egress routes by car, the other on foot, supposed to have a walk around the light plane facility, check general security.

Opium is in his car, noodling along, suddenly there's police everywhere, then fire engines. In the distance is the hangar they're looking for, on fire. More police, and airport security. Thinking okaaay, maybe we should just mosey along, driving around here in a hire car full of tac ops gear. But for now the cops think they are just dealing with a fire in a deserted hangar so they aren't really worried about a little station wagon trying to get out of their way and after a few minutes they are clear of the airport and heading back to Bondi, trying frantically to contact the other half of his team which was caught out on the hoof. But he gets nothing, nada. Radio silence. Something is very, very wrong. Plan is to meet back at the Bondi flat if anything goes wrong, but two hours later, they are still a no show. He is missing three personnel.

Opium comes straight to my place, only place he can think of. Either he is going to a) beat my brains out for setting him up, or b) get my help to find his men. He's decided on b), since I obviously don't know what was happening out at the airport.

"Hangar on fire, cops found your guys wandering around, no airport IDs, took no chances," Jenno guesses. "Cops are a bit tetchy at the moment. We got a terrorist alert on, you might have heard."

"I can't afford police," Opium says, "You got us into this situation, I expect you to get us out of it. I need my team back."

"Soon as I get a chance, we are in the middle of an op ourselves," I promise him. "I guess they can look after themselves, won't say or do anything stupid."

"No, they won't. Their cover is they were looking to book a plane to fly them to the Birdsville Races this weekend. Checking out the different companies. They all have good papers, authentic. But my men are not the biggest problem."

"What then?"

He holds up a green metal cylinder that looks like it has been blown up from the inside, Cyrillic writing on the outside.

"While your police and fire brigade were all busy I used my false ID to go in and look around what was left of the hangar. I found this."

Jenno takes it from him, "Pipe bomb? Looks Russian."

"Flash bang grenade," Opium says. "Russian copy of our M-84."

"What? Now we got Russians chasing him too?" I'm about to pop my cork.

Opium shakes his head, points at the base where there is also some Arabic writing, "No. These are standard Syrian army issue. I checked the serial number with Washington and this consignment fell into the hands of the PKK around Aleppo about a year ago."

We all look at each other, having one of those 'oh, shit' moments.

"I don't know where the Turkish MIT agents have gone, but it's pretty safe to assume your friends from the PKK, who I've been seeing on national TV all day, now have Barrak."

"Oh for godsakes," Now I am mad. "You knew about the Turks hunting Barrak. Turkish MIT going postal on me and Jenno because of Barrak, and you knew but did you tell us? If you had, we could have put him under protection and we might have avoided this!"

"I was going to tell you."

"But you didn't."

"Damn," all Jenno can say. "Honour among thieves. Damn." Jenno again.

Opium looks at me, "You seem a little pale, my friend."

"Me?" get my voice under control, "Nah. Shit like that happens every day here. No such thing as friends in this business. I need to use the toilet."

Bastards. All of them. But I calm down a bit. He really needs us now, thinks his Turkish competitors have his man and have torched their own hideout, are about to get out of town. Might already have left. Plus half his team missing, probably in the lockup out at Bankstown because some local cops smelled a rat. He's desperate.

Step back into my loungeroom, "Who is Barrak, really?"

Opium frowns, "What do you mean *really*?"

"I understand you want him to help find your long lost brother," I say, without much feeling, "But why did the Turks want him?"

Opium shrugs, "Because he's PKK..."

Jenno laughs, "PKK are like flies on a turd on the Turkish border, they don't have to come all the way down here to find one."

Find one. One... special... one. Suddenly the clouds part in my addled mind. Choirs sing. The veil of obfuscation is lifted...

"He was *theirs*," I say.

"What do you mean?" Jenno frowns. Opium gives me a wan smile.

"Barrak was a *Turkish* agent. They found him, turned him, recruited him and for whatever reason, they sent him down here.

183

Somehow they got a hold of that ONA assessment, realised his cover was blown. Had to get him out. Got down here and found you and me nosing around, and tried to put a scare on us."

Jenno is looking like I've lost my mind, "They kidnapped their own man?"

I sit down, "Yes, but they screwed up. Somehow PKK found out where they were holding him. Let's face it, if George found out, pretty much anyone with a bit of leverage could." I look at Opium, "Barrak was a Turkish agent, working for the Turks against the PKK. You knew that all along too, didn't you?"

He waves his hand, "Well, it was a need-to-know kind of thing. Y'all didn't need."

Jenno hasn't had time to pick up his work limo yet so we are both in his purple 2008 V8 Commodore. Could run a small suburb on the power it puts out, but you still have to crank the bloody windows down by hand, and then they stick halfway. Puts it in gear and it sits there thinking about it and then goes, oh alright, let's go then, transmission finally clunks in and Jenno floors it, getting us a satisfying frown from The Pitbull, head of the body corporate for our apartment block, letting herself into the front door, supermarket bag full of gin smalls.

"Women like this car?" I ask him, belting up. Even the seat belt is slack.

"Nah, they bloody hate it mate. Lucky I got buns of steel."

"Nice colour though."

"You like the colour of puke, yeah."

"Fixed the stereo?"

"Nah, can't even get AM now."

"What's the smell?"

"Smell?"

"Kind of burning oil and singed nylon carpet."

Sniffs and looks down under his feet, "That would be burning oil and singed carpet." Hands me a half empty bottle of water from on top of the dashboard. "Thought I'd fixed that. Pour that on the floor would you?"

"Now?"

"Now'd be good. Those bastards!"

"No worries," give the floor a good douse. "Who?"

"Turks. Aren't we on the same side?"

"There are sides?"

Grunts. Takes the center lane between two semis, a space made for a mini. If wing mirrors had bowels, they'd have shat. "I figure, you know, call me naïve, we're all fighting side by side against ISIS in Iraq. We should behave like allies."

"There's no sides in this game mate," I tell him, try to crank the window up, keep the truck fumes out, but the window isn't into the whole up-down thing. Then again, the air outside can't be much more poisonous that the air inside Jenno's Commodore. "Get your arse out from behind that desk you'd see what I've seen – Chinese having drinks with Americans having coffee with Israelis having cocktails with Iranians having dinner with Brits. I think of it more like murder ball in the school yard. Some days you wear shirts, sometimes you wear skins. Either way, you get your arse kicked."

"You're deep, Jones. Still think it's a bit rough, both the Americans and the Turks trying to shut us out," And god love him, he doesn't like it, and he's morally offended, and we can't blame the drugs anymore. Turns to Opium in the back seat, "You think it's all cool though?"

Voice comes cool as you like from the back seat, "That car ahead is stopping."

And with those five words Opium saves us all from a megadeath pileup which would have ended the story right there.

I get back to the office to a scene of major bedlam. Robbo is dancing with Herbal to *Back in the USSR* on his computer. Speed is on the phone. Indistinct chatter is coming over the radio, but I can hear the excitement in the background buzz. Robbo sees me come in, grabs me and tries a fandango with me too, so I knee him in the thigh and he goes down but he's not even feeling it.

"Did the dentist downstairs spring a leak on the happy gas?" I ask.

Lying on the floor, grins up at me, "We got 'em."

"Who?"

"Your barbers. Took Serwan and that Harith guy all the way home, we know where he lives, who's at home, even know what's in the fridge…"

"About bloody time you got it right. How you know they're all there?"

"Look!" he laughs, waving a hand at the computer somewhere behind his prone body.

I walk over, there's a fuzzy JPEG of someone's kitchen, three Arab guys sitting at a kitchen table looking at passports (*Hey stupid, this one looks like you*), a fourth looking in a refrigerator, and the back of a fifth, must be the old bloke Uncle Harith.

"This is inside? You got a camera inside already? How the hell did we get this?"

Herbal sniffs, "Your man Serwan innit? Stupid bastard took a picture with his mobile phone and sent it to us."

Opium looking over my shoulder, "Quite an agent you have there."

"Yeah."

"He has a death wish?"

"Nah, just dumb as a doorpost."

186

Speed puts his hand over the phone, "We got a Police tac ops team outside now, getting ready to go in."

"Tell them to hold," says Opium. "You need to leave your agent in play."

"What the hell," Speed says, "Are *you* doing here?" Looking at Opium. Like he doesn't know. Opium gives a little wave.

I ignore that. "He's right boss," I say. "There's a complication."

Listen more carefully to the radio now, I can hear the police calling in positions and sightings, I know they're only minutes away from moving in.

"Seriously. Pull them back!" I yell.

Robbo standing now, ready for a blue, "Bull shit Jones. All we need to get our boy scout badges from the A-G, is to bag these five bad guys. Which is about to finally happen." Looks across at Opium, "And we don't need your advice ugly."

Opium walks over to Speed, holds out his hand, which Speed shakes warily, "I don't mean to intrude."

"Excuse Robbo, he gets a bit emotional in the middle of a major terrorist op…" Speed says.

"But we need to speak," Opium says urgently, indicating me too, "Somewhere private?"

Speed sighs and stands, "Tell the tac team to hold," he says to Robbo.

"*Why?*" He's whining now.

"Just tell 'em. And call Teflon, let him know the US Defence Clandestine Service has just paid us an official visit with intel that may have a bearing." Cocks his eye at Opium, who nods.

In Speed's office me, Jenno, Opium sit around Speed's desk, "Talk fast, I have some PKK terrorists penned in a takedown zone and an itchy fingered tac team ready to go."

"I do have intel which might be relevant," Opium offers. "And am willing to share, if you just hear me out."

"Listening," Speed says, "But make it quick."

"I am a Southern gentleman," Opium smiles, "Quick is not in our nature."

No one smiles.

"Well alrighty, then. I'll lay it out plainly gentlemen and I hope y'alls will see that I believe our mutual interests have indeed intersected."

Still no one smiling. Jenno frowning.

"I'll start at the top. Those men are holding a hostage somewhere. Merdem Barrak."

Speed goes red at the throat, "That freaking name. Every time I hear it, I get chest pains."

Opium goes on, "Merdem Barrak is a Turkish agent."

"I guessed that," I tell Speed.

"He was recruited by the Turkish MIT in Syria, and tasked with assassinating a leading Jabhat al-Akrad commander. He succeeded in his mission, and for his reward, he was resettled by the MIT here, in Australia."

"So the who traffic cop jail story is just a cover?" I ask.

"No, that is more or less the truth of it, as the best cover stories are. He did a very good job of making it look like there had been a terrible misunderstanding at the jail, and he had to kill the Jabhat al-Akrad commander in self-defence, but that didn't change the fact the Turkish MIT had to get him out of there, with some very angry al-Akradis looking to string him up," Opium says.

Speed looks about to pop a vein, "No offense but I am tired of hearing about you, the Turks and Merdem Barrack. I have five PKK operatives I am more worried about – do you have anything valuable on them, or can we please get on with our jobs and put them in a van?"

Opium holds up his hands, in a placating gesture, "Only this. We've had a signals intercept on the Turkish consulate since we found out they are nosing around Barrak. The other day we picked up a communication which we just decoded, between the MIT officer at the consulate and a Turkish MIT field operations team, telling them to 'give the problem to the PKK'."

I shake my head, "And you didn't share that with us either."

Opium doesn't reply, "Clearly 'the problem' was Merdem Barrak. I found a flash bang grenade at the site of the incident in Bankstown which we've linked to the PKK. They have him."

Speed stands up, "That is what we in Australia call WAG intel. Wild Arsed Guess. Whether or not this particular PKK cell was tipped off about Barrak and grabbed him, we are about to have them all in the bag. We can discuss it with them at leisure."

Speed's right, isn't he? He motions to us to leave, and I stand.

"In the DCS we would want to know where the hostage was, before we arrested the hostage takers," Opium says. "He's not at the house where your agent is, right? How do you know they don't have help? You arrest them, you panic the group, they kill Barrak. They win, you lose." He shrugs.

Now Opium's right.

"We don't *know* they have Barrak!" Speed yells in frustration.

"You don't know they don't. But you have an agent in place who can find out," Opium reasons.

I decide life is too short for this kind of stress. I walk outside and make a phone call.

"Bless me Father for I have sinned…"

"Hello Jones. You know, I don't think the Vatican has actually sanctioned confessions via Skype yet."

"Well this is the 21st century Father, you should have an app for it by now."

Hear him sniff, "Call me a traditionalist. Incense, sombre lighting, sound of candles dripping on the floor – more conducive to repentance I find."

"Father, in a bit of a hurry here, got an op on."

"Yes, I saw the news. Got the bad guys yet?"

"Nearly. Father, I want to marry Karn."

Silence, then, "Oh dear. I thought we had this conversation."

"Lust is my main problem, can we agree on that? I figure I marry her…it's OK to lust after my own wife isn't it?"

"Well yes, but the Catholic ceremony, the union of a man and a woman…"

"Stop right there, Father…"

"You know where I'm going Jones."

"There are other churches father, you aren't the only chapel on the hill you know."

"I believe in one God, Jones, the Father, the Almighty…"

"Yeah yeah."

"…maker of heaven and earth. Yada yada. I believe in one church, the holy Roman Catholic church…remember saying those words?"

"Vaguely."

"Every week?"

"Alright. Yes."

"It's a package deal, the Catholic faith Jones, it's not pick and mix."

"Well, I go to church, I go to confession, I eat mock fish at lent and I don't use condoms, do I Father?"

"That…is well and good, Jones. But marriage, holy matrimony, is…not a joking matter. It is not a state we enter, in order to legitimise our lust."

"Yeah yeah."

"Sublimate."

"Pardon?"

"We've discussed this. Try to divert your sexual energy into your work."

I walk back into the ops room and look at the assembled company, which at the moment comprises Speed, Jenno, Robbo, Opium, and a very diseased Herbal.

"Father, trust me, that is not an attractive idea."

Serwan eventually leaves the apartment at about 10pm, oblivious to the storm of shit that was about to fall down around his ears until Opium intervened. I grab him as soon as he gets off the train and I am sure he is clear and no one is following.

"Oh hey," he says, as I walk up beside him, "Scared the shit out of me, creeping up like that."

"Good job today," I tell him, "Look there's something you should…"

"Something *you* should know," Serwan interrupts, "Before anything else. Those psychos have some guy hostage. Heard them talking. And they want me to get a message back home, ask what they are supposed to do with him."

There's this place on the Balmain peninsula, back of Darling street, on the north side. Streets give up and they can't cram any more houses in, so there's this pointless park there. Got two trees and a bench and a lot of dog shit because the dog walkers they take their dogs as far as the pointless park, let em shit, and turn around, head for home. I like it though. At the end away from the dogshit there's a busted iron railing fence over a sheer fifty foot drop to the harbour and then out there, for a few

191

kilometres over to the other shore, nothing. Blue sky, bobbing waves, seagulls.

First place I saw seagulls in the wild. Behaving like wild animals anyway. A pack of them, working together, slamming down into the water bam bam, scaring a school of fish into the shallow rocks at the bottom of the drop until they had nowhere to go and then the fish killing party started. Brutal. What I learned from that, never take a dumb animal for a dumb animal. Even inside a chip scrounging whinging mongrel there's a killing machine.

Speaking of Serwan, he's keyed. It's late in the evening and not only did the bad arse barbers not kill him outright, they gave him this other job. A memory card with a photo of Barrak, tied to a chair. Even Robbo had to admit this was pretty good evidence the Barbers have Barrak. Serwan's supposed to find a computer, send it to an email address somewhere, bring back the reply. He's getting into position to ask for a lifetime pension now, and we'll give it to him.

This is his big money play and he knows it. All he has to do is screw over five homicidal PKK maniacs and he's home and hosed.

According to what he heard, they got a tip off from 'someone' that Barrak, this guy who was top of the PKK 'Most Wanted' list in Hasakeh Syria, was hiding out in a hangar in Bankstown. They got out there, threw a few smoke flares in, dragged Barrak out and then set fire to the place for good luck. No signs of the Turks who were watching him.

Now isn't that a coincidence? Someone calls a bunch of PKK terrorists and tells them where Barrak is, at the same time as the whole Turkish MIT team apparently decides to go out for a quick feed of *pide* and leave him unguarded? Tells you that if that's how the Turkish MIT treats a friend, you don't want to know what they do to their enemies.

Serwan is bragging about how he took the photo without any of them noticing.

"No Serwan, that was stupid. Don't do that again."

"Oh, I was super cool, they never saw. Took it through the zipper of me jeans."

"Shut up."

"Got a hole in the pocket from me keys, put the phone in there and just whipped it out when I was taking a piss, took the picture straight out the dunny door while I was flushing."

"Too much detail."

"Pretty smooth eh?"

"Dead smooth," I nod. "We need to know what they plan to do with him."

"Dunno."

"I know you dunno. Next time you go back in, you try to find out, then you come *straight* to us."

"Could be tricky, how bout I just text you? On the phone?"

"From the toilet?"

"Best place. Close the door this time."

"You do that."

"Beaudy."

"Be cheaper for us."

"What?"

"They find your phone, read your messages, kill you, then we don't have to pay you anything."

We find an internet café and Serwan sets up a new mail account, sends the picture of Barrak off to the address they gave him which is just a bunch of numbers at a webmail domain.

"They told me to wait for an answer," he says. Starts playing online poker, which says it all really.

About a half hour later the reply pings into the mailbox and he opens it, calls me over from where I'm standing staring out a window. Points at the screen. "Looks too simple," he says, "Not much to go on. Must be code or something."

On the screen it says:

To: SexySal@Qmail.com

From: 341341gagfa@bluenet.com

Subject: Re: Our friend

Text: Kill him.

And that's all it says. Well, he's half right, it is pretty simple.

Back at the safe house I use with Serwan he looks at me, looks at himself in a mirror, doesn't have any clue what I am telling him.

"Serwan. You go through with this, it's goodbye. Goodbye Sydney. Goodbye all your mates. Goodbye to your girlfriends. I know you have no mother or father here, but it's goodbye Uncle Benny and Aunty Fatima. Was me, I'd go to Birmingham Alabama to hide, but you want to go to Surfers or the Gold Coast, fine. But not Newcastle, or bloody Wollongong. You do this, you'll get your fee, deed to a property, reward money, a new identity, but Serwan Askari is gone forever."

Looks at the mirror again. Turns his head one way, then the other.

"What's a good surfer name?" he asks.

"Surfie. Not surfer."

"Yeah. A good surfie name."

"Uhm, anything ending in 'O'?"

"Like Lebbo?"

"No. Like Johnno, Robbo or Wibbo..."

"Wibbo is short for Wilson, yeah? I could be like, you know, Sean Wilson." Takes a big breath, says to the mirror, "Goodbye Serwan."

"Hello... *Wibbo?*"

"Hello Wibbo," he says.

Goes back into the House of PKK to deliver the message he received. We got it have locked up tighter than a drum, 360 degrees. He sends me an SMS after about three hours.

Now they want gun, drop sheet n hacksaw. Cmng out now. CU. Wibbo.

I got time for a quick swing past Karn's work before the next bit goes down. Say hi, kill an hour. I need it. Funny, I don't want to be all melodramatic about it all but I do want to see a friendly, or at least familiar hostile face, right now.

Walk in, her business partner Suze is in the room they call The Sconce with people who must be financiers because Suze is in her short skirt today. Nice pins tho, worth giving a bit of air. Gives me a discreet wave. Put a finger to my lips like, shhhh, I want to surprise Karn. They call it The Sconce because that's where they go when they can't be disturbed – ensconced, get it? Great idea though, big double glass cube in the middle of the mess of their workshop, just a table for talking and a bar for drinks and fruit and espresso.

Karn is over at her design desk, one of her Veneto ladies watching as some new detail flows out of Karn's fingers, though the charcoal and onto the page. Some detail they'd buggered up, she has to put right, I can hear. She's got the long black lace Elvira dress on today, split to the waist. I can't believe how she gets away with it, with the Veneto ladies, these Italian seamstresses - all God fearing Catholic ladies old enough to be her Nonna - but they all love her. They have a room downstairs

195

where they turn the charcoal and butchers paper into Rigoletto and La Boheme and The Handmaids Tale in silk and nylon and satin.

So I can't help wonder, when she turns around, sees me there, is she going to look happy? Not like I have an appointment, after all. The other night, she got a cab outside the karaoke bar, she gave me a big lusty kiss, breathed, "Jones, we need to talk, this is starting to get annoying."

"You mean, enchanting-annoying."

"No, I mean, uhm, confusing."

"Like, delightfully-confusing."

"No, annoying-confusing. I need… clarity."

See, I happen to think clarity is the mortal enemy of love. Clarity killed the cat that ate passion. Clarity is the point where someone discovers actually they need a little time for themselves, that really they always wanted to travel to Goa and now is that time, that maybe what they need is to try sleeping with other men, women, sheep.

So last time I saw her was on my birthday, and I was left with a lingering kiss and the threat of clarity.

She sees Nonna Campione looking over her shoulder at me and turns.

The indicator, for me, is will she be friendly and physical in front of Nonna Campione there, or will she just be like, 'Oh hi, Jonesy, how are you?' give me air kisses like I'm just some friend sort of thing.

She smiles. She's got a light poncho thing around her shoulders and pulls it closed, covering her cleavage.

Nonna approves of that, I can see. That's not good.

She takes two steps. She's so close now I can smell camomile tea and cigarettes.

Nonna is watching, she's wondering what happens next as well.

She puts an arm around my neck. Her emerald eyes regard me like I'm a shell she found on a beach.

Nonna is all like, 'madre de dios…'

She kisses me. And her bare right leg lifts from the floor, just a smidge, slides up my thigh.

Nonna Campione looks away and blushes.

It's Good.

Still thinking about that kiss, six o'clock, I'm sitting in the van again.

Still thinking about it, eight o'clock, Serwan is in the park in Rose Bay now, sitting on a bench up on the bend where the good view of the New Year's fireworks is. Not quite dark yet, not light. Good time of a summer's eve for skulduggery. Serwan has a duffel bag with a doctored gun, a drop sheet and hacksaw on the bench beside him and any minute now someone, probably one of the team who has Barrak, is going to come sidling up to him and have a chat and walk off with that bag.

We're still watching the barbers' apartment, and they haven't moved, so it's someone else who's coming. Opium was right again, they do have helpers. There is more than one PKK cell in play.

Remember back at the mosque, I said, that was As Big As It Could Get? I was wrong. *This*, this is big. Back at PKK HQ Cops have got a 20 man SPG tac team onsite and we've got another two teams here, plus there's Opium, and three of his guys from the embassy here as 'observers' (after we got them out of the lockup at Bankstown local police station). In the van, fully digital and in surround sound, are me and Speed and Jenno. And up on New South Head Road an ice cream truck full of uniform cops in riot gear, with dogs, ready to secure the scene and on the water two boatfulls of Water Police and we've got not one but two birds in the air too because tonight there is going to be nobody climbing doing the switcheroo on trains or disappearing into ethnic poker machine clubs.

We wait, and then suddenly the waiting is over.

I could describe what happens next in slow motion and still not get it right, but here goes. There is a jogger and he comes jogging right past Serwan, doesn't even look at him, just keeps going (he's not one of the Kurdish barbers anyway), and while this is happening there is a little one masted sailing boat puttering up the bay like it wants to tie up for the evening and two guys on the deck pissing around with ropes and stuff and one guy steering and they're laughing, probably pissed I think to myself, and the guy jogging he's done a lap of the elbow shaped park and he's coming back around the second time, about to come past Serwan, but I've got the binos on a guy walking his dog. Thinking about him, and then the binos catch the smallest movement near Serwan, he's bent over now and the jogger is fighting him for the bag. Serwan has his hand in the bag, pulls out the gun, then the jogger is throwing the bag through the air to the guys on the sailing boat which is suddenly accelerating through the moorings and swinging around heading for the western shore and the harbour on the other side.

Serwan is down. I see that and before I even think it, I'm out of the van and running for Serwan. Jenno is yelling into a mike telling the Water Rats they got at least three guys on a yacht coming their way. Full points to Jenno, he thought of having the water police out there.

Takes me forever to reach Serwan and by then the jogger is on the other side of the park, going up steps three at a time.

"Knife." All he can say. No blood that I can see, but the poor bugger is pale as. I pull the gun out of his hand, then I'm away across the path after the jogger.

Pray there is a car full of cops after me.

Pray there is a chopper in the sky watching me.

Pray someone has the brains to call an ambulance for Serwan.

The jogger is away down a small side street now, full of lock up garages and garbage bins, arms pumping, looks over his shoulder, sees me and buggered if he doesn't stop. Dead end.

I point the gun at him. Lot of good it will do me, firing pin disabled. But he doesn't know that.

No panic in his face, he just walks a few steps and his hand flicks forward with a knife and then he starts running back up the street at me. By which, I work out, I'm all alone and he figures he can take me, or die trying.

I got time to see his shirt has come untucked. Brand of his running shoes. Parts his hair in the middle. That's how slow everything is moving now. I yell something at him, can't even remember what. I keep the gun on him, what else can I do? He doesn't care.

And *then* it all starts to happen really fast.

He's on me like *that*.

BANG.

And he's down like *that*. His knife hand slams low, into my thigh instead of my guts. He rolls into a ball.

I look at the gun. It couldn't have fired! It has no firing pin and it's not loaded. Then I turn around and there's Opium about ten metres away to my side, with a pistol in his mitt.

Opium looks at the jogger, looks at me, looks at his gun, "Darn it. This could get rather complicated for me," he says, still panting from running up the hill.

I hold out my hand, "Or me."

He hands me his pistol, still warm, and I give him mine.

"You are bleeding," he points at my groin, red stain starting to flower.

"You better get out of here, someone will come soon."

Watch him go.

That's when my legs give. And some arsehole who was about to put out his garbage, and didn't quite see what happened, still manages to whip out his mobile phone and get a video of me falling to my knees, with a gun in my hand, next to a dead terrorist, before he bolts back up to his flat.

And calls Channel 9.

Jenno finds me sitting next to the dead jogger, trying to press down on my bleeding leg with one hand, and I just have it left in me to give him the gun so I don't shoot myself. Then it's lights out for me. Again. Again.

Day like that doesn't finish early. First I'm off to the hospital. Know it so well, got my own bed with my name plate on it there now. Nurses in emergency know me soon as I stagger in, plus I'm on all the news bulletins, so I get lots of attention, and pretty quick they work out it isn't my femoral artery bleeding out, just a nice little slice across the top of my thigh. Put my neck in a brace. I can't even remember, did I hit my head or do they just do that with everyone? Cops are talking to me in one ear while the nurse is untying my shoes and a forensics guy is testing my hands for black powder residues, keeps asking me who shot the kid with the knife and I'm saying, well I had the gun, you work it out Sherlock. What he expects to find I don't know, my hands covered in blood. Then Jenno comes in with Money and she doesn't know whether to kiss me or hit me. Settles for a hug.

"You're quitting this stupid job Jones," she says, sniffing.

"Hey, I'm just starting to get good at it," I tell her, getting up on one arm. "Don't tell Karn I'm in here again, OK?"

Nurse butts in, "Alright, just lie back please. The blood on your leg is starting to dry, I'm going to have to cut those jeans off, OK? Sorry but I have to get in and clean the wound."

200

Jenno laughs, and hands her the big scissors. "Don't muck about. Go right up the seam," Jenno says, "Shame though, expensive jeans, those."

"Can you all leave us, please?" nurse tells him and the cops and Money. "This isn't a bloody circus. Outside the room."

I lay back, tell Jenno, "Keep laughing, big feller. Mine were dirty. These are your jeans."

The Water Rats find Barrak in the bottom of the boat with a pile of money and three half-wits from a local Lebanese bikie gang. Sitting duct taped to a chair in front of a video camera, PKK flag on the wall behind him.

One of them pulls out a flare gun as the water rats storm aboard and it blows up in his hand, scaring the crap out of both cops and bad guys.

Out in Hurstville, the SPG blow their way into the apartment full of Kurdish barbers they've been watching round the clock, just waiting to swoop.

They get four PKK barbershop terrorists. But Harith The Wrinkled One? He Who Cultivates?

He's gone, goanna. Either wasn't even there, or snuck out in the night through an iron clad ring of hundreds of sleeping police.

The thing about the blood on my jeans. It's mine alright but it didn't all come from the knife wound.

She's a funny bugger, nature.

Nurse peels the jeans away, "I have to take the underpants too," she says.

"No worries," I tell her.

"Sorry."

"No sweat. Nothing you haven't seen a million times. Just mine's prettier."

Clip. The cotton sticks to my groin like the discount label on a CD.

"Oh," she says once she's finally peeled it away. "Uhm, well *that's* good."

"What?"

"You won't need stitches, we can close the cut on your leg with butterflies," she says, and whispers, "And you need a pad. Most of the blood is actually *menstrual…*"

See, at the precise moment Opium shot the Lebanese guy, and he fell forward, his knife slides across my thigh, and his shoulder hits my groin and down in *there*, right *then,* the lining of my uterus which has been building up and getting nice and thick and clotty, it decides to let go and with the help of the blow, and the shock, well it just starts pouring out of me like mud down a Philippino hillside.

Nurse cleans up my cut, and picks up my jeans, "I'll tell the others you need a few minutes," she says quietly. I can hear them muttering away outside the curtain. "There's a shower over there," points at a door. "I'll get you a gown and a pad too."

"Haven't got a tampon?"

"Maybe, I'll ask one of the other girls."

"Thanks mate," I give her a wink and hoik myself off the bed. Thinking *she's* a sweetie.

Pull my t-shirt over my head and unclip my 32D.

And the water feels *good.*

What? I didn't mention I was a girl?

Opium… Well he handed me his gun, I passed out, he melted into the background, did a nice clean interrogation of Barrak under third party supervision and was on the first plane back to Washington.

Yeah sure, like that happened.

Way it happens is, Opium comes to visit me in the hospital after the others are gone. Before Karn gets there. Lying there on top of the bed, just trying to get it all to settle.

Hear his voice, "You are a brave lady, Charlie Johns." See him leaning on the doorway.

"Jones."

"Sorry?"

"My name is Charlie Jones, remember."

"I know," he says. "A boys name."

Prop myself up on some pillows, "Suits me fine. There is supposed to be a cop on that door."

"There is. Tell me what you thought you would do, running after a terrorist in your Blundstone Boots, with a disabled weapon?"

"Well, I just thought…shit I don't know," I laugh, "Just stupid, right?"

"Yes. But lucky. It's the best kind of stupid."

He stands there until I catch up.

"Oh…right. Barrak - he's at the Long Bay jail infirmary. Being debriefed."

"Down near the airport?"

"Yeah. You still want to talk to him, right?"

"I do. I need to know if he knows anything about my brother, Charlie Jones."

Poor guy, chasing the ghost of his disappeared Delta Force brother. Enough to break a girl's heart.

"I'll call ahead, tell them to expect you."

"Thank you."

"Say hello for me. I'm dying to meet that guy again. All the trouble he gave us."

"So am I."

And he's gone, no goodbye, nothing.

Men.

There was a time, I forgot to put the handbrake on my dad's car, I'm at this picnic and while I'm rolling a spliff with my back to it, the car trundles, slow as you like, into a duck pond. That feeling, as I told my dad after, as people started yelling and I realised I didn't put on the handbrake and watched the car roll down the hill? That's the feeling I have now, only, of course, way worse.

Because Jenno has come in, and he's just told me something I don't want to know.

"Serwan's gonna be OK," he says, "Knife didn't hit anything vital. They must've not wanted him around to tell any tales, but they messed that up too."

That's good. The guy will take his money and blow it all at a casino on the Gold Coast, but he earned it. He deserves to live long enough to throw it away.

"You know how I can get in touch with Opium though?" he asks, leafing through my get well cards.

"I just saw him, why?"

"Well, I was in on the debriefing of Barrak," he says. "Got some bad news for Opium."

"Yeah, like what?"

"Like, Barrak didn't just kill that Jabhat al-Akrad commander. He also deliberately killed that Delta Force prisoner they were fighting over."

"*What?*" I prop myself up, fighting the pain killers, thinking, I did not hear that.

"Barrak killed the American soldier, after he killed the al-Akradi commander." he says, "Cold blooded bastard. Tried to make it look like it was the American who killed the al-Akradis. So Opium's brother is KIA, not MIA."

"Oh, hell no."

"Hell no what?"

"About an hour ago I told Opium where to find Barrak and I called Long Bay and authorised him to interview the guy," start fumbling through my jacket for my phone. "Oh shit shit shit shit *shit.*"

"You think Opium already knows this guy killed his brother?" Jenno asks. "Damn. Of course he knows. He always knew – he was just waiting for the guy to surface somewhere."

"Well, duh," is all I say.

Thinking as I punch the numbers, maybe it's OK, hey, they already went and talked to him once, right? Nothing happened. Scared the hell out of the guy, but no bodily damage, right?

"Robbo? Shut up and listen…it's Barrak, can you…he what? When? No, I didn't. Shit, uhm, yeah. Yeah. It would be. Nah I'm fine, just…you know, bit weak still. Yeah you too. Bye."

Jenno is just staring at me. I'm just staring at my phone.

Well, of course they just interviewed him the first time, they had to be sure who he was, make sure they had the right guy, don't want to do grievous harm to a random Syrian-Australian panel beater, that would be awkward. Slight problem though, he disappears and they're racing the Turks to find him but good old Jonesy comes through on that one. Then the PKK bust in and Barrak's gone again. By now Opium's getting really annoyed, has to leave it to us to recover Barrak but miracle of miracles, we do. Walks out of my hospital room, calls his team, "OK, we know where he is now, we're on our way. Warm up the plane will you?"

"They got him." I tell Jenno.

"What's that mean? They got him or they *got* him?" Jenno asks.

"I mean, I told DCS where to find him, and Robbo just told me they walked him out of Long Bay with some phoney papers, and Barrak is bloody *gone*."

"Oh."

"Yeah. Oh."

"No. Oh, as in ohhh, he's gonna *wish* the PKK killed him."

"Thank you Jenno."

"No seriously, slow decapitation with a rusty butter knife has to be better than what Opium and his crew are gonna do to him."

"OK Jenno."

"I mean shit, Delta Force starts *wars* when one of their guys gets taken hostage, imagine what they'll do to a guy who actually killed one of their wounded soldiers in cold blood."

"___"

"And *you* told them where to find him. Whoa."

He's starting to piss me off now.

In the Denzel version I stagger bloodied and beaten to the airport, scanning all the faces at the international terminal, until, through a forest of nicely toned aircrew legs I see Opium and one of his boys, dragging a helpless Barrak to the gate and I leap over startled Japanese tourists to put a gun in his face and he says, cool as anything, "Ah, Ms Jones, a real gun. I see you are learning."

In the reality show that is my life, it doesn't quite go that way. In fact, I never find out what happens to Mr. Barrak, because no one ever sees him again. Air traffic records show about a dozen light planes took off in the window after Barrak got walked out of Long Bay by Opium, any one of them could have been the DCS rendition flight.

Am I crying for Barrak?

Guy was a terrorist, an informer, a stone cold killer, but hey it really seemed he was trying to turn his life around down here. Yeah I should feel a bit bad.

But, no. No tears, big ears.

"Hello Father."

"Jones! Was that you on the news? Were you hurt?"

"Ah, rumours of my death Father, greatly exaggerated, you know..."

"Did you shoot that young man? I saw you on the news...it's playing over and over."

"Well, that's why I'm here ... bless me Father for I have sinned, it is one week since my last confession, here are my sins..."

"My God. Sorry. Go on..."

"Lust, pretty much take that for given Father, sorry."

"And..."

"Well I didn't kill that young man, but I did lie about it and pretend I did, not because I wanted the glory, but to protect the DCS bastard who actually did kill him, because he saved my life."

"Language. Keep your voice down."

"Sorry Father. But then I went and told the DCS bastard where he could find this other murdering bastard he was looking for and I'm pretty sure he's dead now too. Or maybe they took him to Guantanamo Bay to torture him for a few years, before they kill him. So let's say I'm indirectly responsible for one dead guy, and one probably-tortured-probably-dead?"

"Was it your intention in any of this, for these men to die?"

"No, I don't think I thought that far ahead, Father. I was kind of winging it the first time, and on drugs the second. That's going to be my defence in the High Court anyway. "

He summons the Holy Force. Sighs, "For the lust, three Hail Marys. For the rest, I think you need serious spiritual counselling Jones."

"How does that work, Father?"

"You go to a monastery, or, in your case, a convent. You pray for understanding, eat well, sleep soundly, go for long walks and talk to a counsellor."

"Sounds...lengthy, Father. Is there another way?"

"Buddhism?"

"Father."

"Scientology?"

"Very funny."

"Jones, get thee to a nunnery."

Known knowns. I've been trying to put the facts together ever since. Make the story fit.

Somehow, somewhere, someone let slip to the Yanks the Turkish MIT had a man buried in Australia, used to be a PKK infiltrator and probably was the one killed a Delta Force POW. But they don't know where he is, so they park it, waiting for him to surface. Bingo. ONA sends out an intel assessment that the whole world reads, and Barrak is blown, might as well have made a post on the Delta Forces Facebook page.

Turkish MIT reads it too, shits themselves; they know that either the PKK or US Defense would love dearly to get a hold of their guy. So they get on a plane down here, try to work out what to do with their man. Couple days later Opium flies in. Jenno and me start nosing around, MIT gets really nervous, and stupid, and tries to get us to back off. Opium picks up on them and their

208

whole op, now he has to deal with them, with us and still try to get his hands on Barrak.

The Turks are thinking, what should we do with this loser? MIT's already a million bucks in the hole from Barrak's first move. That's alright. Guy did fulfil his mission, killed that militia commander, they owe him even if he did go a bit outside his brief and kill the American. Collateral damage. But now, his cover is blown and they got to move him again, that's another million bucks. This guy is starting to get expensive and he's no longer contributing to the cause.

Then the Turkish operations team sees the terror alert on the news; there's a Kurdish terror cell down here, raising money, recruiting for Peshmerga? Well isn't that convenient. Someone gets a brainwave; hey, here's a way to save the great Turkish taxpayer a lira or two and let the Aussies take the blame – how about we let the PKK know where to find Barrak? Yeah, we kidnap him, make it look like PKK did it, then leave him tied up in a hangar in Bankstown, go out get some coffee. Call Jabhat al-Akrad command back in Aleppo, use the old special codewords, tell them where to find him. Better hurry though, get it done before the Americans find out.

Problem solved. Sit back, grab a salty simit and an iced tea, watch the fun on TV. Go back to selling stationery.

I walk into the lunch room at the rest home and Mum sees me and stands up and starts clapping. The other old dears have no idea what is going on, but they're up for a party, so they all stand and clap too. My mum is beaming. I bung on a bit of a limp. They love it.

And in the Denzel version, he gets the girl.

It's Sunday, I'm out of hospital and Speed has told me to get out of Sydney for a month and while I'm away, talk to a shrink. The AG called, or at least his buddy Alasdair did, but I haven't returned the call. The AG was all over television yesterday, posing with the police commissioner in front of the impounded boat, a table with a few guns and knives on it, and Serwan's 100,000 bucks (though it looked a little light to me). I haven't called back because I'm not sure if the AG wants to congratulate me or fire me, considering we still have no idea where the Big Guy, Harith, is. They keep the terrorist alert at '*Extreme: attack imminent*' while they look for him, but I'm officially out of play.

On top of being way traumatized, I'm still the little girl agent kneeling in her own blood at the side of a dead terrorist, and the media is camped outside the hospital. Right now they just want to know who is this brave and resourceful young officer (OK, my words), and what happened to her? But pretty soon that will turn into *since when did the security service start carrying guns?* And *Oh my god when did they start hiring dykes?* Then it's just a matter of time before the terrorist's family sues me for unlawful killing because yes, sure, he was trying to stab me but only because I scared him with the gun I shouldn't even have been carrying.

So now Karn and I are belting across the Hay Plain in about 39 degrees of sun, one hand on the hot steering wheel, the other resting on Karn's cool freckled thigh.

There's still no danger of actual commitment yet, but hey, Perth is another town.

Book II

Karn and I never did make it to Perth.

Didn't even make it to WA. So now I'm sitting bleeding on a carpet in the dirt at a Musalla (like a Muslim prayer space) in Coober Pedy, watching a big bearded Imam in white robes speaking over a body in a white sheet. It's been a bad few days.

And I'm not sure I can tell this one cause bits of it are pretty ugly and there is a large part at the end where I was out of it. I guess, in the style of *Lemony Snickets*, I should tell you right now the next part of the story, it gets pretty dark and if you liked how the first part ended, you should probably stop reading now.

Take the book, delete it, or if you bought a paper copy, use it to jack up that cupboard in the back room, the one where the door keeps swinging open.

Or you could read on. Take a break though, to help you get the change in mood. If you were drinking red for the first part of the book, pour yourself a scotch now.

But don't worry, it turns out alright, sort of.

I'm still here, right?

Yay.

What happened was, Karn and I are in a service station in Port Augusta. It's been a long trip already but we're in the zone now, got Bob Dylan on the sound system, all we need is to tank up and point the ute west again.

Karn is fixated on hitting the road again as quick as we can, get as much distance as possible between Sydney and us, so I'm the only one sees the news flash on the TV over the cashier desk. There's no sound, so all I can do is read the ticker going across the bottom of the screen, and watch the images of people picking other people, or bits of people, off the street and load them into ambulances. Looks like Damascus, but the dateline says Sydney.

"Shit," I say, tapping her on the shoulder, "Looks like old Harith had a plan B."

Bomb blast at Turkish Consulate

This is ABC News Radio. Two people are dead and three are in a critical condition following an explosion at the Turkish Consulate General in Woollahra Sydney last night.

Eyewitness reports say a car drove through the side fence of the consulate into its back yard and exploded at about 1.30 a.m.

It is not known if the driver was inside the car when it exploded. The dead and wounded are believed to be Consulate staff living at the residence.

While Australian Authorities have not confirmed it yet, ABC sources indicate the attack is linked to the Terrorist Alert issued recently in relation to Kurdish terrorists or supporters believed to be active in Australia, and to the shooting last week by an Australian Security Service officer of a suspected Kurdish terrorist in Sydney.

Turkey is actively involved in the conflict in Syria and Iraq and announced as recently as last week that it had attacked PKK targets inside Syria with its air and ground forces.

"You want the good news or the bad news?" Jenno says when I call him on his mobile.

"Jenno, I'm in a servo in Port Augusta. There's ten truckies perving on Karn, and a Hells Angel bikie just offered to give her a lift to Perth on his Harley. The place stinks of Chico Rolls, and it's about 120 degrees out there. Just give me *all* the news."

"Well," he sounds a little miffed, "I *was* going to say the good news is, Canberra reckons it isn't our fault."

"Why?"

"Cops were the ones watching the Kurdish Barber's apartment right? So your man Harith got away from there without them knowing, it was them who fluffed it, not us."

"*That's* good news?!"

"Not really. The bad news is that everyone blames us for not picking up the fact someone had managed to buy enough ammonium nitrate and diesel to flatten half of Woollahra."

Maybe they have a point. Or maybe the point is, you just can't save the world from itself.

"You there?" Jenno asks.

"Yeah, is there more?"

"More bad news, yeah. We're *all* on the case now, and that means you too. Speed wants to…oh, here he is."

Speed is calm. That's why he is where he is, still at the pointy end after thirty years. He's been there before – 1978 and the Hilton Hotel was the first time. Bali Task Force. Martin Place. Different times, places, different nutters, people just as dead. The world changes, the world stays the same.

He comes on the line, "…sorry to break into your holiday Jones." He's not.

"I got knocked unconscious three times and stabbed. According to the papers, I shot a guy." I remind him. "It's not a holiday, it's post-traumatic stress leave."

"Well, the bar for stress leave just got a little higher. Now…we have more than enough people running around here trying to be helpful, and between you and me it's total effing chaos."

"You don't want me to come back?"

"No, I want you to go to Coober Pedy."

"Where the hell…"

I'm not sure that everyone in the world has heard of Coober Pedy but I have now, so let me take a moment to paint a picture. In 2030 China is planning to send a manned mission to the Moon, to begin building a permanent moon base. They plan to set a record for living on the Moon and so they are doing a lot of practice. In the daylight hours, with no atmosphere to protect it, the surface temperatures on the moon actually get up to 107 degrees. At night they go to 150 below. The Chinese plan to get around this by digging a great big tunnel in the moon's surface, and living in it, which will also help protect them from solar radiation.

After looking at various places including Death Valley in the USA, Siberia, and the Gobi Desert, China has asked the Australian government for permission to train their moon base astronauts in Coober Pedy. That's all you need to know.

I look at a map on the wall of the servo and do some numbers. "I'm 500 kilometres from Coober Pedy!"

"Then you're about 500 kilometres closer than anyone else," he replies. "The cops have an early lead on the detonator, and it was part of a batch sold to an opal dealer in Coober Pedy. He also owns the Coober Pedy Mine Hotel. Shirl has booked you a double room there."

He gives me the guy's name, company name, the address. I look at Karn. She's picking up the vibe that our Perth plan is about to go to sideways, and if it was a cartoon, there would be thunderclouds forming over her head. I cup the phone in my hand, tell Speed, "Tell Shirl to book separate rooms."

Karn takes it very calmly though once I've explained. I'll be on solid food again in no time.

Now her and her alabaster skin are standing in the bleak daylight, waiting outside a Greek café in the main street of Coober Pedy for me to pay the bill and join her. Been here a couple of days already. She's even paler than usual - like that's possible - from the thin white film of dust that coats everything here. Brushes herself down with no visible effect, before closing her eyes and tilting her head back to the sun.

Lined up outside the cafe is a row of battered trucks and utes, looking like they're extras from Mad Max, but each with one thing in common - the hand painted warning posted on a wood or metal sign above the cab, "DANGER: EXPLOSIVES."

As I wait, another four-wheel-drive pulls up outside, engine rattling to a slow death. The door props open and a dog leaps out, gives Karn's boots a quick sniff and then disappears into the cafe. The driver is small, solid and Philippino, about three days late for a shave and just as late for a shower.

He grins at the dog disappearing through the door, then at Karn, "Needs a beer," he says, then leans back into the cabin and pulls a shotgun off the back shelf.

" 'Scuse me," he says, awkwardly pushing past her and then bending over the tray at the back of the truck, dragging the lock off a strongbox and dumping the shotgun inside it. I hear it settle against glass and metal, then with a grunt he slams the box shut and locks it. " 'Scuse again," he smiles politely, the smile of a man uncomfortable around women, edges past her. At the arbitrary line in the sand which marks the sidewalk from the road, he pauses and turns back to her. Under the dirt he could be anywhere between 20 and 40.

"Gonna be a party in here Wednesday night, if you want to come," he says hesitantly.

"Um, have we met?" I hear her ask.

"Nah, but I seen you here yesterday. You're staying at The Mine Hotel with that short chick. The name's Victor," he says, batting a fly away from his face and holding out his hand. "I kinda work there."

She holds out her hand, "I'm Karn. The short chick inside is Charlie." He wipes his hands on his shorts and shakes it. He shrugs, "She can come too, I guess."

I'm listening to this from inside the door, thinking, *Don't do me any favours mate.*

She drops his hand, hot and dry, "We just might."

"Yeah, well," the big man shuffles closer to the door, "Men *and* women."

"Sorry?"

"The party," he explains, "It's not just blokes. There'll be other women there too, in case you're worried about being the only ones."

"Uh, thanks, I *was* wondering," she says.

"Good-o," he says, and disappears inside, brushing past Karn on his way in to the café and past me without saying hi.

I fold the bill into the top pocket of my spiffy new shirt and squint up at the sun, see Karn smiling with the whole of her face.

"What's up?" I ask.

She gestures to the street, the utes, the blasted hills that make up the small opal mining town, "This place. It can't be real."

"Yeah, one of a kind, that's for sure. Shall we go back to the Cave? I have to make a couple of calls," I say, and she nods.

"By the way, we just got invited to a party, at the Taverna Wednesday night," She tells me as we walk back to the ute.

"Yeah, I heard. It's someone's birthday. That Amir guy was telling me about it last night, told me it was going to be quite a bash. Said we should stick around for it."

"Who's Amir?"

"Old guy I met yesterday, you know, the Lebbo who owns The Mine…he seems pretty friendly. You should meet him."

"Me? *Why?*" I can tell she's working herself up about it. "I'm not going to help you with the cloak and dagger crap, I hope you know that. I already got car crashed, had to hide in a shithole flat for a week and watch you get three kinds of crap beaten out of you. I'm *done*. You want to deceive some old age pensioner into helping you out, you do it your..."

"Hey, he seems like a nice old guy. He challenged me to a game of chess. Just thought you might like him, is all."

She grunts, could be a yes, or a no. She's keeping her options open.

"He challenged you to a game of chess? How did that happen?" she asks. Fair question.

"I asked him how he made his money to buy the hotel. He said a bit of prospecting, a bit of gambling. He said he bets big on chess and I told him I play and he said he's happy to take my money any time..."

What Speed wants, is for me to dig around a bit in Coober Pedy (ok, bad pun), before the cops pile in and start asking the hard questions, and everyone clams up. How I do it, he doesn't care. But it's going to be a whole lot easier with Karn for cover. These guys look at Karn and me, they can think a lot of things, but police or Security Service won't be one of them.

"By the way, your disguise hasn't fooled the locals," She says as we reach the car.

I look at her sharpish, "Disguise? What you mean?"

"The hetero look with the new jeans, Blunnies and blue shirt," she teases, "You're trying to look like a sheep farmer or something, but you might as well be wearing a Dykes on Bikes gang patch."

I relax, "They see through me eh?"

"Yep. Of course it could be the Sinead O'Connor haircut and the fact you keep putting your hand on my butt. But you still got an invite to the party. Must see all sorts in this town." The car is an oven and the seat stings her thighs as we sit, "Ow! Anyway, they'll be so busy trying to work out what side you play for, maybe they won't guess you're a spook," she decides.

I grunt as we back into the main street, "Thanks a lot."

Yes, don't be surprised. I like chess. Lots of people like chess. It's very relaxing chess is. Karn does not like chess.

I listen to her on the phone to Sydney as we drive back to the hotel. "Hi Money, it's me…No, actually, we took a detour…Yeah, I saw it on the TV…Yeah, she's OK but she popped her stitches, has to get sewn up again. No, no…because I hit her. Coober bloody Pedy…I know…I know…I know I don't have to…Thanks…No, but…She is…I just thought, well, I just thought…Well, you're not here…I know I can…I know, you're right…I will…yeah, I *will*…so how's…no worries. Yeah, bye."

"What was that about?"

"You."

"I know that, but what?"

She puts her long legs up on the dash and leans back, blows hair out of her eyes, "Before we left Sydney, I bet Money a hundred bucks I could get you to quit your stupid job, for good."

"You…really?"

She doesn't even look at me, just unbuttons the top button on her shirt and starts fanning herself, sweat beading in her cleavage, "Yep."

So it turns out, Amir Wahid is known locally as The Lebbo. In a town with a drifting population of dozens of Lebanese immigrants the title is pretty unremarkable, except that Amir is *The* Lebbo. According to him, first Lebanese migrant to settle in Coober Pedy, 1929, when there was no real town, just a railway siding and a rough pile of tents and trucks parked around holes in the ground.

218

And Amir is the guy they think resold the detonator that was used to blow up the Consulate.

He likes hanging with his guests, and I had a good session with him yesterday over about a litre of homemade red wine (yeah, he's Muslim, and yeah, he drinks. Coober Pedy will do that to you...) and the locals seem to enjoy swapping stories about him, so since we've been here a couple of days I have the public version anyway.

First Amir fact, he likes women. Particularly smart, cheeky women who can drink him under the table. So I can tell he'll like Karn. Amir and I at least have that in common.

He claims sometimes to be 104, sometimes 108. Better not to question this, because Amir goes off when contradicted, and is apparently famous for his sulks. He is easily the biggest bullshitter in town.

This hotel used to be his dugout, the type of underground home favoured by all the old timers in Coober Pedy. It's a maze of cavernous rooms, a new one dug each time he had a child - and there were 9 of them - or for guests, some of whom stayed more or less permanently. Legend had it that every time Amir blasted a new room, he struck a new vein of opal. Whenever a particularly large bill comes in, he still mutters to himself, "More children, I should have had more children." But the bills got bigger and the Opal finds smaller, so he had to turn his place into a hotel.

When I heard that, I had my cover story. I told him I'm looking to start a backpacker joint in Coober Pedy and asked if he was interested in selling? Turns out, maybe yeah, maybe he is.

The place has secure rooms walled off by iron grilles for opal storage. Bathrooms which seem to be placed randomly through the complex, until you look above ground and see they're supplied by water tanks which have to sit on level ground. I have no idea where the waste goes and I do not want to know. A billiard room with full length table, a lounge-bar with built in roulette table which Amir welded solid, immovable, after a particularly bad losing streak in 1958. And the pride of the hotel, a 25 metre underground swimming pool, fed by solar heated recirculated water which he trucks in from Port Augusta, 600 km away if they have a dry season.

In 1984 he blasted a new room to serve as an office, and knowing that his strength was failing, started employing contract miners. His third wife worked as secretary until 2005, when she died. Since then he's done the paperwork himself. This consists of placing all papers into colour coded 44 gallon drums to be dealt with by the accountant who comes up quarterly from Adelaide.

Paranoid about theft, he keeps a single entry to his office, a solitary door in the side of a hill which opens to a wide reception area, filled out with silk plants and velour couches. Between the 1930s and 1950s when it was still a private house this room was also supplied with beer and scotch whisky for those waiting, but Amir stopped this in 1964 when the number of bodies in his lobby every morning when he arrived made him feel his hospitality was being abused. The outer door is always left unlocked, but entry from the waiting room to the main house is only possible via a 30cm thick steel door Amir bought from the defunct Savings Bank of Port Augusta in 1949. Guests love it, opening that combination door with the combination Amir gives them. Makes them feel special.

Well, not a combination, just a set of nine studs on each side which operate the lock. In olden days he would open this manually, but now he can actually do it by remote from almost any room in the house. There is of course not a resident in town who doesn't know the combination and Amir hates that but he can't be bothered changing it because then he'd have to recode his remote too, and he forgot how to do that. He's been waiting 40 years for another bank to close in Port Augusta or Alice Springs so that he can get a new door. A lighter one. Beyond that is a short, narrow corridor, which he increasingly fortified as technology has progressed. In its day, it was lined with sound detectors, laser lights, movement sensors, all defunct now except the rumour around town, which Amir is careful to frequently deny, is that these are kind of faulty and could still set off a spray of tear-gas, or even better, a bomb any time someone tries to sneak through.

In 1997 Amir had a video camera installed in the waiting room so that he could see who was calling. In 1998 he removed that because his friend Anton kept smashing it for invading his privacy. Amir ripped the wires out of the back of the movement sensors in 1999 after five nights of broken sleep from alarms going off – given all the blasting going on in Coober Pedy they drove him batshit.

From down in this bunker he runs not only the hotel, but about half a dozen mining operations around Coober Pedy. He says he has hundreds of guys working for him, but from what I can tell it's more like two full timers (his right hand man, Victor, and his step-brother, Bob) and the rest are contractors. Oh, there's one other employee.

At the other end of this corridor, behind the metal door of Amir's office sits Gaddafi. Gaddafi is Amir's protection. Gaddafi knows everyone who comes to visit Amir. If they are new friends and Amir *wants* them to visit again, he introduces them to Gaddafi and Gaddafi memorises their scent. Gaddafi has a remarkable memory, remembers how they carry their weight on their feet coming down the corridor, the timbre of their voices. He's not real bright, but he is loyal. He doesn't take bribes and can't be distracted by beauty. You can go anywhere in the hotel, and Gaddafi doesn't care, but if you try to go into the office or Amir's private rooms, Gaddafi doesn't recognise you and you try to get past him, he *will* rip your throat out. He's part dingo, part Doberman, a real ugly mutt.

Karn and I sit on a purple velour couch under a picture of Queen Elizabeth and wait for the heavy click of the bolts in the door to welcome us in.

During the day Amir's office is busy, staff regularly tramping in with news, or for instructions, and Amir sits in his wheelchair, cordless telephone in his lap, alongside it the remote control for the door and intercom, and on the table in front of him a chess problem he takes from the newspapers.

No way is he as old as he says, though the hair is white. The eyebrows are shockers. He could just about plait them together with the hairs growing out his ears. Stained khaki overalls, he probably sleeps in too.

"This Ukrainian kid is a new breed," he says to us without looking up, as we walk in. Gaddafi has already clocked us through the door and decided yeah, OK, these are those girls from yesterday. Puts his head back down on his paws and goes back to dreaming about eviscerating kangaroos.

Amir's eyes are fixed on the board and he waves a thick knobby forefinger over the pieces. "Most of these bloody prodigies lack control! But this Karjakin kid, he's something!"

He looks straight at me, "You know what I'm talking about, right?"

I smile at the puffy white tufts of hair above his ears, the heavy jowls, and eyebrows which form a thick veranda over the slightly glutinous eyes. Right now there is a sparkle behind those eyes, for Karn, anyway. Randy old goat. Shake my head, "Karjakin is a robot. No creativity."

"Hah! Creativity!" he laughs. "Allah be praised, you do know chess." He turns to Karn, "And you must be Karen, yes?" Still sitting, holds out his hand, then points to the chairs on the other side of his desk, so we sit.

"Karn, actually, no 'e'. Don't ask me why," she says, parking herself in a chair.

"Amir challenged me to a best of three chess match tonight." I spring it on her.

"What about that party?" she asks, looking at Amir, "At the Tavern. I thought the whole town was going?"

"Pah. I don't go to parties now. Every week some new party." He wrinkles his brow, "Do you know how often I get to play against a good chess player in this town?" Thumps the table, "2003 was

222

the last time - some Cuban geologist was staying here. Stupid bastard fell down a hole in his third week and that was the end of that." Does a slow calculation on gnarled fingers, "More than a decade! You don't think a piss-up in a Greek restaurant is going to come before that I hope?."

"I think Charlie is planning to go," she nudges my leg. "To the party. I'm not going to go alone."

"Fine," the old man waves his wrist, "She can go after we play. I'll make sure you're not alone. My niece Sharon is going, I introduce you, you go with her. She'll look after you until Miss Johns gets there. Hah!" He winks. Presses a buzzer on his desk and shouts into an intercom, "Victor! Tell Sharon get the bloody hell in here!"

A minute later a tall thin girl, all teeth, elbows and knees, couple of years older than me comes in. Amir tells her she is chaperoning Karn to the party. She can't get a word in but doesn't look too bothered. Like this is just another day at the office, taking some random hotel guest to a party. "Now, you like to swim? We have pool! Sharon, take Miss Karen for swim! Show her the place. I have to talk business with Miss Johns!"

Karn stands up and the skinny girl smiles shyly, "We don't have to have a swim. Let me show you around a bit – we just got a new coffee machine. I make a killer cappo. On the house." Karn shrugs and follows her out, but looks back over her shoulder at me as she's leaving the room and her look has the promise of pain in it.

As soon as Karn walks out, Amir rounds on me, "So you want to buy Amir's place eh?"

"Well, I…"

"I show you round yesterday, is good place, right? Fifty rooms, 20 rooms underground! Good kitchen for breakfast, games room, café."

"What I'm looking for…"

"Swimming pool too, only underground pool in all Australia, I bet. Put *that* on Facebook, eh?"

"What your average backpacker is looking for is…"

"Too bad. I don't sell it."

OK, so much for that cover. *So Jones, what did you learn about the explosives dealer. Well sir, he likes chess, runs a nice hotel, and his best mate is a feral dog. I think he definitely did it.* I start mentally checking out of the hotel. Let the police come in here and kick a few doors in.

"You're aren't interested in selling?" I try to sound ruined, give him the big blue eyes treatment, like the cat out of Shrek.

"What is wrong with your eyes? You need some drops? No, I would sell this hole in the ground like *that!*" snaps his fingers, "You give me the right price. But see, I promise this place to my step brother Bob. When I die this year, the place is his. I told him that, and Amir never goes back on his word."

"Bob?"

"Bob. You know Sharon, the girl you just met? Her father Bob is my step brother. Same mother different father sort of thing. This place, my business, these are his when I die, it's all arranged. I already did the papers."

"Wait, you're *dying?*"

"Sure, this year. Of course, doc said that last year, but this year for sure. Girl, when you get over 100, it's no sentence, it's a relief…"

"You aren't…" I'm going to say *you aren't over 100*, but then I remember about the sulks, change it to, "You don't…look sick to me."

"I bloody better be," he growls, "All the medicine that freaking doctor makes me take. No, you have to talk to Bob. Now I don't promise anything, but you make a good offer, maybe Bob is interested, right?"

"And you don't mind me dealing with him on this?"

"Deal, deal, what do I care anymore, I'm dead, right? I already paid the funeral home, picked out my spot in town. Close to my second wife, best of the three. Make them move the first one over the other side of the cemetery. Bitch."

"Ok, well, I hope I can still come to you for some information about the place, maybe…"

But he's lost interest now, leaning back in his chair.

"Only thing, I always wanted to be buried in a snowy place. Cold. Not the heat and bulldust like here. Do you know how long since I saw the snow in Lebanon?"

"No. I didn't even know there was snow in Lebanon."

"What? One hour from Beirut, straight up the mountains. Best snow outside Switzerland…1948 is how long."

"I thought you came here after the first war?" It was a story he told me yesterday. How he was fighting with the French in Verdun and got trapped in a hole with two Aussies. One was killed and he took his helmet. The other was killed and he took his tunic, just because it was dry. Into the neck of the tunic a thoughtful wife had sewn, "Mick Turner, Sgt., II Batt. RAIF." Then he got knocked out by a shell, and woke up on a hospital ship bound for Australia. With no family in Lebanon to worry about, he accepted it as fate. When 'Mick Turner' landed in Melbourne he took off the khaki and made straight for the Outback. Bullshit – he wasn't even alive back then - but it's a good story

"Yes, yes," he says, a little irritated, "But I went *back* for the second war. Fought with The British against the Vichy in Lebanon and Syria, then in the Western Desert campaign. You could say I had a grudge against the Germans." Sighs, "We don't talk about that," he says firmly. He points at the wall, in the direction of town, "Do you know, the last time I left this house was in 2013. They were having a meeting at the Mediterranean Club, some idiot wanted to change the name."

"Why?"

"We were all members there, " Amir explains, "Greeks, Macedonians, Libyans, Cypriots, Turks, Lebanese, it was like the United Nations of Coober Pedy. I went there and sat at the front in my usual chair and said nothing while this idiot raved about how the club should change its name and its rules because ninety percent of the members, they were Greek. Since the Italians have the Italian Club, the Croatians have the Croatian Club, the Serbs have the Serbian club and a club full of Greeks, they should call it the Greek club."

He snorts, "Gah. Such words from a youngster just 58 years old. What does he know. Sure now there's more Greeks than Lebanese in Coober Pedy, but it was the Afghans and Lebanese who was here first. It was Afghans and Lebanese and Syrians *started* the club, in 1929!" He bangs the table, "Now the Greeks want to take it over?"

"You must have lost the argument," I say, "Since I drove past the sign saying 'Greek Club' on the way in."

"I didn't lose," he says. "I didn't fight. The local police were there, and an inspector from Adelaide, just sitting up the back saying nothing. Ha, probably they thought we were all going to start shooting each other. So when this Greek idiot finished his speech and all the other Greeks are ready to vote themselves a new club I rolled up to the microphone and they were all quiet. They still respected me back then," he says stiffly. "I looked around the room and said, 'I'm not a Greek, so you change the name, and I don't ever come to this club no more. And I left, and they changed it and I never went there again."

Stops and looks at me like he's trying to remember something. "It's all bullshit. Anyway, you want to meet Bob." He grins up at me, a gold tooth glinting in his mouth. "Now, how much you want to play for tonight?"

I've already met Bob. I'd gone up the top of the hotel to try to get a better phone signal, and he was up there, with Victor, though I didn't know him yet. Well, I guess you'd call it a roof,

226

but it was just the top of the mound the hotel was buried under. There's an overhang made by a truck bonnet propped against a fence. Say it's about 48C in the sun. Victor Diego and Bob Jaloubi stand in the shade, round them a graveyard of old household appliances and clapped out cars. Underneath, on a table that is bright and clean, Victor is putting together mining explosives for Amir's contractors.

I'm in the shade, they don't see me, or don't mind I'm there.

Bob watching as Victor packs a tube made out of glued newspaper with a mixture of powdered fertiliser and diesel oil, squashes it tight into the tube with a big black thumb, then puts a blasting cap and fuse in the top before taping it shut. He lays it on a pile of about ten other tubes and reaches for more paper.

"I never paid attention. You use lead or sodium caps in there?" Jaloubi asks him.

Victor looks at him out of the corner of his eye, fills the tube with some more fertiliser mix, "Lead. Cheaper."

"And why don't you use kero instead of diesel? It's more powerful."

Victor stops, pinches the top of the tube and looks up, "Yeah, but kero's more expensive and not so handy - everyone round here has a drum of diesel handy," he says. "Since when you know so much anyway Bob? Thought you was a mechanic?"

"Army engineer once," Jaloubi says, "Long time ago. Kero's not that expensive is it?"

"Mate, when you're stony freaking broke every bloody thing's expensive, that's why we make our own charges."

Jaloubi raises an eyebrow, "I thought Amir was doing OK. Keeps telling me how grateful I should be, taking over the business."

"*He* might be doing OK mate, but he don't waste a chance to make money. You contract for Amir, you buy your explosives off me. I make 'em cheap as I can and make 'em pay ten times what it costs us. How you think he got rich? Not on opal. Not on this stupid hotel. On selling shit to other fools who wanted to get rich on opal." he finishes a charge and puts it on the pile. Picks up another tube. "'Cept now even the fertiliser is gettin' bloody expensive. Damn wheatgrowers laid in a huge wheat crop this year and this stuff has gone up $5 a kilo."

"You could try a bit of aluminium powder, to boost it. Wouldn't need as much fertiliser. Charge even more for the ones with the booster in. You could have like, standard charges, and booster charges." He's kind of joking but Victor likes that idea.

"Booster charges?"

"Powdered aluminium. Two percent aluminium powder in your mix and you'd only need a third as much fertiliser. Could make them smaller, but more powerful."

Victor smiles, "That so Einstein? An' just where would I get powdered freaken' aluminium out here?"

Jaloubi points to a wrecked XE station wagon sitting beside the lean-to, bonnet in the air. "Right over there. That's got an aluminium head. All you need is a grinder. Enough there for hundreds of charges once you grind it down."

Victor looks over his shoulder and shrugs, "Might try it later. You can show us how much to use."

"I'll be here," he sighs, "Not going anywhere am I?" Heads off down the mound to the hotel entrance.

So I'm leaned up against a pole in the shade listening to this and I take a step back and then after Bob disappears, I go back down too. *O-kaaaaay.* Two guys standing around making bombs, talking about the best way to blow stuff up. Out of context, you might call that 'intel'. Except just about everyone in this bloody town blows stuff up for a living. It tells me is that Amir is a crafty businessman, not digging for opal himself, making his real money off other people's dreams. It tells me Victor makes Amir's explosives, so he's the one with the access to detonators and blasting caps, probably he's the one doing the buying too. But Bob was an Army Engineer? I'm starting to think maybe Speed sent me to the right place after all.

***

Later that night, after a party she can't even describe at the Greek Tavern, Karn lies on her back on the warm bonnet of an old Toyota, windshield wipers making red pressure welts on her back but she doesn't care. The moon is bright and cold like an ivory button and the air temperature falling towards zero, but this too is unimportant. She's staring up at twin mountains, sitting like scoops of icecream in the impossible red, white and brown of the desert at night. Bob's sister Sharon sleeps beside her, cradling the bottle of port they took away with them from the party at the Taverna.

When Sharon first arrived in Coober Pedy apparently she looked thin and weak, but in just a few months she has changed. She has taken the warm dry air and sunshine and poured it into her flesh. She's wiry and strong now. Hair tied in a tight ponytail glossy as a black cockatoo's wing. Lean brown legs in leather sandals dangle over the side of the bonnet, and arms toned by constantly lifting Bob off the floor and into bed after a binge. At the party she danced and drank and giggled like such a maniac it made Karn think it must have been a long long time between laughs. Now she is spent and sleeping with a smile.

A Miles Davis trumpet line drifts from the windows of the car and out across the sand, and Karn imagines she could ride the notes up through the air across the flat land and up the salt and pepper slopes of the twin crested hills to stand on their summit.

Her Irish granddad (where she got the red hair) described desert to her once, the desert of Northern Africa. But it was nothing like this. He described towering dunes and the orgasmic sweetness of dates and fresh cool water held a while in a dry mouth. He described Bedouin appearing in the quiet of the night to share a fire, then disappearing again with the dawn. Not this bleak and terrible flat nothingness, broken only by brief and improbable mountains.

229

Not this silence. A silence like a pressure on the ears so great she finds herself coughing to relieve it. A silence so wrong to her city senses she needs the music to make herself feel safe.

Now the alcohol and the intensity of the experience are giving her fantasies. She lies with the side of her face against the cold glass of the windscreen and watches as the horizon seems to come alive. A low mountain range in the distance shifts, and begins to move toward her, swaying and dipping with a steady gait, black shadows against the black land. Time seems to slow, and the dark shapes continue their creep toward her, slowly separating as they get closer into a line of four peaks. There is a spit, and a grunt, and then the shadow nearest her lifts itself from the skyline onto four knobbed, skinny legs and comes to a halt about 10 metres from the car.

Am I imagining camels? she thinks to herself. Or maybe she said it out loud because Sharon stirs without waking, and the animal nearest her looks around at its comrades, like it's a bit weirded out, before looking back at her again. She can smell a musky rough odour, see the muscular sweep of its nostrils twitch as it takes in the scent of the car, and even imagine it tilting its ear to the music, before it grunts again and with a sway of its hump, leads the others around them and away. It takes ten minutes before she loses the hindquarters of the rearmost animal in the darkness. But she can hear the steady thump of their feet a full five minutes more.

It's nearly dawn when she slides into bed beside Jones. It's her new favourite thing, sleeping with Charlie.

"Hi," Jones says, making room for her. "Great party huh? Where'd you and Sharon get to?"

She stays quiet. Sometimes she doesn't want to talk. Sometimes you can't really explain why you need to be apart from someone, can you? All she says is, "Sharon and I saw camels. Now, kiss me."

"Are you able to accept a reverse charge call from Coober Pedy?"

"From who?"

"Uh, let me see...one Charlie Jones."

"..."

"Hello? Sir?"

"Oh for heaven's sake, yes, put it through."

"Connecting you..."

"Hey there Father! Bless me Father for I have sinned etc., etc..."

"Jones, why am I paying for this?"

"Well, if I charged it to the Great Australian Taxpayer Father, that would be like stealing, wouldn't it?"

"Hmm. How is Perth?"

"Not there yet Father, see, here's the problem. I have been lying to this nice old Lebanese guy to make him think I want to buy his hotel."

"And why would you be doing that Charlie?"

"So I can get to know him. Get a peek at the customers he has on his books. Not the hotel books, the 'I sell explosives on the side' books."

"So that..."

"So that I can find out who he's been selling explosives to."

"Nice old Lebanese guy selling explosives. You are working aren't you Jones...don't answer that. Doesn't the government keep records of that sort of thing?"

"Well, there are records, and then there are records, right Father?"

"Of course."

"Like, I'm sure the Church tells the government about *all* the money that goes into the collection tins, right Father?"

"Jones, we are talking about you, not the Church. Your sin is?"

231

"Well, until now, just lying I think. No one has been shot or blown up so far… yet."

"And there is no chance you can be honest with this old man? Just ask him straight out what you want to know?"

"Well, after I've seen his books, I will probably ask him straight out. But he has a very big dog, so I might not."

"Five Hail Marys Jones, and I want you to tell him the truth, face to face, as soon as you can. You have to stop lying, even in the national interest."

"Would you lie to protect the Pope Father? Say someone was going to kill him and by lying you could save him?"

"Fair question. Yes, I would."

"OK, now say you could stop it happening by killing the person who was going to kill the Pope. Would you do that?"

"How did this become about *me*?" he asks.

"Don't avoid the question."

"Yes, I probably would. And I would atone for it later."

"Then how about ten Hail Marys, I bring this guy down, and I let someone else tell him about it?"

"You can't bargain with God, Jones."

"Did I mention the dog Father?"

"Ha! I have at last worked you out," Amir says to me. His hand hovers over the board before he dramatically castles his king, like drama alone is enough to win him the game. We agreed that until we get the measure of each other, we should start with low stakes. Low stakes for him is $100 a game, best of three wins $300. Right now I am one game up.

Drop my hand on my chin and study the board, "Yeah, right."

232

"Yes yes, a little disappointing, I must admit. Someone who plays chess with just one philosophy, well, she cannot provide a lasting challenge." Amir sighs and drains the port at his elbow, leans down for the bottle beside his chair wheel and then refills our glasses.

"And I worked out *your* philosophy the first time we met," I smile, moving a pawn to cover his threatening bishop. "You like to get your opponent drunk so that she makes mistakes."

The old man laughs, "I drink the same as you."

"Yes but I'm just a little girl, and for all I know you probably had your stomach removed by now and the port just goes straight down your gullet, out a tube and into a colostomy bag in your pocket."

Amir pats his large stomach and moves his castle, "This is where I keep my port. No, you are just being rude because you are going to lose."

"So you keep saying." I study the game a moment and though I'm no chess genius, to me it seems like I have the upper hand, because I've captured the old man's queen and two knights. So he's just bullshitting to try to throw me. "If you're so clever, how come you don't always win?" I point out to him.

"Well. We learned in Tripoli in 1943 that it is bad policy to demoralise one's guests," Amir laughs and suddenly his eyes are locked on mine. Rheumy eyes, often cloudy and unfocussed, suddenly sharp brown and bright. He waves his hand over the board again, "Do you live your life like this?"

Lift my port glass, look at the old man over the rim as I take a sip, "Like what?"

"This. This," the old man points down at the board with an emphatic gesture. "You don't force the game, you just react, without a plan. My move, your countermove. You know the way a person plays chess reflects the way that she lives her life."

I consider before answering. "Unfair question. *You* put me in a little box, and then ask me to explain why I'm there."

233

A broad grin on the cracked brown face, "Ho! Very good, very good. But I did not make this box for you. You made it for yourself."

Lean my head back and groan at the ceiling, "Amir, I'm not so good at these conversations at two in the morning."

"No? So then, just listen to an old man. I talked to my nephew, Bob Jaloubi. What sort of a name is Bob for a man with Lebanese blood, anyway? But that's another conversation. He tells me you talk to him?"

Think back to my quick conversation at the bar this afternoon with Bob. I kept it simple, stuck to the script, mostly just questions about the Hotel, occupancy, seasonality, where the guests come from blah blah.

"A little," I say, "We just had time for a couple of drinks."

"Hmm. He said you ask a lot of questions. Questions not just about the hotel."

Uh oh. Thinking I didn't have too much time to set up the backpacker cover. Fake business cards, fake telephone service, got a friendly backpacker hostel owner to agree he would vouch for me, but would it hold?

"Ah this interests you," Amir laughs, "Yes. It should. You seem to be a perceptive lady Miss Johns."

"Thank you. I guess," I lift my glass in a mock toast.

"OK, my move. You should know, I say to my nephew, you talk business with this Johns, you drink beer and play pool with her and you tell me all about her. Also, Amir has friends in Sydney. So I ask some questions about Miss Johns back in Sydney and well, everything checks OK about the backpacker business. Seems legit. Meanwhile I talk with you, and *you* tell me, the beautiful Karn and me, *we are just friends...*" Amir says sarcastically and pauses. For effect, for balance, his eyes hard on mine. He waits long enough to get me annoyed before continuing. "Not just friends – *girlfriends*, no? Aha! Yes."

He takes a slug of port and continues, "Before, I am thinking, two pretty young ladies want to buy hole in the ground? I don't

234

think so. But now I learn Johns is dyke? Many dykes I know run pubs and clubs. You open backpacker place for dykes. Do dyke desert tours. American and European dykes come like flies. Yes?"

I'm not going there. I give him a kind of smile. Just as well. He's just testing.

"Yeah, but no. I don't think so. You see, I cannot move around any more, so mostly I just sit, and think." he says.

Oh for God's sake. I look down quickly and move a piece. The pressure of the old man's gaze is like a hand on my chest. *Beam me up Scotty,* I think to myself.

Amir holds up a finger cracked and callused, as though he has dug for his opals with his bare hands, "Ms. Johns says she want to buy my hotel, turn this place into some sort of underground dyke desert experience thing? Fine by me, if she can talk Bob into it."

"But…"

"But there is something else. What, I don't know yet." Looks at me, I look at him. Look at us, sitting here, looking at each other. "*More* than the hotel. Yeah. Amir lived this long because he is one suspicious mother." He moves his piece and leans back, satisfied, "Ha. Check!"

Sharon and Karn swim lazily, languorously, in the warm water of Amir's pool. It is lit from below with luminescent lights that make the lines of the body in the water blur, as though viewed through speckled glass. It is the first time that she has really looked at the other woman. The other night at the cafe they danced together in summer frocks and shoeless feet, but she realises that she never really looked in Sharon's face, never really got the chance to talk to her.

Sharon Jaloubi is in her late 20s, her skin deep brown thanks to a combination of Middle Eastern DNA and Coober Pedy sun. A delicate marbling of tan lines running across her stomach and breasts, and a small round belly that would fit nicely in the palm of a hand, but otherwise she's long and lean like her brother Bob. Only her face is about ten years older than her body.

Karn hasn't seen Bob Jaloubi belly laugh, but this girl has a laugh that bends her double, knees collapsing inward, until she rises breathless with tears in her eyes. It comes on her sudden, a couple of warning giggles then bam, just the eyes as the joke registers, and then the huge laugh. The grateful laugh of a woman who's had a lot to cry about.

Her hair is cut short and curly, a sexy contrast to her long limbs, a style that suits her, but Karn could never wear. And now she floats face down in the middle of the pool, arms flung out wide, playing dead, her head a fuzzy anemone at the top of her neck. Karn swims up beside her and waits for her to run out of breath. Finally she rolls over, coughing and spluttering into a back stroke and sees Karn beside her.

"Did I fool you?"

"Oh yeah," Karn says, nodding seriously, "I was just about to give you the kiss of life..."

"Ugh, thanks...not." Treads water slowly, using her hands to squirt little jets of water into the air. "I mean. You know I'm not..."

"What?"

"I like guys, like that."

"Me too."

"You do?"

"Sure."

"Sorry, I thought...you know...you and Charlie?"

"Yeah. I like Charlie like that too."

"Oh."

Karn laughs, "Don't worry. *I'm* still working it all out. I don't expect anyone else to understand."

My spidey sense is telling me Jenno is pissed off. "Having fun out there in desert are we?" he asks.

"Not really. Why?"

"Know who I'm working with on this? Freaking Witfield is who. You're off drinking yourself stupid in the Opal Field Arms every night, whatever they call it there, shagging Karn, and I'm sharing a car with *Witfield*. He flosses for God's sake."

"Lots of people floss Jenno."

"Not in my freaking car they don't!"

"So what's happening?"

"What you'd expect. First everyone pointed fingers at each other, then we were all great mates for a few days, now the cops are back to telling us nothing."

"NSW or FedPol?"

"And SA police. What we do know, the car used for the bombing was stolen from a panel beater in Bankstown. Got some prints, match the driver who killed himself. Else, we got nada."

"So we aren't off the hook after all."

"Nah, looks like we rolled up the small fry, but we left some heavy hitters in play. Who knew it was bigger than just a few guys trying to score some cash?"

"Anything more on the explosives?"

"Nope, just your detonator. That's still solid. Rest was homemade and we have no lead on where they sourced the chemicals. Hey you getting anywhere with that detonator? Speed wants to know why you're taking so long."

"Well, we can put this Amir guy against a wall and get nothing or go softly, and maybe get a lot," I tell him.

"Better hurry up is all. Cops want to send the SA Star Force in and lock down the whole of Coober Pedy. They have a freaking army ready to head your way. Teflon is holding them back but he said to tell you he can't hold em forever."

"OK. Want to know how to manage Witfield?"

"Any and all advice welcome."

"Tell him all this time in close proximity, you're starting to find him physically attractive."

Bob Jaloubi and me stand over tinned beers at the bar of the Coober Pedy Italian club, sipping and watching cricket on the box.

"So now you know why I'm here. Screwed up, lost the wife and kids, found a place here with Amir. Simple story." Jaloubi says after a long silence, "Why are you here?"

I sigh, "Here in Coober Pedy? Here in this business? Here on this planet? How deep do you want to go?"

The older man leans one elbow on the bar, "No, serious. How did you get into the hospitality business? Kind of young for a property developer."

Maybe he is genuinely interested. Looks at me with brown pupils shot with grey lines, unblinking.

"Would you believe, my old man was a communist?" I say. It's the truth, god rest his rotten red soul. Sorry Mum.

"Yeah, actually, that I believe."

"Well he was," I say, "Dock foreman. Stevedores union delegate, and secretary of the Summer Hill branch of the CPA from '55 to '70."

Jaloubi smiles, "So you became Gordon the Gecko Capitalist to piss him off."

"Something like that," I smile too. If only it was that simple. But I'm keen to get back to what we were talking about. "Nah. He owned a couple of pubs. I inherited them. You say your wife was Indonesian?"

"Yeah, met her in Jakarta in '93 on a trip for Bayer, told you I worked there?"

"Yep."

"Yeah, her dad had an agriculture supply business in Solo, so she was up talking to some suppliers. I met her at customer do. Kept it going over the next year or so and next thing I knew I was down in Solo asking her Dad for permission!"

"Solo, that's…isn't that the Muslim extremist hotbed?"

"Nah, that's all hype mate. They're just like all the other Indons, just scratching around trying to make a living."

"Did you live there?"

"Got married there, the whole deal, 12 years. Idea was I would take over the family business – you know, the genius son in law businessman. Didn't work out."

Give him the long, 'trust me' look. It just makes him uncomfortable, turn back to the TV. "Shit, another wicket."

I get Shirl to run Bob Jaloubi through the database. I'm not one to look an obvious clue in the face. Man married a girl from Solo, lived in Indonesia 12 years. Extremist central, that's what Solo is, despite what he says. Man works with Amir, who employs Victor, who I'm guessing probably sold the detonator that did the job in Sydney. But someone needed to get it from Victor to the Kurds. A middle man. Maybe a man who knows that adding aluminium powder to ammonium nitrate makes for a bigger bang. Snap.

Send in the Star Force. Grab Karn, point the ute at Perth.

Except, how come he doesn't look or act like he even heard about the Turkish Consulate bombing. Hasn't mentioned it once, doesn't look the least bit shifty. Isn't a true believer, in anything in particular, far as I can see.

Bugger, here we go again. A world full of known unknowns.

A mild grey sky has drifted over the town, but a hot breeze scuds beneath it. Temperatures already rising into the high thirties, so I pull on shorts and a singlet and leave Karn in bed, walk down to Main Street for the newspaper.

It's barely 8 a.m., road is empty except for the cars of shopkeepers and tourists topping up on petrol and water before leaving town. Aboriginal woman opening a gallery nods a friendly g'day to me, two sandy haired kids clinging to her skirts.

Outside a backpackers' lodge I see greasy haired young Europeans shrug into their packs, stand squinting in the bright light. I spot a group of Dutch, gutteral language drifting across white sand and red stones that seems like you should be able to understand some of it, but I don't understand a single word.

From the Crusts Outback Bakery at the bottom of the road I catch the warm smell of pastries and bread and checking my pocket for cash walk down to pick up some breakfast. No chance of a good espresso here, but at least the rolls will be fresh. Nice coincidence, the only other customer in the tin shed is Bob Jaloubi. He smiles as I enter and I'm thinking, actually he looks a bit like my old dad. Same tough skin and soft eyes, broad hands, way of getting sand or dust or cobwebs on his clothes that makes you want to take a brush to him. Might also explain why I'm so suspicious of him.

"Hi Bob."

"Charlie Johns," he nods to me, then takes a brown paper bag from the girl behind the counter. "A couple of pasties for us oldies and a spinach and feta for Shazza."

I peek into the bag at the mess of flaky pastry, and tomato sauce, "Pasties. For breakfast?"

He shrugs, "We've been up a while. Shazza - you know how it is."

"No, who? Sharon?"

"Sorry, thought you knew. It's no secret. Drugs. Brought her here to dry out." Just says it straight out likes it's migraines, or piles, or a bad period or something. "Amir's name means something here. No one would dare sell her anything – that's half the battle. Victor looks after that for us, he just has to say boo to the dealers and they shit 'emselves. But some nights are worse than others."

"I…guess so. So, um, what are you guys up to today?"

"I've got the day off. I'm going to take a spin up to the Mound Spring this afternoon, have a look. Sharon is going to the hospital for, you know, her methadone, so she'll be out of it. "

I see a chance, "Actually, if you'd like some company I wouldn't mind a drive. I still have a lot of questions about the hotel and Amir keeps referring me to you. I've only got a couple of days to decide if there is potential here or not, then I'm gone."

For a moment I think he's going to get windy, me inviting myself on his sightseeing trip. There is a definite hesitation in his face, a frown, but it passes quickly and he smiles, "That'd be fine, I could do with a bit of company." He walks to the door as I search my pocket for change for the rolls, "I'd better get these back while they're hot. I'll come past your place about 3 o'clock, OK? Pack your camera."

Amir is arranging pieces of a puzzle on a sheet of paper. It's an old game of his. Sentences written in Arabic and then cut out. He turns them over, mixes them up and then turns them over again. Reads them from top to bottom, and then in reverse. In his head, and then out loud. Sometimes meaning emerges, but often not.

241

He regards it as a kind of poetry also but he knows many would probably regard it as senility.

He finishes gluing in the last sentence and runs the heel of his hand across the page to smooth out the paper. Dabs away the excess glue.

She reminds me of Farouk before Farouk deserted

Hatred, shame, betrayal, disappointment by a father

She has breasts and hips like my beautiful Sheera

There are too many secrets

A woman's blood is the key to her heart

There is fire here

I am too old and they are too young to be careful

If you hurt her she will leave

The only person we can really deceive is ourself.

The Arabic words flow easily from his tongue, though he goes weeks without speaking them now. For something different he closes his eyes, spins the paper and then runs a stubby finger down the page, feeling the slightly raised edges of each sentence slide underneath and then up again, stopping at random on the page.

There is fire here.

An omen or a prophecy? He hopes not. A fire in the desert burns briefly but the heat is more fierce. He has become increasingly superstitious of late. In the corner of the page he writes the date, then places the paper in an old leather folder thick with similar meditations.

Later he will tell Victor to check the hoses and taps for all the gas bottles. Fire. He shudders. You never know.

"You meditating about us?" Karn says over my shoulder, while I sit in the kitchen of our room in dugout staring at the wall. It's like the kitchen in an office block, compact and windowless. The floor is tiled and the walls are a honeycomb cream, sealed with a silicon spray so that the natural tones of the stone give the room a warm glow. She lays a coffee cup at my elbow, rests her hand on the back of my neck.

"Yeah, just thinking, the idea was we'd both get out of Sydney, clear our heads, lie on a beach. Instead we're here."

"There are worse places," she says, lifting her hand and kissing my neck where her hand was. "I'll just have a quick shower. You want to go get lunch?"

"Cool. Hey, Bob's taking a drive out to some hot springs this afternoon, I invited myself along for the ride," I tell her.

She frowns, "Work, or am I invited too? Can you swim in these hot springs?"

"No, it's more like a stinky patch of mud. Not really a social outing. "

"Whatever. We'll have lunch then you can go do your spook thing, I'll go to the town library to find a book." Throws me a towel and wanders off. "If this place even *has* a library…"

I call out after her, "Wait, did you say 'there are worse places than this'?"

"Maybe."

"Who are you and what did you do with Karn?"

Of course there's something you *should* know about Bob. I didn't know it at the time, but give me credit, I was starting to suspect. Maybe you already guessed?

Yeah, he was in Java, like he said. And before that, in a suit and tie and working for Bayer. But before *that*, funny enough, he was in Europe running drugs. Yep. The reason his sister Sharon ended up a junkie? She was buying from her own brother at wholesale prices.

But that was a whole different place and time. Back to today. Bob driving an old Toyota Landcruiser when he pulls up outside the Mine hotel. Like all the others around here, it has a hand painted sign on the roof calmly saying "Explosives." He leans over and pushes at the heavy door with his fingertips, which opens an inch or two so I heave it open the rest of the way. Climbing up into the cabin is like climbing up into a truck. Throw my day pack into the back seat, "Sharon's little Toyota has been taking steroids," I observe.

Bob smiles, "Yeah. Amir's let me have one of his troopies for the day. Said there's some soft sand out where we're going and we might need a four wheel drive." He pushes the long gear lever into first and lets the clutch out with a bang and a lurch, but the engine rattles to a stop before they get moving. "Old troopies," Bob grunts, "You got to warm them up properly before you go anywhere." The starter clicks unsuccessfully a few times before the engine catches and he lets it idle a while before throwing it into gear again and guiding it out onto the road. "Now we're rolling."

Look kind of nervously over my shoulder. The back of the troopie is crammed with mining equipment. Racks of plastic and steel pipe line the windows, and timber and tool boxes are piled high on the floor. A scarred, well used .22 rifle rests casually in the racks alongside the pipe and there's a locked strongbox beside it. "There's no explosive in there is there?"

He looks over his shoulder to where I'm pointing. Shrugs. "Don't worry. If there is, it'll be safe. These boys aren't stupid. Don't go round blowing themselves up." He puts a hand on the gear stick, "If it really worries you we can stop and have a look, the key is probably on the keyring."

"No, just wondering, that's all" Settle lower in my seat as we hit the black top of the highway. "How far is it? I mean, how long to get there?"

"Well, there's only one within a bulls roar of here. The one most people know is up near Marla, but there's another not quite so far away that Amir told me about – I never been there. Maybe an hour." He tips his finger to his nose. "We are sworn to secrecy though. He only drew me a map because I'm a blood relative."

I don't doubt this oath was administered in all seriousness by the old Lebbo, "What exactly is a mound spring anyway? Like in Rotorua, some bubbling hole in the ground?"

"Well, I've never seen one myself, but don't get too excited. It's not exactly a bubbling spring. I mean yeah, the water is warm from being forced up from deep in the ground but you can't swim in it. Amir showed me a photo he took. It's more like a big mound of wet grass."

"You're driving out into the desert to look at a big mound of wet grass?"

"Ah now, would I be going all the way out there just to look at a mound of wet grass?" He asks, winking at me again.

"Well, Bob, I don't know much about you. Maybe that's your idea of a good time."

Karn is sitting on the bed at the hotel. The library was shut of course, so she just grabbed a novel at the servo on the highway. She's just getting into it, or actually wondering if it was a waste of money, when the phone rings.

"Miss Karen?" Amir asks.

"Karn," she says. "Hello Amir."

"Yes, Karen. Look, have you seen Sharon?"

"No sorry. Charlie said she was at the medical center earlier..." Doesn't he know she's been off to get her methadone and is

245

probably lying zonked out in her room? If he doesn't, then she decides it isn't her job to tell him.

"Ah, yes. Yes. So you won't be seeing her?"

"Haven't arranged to. What's up?"

"No, no you are a guest, it is not your problem…"

She can hear he needs something. Sighs, "No, that's alright, can I help with something?"

"Well, Victor has pissed off, and so has Bob. It's a thing I can't ask the staff here…usually Sharon helps me if the others aren't here."

She starts to get a bit nervous. Like is he going to ask her to help change his catheter or something gross?

"Uh, OK. What is it?" she asks nervously.

"I need someone to take Gaddafi outside for a walk. The staff are too scared of him. But he likes you, I can tell."

The troop carrier heaves like a ship in a storm as Bob and I turn off the bitumen and onto a dirt track, unmarked except for a bullet-holed refrigerator, serving as a mailbox for one of the cattle stations.

We've been driving nearly an hour, and I'm holding Amir's scrawled map in my lap, trying to read it as it jumps around. Look back over my shoulder at the refrigerator, "That must be it, there can't be too many other mail boxes like that…"

Jaloubi slots the car into some well worn ruts in the hard red sand of the road and loosens his grip on the wheel. Like a train on tracks the wheels stick to the ruts and the ride evens out until the troopie feels like a boat skimming across a lake of dust. Behind us a thick red comet tail plume hangs in the air. The air-conditioning in the car is going full bore, but I can still feel the air hang in a hot dry pillow in the space behind my head. Tempted to open the window a crack but that would just fill the car with flying grit. I lean forward and adjust the vents in the dashboard to give a bit more relief.

"Only another few minutes of this!" Bob yells cheerfully, enjoying himself.

"Rock and roll," I yell back. I look at the unbroken horizon thinking there are a million directions on this continent, and isn't it strange me and Karn chose this one.

Or it chose us.

Karn isn't a dog person. In fact, she's not a cat, bunny, bird or fish person either. Karn is a cocktails-and-rooftop-bar kind of person and you don't see too many people wandering around them with a small black plastic bag in their hand picking up poop. Or if you do, their behaviour is chemically induced.

But weirdly enough, Amir was right. This brutal mongrel actually does like her. When Amir handed her the leash, he scampered over like a little pup and started licking her hand and let her put the leash on his collar without any complaint before virtually pulling her arms out of her sockets trying to get out the door.

"Hey, just don't let him go near any other dogs!" is all Amir says as they disappear out his office door, "I can't afford the bloody compensation."

She doesn't have to decide where to take him, he seems to have his own route already planned and she just follows along as he moves from building to building, fence to fence, picking up scents and leaving the odd doggie email. There was one thing, when a stray came around the corner, about fifty metres down the road, and Gaddafi got all tense and started licking his chops, but the other dog had apparently been Gaddafied before, and it took one sniff upwind and turned and ran.

She can't help notice the locals are also pretty quick to cross the road or move out of the way when they come past too.

Freaking fairy bells, she thinks. *I'm walking a killer guard dog through a desert mining town for an Arab terrorist while I wait for my lover the lady spy to get back from work and take me to a pub for a schnitzel.*

She watches as Gaddafi stops at a driveway with one of those rubberised solid metal link chains across it, and starts chewing the chain like he expects to be able to chomp through it. And it wouldn't surprise her if he could.

Jones, you better turn out to be a keeper.

Bob and I coast to a halt at a gate about 12km off the bitumen, along the old survey road they had been driving down. We travelled nearly 10km without a single bend in the track, and I was beginning to think it would never end. There was nothing to tell the view out one side of the car from the other. Low blasted scrub was scattered sparsely across the red sand in every direction and nothing higher than a termite mound broke the skyline in any direction.

I'm asking him about the hotel, trying to get onto the whole Opal mining thing. Isn't it dangerous, all those explosives? Who manages the explosives, is it Victor, or someone else? Do they have to be registered? Can guests bring them into the bar at the hotel, kind of thing or do they have to check them at the door? I'm trying to keep it light, keep it connected to the hotel, but I'm narrowing it down. Jaloubi might be an ex-army sapper, but you ask me, it's Victor who controls the boom-sticks for Amir.

Yeah, I'm thinking Victor is our man.

The only life we see, apart from skittish kangaroos and rabbits, is a huge wedge tailed eagle, bored shitless sitting on a low bush, that lifts itself into the air with a single flap of its wings and immediately catches an air current that sends it circling high behind us. I watch it until it spirals out of sight and get depressed the moment it fades from view, because there is nothing to replace it. But the track at last ends, terminating at the gate in a sharp elbow, which then spears off to the north, without deviation, until it disappears over the horizon again. Around one dry and cracked gatepost a single piece of red reflective tape flaps a little in the hot wind.

"I thought Amir's directions said *yellow* tape," Bob says, taking the map from me. "No, red tape. This is the right place. Open the gate will you, and close it after I go through."

I open the door and jump out of the troopie, diving into the heat is like diving into a pond. My hair crackles with static and I can feel my skin begin immediately to burn. The gate is fixed with a messed up arrangement of wire and wooden sticks and I fumble with it for a while, looking up once or twice to the troopie for help but he's just smiling, bastard, before it finally falls free and Jaloubi drives through. Shut it again with only slightly less difficulty and with relief climb back into the cab. Now I'm really loving the pitiful puffs of cool air dribbling out of the console.

"Why close the gate? There's nothing around here for a million miles!" I ask him, hanging my head in front of one of the louvers.

"Well, we don't want to let all the rabbits out, do we?" Bob laughs.

I look at him mystified, and he just shakes his head, "Never mind. Old joke. This isn't desert out here, this is the rangelands - cattle country. Got to close the gates." He consults the ball compass mounted on the dashboard, and points the nose of the troopie to something close to N-NW. "Amir says we go about 1 km on this heading and look for a tall pole with a flag on it. That's where we stop."

I lean forward in anticipation, but I'm soon buckling my belt back on, and bracing myself with knees and arms, as the troopie scrapes slowly forward over rocks and scrub and the wiry fallen trunks of long dead trees. The line we take is far from straight and there is no track to follow now. More than once we have to back out of dangerous ground when one wheel of the vehicle drops into a rabbit warren. Looking closely at the ground I can see the surface pockmarked by dozens of burrows, but in this sun nothing is moving above ground. After 5 minutes I lean over to look at the odometer, "We must have gone a kilometre by now."

Bob flicks his eyes down to the dashboard and then back to the scrub in front of us, licking his dry lips. "Just about. You keep your eye out for that pole on your side. It may be a way off. We've had to make a few detours..."

But I can't see anything and as the odometer clicks over the 1 km mark he lets the car roll to a halt, gazing around him. "I'll get out and climb onto the roof. Might see it from up there." A brief gust of baking air and he is clambering up the side of the cabin and onto the rack on the roof. I lean back and puff hair out of my eyes. Not that I'm worried I won't see this mound spring thing. More annoyed. To think we might have come all this way, through the toughest country I have ever seen, look at nothing, and all I found out, Bob Jaloubi is no terrorist. Freaking typical.

A pair of brown legs lower themselves down past the driver's side window and he jumps down. He takes about three steps into the scrub and bends down, then stands again, clutching a white metal golf flag, tattered yellow banner on top, and waves it over his head. He takes up a rock and pounds it into the sand again, then climbs back up into the cab next to me. "You wouldn't believe it! Talk about a navigator, we nearly ran over the bloody thing! What are the chances of that?" He is hot, sweaty and proud of himself and I can't help smiling. He reaches down to the ignition, and kills the engine. The air conditioner falls silent and though I want to get out and stretch my aching back, I'm not in a hurry to leave the cool cab.

"So now what?" I ask.

"Now? Now we have a drink, put on our hats, and go for a wander. I think I could see the spring that way, from up on the roof of the cab," he says, pointing in the direction we had been driving. "There's little white rocks showing the way. This is as close as we go with the car. Don't want to get bogged.."

I reach into the day pack and drag out the creased floppy straw hat I carried with me all the way from Sydney to this baked clay arsehole of the continent. He smiles a little as he jams an old oily stockman's hat on his head, but I have to comfort myself with the thought that while it might not win the outback credibility stakes, mine gives a lot more shade. Swig some water from the canteen and together we step out into the sun. The heat lifts in waves from the sand, onion layers of roasting air, but it is better as we step away from the glaring metal of the car, and start walking. I'm guessing we've arrived just after the hottest part of the afternoon, and that from now on the sun will wane, but looking around I see no cover at all. Perhaps it'll be a very short sightseeing trip. As I wave a cloud of flies from my face, seemingly appearing out of the air itself, I'm thinking a shorter trip might not be so bad.

After about five minutes of following him through the rolling sandy scrub he calls out and points again, and I see a low mound ahead in the middle of a sandy bog. It's about knee high, an ellipse about ten metres long, and bright scrubby green grass like a punk's haircut across the top. Off to the right I see another similar, but much smaller mound. The sand around them is a darker brown or red, and as we step through it I can see it is moisture in the dirt that darkens it. The air is vaguely sulphurous and as I get close I wrinkle my nose.

"I call this a bloody miracle," Jaloubi says kneeling on the biggest of the mounds. "Feel this here."

"I would call this 'whiffy'," I tell him. I kneel beside him and push my hand through the grass to where his hand rests near the roots. Close to the ground I can feel a wetness, and pushing harder, spongy mossy grass giving way to water pulsing through my fingers.

"Can you believe that? Water! It must be 45 degrees out here!"

I lift my hand out of the grass and my whole palm is wet. Lifting the fingers to my mouth makes me gag because of the brackish smell, but I force myself to lick my fingers and taste the water. Spit in disgust, "Shit! That's terrible."

He tastes his fingertips himself, "Yeah. Probably way too salty for us to drink, maybe for cattle too, but that's not a bad thing. Cattle and humans aren't the only things that live out here."

251

Look around at the bare earth, dead twigs of trees and dry brittle grasses, "Nothing lives out here."

"You might be surprised… OK back to the car. We have to set up a little camp and get ready for dusk. Judging by the tracks the camels are regulars here."

Tracks? What tracks. Looking back behind us I see our footprints in the wet sand, and then I see them, the fat flat hoof prints of camels. I look up at the sun, and the idea of another couple of hours beside a sulphurous hole just to see a few more camels, well, it isn't singing to me. The idea of a cold Coopers underground, now *that's* an idea. "Actually, I saw some camels the other day Bob. So I don't want you hanging around here just to get a picture for my sake…"

He laughs, "Picture? You think I came all the way out here for a picture? I'm going to *shoot* one of the bastards, girl! There's a month's eating on a camel. But you can't shoot 'em close to town, someone might own 'em. Got to shoot a wild one. Two ways to do that. Get yourself a helo and go looking for 'em, or come here and wait for them to come to us. Now, you wait until you taste my Halib Geyl…"

"Sit sit!" Amir says as Karn gets back and slips his bodyguard off its leash. The killer gives her hand another grateful lick and then slopes over to its blanket by his desk and resumes its watch. "You want to eat, I'll get us some food. You like prawns? I'm having prawns – fresh, not frozen, straight up from Spencer Gulf today. You have some prawns." He gets on the phone and orders up some prawns, hummus, tabbouleh, bread, lemon, olives and white wine from his kitchen.

"Prawns it is," Karn quips, "Why not?"

They chat a little and then the kitchen staffer comes in with the food on a trolley, the wine in an ice bucket. The old man likes his wine this way. "You Australians drink the wine too warm," he says, pouring her a glass. "Room temperature' does not mean 30 bloody degrees!." Red or white, he puts them both on ice.

"Wonder how Jones is doing," Karn thinks out loud, leaning back in her chair. Sightseeing with Bob. Hopefully Jones will get what she needs, so that they can both get out of here.

"You worry about her?" Amir asks.

"Her? No, she's a big girl."

"It is not a good idea to worry too much about other people," Amir waves his hand dismissively, forking some food onto a plate for her. "You cannot alter fate - I learned that a long time ago. Allah wills it, and so it will be, or not. Did I ever tell you about the time the German army had me stuck up a pole for 14 hours?"

She leans back in her chair as the old man talks, waiting for the moral that undoubtedly lurks in the tale, because Amir never tells a tale without a moral. She can see he's settling in for an ear bender.

1943, Libya, he says. The British had the Germans backed into Tripoli, and they wanted him to get into the port and scout around, see if they were digging in, or getting ready to ship out. But he'd had enough of war; he wasn't a regular soldier and he had no intention of going back to the British. He wanted to get out to Alexandria, work his way on a boat to Britain. Still had his Australian Commonwealth passport.

There was panic and chaos everywhere in Tripoli, a tidal wave of anarchy that flowed over the city in waves that matched the allied bombing. He got to the port in the early hours of the night, planning to bribe a fisherman to get him out, but the port was packed with refugees and a small company of German troops had blocked the access road to the docks, firing shots into the air occasionally to keep the wall of desperate people at bay. Amir guessed the refugees were German sympathisers and collaborators, sensing the Germans were about to flee and terrified of the revenge that repressed Tripoli residents would bring down on them. People at the back were shouting and cursing those in front, urging them forward into the guns. The whole scene was lit with big arc lights, the shadows making the crowd look double the size and menace that it was.

Amir had climbed a dock crane to get a better view, the crowd surged forward and then the troops started firing into the crowd. Men, children, old women, fell to the ground scared or hurt or dead. The volley of shots died and Amir watched amazed as total silence fell over the docks. A few of the German troops, mostly just frightened boys, tipped back their helmets and stared shocked at what they had done. A German officer in the uniform of an air force pilot was the first to break the silence. He had been crouched with his pistol in a firing stance, but now he stood and held it out in front of him gripped in both hands. Waving it slowly back and forth over the hundreds of refugees lying prone on the ground, in rough Arabic he yelled out that anyone who was still on the docks in five minutes would be shot. Like grain sliding off a table, the crowd fell away from the back first, people crouching low and running, leaving clothes and bags behind. Those toward the front dragged the wounded or dead away with them.

Amir looked about for a way to climb down without attracting any attention from the Germans, then noticed that the boom of the crane was hanging just above the roof of a low warehouse. If he could make it to the warehouse roof, he could bypass the troops at the entrance to the docks, and perhaps make it to one of the boats, bobbing tantalisingly beyond, crews working feverishly to get away. The German officer was now organising his boys to set up a proper barricade. They dragged oil barrels and razor wire part way across the road and set a heavy iron bar across the gap to form a gate. A few of the wounded were still lying moaning on the road, or trying to crawl away, and Amir watched fascinated, hugging himself behind the latticework of the crane, as the German officer sent a team of medics out to tend to the wounded. Some, bandaged and limping, eventually stood and staggered away. Others, about five, were carried by stretcher beyond the barricade into the shelter of a brightly lit shed without walls and made comfortable, then left to their fate.

"I always respected the Germans for that," he said. "The British would have let them all just lie there. Filthy Arabs."

As he crouched in the ironwork of the crane, waiting for his chance to move, Amir fixed his attention on the five wounded in the shed, watching their every movement, trying to stay awake by guessing which would die first.

"A morbid game," he admits.

"Well, we do strange things when we're under stress." Karn tells him.

"Yes. We do. You know, I laughed. Me, the dreaded spy, liberator and warrior, stuck up a pole like a boy in an apple tree."

Surrounded by the dead and dying, the Germans prepared to evacuate Tripoli port. Grey trucks started to rumble into the port, past the barricade, unloading troops and crates onto small freighters and fishing boats. The air force officer had been replaced at the barricade by a Wehrmacht captain in a uniform new and clean. In fact, Amir noticed most of the troops looked young and fresh, scared, but not bloodied or even tired. It was very strange to him, watching this undefeated Teutonic garrison army abandon the city to the pale, skinny, half starved boys of the British 8th. He knew it had more to do with the American landings, but still it filled him with a savage pride to watch them file through the barricade and onto the boats. His French Lebanese mother would finally be thinking, up there in heaven, OK Amir, now you've done enough.

After another four hours, during which daylight arrived, and he found a way to wedge himself between spars so that he could sit out of sight and doze without fear of falling, there were only two of the five wounded still moving. Three had not shifted their places for so long Amir had no doubt they were dead. The two who were still alive were lying side by side, a young woman, about 20, and an older man in his fifties. She was partly conscious, shot in the side. A lot of blood making a black stain on her burka, torn open where the medics had applied a pressure bandage. She lay on the uninjured side, facing the old man and held his hand. Amir couldn't know whether she knew the old man, but he guessed not. The girl looked well dressed, good shoes - a city girl, someone's daughter - caught in the surge to the port and then felled. The man looked like a farm labourer. He had no shoes on his feet and his pants were more patches than cloth. He had been shot in the stomach. His head rolled from side to side as he talked softly to himself, but he never opened his eyes.

These two stayed alive a long while. The man would lie still for a while, then move his head fitfully, mumbling to himself, and the girl would stir, her hand clenching his, her voice weak but trying to reassure him. Then they would both fall quiet awhile until the man cried out again. He tried to catch a glimpse of her turned face, and found himself deeply upset by the savage slash in her brown burka, the top of her underpants just visible beside the bloodied bandage against her skin. He had no sister himself, nor girlfriend, but he could imagine that this girl had a brother or a father somewhere, once they would have been sitting at a kitchen table smoking and looking at the clock wondering where was she. Now they were probably dead. He had to divide his attention between the girl, and the activity on the dock, but he returned his gaze to her as often as he could, as though just watching her might keep her alive.

After some hours, when the man had failed to move, Amir decided he was dead - though the girl kept talking to him; crying, and talking. Boats started to pull away from the docks, wallowing in the water until they found way, overloaded with men and crates, their bows dipping dangerously low in the water. There was one moment when Amir nearly cried out. Sometime near lunch, one of the guards at the barricade, bored during a lull in the activity, walked over to look at the wounded civilians. Without compunction he dug a toe into the ribs of each of the dead, and then went through their pockets. He did the same with the man with the head wound, and the man didn't stir, so he went through the man's pockets, but found nothing, and stood. The girl was not unconscious at that stage, but she was trying to look like it, and though the soldier nudged her with his boot, she didn't move. Amir hoped she truly was unconscious, and not lying with her eyes closed, waiting for the worst. Then from the waistband at his back the soldier pulled a pistol and pointed it down at her head. This was when Amir nearly gave himself away. He wanted to cry out, "No!" But instead he turned his head away and closed his eyes, waiting for the shot.

"Probably saw her breathing, just wanted to end her suffering," Karn observes.

"That girl, you have no idea how brave she was. She did not make a sound."

But no shot came, and when Amir looked back again, the boy was sauntering back to the barricade, juggling in his hands the few things he had taken from the bodies. Obviously he could not bring himself to shoot. Then as the sun tipped over in the sky and started to drop toward the sea, a large lumbering convoy of lorries belching diesel smoke arrived at the barricade and began pouring out tired and dirty German troops and bellowing sergeants. Amir could see that these troops had been fighting; some were carried, some helped their comrades limp towards the last two small boats. These were the last to arrive, and Amir saw some despair in their activity as they crowded around the last fishing boats, which were obviously inadequate to carry all the men and their equipment. All but two of the soldiers abandoned the barricade too, jostling to try to secure themselves a place on the boats. The new troops set to stripping equipment from the boats, clearing every available space on the decks.

Amir realised this was his moment to escape, while the departing troops were frantically occupied, and before the jubilant British came in to claim the town. Getting a boat was now out of the question, but he had made his break with Britain and had no desire to get entangled again. But just then the girl moved again, and cried out sharply. Her breathing was laboured and without really thinking, Amir abandoned his perch, crawled out along the boom of the crane and dropped down onto the roof of the warehouse alongside. Crouching low he ran along the grey rusted roof, heedless of the noise of his boots, trusting the clamour of the troops, and jockeying lorries, to cover him. Past the barricade, and another hundred metres along where the building ended, and Amir slid down to the edge of the roof and looked over. He was about six metres off the ground, and directly over the hard wooden rails of the dock. There was no ladder down, and he knew the drop would probably break his ankles. Beyond the dock the cold water glittered in the sun, and the next thing he knew was the shock of his breath exploding from his lungs as he crashed, legs and arms splayed, into the sea. He emerged gasping and spluttering and dragged himself through the oil and garbage to the pontoons of the dock and hauled himself up a ladder. His body was shaking with cold but he waited below the lip of the dock and listened for the sound of running boots, coming to investigate the splash. There were none. One arm hooked over a rung of the ladder to make sure he didn't fall, he hung steaming in the sun and let some warmth come back to his bones.

The space between the warehouses was narrow and dark, and empty. He edged between them and halted at the road across which the barricade had been thrown. He was about a hundred metres down from the barricade, and both of the soldiers still there were facing him, smoking nervously and watching the commotion at the docks, no doubt trying to judge the last moment when they could leave the barricade, and still make it to the boats. For five agonising minutes Amir hung back behind the corner of the warehouse, edging his head into view every now and then to check whether he could make it across to the warehouse opposite. Expecting any moment that someone would spot him.

Then the refugee mob returned. A hundred strong, mostly men. They had obviously been watching the scene on the dock and realised their last chance to escape was about to disappear. Their fear of the British liberators greater than their fear of the German rifles, they made a last desperate bid for the boats. And this time, as the leading ranks charged at the barricades, and the two German boy soldiers left there raised their guns in panic, petrol bombs flew through the air and exploded; short of the wire, but throwing a black oily smoke over the scene. In that second Amir ducked low and ran across the road to the gap between the warehouses opposite, throwing himself gasping to the ground, looking back over his shoulder in time to see the boots and coats of German soldiers pounding down the road toward the smoke and fire. He heard the whoosh of another petrol bomb then a disciplined volley of rifle fire as the battle hardened German troops took up positions at the barrels again. With his nose in the dirt and weeds he crawled close to the walls of the warehouse, moving slowly and hoping the darkness would hide him from the troops he could hear running to reinforce their comrades. With a gasp of relief he finally edged around the corner, into a narrow alley between a wall and the warehouse, high with neglected weeds and grass, and along this he scuttled, parallel to the fighting, wondering how long it would be before the Germans realised they could outflank the mob by doing the same thing.

Without realising it he came suddenly to the end of the warehouse, where it became the large open shed in which the girl lay, and found himself standing completely exposed, wide eyed and staring stupidly at the furious battle going on just fifty metres away. Behind blazing oil barrels and melting wire, German troops lay prone, firing blindly through the flames. Fifty metres up the road, men with knives and iron bars crawled slowly forward. All were focused on the danger straight in front of them, and none looked his way. Feeling numb and foolish he slowly lowered himself to the ground and began to crawl over to where the girl lay.

She lay on her back, her face toward the fighting, one hand at her mouth, white. Her chest heaving as she tried to drag air into her lungs, air fouled now with smoke. As he came closer he could hear a gurgling sound with each breath, as she pulled the air through phlegm and blood. Bullets were flying around them, spanging off the metal and concrete.

"Why did you bother? Why not just hide until the fighting was over?"

"She was dying. I don't know why, but I didn't want her to die."

"Brave man."

"No. If it was the old farm labourer, and not the young girl, I would have stayed up my pole. I am soft that way, about women."

As he came close to her, she heard him and twisted her head to look at him. Wet, dirty, wide eyed and breathing heavily himself, he terrified her and she gasped in Arabic, "No! Please....oh, by the Prophet please don't." A local girl, he guessed from her accent. "It's alright," he said, rolling alongside her, "I'm a friend. I have to move you." The Arabic he spoke reassured her and for a brief moment, a moment that would always live with him, she stared into his eyes, and smiled weakly. Then coughed, and a thin spray of blood laced her chin. He stood then, put his arms under her shoulders, and started to drag her towards the weedy shrubs and bushes by the dock wall, where they would both be hidden from view, and perhaps safe for a while.

The bullet struck him in the left shoulder, coming from up the alley where, as he had feared, a platoon of Germans had finally moved to flank the fighting. The arm fell numb and lifeless and he dropped the girl, then clapping his hand to the back of his head, started to feel faint, realising that the bullet had ricocheted off his shattered shoulder and cut a deep furrow through the scalp and bone at the bottom of his skull. He dropped to his knees, a mighty pounding in his head, staring at the blood on his right hand, then fell face forward into the dirt.

"The second time in my life I was shot. Pah. That one really hurt." Rolls up his sleeve and shows Karn the smooth round scar on the wrinkled skin of his left shoulder, a wound that looks suspiciously like a vaccination scar.

"Nice one, what about the girl?"

"It was dark when I woke and my shirt was stuck to my neck with my own blood. I must have looked dead. The Germans were gone. Away on their little boats. There were bodies all over the docks. Locals, Germans. One woman, her head shaved and her dress torn off, had already been hung from the crane where I had hidden, so the local mob had obviously been in action. I'd been knocked out the whole day."

"And the girl?"

Amir looks at Karn, shakes his head, "Dead. Of course. I saw her lying beside me but I couldn't look at her. Maybe another bullet from the Germans, probably she just drowned in her own fluids. It was as Allah willed it."

Karn reaches for her wine and takes a gulp, "Jesus Amir, did you ever hear of happy endings? You and her are supposed to wake up in hospital together, get married, have a brace of chubby little Lebbos and spend your golden years arguing over whether to be Sunni or Shiite."

Setting his glass down, Amir sighs, "I have not shared that story with anyone since my first wife. Do you know that? And bah to happy endings. Some things are just ordained to happen. The girl was meant to die, and all my worrying, my stupid heroics, could not change that. I was meant to live, and probably I could have dropped out of that crane onto the heads of the Germans and still got away."

"I don't believe that. I'm not a fatalist," Karn tells him.

"That," Amir says without looking at her, "Is why you fit together so well with Charlie Johns, yes?"

"Well, anyway, let's get some tucker ready now," Bob says, picking up an esky and dragging it out from under a canvas, "Just unroll that will you? Get us a bit of shade. We need to get settled and stay quiet or they won't come close enough."

"Big four wheel drive parked right beside their water hole won't be enough to scare them off?" I ask.

"Nah. Not real cautious, your camel. No predators out here," he smiles, "'Cept us."

I stand and stretch, start kicking the sausage of canvas out flat.

He clips the canvas to the roof rack of the troopie, then sniffs the air, "You know, I can smell petrol." He drops onto one knee and peers underneath the four wheel drive. Peers into the darkness a moment, then his eyes adjust, "Ah, shit. We must've put a stick or a rock through one of the tanks," he says.

I kneel down beside him and see the large dark stain in the sand underneath the car, petrol still dripping silently from a puckered rip.

"Is it bad? Are we stuck here?" It's my first thought. Hundreds of kilometres from the highway, and not another soul around, I'm afraid we'll be stranded.

He gets up again, "Nah. No, don't worry. There's two tanks. I think only one is leaking and I filled them both. Plus there's forty litres in jerry cans in the back. I filled those too." He claps me on the shoulder. "But the other tank is just a reserve and it will be a pain in the arse stopping every 80 or 100 km to fill it up again. I'll just see if I can patch up the hole before it leaks out totally, it doesn't look too big."

He opens the rear door of the wagon and rummages through a tool box, coming up with some putty and duct tape. "Yep, this is what we need. I'll have to move the troopie. I need to find some solid ground so that I can jack it up. Pull the food and stuff away from the car will you?" Jaloubi says, climbing into the cabin and slamming the door behind him as I drag esky and chairs through the sand. He cranks the engine a couple of times, but it doesn't catch. Frowning, he cranks it again for a solid minute, and from twenty feet away, standing near the esky I can hear his foot pumping the gas pedal as the starter motor clicks and whirs. He waits and tries again, again without luck. Finally, he reaches down and yanks the bonnet open.

He climbs back out of the cab, muttering, "Bloody Amir. Starter's been a bit dodgy, but Victor fixed it, don't worry he says. My arse." I hear more cursing, and squat down beside the esky to take out some ice, rub it on my face and neck, drip it into my hair. See him reach under the bonnet for the release, start heaving it up.

It happens in a second. The click and pop of something in the big box behind the driver's cab. Then the explosive in the box detonates and I'm picked up in a tangle of canvas and rope and flung into the scrub.

Kyle Murphy, driver on the Adelaide to Alice Springs passenger train, The Ghan, is stirring a cup of instant coffee when he sees the thin column of smoke rising into the air. Could be anything from 50 to 100km away he judges. But it is the only thing in 360 degrees of horizon, and he watches it for a few minutes to see if it'll disappear. Some grazier burning rubbish, could be. The smoke changes from thin white to an angry black and starts to thicken. Kyle watches it another five minutes, then the smoke starts to thin again and disappears. Yeah, just some cocky.

He settles into his chair for the last two hours of his shift, eight hours out of Port Pirie and another ten to Alice, most of which he'll do on autopilot. People ask him how he stands the boredom, and staring out the window at the blasted plains around him he kind of understands why, but he explains to them his job is no different to the driver of a 747 Jumbo, and no-one asks them about boredom.

There is activity, negotiating the sidings at places like Coonamie, Pimba, Kingoonya, Tarcoola, Marla, Adelaide and Alice. The rest of the 20 hour trip they are on 'autopilot' so the driver's job is no different to an airline pilot who only has to wake up for take offs and landings, and as he likes to say, his trip takes nearly as long as it takes a jumbo to fly from Sydney to London.

Besides, he likes the outback. Likes the surprises that only rangelands and desert can offer. Camels or cattle on the tracks, eagles cruising parallel with his windows, roos and rabbits scattering like a bow wave ahead of the train's headlights. Likes the history too, his train named after the Afghan cameleers who used to make the big supply trip north, an epic zig zag journey from sheep country to cattle country, from homestead to homestead, that would take them months. He'd never say it in front of his mates, it's a bit corny, but he tells his kids he drives 'the camel train'. A real modern day Afghan.

He looks back to where the smoke had come from and squints. At 100 km/h they are nearly out of sight already, but with a frown he sees more smoke starting to rise. Broader and flatter this time, like it is spreading over a wider area. A grass fire maybe. He'd better call it in after all.

He takes another sip of coffee and lifts the radio telephone.

"So," Karn looks for something to say, "Charlie's OK out bush with Bob? I mean, you know him…he's your stepbrother and stuff."

He laughs, "Do I know Bob? I know him. Bob is a piece of human waste who brings nothing but trouble, to everyone he meets. His own sister, a junkie, and you know who sells her the drugs?"

She blinks, "No, but I guess they aren't hard to find."

"Bob. His own family and he sells her drugs. What did they tell you, why he was in Indonesia?"

"Well, Sharon said he married an Indonesian woman, lived a while up there…"

Amir spits, "He was a drug courier. Married a prostitute. She brought him into the family business – heroin. Sharon, his little sister, comes to visit and he gets her hooked. My own half brother, a piece of shit."

"She didn't tell me that…"

"Obviously. His wife, the prostitute and his child, killed by Indonesian special forces, the Kompassus, when they raid the drug camp? No, I can see she didn't mention that either. I am the one who brought little Sharon here. Get her straight. Then he turns up, and hangs around, waiting for me to die." The old man shrugs, pushes his plate away, dabs his mouth with a napkin, "Pretty lady, you and Charlie Johns are not here to buy my business."

"No?"

"You are not going to sell its bits off and turn this dugout into a hostel."

264

It's not a question. "We're not?"

"You are here for me."

As he says it, she knows of course he's right. Jones has been fixated on Bob, who strikes her as a guy who couldn't organise his sock drawer, while old Amir...

"Look..." she starts protesting. "*I'm* not part of anything..."

He reaches across the table, and places his old brown hand on hers, "Of course not," he says, not very convincingly, "There is someone here who wants to meet you." He rolls his chair back and knocks on the wall beside him.

From the door behind Amir, leading into his bedroom, steps an old middle eastern man. She jumps to her feet, knocks his chessboard flying. She doesn't know who the guy is, but suddenly there are two old wrinkly blokes to worry about instead of just one, and she doesn't like the odds. Grabs the only thing near to hand, an old ashtray stand, and holds it across her chest like a shield.

She hears Gaddafi's paws on the tiles behind her and turns to face him. The dog's look takes in the room, the chess board lying askew on the floor, one hinge broken, and he stands there with his head tilted, big dark eyes asking a question at Amir. He's not a smart dog, for a second he seems confused, and sits back on his haunches. Maybe he's got mixed loyalties – after all, she just took him walkies.

She turns back to the two old men.

Which is when 20kg of Canine Cruise Missile hits her square in the back, and sends her face first onto the table, cracking her forehead cleanly across the edge.

Rex Williams is ten metres up a windmill, fixing the head on a bore pump, when he hears the crackle of the radio in his Cessna. With a curse he cocks his ear, but from fifty metres away, in the clearing he uses as an airstrip, the noise is only so much static.

It's Murphy's law, he knows that, that he can be flying around the property for three hours without a peep, but the minute he lands and then gets into a job, someone will come looking for him. He waits a moment in case whoever it is gives up, but after a minute or so he hears the crackle again.

Wearily dropping a heavy wrench to the floor he lowers himself over the platform and climbs to the ground. It's been a long hot day, and at 68, he doesn't move so quick anymore. Gone are the days when he had permanent help, when there were twenty people or more living on the station. They had nearly enough for two full cricket sides back thirty years ago. Four families and a dozen kids. Now even half a dozen stations together couldn't raise a cricket team between them. The 390 square kilometres of Mulga Downs is just him and Dawn and Allan, their grandson, now - and Allan going off to Roseworthy College in Adelaide next year. His son the banker, already living down in Adelaide with his wife, is always onto him to get in a manager and retire to the coast, but what the hell would he do? So he hires help when they have to shift the cattle, and flies all the fences and bores himself.

The radio crackles again - whoever it is, is persistent. Hauling open the pilots' side door he leans in and hears his wife's voice coming through on the tinny speaker above the seat.

"Rex, this is Dawn, over. Rex, are you there?"

He grabs the hand piece, flicks a switch, "Rex here Dawnie, what's up girl?"

"Oh Rex, got you at last. Rex, the Fullarton's have got a fire somewhere in their Long Hundred paddock. The Ghan driver reported it about 4 o'clock."

He looks at his watch, it is nearly twenty minutes after that already, "Where's Tom Fullarton?" he asks tiredly. A fire is not necessarily a disaster, unless it's near stock, or a water. He knows Tom has his own plane and could check it out quicker than him. He is a good 90km from the Long Hundred paddock.

"Cath says he's flown to Alice today to look at a new car. She's sent young Tom out with a water tank, but he'll take an hour or more to get there, and he might need help. Marla CFS are waiting for someone to tell them if we need them. Can you get out there and have a look?"

"Guess I'll have to."

"Guess you will. Out."

"Righto. Out."

It takes him ten minutes to climb the windmill again, pack his tools, climb down, throw them back into his Cessna, and complete a quick preflight. He fires the engine and points the nose down the red dirt runway into the wind, running the revs high before he lets go on the wheel brakes, because taking off from this strip is always a bastard. He skips across the dirt and just before the myalls at the end of the strip hauls the nose into the air and begins a slow climbing turn to the southeast and Fullarton's place.

I wake in a world of pain. I just remember a flash, an explosion, nothing else. I try to move but my whole body feels bruised and for a disorienting moment have no idea what's happened. Every small movement results in deep muscle pain, but everything around me is grey-black; I can't see. From the sound, and the harsh scratching in my back I can tell I'm lying across a broken bush or tree. My right arm and shoulder are twisted around a branch, and I can feel other branches or parts of the trunk pushing against my skin low, near the base of my spine. Slowly, moving my left hand around in front of me I feel first wood, and then cloth, canvas, and slowly it dawns on me that I'm not blind, just wrapped in the awning I was rolling out when the explosion came. Blinking the pain and tears from my eyes I can see little points of light through the material now, and using my free left hand again, try to bat it away from me. It falls back, still twisted around my legs, and the sudden light causes me to screw my eyes shut, but after a moment I can open them again and turn to look for the source of the pain in my shoulder.

I see immediately that I've landed heavily. A bush lies smashed beneath me and a small spike of broken branch, about half a centimetre round, is stuck in the fleshy part of my upper arm. With a jerk I pull it free, blood pulsing from around the small wound, and I scream. I half roll, half fall away from the bush, sticks and branches that are stuck through the shirt of my back snapping and tearing as I move. Now I can drag myself free of the canvas around my legs and I back out of it slowly, one of my legs numb and useless.

Something, probably a piece of metal from the truck, has sliced along my left calf like a butcher's knife. Diagonally across my Achilles tendon, just above the heel, slicing it in two, then up the muscle of the leg, a deep cut ten centimetres long and about a centimetre deep. My foot is soaked in blood already and without even trying I know I can't walk. It's been bleeding, but it's not like it's gushing out now. I feel weak suddenly, and very tired, and lie back on the sand. The pain seems to come from everywhere, and reaching up to my face I find a small cube of glass stuck deep in my forehead, then another in my cheek. Probably the canvas protected me from most of this. Perhaps I faint then, because the next thought I have is that I'm choking, sitting up again and choking on thick smoke.

I'm propped up on one elbow and look around myself through eyes blurred with water, and see flame, sparks shooting into the air, moving toward me from around the blasted hulk of the wagon. Paper dry grass and scrub has burst into fire around the wreck, and I watch helplessly as the wind sweeps the smoke over me. Grabbing the canvas I just have time to haul it over me before the fire front, gaining heat and momentum, jumps over me and begins to move away. Looking out from under the canvas I see that in half a minute it's already fifty metres away.

Gasping in air and smoke, baking under the canvas, too scared and tired to move, I slowly look myself over, find no more injuries. But blood is pooling under my ankle, and finally it occurs to me I should do something about that. My right sleeve is already ripped, and I pull it free, winding it tight around my thigh to make a pressure bandage. I know I should try to keep it up, until the bleeding stops, but worry about what has happened to Bob takes over, and I call out, weakly at first, because my mouth is dry and choked with dust and smoke, then more strongly, "Bob? Are you alright? Bob!"

From where I lie, I can see only the still burning wreck of the troopie above smouldering bushes and grass. It stands exactly where it was, the four tires burning fiercely and spewing black smoke, the front end still mostly intact and sitting on a skeletal chassis, as though the rest of the car has been stripped by carrion birds. Biting my lip against the pain, I lever myself up onto my right leg, screaming in pain as I accidentally try to take some weight on my left leg and feel the joint flex sickeningly, without the Achilles to brace it. But half hopping, and half dragging my useless leg, I move closer to the wagon.

From about five metres away I can see him. A huddled shape, curled in a ball just in front of the car. He's lying with his feet toward me and looks remarkably untouched. His boots and legs and shorts are unmarked with blood, or even dirt, and as I watch he moves one foot, as though making himself a little more comfortable. I call to him, "Bob! Are you alright? Can you help me? I can't walk! Bob?!"

But he doesn't move, doesn't respond. Looking around me in the smoking grass, I see a short thick stick that might take some weight, and with a wince, use it as a crutch and drag myself closer to Jaloubi. Now I can see why he doesn't move, doesn't speak. From the waist up he's naked. His shirt and hat have disappeared, and he lies curled into himself, rocking slightly. The grey-brown hair on his head has been burned to the scalp. And as I get close enough, I can see that his head, twisted away from his body in agony, is a mass of blisters, welts and cuts, and windscreen glass pebbles the flesh of his chest and arms. His upper torso must have taken the full force of the explosion blowing out through the windscreen. But, except for the initial blistering flash burn when the petrol ignited, his neck and face seem unscathed.

"Shit Bob." It's all I can say, my own pain forgotten for a moment, and lowering myself down to the ground at his back, I reach out a hand to touch him...where? Finally I reach down and rest my hand on his waist, the skin of his back still downy and warm and brown, and I hold it there, hoping he can feel it. "Can you hear me?" He shudders, and clutches his arms tighter to his stomach, jerks his knees up. I lean back a little to look at him again, and it's then I see the dark stain in the red sand beneath him. A wide black patch extending out from the small of his back, from somewhere beneath the clenched arms.

He shakes again, and without opening his eyes, says just one word, "Cold." The sun is still bright, though getting lower in the sky, but I take off the rest of my shirt and lay it across his back. Leaning over him a little I can see his forearms are glistening red, as is the front of his shorts. Something has ripped into his guts and laid him open, I can see that from the amount of blood.

And now I shudder, as the horror and the fear and the pain take hold of me again.

After about thirty minutes, Rex Williams can see the low curtain of smoke on the horizon that must be a grass fire. Still about thirty kilometres away, and about ten degrees to the left of him, he drops one wing and heads toward it. In another ten minutes he is close to it, and due east, in the direction it is moving, the plane bucking and jumping a bit in the superheated air. He stays in front of it for a while, then flies along it, trying to guess its direction, its strength, and the amount of fuel on the ground in front of it, to feed it. At its north and south edges Rex can see it is already dying off, and moving ahead of the front about a kilometre, he sees it will soon run into a wide sandy creek bed, long dry and bare of trees or even fallen wood. There are no cattle in sight.

Spinning the plane around like a top he looks out for the telltale dust plume of Tom Fullarton's ute, and sees that too, about twenty kilometres away and moving parallel to the fire along an old survey road. Pulling the headphones over his ears, he turns the radio to the local CB frequency. "Tom, this is Rex, over. Tom, this is Rex, over."

The sound in his ears is so clear he could almost imagine he was racing along the track inside the ute with the stockman, "Yeah Rex, I see you up there, warm enough are you?"

Rex smiles into his mike, "I don't plan to get any closer, if that's what you mean. It's not too bad Tom. Seems to be pretty small, and it's heading for a river bed which ought to hold it up a bit. You got any stock in here?"

"Nah mate. Moved 'em out a month ago. Got a water and some yards about five miles south of you though. Uh, what do you reckon?"

Rex looks in that direction and sees the fire is moving away from it. "I say let it go. There's not much in this wind, and those yards aren't in any danger."

"Righto then. I'll just head for the yards anyway, 'case the wind changes. See what it does."

"I'll head back and see where it started. You got any campers in here you know about, could've started it?"

"Nah mate. But the mound spring is back there. Could be some bloody greenie or public servant poking around."

"I'll have a look. Out."

"OK then. Out."

Heading north to avoid passing over the top of the fire, he tilts the Cessna onto its left wing, kicking in plenty of right rudder so that he can crab along in a straight line and get a good look at the flames. In 68 years he has seen a lot of fires, most started by electrical storms, but a lot by idiots camping too, and this is not one of the worst. Out in the open paddock like this, with no stock or equipment threatened, they can burn for a couple of days without doing any damage. This one looks like it is already running out of momentum.

He rounds the northern front of the fire, and from five hundred feet up, can see clearly where the fire began. The smouldering path of the blaze is like an fan, wide at the front, then narrowing as it grows closer to the spot where it started - an arrowhead of blame pointing back about five kilometres. The sparkle of light on glass catches his eye, as does a feather of black smoke still rising into the air where everything else is smoking low and white. He turns the plane toward it, dropping a little low as he gets closer, frowning, trying to make tired old eyes that really need new glasses work harder than they are used to.

As he gets to a point about 500m back from the big mound spring, he can see the blasted troopie, smoke still rising from burning tires, and on the ground in front of it, two bodies. One, a man naked except for shorts and boots, curled into a ball, and another, a boy or girl in a singlet and not much else, startling and bright and white amid the carnage, cradling the man's head in her lap. He tips the Cessna over onto its left wing again and pivots around the accident site, making sure of what he sees. As he does, the girl looks up at him, without relief, without recognition, without waving. She watches him spin in the sky above her for a minute or so, then lowers her head again, holding a hand to shade the face of the man in her lap. Even from two hundred feet in the air, Rex Williams can see the blood.

Jesus Christ. What could make a car blow up like that? He can see pieces of wreckage lying in a semicircle out from the back of the troopie, as far as two hundred metres away. Glass from the shattered windows lies in glittering cubes in a perfect circle around them. And they are obviously very badly hurt, both of them, or they would be waving to him for help. He goes into a climbing turn and looks around desperately for a place to set the aircraft down, but the paddock is unfamiliar and he can't see a landing strip cut anywhere. He follows a heavily worked stock track desperately for a couple of minutes, hoping it will lead him to a stretch of dirt big enough for him to set down, but after five minutes, it is still meandering toward the horizon with no sign of ending, and he picks up the radio again.

"Tom, this Rex. Tom, are you there?"

"Yeah Rex, hang on..." The laconic voice is lost in a loud rattle and then a thump, then comes on again, "Sorry mate, track's a bit rough here."

"OK Tom. Listen, there's been an accident near the mound spring. A vehicle fire, and it looks like a couple of people hurt."

"Jesus, who...how bad? Are you on the ground now? I can't see you." There is another curse as the boy hits some rough road and static as the radio in his car is thrown around. "Sorry Rex, I wasn't watching the road..."

Rex cuts in over the top of the young man, "Just calm down son, and pull over, alright?"

"Righto Rex," he sounds worried, but Rex can hear his vehicle rattle to a halt, his thumb still on the call button. He comes on again, "OK, what's happening?"

"I'm still airborne, about ten kilometres south of the mound spring, but I can't see anywhere to put the plane down. Have you got a strip in here somewhere? What about that water you were talking about?"

"No, that's no good mate. We don't use it much now, if there was a strip there it's grown over by now."

The Cessna is still spinning sickeningly in the sky, horizon swinging around him as he searches for a road, some bare ground, a cleared fence line . . . Nothing.

"Help me out here Tom, I have to be able to put down somewhere!"

There is an agonising silence for a while, then the radio crackles again, "The only thing I can think of is the old survey road. It starts about 10 km southwest of the mound spring."

Flattening the plane out straight away, Rex can see the thin ribbon of dirt in the distance - it seems barely wide enough for a car, let alone an aircraft, "It's too narrow Tom, is there anything else?"

"No, no, it's not, it .... if you follow it for about 20km you'll come to a part where it widens out. We were ripping some warrens and had a D6 camped there for a few days. There's a couple of hundred metres where it's twice as wide and dead flat."

Ten kilometres to the road, twenty until he could land. Thirty kilometres from the accident. It was the best they could do.

"OK, but I need you to meet me there, we'll need your ute to get them back to the plane."

He can hear the other man's engine growl to life again, "It's that bad? I'm on my way mate - I reckon about twenty minutes. Out."

The Cessna, still only a couple of hundred feet above the ground, dips and bobs in the warm air. His hand slipping as he turns the radio frequency dial, Rex curses and then gets the frequency he wants, "Dawn, are you there luv? Come in Dawn."

She is obviously still sitting at the radio, waiting for news, because she comes on immediately, "Dawn here Rex, how is it? I've got Cath on the phone at the moment."

"Forget Cath. There's been an accident by Fullarton's mound spring. Vehicle fire. Looks like two people hurt, and we're going to need the Flying Doctor Dawnie."

"My God Rex, who's hurt?"

"Don't know luv. I'm still in the air, and I'm just about to put down about thirty km southwest of them. Young Tom is going to meet me there and we'll head out to the accident, and...bring the people back to my plane." He thinks hard, racking his memory for a nearby landmark the air ambulance pilot would know, "Uh...tell the air ambulance to go to the Fullarton's old homestead and call us when they get there, we'll....we'll give them directions from there. I'd fly 'em straight to Coober Pedy, but I don't know how bad they are."

"Right Rex. You OK luv? You sound a bit..." she lets the words hang, knows he doesn't like it when she worries.

He looks through the windscreen at the swaying horizon and thin red ribbon of road in front of him, "I'm alright. Even from up here...there was a lot of blood, Dawn."

Bob Jaloubi is in a world *beyond* pain. There is only good and bad. The soft pillow of the girl's legs under his head, that is good. The bright sun on his face, when her hand moves, that is bad. The feeling in his torso, though he couldn't call it pain, he knows is bad, but if he keeps his knees pulled up high and his arms clenched tight around his middle, that's good. He's still cold, but that's OK, and he could open his eyes but he doesn't want to.

He can't focus on one thought for very long, doesn't really comprehend what has happened, but some part of him, separate from everything else, realises with clarity that he is dying. This part of him is sad. The sadness of a journey incomplete, interrupted. Things undone. Things done which can't be undone. Things not said. Never said. A deep grief over time wasted. An urgency comes over him now and he opens his eyes, seeing but not seeing. Light filtering through fingers hovering above his brow, and beyond them the girl. Sharon?

He hears a voice, a girl's voice, reply to him, but the words mean nothing. He doesn't know if he is talking, or thinking, but he wills her to hear. There is so much she should know. He doesn't want Sharon to live without knowing any more. To hear things after he is gone, and wonder why he never told her. Maybe be hurt. Maybe not understand.

A spasm runs the length of his body and he lets it pass, knowing it hurts, but somehow standing outside it, observing quietly until it passes. Her fingers flutter over his eyes, and the light is like light through the green leaves of trees, flickering and warm. Her voice stirs him again. So much unsaid. Can she hear him? Does she understand? It doesn't matter, she'll understand one day.

I look down at Bob, his mouth running out an endless string of words that make no sense. I want to jam my ears shut against him unburdening. He thinks I'm Sharon, so I can't do anything but listen.

I look up to the sky again and see an aircraft disappear into the haze. Neither its appearance nor disappearance have any meaning. I'm too tired and hurt to give a shit. If rescue comes now or in the night, it'll come too late. I shift my leg a little and Bob stops talking, groans, starts mumbling again..

I try to soothe his face. Holding my hand out to block the worst of the sun, blowing with dry cracking lips across his blistered forehead. But the blowing just dries my mouth even more and I start to feel frantic, panicky. I need water, but where? All our water was in the wagon and it's a freaking wreck, there would be no water left there would there? In the radiator...could I drink that? Or the little tank of water for the wipers? Then I realise the esky is still sitting where we left it, green and bright and untouched by blast or debris. It's about ten metres away, and easing myself out from under Bob, I strip off my singlet and make it into a small pillow for his head. It takes me five minutes to drag myself over to the esky. Lifting the lid, a column of cool air spills out to greet me and I fan it over my body. I grab a handful of ice and water and pour it over my head and neck, grab ice and rub it on my shoulders, burned dark red by the flames. The cold shocks me, brings me back to life, and I plunge my hand in again, pouring the water into my mouth, face, down my chest.

Bob. Got to get some to Bob. Now I pull myself onto my right foot, stand again, feeling stronger. Thanking heaven and earth I'm alive, not badly hurt, not dying yet, like him... I shrug the thought away, and shuffle the esky closer to Bob, hopping on my right leg, my left foot hanging limp and useless. Then, while I'm still up, still mobile, and still have this burst of bloody minded energy, I take up the branch I used as a crutch before and limp back to the canvas tarpaulin. With an effort that nearly makes me puke, I drag this over to Bob too, and throw it across him, dragging the esky near his head to keep the tarp from coming into contact with his blood wet scalp. There is enough scrub around us that I can attach a couple of corners onto nearby bushes to make a low tent, and I crawl in and collapse next to him. His lips are still moving but his voice is faint and hoarse, and lifting the esky lid again I pull out some chunks of ice, running one across his lips. His tongue darts out hungrily and I cup my hand into the water and lift out a palm full, dribbling it slowly into his mouth. He coughs, but swallows, and I give him two or three more before finally it seems he has had enough. Then, taking a chilled bottle from deep in the water, I roll it over his scalded cheeks and forehead. Some skin sticks to the plastic but he doesn't seem to notice.

His eyes, which had been tightly closed, relax a little, fluttering slightly, but he doesn't open them.

Sleep, now that seems like a good idea.

Hot air rising from the ground is like a foam cushion underneath the Cessna as Rex Williams tries to persuade it to land on the short dirt clearing in front of him. He is trying to set down on a straight strip of about two hundred metres in length, but it is only twenty metres wide, and the westerly wind is intent on pushing him into the scrub. At each end of the strip, the survey road it is made out of begins again and the scrub closes in abruptly. The Cessna is nearly diagonal to the line of landing as he makes his final approach, and the hot air is bumping the aircraft up and down dramatically. Picking his moment, on the edge of a stall, he cuts power to the engine, letting the weight of the plane force it down to earth the last few feet and with a thud his right wheel hits, and he scuds along the dirt for about twenty metres before his left wheel slams down too and the world behind him is suddenly a storm of billowing dust and tumbling brush. He pulls up with a good eighty metres to spare, realising that he'll need all of it to get off again, but thankful that the widened section of road looks big enough for the Flying Doctor's Twin Beech to set down on too. He taxis his plane to the very end of the strip and tickling the throttle gently, pushes the nose into the uncleared, single width of the old survey road, trying to keep as much of the strip free as he can. When he can't push in any further without chopping trees and shrubs with his prop, he cuts the engine.

He calls his wife to make sure the doctor is on the way, and then clambers from the plane. Then there is nothing for him to do except pace up and down in the shade underneath the wings until, with a far off rumble, he see the approaching dust plume of Tom Fullarton's ute. The flat-bed troopie, a big fire-fighting tank and pump unit loaded on the back, pulls up behind his plane and Rex jogs over to the passenger door and throws himself in.

It is no cooler inside the cab than out, and a thick layer of red dirt covers everything. Young Tom is about 28, wearing a clean blue-checked shirt and filthy jeans, the arse of which Rex knows by experience, will hang halfway down his backside when he stands up. His elbows and knuckles are made for brawling, sharp and strong, and as he grips the wheel and spins the troopie around, Rex can see his hands are white. His face is lean and brown and the pupils in his dark eyes are wide with adrenaline from the frantic driving. He nods to the older man, "Rex."

"Tom," Rex leans down to check the radio, "This switched on? Flying doctor might call in..."

"Yeah, 'course."

As they head up the road they are heading toward a horizon of smoke. They say nothing to each other for fifteen minutes until they are through the gate at the bend in the survey road. Rex, knowing the paddock is empty of cattle, hauling the gate open and leaving it hanging wide before climbing back into the cab.

"Better hang on tight, there's no track here," Tom says tightly, as he begins to bash through the scrub, only diverting for the biggest logs or rabbit warrens. Rex, who in the '60s did some time in the army as loader in a Centurion tank, feels a sense of deja vu as he is catapulted around the bare tin cab of the Toyota. Tools, dirt and rust from the floor are jumping in the air around his knees, and pipes and fencing wire behind their seats are threatening to bludgeon them in the back of the neck. But Tom keeps the nose of the ute pointed at the thin column of black smoke about ten kilometres away and soon they are coming up on it.

Tom slows down instinctively as they close the last 100 metres. The burnt out wreck has its back to them and they can see the whole rear end has disappeared, leaving only the burning wheels on the chassis. Tom knows that a fire in a petrol tank can't do that, cars only explode in American movies, so this must have been something more. The glass in all the windows has been blown out too, and the cabin of the ute itself is canted forward, as though pushed with a giant hand.

Rex recognises the signs. "Coober Pedy miner," he says.

"You reckon?"

The bonnet has been flung open too, and is charred black from a fire in the engine space. As he pulls up a few metres away from the front of the wreck, he can see a tarp slung over some bush, and two figures huddled underneath.

Rex climbs from the car, standing tentatively with the door still open, one foot still in the cab, as though afraid to go closer, "Hello!" he calls, "You need some help there?" It's a stupid question, he realises, but what else should he say? *Hello, are you alive?* There is no reply and he and Tom exchange a look, then run quickly over to the canvas. Squatting down Rex can see two heads lying side by side, one raw and burned, the other, a woman or girl, twists toward him at the sound of his feet and she tilts her face up to his. Her eyes gaze blankly at him for a while, a startling blue, then she blinks and lowers her head to the ground again.

"Let's get this off Rex," Tom says, standing and pointing to the tarpaulin, and each grabbing a corner they haul it back. Rex Williams will never forget the horror of that moment, so unprepared is he for what he sees. He has butchered cattle himself for the homestead, so he is used to blood, but he had no idea the human body held so much, or could lose so much. The man is hunched in a foetal curl, a circle of blood soaking the sand around his waist out to about two feet. Close to him it is thick and red, further away already dark and dry. A mass of flies have gathered. And the small woman, naked except for boots, bra and shorts, lying on her side, her shoulders and back scarred and cut, her torso sticky with the man's blood, a rough reddened bandage

279

over her upper left leg showing that she has been hurt too. Another pool of blood lies at her feet.

Rex kneels down at her head again. The sun is not so strong now, a warm soft glow in the lower west that makes long shadows from the scrub. Where should he touch her? He settles for resting a hand on her short cropped hair, "Can you hear me lass? Where are you hurt?"

She twists her neck to look up at him again, staring at him for a moment and then replying tonelessly, "My leg is hurt. I can't walk."

"OK, we can carry you. The air ambulance is on its way, but we have to take you in the car for a bit. Is it OK if we lift you?"

She nods, lowering her head again and hugging her arms to her bare chest in an act of modesty that breaks his heart. He stands and pops the pearl buttons on his own shirt as he quickly tears it off, draping it gently over the cuts and blood on her back. Gesturing to Tom to help with her leg, Rex bends down to take her under the shoulders and waist and lift her up. He tries to slide his hand under her, but her skin is sticky with blood and when he pulls it away it is wet and caked in clotted sand. Suddenly his stomach rises into his throat and he turns, retching into the dirt.

"It's OK Rex, I got her," Tom says softly, bending and lifting Jones in one easy motion. Her body smells of sweat, sand and wood smoke, and he sees her wince as he walks slowly to the ute. "You'll be right," he says, "You're going to be fine now." Her head lolls against his shoulder and he can feel her thighs slick his arms with sweat. He lowers her into the passenger seat of the ute, throwing out the crap on the floor to make room for her injured leg. He is about to walk back to Rex when he notices she is still sitting with her arms crossed over her chest. The other man's shirt flapping loose across her front.

"Here, we can put this on a bit better." She sits looking at him numbly, so he takes one of her arms, guiding it into the sleeve. He lifts it carefully off her shoulders so that it won't drag on the skin and guides her other arm into the sleeve and then buttons it in front. . "You're going to be OK," he says again.

Rex is kneeling by the wounded man, and turns and shouts to Tom, "He's unconscious. Jesus, it's all blood...ask her where he's hurt. Maybe we shouldn't move him."

Tom is about to speak, but Jones, staring out blankly through the windscreen, has heard and she cuts him short, "He's dead. Died a while ago."

Just then the radio in the ute crackles to life and Tom leans across her to pick up the handset. "Tom Fullarton here, over."

Another crackle, and then a voice breaks through the static, ."...ing Doctor, Carlo here Tom. We're circling over the old homestead now mate, can you tell us where to go from here? Over"

Picturing a route in his mind's eye, Tom gives the pilot a series of landmarks that will take him to the old survey road. "Follow that north for about fifty klicks and you'll see Rex Williams plane parked at one end of a wider part of the road. You should be able to put down there. We'll meet you with the injured."

"Wait on Tom...just fill me in a bit first, what have you got there? Dawn reported a vehicle fire. Over." The concern in the dcotor's voice is evident, obviously he is also worried they might hurt critically injured patients by trying to move them.

Tom turns his back on Jones, dropping his voice and holding the handset close to his mouth, "There's a girl with a bad injury in her leg, she's lost some blood, she's a bit cut up but she's not bleeding now. She can't talk much. Maybe shock or something." He looks over to Rex again, who is now sitting on the roo-bar of the burned out troopie with his head in his hands. It is hard to say from this distance, but he thinks the old man is crying. "But the other bloke is dead. Looks like there was an explosion in the back of their car. That's all Carlo."

"OK Tom. Can you take a pulse? Check he is dead will you? She might have made a mistake. And don't move him, we'll have to check for ourselves, or the cops will. Talk to you in a few minutes. Out... Hang, on, you still there Tom?"

"Yeah Carlo."

"Find out their names, we'll radio through to Coober Pedy police. Out."

"Righto. Out." Tom hangs the handset back in its cradle and sees Jones is crying silently. Thin white lines of water running through the dirt and smoke on her cheeks. He takes her chin in his hand and turns her face to look at him.

"What's your name?" he asks softly.

The tears stop, "Charlie Jones."

"I'm going to take you to the doctor now Charlie. What's your friend's name?"

"He's dead."

"I know. But we have to tell the police. What's his name?"

She pulls her chin out of his hand and stares ahead again, silent. There are a million other questions he wants to ask her. What were you doing messing around out here? How did the car blow up? What the hell happened?... but instead he walks back to Rex, carefully not looking at the body of Bob Jaloubi, stopping beside the old pastoralist to put a hand on his shoulder before leaning down to put two fingers against the dead man's peeling neck. The skin is still warm, but there is no pulse, and Tom can see he isn't breathing.

"We have to go Rex. Carlo called in and I gave him the story. He said to leave this fella here," Tom says. "He also asked if we could get their names, for the police."

Rex takes a deep breath and stands, brushing his hands on his jeans, "Yep. Fine. He's dead all right. Did you find out who they are?"

Tom shakes his head as they walk to the ute, "She's in shock I reckon. Not saying much." As they get to the car Tom points to the tray behind, "You'll have to ride in the back Rex. 'Less you want to drive..."

"No, that's fine," Rex says and walks around to the back. He is about to haul himself up onto the tray top when he has an idea. Walks back around to the driver's side window, "You have a pen there Tom? I'll just get the car rego off the front. Maybe the police can use that to work out who these blokes are."

"Good thinking mate," Tom says, leaning over to the glovebox and pawing through it to find a chewed pencil and some paper.

When Karn comes to, she's lying on a cot in Amir's office. She's not tied down or anything, but Victor is sitting there behind the desk, with Gaddafi beside him. She sits up, and the dog looks at her, but he doesn't growl. Doesn't need to.

"Man, youse really screwed up," Victor says, like it's something to be admired. "You're running around like blue arsed flies, while the whole time you had the freaking PKK staying in the same hotel as you."

She doesn't get it at all, still a bit groggy. "I have no idea what you're on about. Where's Charlie?"

He leers, "Your *girlfriend?* Man I wish I had video of you two going at it. Hate to be the one to tell you, but she's dead by now. Amir told me to take care of her and his piece of shit druggie brother in law, so I did. Ka-boom." He grins.

"What the hell does that mean?"

"Means when we found out him and your girlfriend were going bush, I rigged their troopie with enough ANFO to shred anything within a hundred yards. Fixed the det to a timer, set to blow around the time they got out to the mound spring, no help around for miles...yeah, they're history."

He's talking like she should be impressed how clever he is. She doesn't start crying. Deep down she just doesn't believe him... Levers herself up onto an elbow, "So, why am *I* alive?"

283

Victor shrugs, "Beats the shit outa me. Amir must like you. I'd have knocked you on the head and thrown you down a hole by now. But he said call him when you wake up because he wants to say goodbye personally."

Goodbye because he's leaving, or goodbye because I am, she wonders.

He reads her mind. "Dunno what the plan is for you," he shrugs, "But we're outa here, bags all packed, and a plane waiting for us, is all I know."

She knows she should be scared. But she has a blinding headache and this whole scene is too surreal. She's wondering how long she's got to wait, when the door opens and Amir wheels in.

"Ah, beautiful lady, you are awake." He throws some papers and Jones' laptop and bag on her bed, which he's apparently had taken out of their hotel room. He holds up Jones' Security Service ID, then throws it on the bed too.

"Hey, I'm not..."

"Not with the mukhabarat? The secret police? I know," he says, "Harith thought maybe you were but then the idea of two such ladies in the spy service, it is just not probable except in Hollywood. We find only Charlie Johns' papers in your room, so for you we think, OK, she really is just the girlfriend."

Just the girlfriend. In another life, she'd hit him for that. Cripple or not.

"Johns would have fooled old Amir you know, with this whole routine of buying the hotel. Unlucky for you, Harith is watching my video cameras one day and sees you and Johns walking in. Says to himself, hey, isn't that the girl we whacked on the head in the barber shop and threw her in the wheelie bin? The girl who said she was with that traitor Serwan. The girl he saw on television every night for a week, shooting one of his men."

Freaking Jones, Youtube mega star. She butts in, "Harith who?"

He cocks his head, "Of course, you were not introduced properly. Soon you will be. We wait for Harith."

"For what?"

284

"To...decide."

She stares at him, old man sitting there in his wheelchair. Victor picking dirt from his fingernails. Gaddafi licking his chops.

"What the *hell* is this all about?"

He looks up. Cocks an eyebrow, "It is simple, no? There is a war, Australia is a part of that war, I am a soldier in it. As is Victor," Victor gives a dirty thumbs up. "You, beautiful lady, are what they call collateral damage."

"You're Australian for God's sake! Who made it your war?"

"Lebanese Australian."

"Australia is at war with Lebanon?"

"Me against my brother. Me and my brother against my cousin. Me, my brother and cousin against our neighbours," he shrugs, then nods at Victor, "Not him though. He's with Islamic Liberation Front, from the Philippines. You know it?"

"No."

"They are freedom fighters. I send them money. I send the Kurds some money too. Well, a lot of money. Then they come to me, say they need explosives, I say why not. Harith needs somewhere to hide, I say sure, come here, I got swimming pool!" he laughs. "Harith has grandchildren you know, two of them. Girls. He made a call to them. They say to him Grandfather, watch out for sharks down there." He cackles, "Ha! Sharks..."

"I still don't get..."

"What? You think I owe this country something? Everything I got here, I dug out the ground myself. Maybe there was a time I think, yeah, I'm an Aussie. Then the Americans go after the oil and start killing Muslims – Iraq, Afghanistan, now Syria, Australia standing there under the American flag. Amir has to choose sides. Is he nobody, or is he Muslim? You remember about the girl in Tripoli?"

"I remember."

"I let her die. I said to myself, Amir, they are killing your people again. Do something this time, don't just hide up a crane, or down a hole."

"Well, you did something. All those people dead in Sydney, happy now?" Gaddafi growls at her tone, so she scowls back at him.

Amir stares at her a while, "Five dead is nothing. Ten thousand is nothing. You compare five dead to 100,000 Muslims dead in Iraq, another 50,000 in Afghanistan? Libya? Syria? Where is next? Shall I tell you? Iran, trying to build a bomb to defend itself and waiting to be attacked by the Americans every day. How many dead Muslims when Israel or America go into Iran eh?"

He believes what he is saying, she can see that in his eyes, "I get it, you put it that way." *Go with it Karn.* But he doesn't buy it.

"No, you don't, but maybe when you get to heaven you will see, ah, that old Lebbo, he was bloody right!" He thumps his fist down on the table. Victor looks up from picking his nails and nods. Hell yes.

Gaddafi wags his tail, enjoying the sound of his master's conviction.

And then the old wrinkled man who must be Harith walks in, kindly old grandfather with his two grand-daughters, part time Kurdish barber and terrorist. He shuts the big soundproof bank vault door behind him.

Smiles hello at Amir, takes a handgun out of his waistband and shoots Gaddafi in the head. Then Victor, in the chest. Then, as he glares angrily at him from his wheelchair, Amir. Twice.

You want to know what it's like when a big handgun goes off inside a five meter by five meter underground office?

Put a tin rubbish bin on your head, and then bang it with a crowbar. That's what.

Harith pushes Victor's body off the chair and sits down at the desk. Brown, wrinkled, grey pepperpot stubbly hair and jaws. Tired eyes.

"Hello, friend of the brave little mukhabarat girl."

At least, Karn thinks that is what he says, if she could concentrate through her ears ringing, her blinding headache and the feeling of warm piss pooling on the mattress under her.

"If you were counting, that was four shots. This is a nine round magazine," he looks down at his gun. "But I will only need one more," he says, as though this is supposed to be a comfort. So what is he freaking waiting for?

He looks at the carnage on the floor, at Amir slumped in his chair, blood spreading from the holes in his chest. He shrugs, "Loose ends. We cannot have loose ends."

He gets up and walks over to the bed, picks up Charlie's ID, "I am sorry about your friend. More loose ends. My condolences for her death, she was very brave, but she knew the danger."

"She's not dead you arsehole. I don't believe it." She still doesn't.

He looks at her curiously, "You have spirit to match the colour of your hair. And, Amir told me, smart too. I have a favour to ask you. You would be smart to agree."

She looks at him, "You have the gun."

He looks at it. "Yes, I do." From his back pocket he pulls photographs of two small children. "My grand daughters," he says, handing the photos to her.

She takes them, hands shaking despite her bravado, "Amir told me."

"Turn them over," he says, making a circling motion with his finger.

On the back she sees names, and what look like the words Red Crescent, and some addresses and telephone numbers.

287

"They are in a camp in Jordan," he explains. "Their mother and father are dead. Killed by Turkish bombs. Or American. Or Russian. It doesn't matter."

She looks down at the two small round faces, little girls like a million others, dressed in party dresses, pink and green.

"Happier times," he says, watching her.

"What do you want from me?" she asks.

"I will let you live," he says simply, "If you promise me to get this package to them." From his pocket he takes a thick envelope. "If I just put it in the post, it will never find them. But you have honest eyes. I think if you promise me you will get them this package, then probably you will try." He hands it to her.

She takes it, sees the same names and addresses printed on the envelope, money inside.

He points the pistol at her now, "Do you promise?"

She swallows, or tries to, "I promise. Yes."

He looks a little sad. "Good. I know you will honour your word. They are good girls," he smiles. "You will like them." Makes a small circle around her face with the gun, "God is Great, yes?"

"Sure."

And puts the gun in his mouth.

Bang.

The truth is just a story that fits the facts. The way this story goes, you've got five cashed up Kurdish PKK fighters who want to blow up the Turkish Consulate. Their cover is they're just down here to recruit a few warm bodies for the cause, but they've got their target sussed, they've got the vehicle and the Consulate is a nice soft target, low fences, not reinforced, you can drive right up to the back door. They need money, but they get that organised too, thanks to Serwan and his crew. Then they get a phone call from Erbil in Iraq, get told to take care of the thing with Barrak, but that's a sideshow, and they hand him off to some local support to deal with. A little favour to Jabhat al-Akrad is always useful.

Now they need about a tonne of Ammonium Nitrate Fuel Oil explosive but their cover is blown, the police are looking for them, they can't get the ingredients on the open market. So a contact puts them in touch with Amir. Explosives? No problem. He sorts them out with some amped up ANFO in 44 gallon drums, detonators and timers – gets it driven to Sydney overnight.

Then the mukhabarat close on them. Harith loses his best men. But not all of them. There are still enough to carry it through, and one who will drive the suicide car. It is done.

Now Harith needs somewhere to lay low, to work out how he can get back to Iraq, but he's hardly in Coober Pedy a couple of days and sees Charlie Jones of the mukhabarat sniffing around old Amir and his crew. It's all too messy.

Time to put everyone on the Paradise Express.

Epilogue

So I sit in the hot evening stillness of a Musalla courtyard, listening to an Imam drone his way through the Salat al-Janazah, the funeral service, my eyes keep getting drawn to Karn. It's only been two days and I had to make a scene to get let out of hospital but what could they do?

Muslims have to bury their dead within three. Bob, Amir, Victor. Old Harith isn't going to paradise on a direct flight, the police have impounded his body.

When Karn got to the hospital at Port Augusta, she kind of lost it. I'm a bit of a train wreck. Leg in bandages, got a thin zipper-like cut down the side of my neck from a flying fragment of burning metal. Doctor told me it will fade with time – I have to stay out of the sun, rub it with vitamin E cream. Karn spent about twenty minutes going over the other marks. The puckered ridge of the wound on the back of my leg. The pinpricks and dots across my stomach and back, where they spent hours pulling tiny pieces of shrapnel from me, using an ultrasound wand like a metal detector, but leaving anything smaller than a pinhead to work its own way out. I made a joke about how we both have freckles now, but she wasn't laughing.

Shirley flew over and signed me out of the hospital, hired us a car and then drove me and Karn back up here. Karn filled me in on the whole scene back at the hotel. Shirley kept asking, did we need to see a shrink, a counsellor. Karn said no, but made her stop at a bottle shop and we got a bottle of bourbon and we drank that and passed out somewhere near Woomera. We had a police escort, but I think that was more to make sure we didn't disappear before they'd asked all their questions.

Shirley dropped me off at the police station, and then she and Karn went to the hotel to get Sharon. *Sharon's* hotel now, since Amir actually left it to her, not Bob. Yeah, she's freaking out at the thought of that. Said she's definitely going to sell it, thinks there is no way she could run it. I think she could.

We all sit on carpets in the women's row at the back. First two rows full of men, miners mostly. Staff from the hotel, Amir's contractors. Locals who don't mind kneeling on carpets in the dirt at the back of a tin shed which is the closest Coober Pedy has to a mosque.

The Imam from Adelaide is praying, some of the people following along, most with no clue what's going on. Star Force cops are here, looking like storm troopers, about ten of them. The rest of the SA police force has Coober Pedy in lock down. Media everywhere, interviewing anything that moves.

Sharon starts to cry and Karn pulls her head onto her shoulder. I thought she'd blame us for everything, but with Amir and Bob gone, she's crawled into Karn's nice strong arms and that's probably the only reason she hasn't gone off and overdosed on something. Shirley reaches out and takes my hand, makes me feel like a schoolgirl.

This sucks. For me, for Bob, for Sharon, for Amir's damned soul. For the people who died in the bombing and the ones who killed them. For a dead Kurdish kid with a knife. The two little girls whose pictures Karn has in her purse. For Barrak the panel beater and the Delta Forces soldier.

For everyone destroyed by this freaking endless miserable war, including myself.

I can feel the eyes of the small crowd on me. Glances over shoulders, sideways looks. Burning into my neck in the courtyard of the Musalla, staring at me from under sun-bleached towelling hats or black police helmets. My presence is a flag of guilt flapping in the wind of their suspicion. To the locals, I'm the reason the town is like a prison camp now. To the police, I'm the one who screwed up the whole operation, left them with four dead terrorists and a headless dog.

Screw 'em. I'm the one has to get through this.

And when I do, I'm going to take Karn and make an honest woman out of her, somewhere a long long way from here.

From the Author

Thanks very much for supporting 'Direct Publishing' as a way for authors to see their works come to life without the barrier of finding an agent or publisher.

I would love to hear from you on the Charlie Jones Facebook page

https://www.facebook.com/teejayslee/

or on my Goodreads author page

https://www.goodreads.com/teejayslee

Where you will also be able to read excerpts from the next title in the Charlie Jones series: '*Cloister*'.

Cheers

TJ

Preview of 'Cloister', volume II in the Charlie Jones series.

2 years later...

Of course, you know it's not going to be just another day at the convent when the Archbishop calls you and starts the conversation with, "Sister Jones, is it true you used to work for the Security Service?"

"Yes, your honour."

"It's *Your Eminence*, Jones. You call a judge Your Honour."

"Sorry Your Eminence, still getting into the habit."

"Yes. But you have started your novitiate have you not?"

"About six months and 200 bedpans ago, Your Eminence."

"Do I detect a hint of a whinge there Sister?"

"No Your Eminence, you detect a blatant whine. You didn't get the pun, did you? *Getting into the habit?*"

"Mercy nuns don't wear a habit Sister."

"Still. I've been wanting to say that for ages. I knew I should have said, 'so to speak'."

"Quite. Well, we have a situation Sister Jones, and I need to talk to you about how we might use your, uhm, special skills."

I have to think about this for a minute. After all, I left the Security Service for some pretty good reasons.

Namely, the fact that in the space of a few weeks toward the end there, I was knocked unconscious three times, stabbed once, and had my girlfriend kidnapped and then blown up.

Yes, I said girlfriend. And yes, I eschewed all that when I started my novitiate. (Eschewed being the word Father Thomas used in my spiritual counselling sessions, it being more final sounding than the one I preferred, which was 'parked'.)

OK, minute's up.

"Well Your Eminence, I have some wet sheets and a pile of laundry waiting, but I think I can fit you in. Would now be convenient?"

I've never met the man before, and I don't know what you think a Catholic Archbishop's private digs should look like, but personally I was expecting Point Piper, or Mosman, big round driveway with perfectly manicured lawns, monsignor at the door acting as a butler and a spry little old lady who's a dab hand at scones, serving us tea with slices of lemon.

The Arch meets me himself, at the door of a house in Parramatta that looks like a red brick knock down, it's ten a.m. on a Tuesday and he's dressed in a cardie.

"Oh, hello you... must be...Sister Jones," he says, as though he's surprised. Maybe it's my height. I've learned over the years that people expect me to be taller. Blame James Bond. Or maybe it's the fact I arrived on a Vespa, wearing black bike leathers, taking off my helmet to reveal cropped hair and a diamond nose stud.

Hold out my hand, "In the flesh."

"Yes, come in," he ushers me into the cramped hallway and watches while I dump all my gear. "I can uhm, see why you chose the Order of the Sisters of Mercy."

"Your Eminence, have you ever tried on a Dominican nun's habit?"

"No! Well, no, of course not."

"The skirt's like a cooking apron. Blouse like a...like a...well, a blouse. And it's not that I mind shaving my head, obviously, to get the veil on, but it gets so sweaty up there you end up scratching like you've got nits. Mercy Sisters go mufti, it's a better fit."

He cocks his head and smiles, "Most of us are guided in our choice of Order by a deep spiritual affinity with its ethos, or its founder, or divine intervention by a Saint...I suspect only a few are guided by fashion. No matter, I agree, at first blush the Mercy Sisters are probably a good fit."

"See, there you go," I say, as we walk into a small study. "And would I be right in saying that, judging by the way you use words like *affinity*, and *ethos*, that you are a Jesuit?"

He reaches for a pair of reading glasses on his desk, gesturing to a chair for me to sit, "Very good Jones, you've been doing your homework?"

"No, actually," I admit, "I knew an old spook who studied for the Jesuit order before he dropped out and became a spook."

"I think I may have heard that..."

"He also used words like ethos. Used to routinely correct my split infinitives."

"Uhm, *routinely to correct*, I think you'll find..."

"See, you guys can't resist. We called him the Black Pope."

"I didn't hear that," he smiles again. Not sure if it's a warm smile, a patronising smile, a worried smile or a token smile, "Now, to business."

Token smile.

I'm wondering, actually, as we sit in his little cosy study, why we are not meeting at the big office I know he has on Macquarie Street, where he would be kitted out in at least his black robes and I'm sure he has a personal assistant who should be briefing me instead.

Why, Jones, are we getting the fireside chat in front of no witnesses?

"You may have heard that Pope Michael the First will be visiting Australia," he says, smiling at his own understatement.

Duh. I'm a nun - it's a fair bet I've heard that el Papa is coming to town. OK, he's not Bono, but amongst the girls in the convent he's the closest thing to a rock star we're going to get. Plus I think old Sister Angela has the hots for him. It's the Portuguese accent.

"Yes, I did hear that. In fact, Father Thomas has installed a fluorescent countdown timer behind the pulpit which he watches when no one is looking. '28 Days-To-Go', right?"

"Is it that soon, oh dear," he says, ruffling through some papers. He hands me a folder, "And now it seems we have what your former colleagues are calling, A Credible Threat."

I take the folder, sit it in my lap. Look at him.

"You aren't reading it," he observes. Good skills, guess that's why he gets the big bucks. "If you look on the first page…"

"No. First," I raise my finger, "There is something you should know."

He blinks, "Oh. No, well, I think I probably do know," he says. Reaches into his desk, pulls out another folder from a drawer. Opens it up and reads, "Sister Charlie Jones. Yes…uhm… Bachelor of Arts Politics, student activist…researcher for the State Minister of Housing…joined the Security Service…four years in surveillance, two years as an uhm, case officer…"

He holds a newspaper clipping up and shows it to me (*picture of a girl with a gun, on her knees in a pool of her own blood, beside a dead terrorist*), the headline says, "WHO IS SHE?" Underneath that (I know it by heart, don't have to try to read it), "She gunned down a terrorist in broad daylight and the video taken by a witness went viral, but the Security Service won't confirm she exists. This brave girl may have saved Sydney from a major terrorist attack but we might never find out her identity."

"Not my best day," I grimace, "And I didn't actually shoot him…it was…more complicated than it looked on TV." I tell him. No one ever believes that, true as it is. I look at the picture again. Secretly I love the fact I made the front page, and I think the photo looks pretty cool. It's a grainy shot taken from the video, but it's from the side so you can't see my big ass. My hair was cropped even shorter back then. I was wearing tight black jeans, a white T-shirt and Doc Martin boots. You ask me, I look a bit like Natalie Portman from that movie '*V' for Vendetta*. With a gun. And a limp. Less bosom. OK, nothing like her.

He looks back at his folder, "Just weeks later, you're…uhm…"

"In Coober Pedy, where I got blown up?"

"Yes…hurt in an explosion…and your *companion* …"

"Girlfriend, in the biblical sense…"

"…uh…was lucky to escape with her life."

"It was the same fools. We got a couple of them, but their B team was still in play. Bunch of dickless wonders."

"Quite, Sister." Pulls his glasses over his nose, frowns. "But she…your friend… survived."

"And I've forgiven them for that."

"I…yes, very Christian of you."

"*She* hasn't though. She's a redhead. You know what they're like. Last time we spoke she said if I come near her again, she will gut me with a pair of dress scissors and make my hide into a tutu."

"…"

"She's a set designer, your Holiness," I explain.

Pushes his glasses back up, "Call me Cardinal, it will be simpler."

"Cardinal?"

"It's my title."

"Right you are, Cardinal, Sir."

He looks at me, "Or Brian. It might be easier." Returns to his personnel file, "Father Thomas recommended you for vocation…and here you are, a novitiate."

"Here I am. And it hasn't been an easy road, let me tell you, Cardinal."

He raises an eyebrow, "Really?"

"Oh, was that sarcasm?"

"Not at all. Worldly desires, left behind Sister. Vows of devotion unto and only to God? Ring a bell?"

I lean across his desk, "Still a Novice Cardinal. Vows come later. This is just my second year, and putting rosary beads around your neck doesn't take away your libido - it just makes you less stressed about the whole 'is-she isn't-she' thing."

He stands, gives a little 'lets get this back on track' cough, "Erm. So, there was something else I should know?"

"Yes."

"Yes?"

"Yes. I'm done with all that crap, Cardinal. I came into the Mercy Sisters to find a different life. Father Thomas says it's a calling, I call it a life-choice but in the end it's the same." I grab the newspaper clipping from the desk. "This isn't me. This is some screwed up idiot who thought the world was just good guys and bad guys and being one of the good guys was all you needed in life."

I rip it in half. Pretty cool really, except I don't rip it all the way through, so I rip it again for emphasis. I continue, "OK, changing bed pans and making broccoli soup in between mass and scripture lessons isn't exactly my dream job, but every club has its initiation, and I'm getting through it. It's all I want right now."

"Someone wants to kill the Pope when he visits Australia," he says simply. Looks at me like he expects me to wig out.

I'm supposed to be shocked? It's the *Pope* - he must be an equal first on the assassins club Top 10 wish list with the President of the US of A and Vlad Putin. Neo conservative loonies are lining up to kill him for being too lenient on contraception, liberal loonies lining up to kill him for being anti choice, and loony loonies lining up just to get their names in the history books for killing a Pope.

"So?" I shrug.

"So!?" he sputters, "The Holy Father is coming to Australia and a plot to kill him has been uncovered and you say...*so?!*"

"Look, don't get me wrong. I wish his Holiness a long and

fruitful Popeship. But I am a Mercy Sister novitiate who spends her day changing the nappies on the old dears at the convent and her nights picking kids out of doorways in Newtown."

"Well, yes, but..."

"*Sooooo...* what has this got to do with me?"

He stands and goes to the window, contemplating the view over the back yard full of weeds. "My office has been overrun. They've set up a situation room in the boys dorm..."

"They what?"

"An unused dorm, of the Boy's College. You know, behind the Cathedral. With the visit of his Holy Father to organise it was the only space that could disceetly be used! I didn't want them in our admin offices on Liverpool Street, scaring everyone to death. The dorm has fibre to the node broadband now!"

I smile, "Well that could come in handy later for the boys when they want watch those naughty videos."

"That's not amusing. The Police are trying to alter the Pope's itinerary - an itinerary it has taken years to agree." He is babbling now, "And they insist we cannot advise people why the itinerary must be changed, just that it must. The restrictions are extraordinary, They are demanding to know who is on the guest list for every single event at which His Holiness will be present, and they will conduct background checks...but will it be possible to complete all of these background checks in time for the actual events? Oh, no, they can't guarantee that, so there may be some people who will miss out, you'll just have to find some excuse for them...as though I can just say to the Archbishop of Tonga, I'm sorry, the police weren't able to interview your referees in time, being as you are from *Tonga*, you'll just have to go home without meeting Pope Michael..."

I cough, "You're raving Cardinal, Brian, Sir."

He turns and smooths his shirt, "You're right, I am. And that is because I find since this, plot, has emerged, I have lost all control over the Holy Father's visit and this is not a situation I can accept. The Protocol Team of the Holy See arrived in town a few days ago. Poking their noses into everything, demanding access to every single building, road or tree the Pope might sit under. Worse than the police. They are treating me like an idiot, giving me a five minute briefing every day, while I run around fielding phone calls from clergy all over the diocese who are being interviewed like they are criminals. And I always find out what they are doing, *after* they've gone and done it!"

I try to help him along, "Soooooo..."

"Then I get a call from the Vatican," he sounds mortified.

I point at the ceiling, "Him?"

"What? No! Not from the Holy Father, from the head of Papal security. Lieutenant Colonel Marder of the Swiss Guard. And he's annoyed. His Protocol Team has been onto him and told him the Police are investigating a threat to the Pope and how come he hadn't been notified? He's demanding to speak to my head of security, and there's a telecon set up for Thursday!"

He sits. Somewhere, a clock chimes. Who, except Archbishops, still have clocks that chime?

"And?"

He opens his palms helplessly, "I don't *have* a head of security Sister - I have Wissant, my Chancellor who's exec admin for this visit, he's been handling all the police stuff to do with the visit until now. But this is out of his league. I need someone who can get on top of these cowboys in the police so that I can convince the Vatican that we have everything under control. It has taken me years to get this visit organised. This Papal security chap could cancel it in a minute if he thought there was a real risk."

I pick up the ripped newspaper clipping from the floor. There's the picture of me, kneeling in a pool of blood beside a dead terrorist I didn't shoot. But the whole world thinks I did, including the Archbishop. I can almost hear Father Thomas in my ear...*Jones, this is your calling. He led you into the security services and He led you into the faith, and now He has led you here...*

The Arch waits. Oh, what the hell. I think on it. It's my turn to stare out the window. I'm not a big thinker though. It doesn't take long. He's about to say something, but I hold up my hand, "I need two…no I need three things and you can't say no."

He nods, "Such as?" He picks up a pencil.

"I want my own office, on the same floor as the Police situation room. It's somewhere in the College building behind the Cathedral? So, I want my office to be bigger than theirs even if you do have space issues. And I want an assistant seconded from the Security Service. I'll pick her…in fact…I already have, while you were raving. I'll give her boss a call, you sort it out with the Regional Director or Attorney General, whoever it takes." I take a breath, plough on, "And I want a business card with a title on it so long that it hardly fits the card, like *Senior Executive Security Advisor to the Visit of His Holiness Pope Michael I Down Under.*"

He looks down at the paper, "That's more than three things…"

I keep thinking, "I haven't finished. I want a meeting table in my big office big enough for about 15 people, so that the Police Commissioner can turn up with his five flunkies and I can still fill the room with enough flunkies of my own to scare the crap out of him."

"I don't…"

"Which means I will need ready access to a cast of flunkies from your volunteer pool. All they have to do is walk in with manila folders and say yes when I ask them to do stuff…after that they can go back to organising *I Heart the Pope* t-shirts or whatever they were doing."

"This sounds…"

"Ridiculous? Welcome to their world, your Archness. This is the price of coming in late and trying to make them listen. You want them to back off? This is how. And a laptop, and a data projector so that I can do web meetings, which means I need High Speed cable too."

He blows out his cheeks, "I suppose we could move the Papal Visit Call Center to one of the priory schools..."

"Move it to India for all I care, everyone else does. And a cappuccino machine. Nothing fancy, just one of those that takes pods. With a milk frother."

"*What?*"

"Brian, the Senior Executive Security Advisor to the Visit of His Holiness Pope Michael I Down Under, does not drink instant coffee."

You can download or buy 'Cloister' from your favourite e-book outlet today

CPSIA information can be obtained
at www.ICGtesting.com
Printed in the USA
VOW04s1737190716
926LV00026B/1449/P